THE WELL OF MIMIR

MATT LARKIN

THE WELL OF MIMIR

Gods of the Ragnarok Era Book 5

MATT LARKIN

This is a work of fiction. Names, characters, organizations, businesses, places, events and incidents either are the product of the author's imagination or are used fictitiously.

Published by Incandescent Phoenix Books

CONTENTS

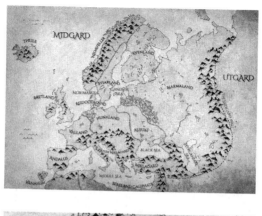

For more maps, join the Skalds' Tribe and get a free codex of
The Ragnarok Era:

http://www.mattlarkinbooks.com/go-ragnarok/

PROLOGUE

Year 33, Age of the Aesir
(Two Years After *The High Seat of Asgard*)

SUNLIGHT GLINTED off the gold-plated roof of Sessrumnir, bright enough to sting Loki's eyes despite the ivy covering large swathes of it. This place, the Vanr archives and the school they represented, had caused both great weal and great woe across Midgard. Maybe it would have served his people better had Odin torn it down with the rest of the halls on Vanaheim.

But then, Loki had always known he wouldn't. The web of urd twisted and bound all men to their cruel fates, oft unaware of the strands that bound them. Blissfully unaware, perhaps. The few like Loki, who glimpsed the truth, had to live in unrelieved horror at such revelations.

The flames told him a great many things. Most, he might rather have not known.

Some men thought they'd rather know beforehand the

tribulations they'd face. They thought this because they had not considered the disquiet engendered by knowing the future and yet remaining powerless to avert it. That was the worst of torments.

Loki trod up the mountain, not lifting his gaze from Sessrumnir despite the burning in his eyes. This place was still working its way through the web. Still spinning, twisting. It had wrought so much ill. And more would come.

At the peak, he threw open the great double doors. As expected, Sigyn appeared at the balustrade of the upper level, looking down on him. That first flush in her cheeks, that unabashed smile at his presence before she caught herself and remembered all that had gone—those things he wished he could savor forever. To grab hold and never let go.

To pretend the future wasn't hurtling ever closer.

But of course, Sigyn's smile fell. Of course, she remembered what had happened. And while she lacked the Sight, on some level, her own intuitive sense probably told her a hint of what must soon unfold.

Ages of practice let Loki keep his own smile in place as he climbed the stairs up to her.

Pyromancy didn't oft reveal specifics. Not context, nor exact timing. Just shadows on the wall, dancing and leaving the viewer to guess at their meaning. Some revelations proved clearer than others.

"I've missed you," he said.

Sigyn nodded, bit her lip, then embraced him. Despite the warmth, she held something back. She blamed him, as if, in knowing some misfortune impended, he ought to have been able to avert it.

A death. A plague. A child born blind.

As if any of them were truly gods.

"You were gone a long time," Sigyn said, her voice tinged with a hint of reproach.

"I know." He patted her shoulder. "There's always so many things to do."

"Pieces to move about the board."

Loki ignored the snipe. Sigyn meant it less spitefully than it sounded, he knew. A parent in pain could barely control her actions. Or his. "I fear you're spending rather too much time in this place."

Sigyn pulled away, turning her back, maybe just to keep him from reading her face. "The answers are in here."

"Maybe not to the questions you truly want to ask. Certainly not to those you ought to ask."

"I don't have time for riddles." Still refusing to look at him, her shoulders tensed.

"You used to love them."

Now she did spin on him. "That was before my son was born this way. One of us has to find a way to help him."

"If you turn to the Art, you will pay a price. One greater than aught you hope to achieve with it."

Sigyn glared at him. "No price is too high for my child."

Loki shook his head sadly. Many would have claimed the same, before realizing what the price might be.

He reached for Sigyn's hand, but she jerked it away and stormed off into the archives.

Leaving him as trapped by the future as ever.

PART I

Year 49, Age of the Aesir

Winter

(Eighteen Years After *The High Seat of Asgard*)

*H*unaland stretched as far south as the Sudurberks, encompassing vast swathes of land into five kingdoms of the Huns. A century and a half ago, they had swept in and conquered the native Siklings, prompting the Great March of Odin's ancestors along the way. One might say then, that the Huns had made Vingethor the last king before Odin and perhaps led to his own rise.

On a peak in the Sudurberks, Odin sat staring at the blood moon above Hunaland. It was larger than he ever remembered seeing, though what it portended he didn't know. Its ominous red color filled the sky and left him shuddering slightly, as if the Veil had grown thin. Part of him longed to embrace the Sight and glimpse the ghosts that no doubt flitted about these snows, equally drawn by the moon. But to see them was to be *seen* by them, and Odin did not care for the burden at present.

Sigyn had predicted this night would come. Vanr astrology, she'd said, claimed the great blood moon would rise. She had even predicted Hunaland might offer the best view, back three moons ago. She busied herself with such things, perhaps, to distract her from her own pain. Odin empathized.

Years ago, the völvur would have sacrificed criminals under a blood moon in the hopes of appeasing Njord and the other Vanir. In the hopes of buying respite from the mists. A vain hope, of course. And Odin had killed Njord, though that felt another lifetime ago.

A raven's cry broke through the stillness, followed by muffled whimpers. Odin shut his eyes and let his raven's vision feed his own. In truth, Valravn controlled the ravens, but Odin had stolen the vaettr from Gjuki, and now the birds served as Odin's eyes and ears while away from the High Seat. He called them Huginn and Muninn, thought and memory, fallible as both were.

Through their eyes, he spied the shadowed figure drifting up from a crevasse, a flailing girl tucked under his arm. Ashen-skinned, with hair and eyes jet-black, the svartalf drew up alongside Odin, the play of shadows concealing his features even in the bright moonlight.

He cast the bundle at Odin's feet, and she crunched down in the snow. Then she turned over, a girl, maybe sixteen winters behind her. Dust and grime matted hair that might have once been sandy. Streaks of red rimmed her eyes. A rope gag had worn the sides of her mouth so raw they bled, as did her wrists, bound behind her back. Her blood stained the white snows to match the crimson moon above.

"What is this, Volund?" Odin demanded.

"Oh, you already know. There is truth in the old ways."

"There is barbarism."

Volund cackled, the sound grating on Odin's mind, a

twinge of inhuman cruelty behind it. "As if you have not drenched your hands in a sea of blood."

"I sacrifice where sacrifice is warranted. I do not touch sorcery without direst need of it."

The svartalf snickered and looked to the girl. "See how he casts himself as a hero? This man who would be king and god of all Midgard? A murderer. A liar. A thief. A breaker of all faith." Now he looked to Odin. "The only difference between us is I do not cloak my darkness in hypocrisy."

The woman whimpered again.

"Trust me, Ás, you'll want a sacrifice before the night is done. I have brought you what you sought, but you must shed blood to truly gain its benefit, and you must do so this night." He shrugged. "And virgins make wonderful sacrifices."

Odin groaned. "A virgin." A child.

Volund snickered. "Well, she was."

Now Odin lunged at the svartalf. Volund melted away in shadow, only to form up a few feet from where he'd stood.

"You rapist!" Odin spat at him.

The svartlaf snorted. "There was time to pass while the cursed sun blazed."

"You sick son of a—"

"Please. Spare me the sanctimony, Ás. We are forged by agonies. It the very essence of our existence. The more we suffer, the stronger we become. Those who break are unworthy of aught save their uses to those who weather the cycles of pain and damnation. I do naught which has not been done to me and made me strong. And you, who have sucked the very souls out of hundreds of victims and damned them to eternal torment, would condemn *me* for visiting transitory suffering upon one soon to die to sate your more profane needs?"

"I should have killed you long ago."

Volund chuckled and opened one hand to reveal a golden ring, glittering in the moonlight, engraved with faint runes, a swan-like design encircling it. "Had you done so—or tried—you would not now have before you Draupnir. The culmination of our bargain and of your chance to hold the dead under your grasp."

Odin grimaced, unable to look away from the entrancing golden sight. "I already provided you with souls for that."

"To forge it. But if you would draw out its true potential, you must feed it, and under a blood moon such as this. Do you think traditions came from nowhere? Do you think they matter naught?"

Finding it hard to swallow, Odin turned his gaze upon the girl squirming on the ground. Damn Volund. And damn Odin himself for employing the dark smith. Without such treasures, Ragnarok would be lost. All of Midgard might fall. What was one girl's life—or terror—compared to the lives of an entire world? Maybe if she understood, she'd have paid willingly.

Or maybe not.

"Give it to me." His words sounded almost a growl in his own ears. Draupnir. The Dripper. The ring that would bring him one step closer to victory. If he could but bear the price.

"My payment," Volund said.

From nowhere, shadows seemed to tickle Odin's sides, probing into his satchel. Seeking the grimoire. That book, taken from Grimhild, belonged in no one's hands, least of all a monster like Volund. But the ring ... Oh, if only Volund had been able to replicate Andvarinaut, maybe none of his other works would be needful. But wishing for it would not make it so.

Disgusted as much with himself as the svartalf, Odin

flung the satchel at the creature's feet. Sneering, he dared Volund to claim his prize.

Without hesitation nor any hint of shame, the svartalf snatched up the bag. "Use it wisely, oh king." He flicked the ring through the air and Odin caught it, overcome by its sudden warmth. "For it is the last craft I shall make for you."

"No, smith. We are not done yet. Not while Ragnarok looms over our heads."

Volund grinned. "The Mortal Realm concerns me less and less. I have my own kingdom to attend to."

Odin took a step toward him. Volund fell back, shadows swarming up around him. The gleam of his eyes lingered an instant after his form had descended into darkness. His dry, mind-twisting chuckles remained longer, echoing off the empty mountainside.

With a groan, Odin looked down at Draupnir, warm and gleaming in his palm. Supernal runes lined it, beckoning powers Odin could barely dream of understanding. "Damn you, Volund ..."

After a moment of self-loathing, Odin looked to the girl. She moaned, the sound muffled by her gag. Then she flopped around, squirming toward the edge of the slope, as if she might escape by flinging herself down into a ravine.

Odin sighed, wishing—not for the first time—he had some gods left from which he could ask for forgiveness. History judges men. But what of the one burdened to ensure history continues at all? Maybe that had been Loki's true onus all along.

Seeing no alternative, Odin grabbed the girl by the back of her shirt and hauled her up onto her feet. Those were bound too, so she couldn't have stood without him supporting her. He turned her about to face him. The least he could do for her, really. "I know it's not much comfort, but your death may allow future generations to live."

She whimpered.

Truly a small comfort, even given that she probably had no idea the horrors that lay in store for the dead. Men were blessed with not understanding what truly lay beyond the Veil, an ignorance Odin sometimes envied them.

He eased the girl down to the ground, then slipped Draupnir onto his finger and blew out a long breath.

As he pulled a knife from his belt, tears begin to stream down the girl's face. But sadly, Volund had spoken the truth: Odin had slain a great many for his ends. The king of gods and men could not afford pity if it might cost the world itself.

Grimacing, he drew the knife along the girl's throat. Hot blood oozed from the line he'd cut, and he let it dribble down over his fingers, over Draupnir.

Her eyes glazed over, and she fell back into the snow, convulsing lightly.

Draupnir grew warmer, hot even, as hot as molten gold it seemed. It glowed incandescent, then white hot. Odin grunted in pain as it seared his flesh.

Every instinct screamed in his mind to tear the blistering ring from his finger. Instead, he closed his fist—as much to steel his own will as for any need—and held it before his face. Liquid gold seeped from between his clenched fingers and dribbled down his arm.

Odin gasped at the agony as his flesh bubbled and popped from the heat of it. He threw back his head, choking on his own screams. The gold dripped down from the ring and landed sizzling in the snow.

Drop after drop fell, hissing. They threw up curtains of

steam hot enough to burn away the mist drifting over the mountain.

Finally, the heat faded. The last dribble of gold fell from Odin's elbow, and he collapsed to his knees, clutching his arm. Rivulets of raw, blistered flesh ran down the back of it in bloody deltas. The flesh around his finger had bubbled and burst, scorched and agonizing.

Odin groaned, then thrust his burning hand and arm into the snows. It stung like the spit of Hel. He gasped, letting the coldness offer him slow relief.

Immortality would ensure such wounds didn't kill him. His flesh would heal in a few days, in fact. It hardly lessened the suffering of having his skin burned off. Almost, it seemed a blessing he could only achieve this during a blood moon. It obviated the guilt of not doing so more often.

Coughing, Odin swept away the snow where the drops of gold had fallen. The heated metal had melted straight down to the mountainside, leaving the droplets sitting in pools of rapidly cooling water. And inside each pool lay a ring, a nigh duplicate of his own, and so very similar to the one Svanhit had once entrusted to him.

A ring of valkyries.

And it had spawned eight copies, each glittering in the moonlight. Eight rings to bind the choosers of the slain.

Odin scooped them up and deposited them in a pouch. He'd need to burn the girl's body to ensure she couldn't rise as a draug. And then ... then he had a great deal of work to do.

2

Eighteen Years Ago

*T*he vagaries of time stripped away the truth of memory and left it a shadow of reality, much like the Penumbra that haunted Odin's dreams. How many times had he descended into the deep forge, seeking the svartalf smith? How many interminable winters had passed while Odin strived after scheme upon scheme, seeking knowledge or artifacts that might unravel even a single strand of the weave of urd?

Memory lies, Valravn said in Odin's mind. The raven spirit he'd taken from Gjuki did not oft speak to him directly, rather relaying the sights beheld by its minions.

A good many moons he had poured over Grimhild's tome, lost in the mud when Skadi fled from Loki's implacable flame. The cryptic and mind-shredding writings had whispered strange truths to him, even as the wraith inside Odin taunted him of the grimoire's potential.

Older than old ... Audr said.

Older than the Niflungar, if that was to be believed.

Older than either Valravn or Audr. Perhaps even written by Hel herself when she yet lived. The daughter of Loki, in another era, long before the coming of the mists. A book out of time, older than the world itself.

Shadows loomed around Odin as he stalked down into Volund's forge, ever dancing, seeming to watch his progress and report back to their twisted master.

Perhaps they even sensed the vile grimoire within Odin's satchel. The book had held more questions than answers, but, if Loki had taught Odin aught, he had taught him the value of questions. *Questions* might spark revelation where answers but compounded bemusement. If prompted to the right question, knowledge unsought might come to the student.

As the grimoire had instructed Odin, even while refusing to reveal the depths of its secrets.

Dozens of different hands had scrawled notes in the book, explanations even Audr could not unravel, for they had belonged to languages dead thousands of years before the Old Kingdoms. But in the fleeting shadow of his memories, his past lives, Odin could recognize hints, glimpses of tongues spoken in forgotten lands by races turned to dust.

Witchcraft, foul Art stretching back to the beginning of time. To the beginning of all things, perhaps. The darkness that consumed memories and thought. Odin might spend a thousand years studying this grimoire, might lose himself in that darkness, and still not fathom the depth of Hel's vile power.

"He sees it ..." the shadows whispered. "*The beginning. The end. The cycle ...*"

The longer Odin listened to Audr, the more the wraith's words spiraled around in his mind, unravelling secrets mortal man was never meant to know. Or perhaps unravelling the fragile thread of Odin's sanity. So many sorcerers went insane from the voices in their heads, the vaettir they bound in an unending search for ever greater power.

We lose bits of ourselves ... Audr said.

Until we no longer care, Valravn said.

Sometimes, Odin could not say whether they spoke to him or to each other.

Deeper into the dark tunnel Odin walked, until he came to the forge, lit by the flicker of a furnace. Drenched in swirling shadows, Volund sat upon a chair of bone Odin might have easily mistaken for a throne.

The svartalf leaned forward, fingers steepled, staring at Odin. "I've waited for you. You wander slowly in my realm."

"I am known to wander."

"But this time you come bearing gifts."

Odin sneered. The svartalf always knew more than he ought to and oft pushed the limits of Odin's patience. More than once, Odin had considered ending the creature before him. Volund played his own game of tafl, manipulating the board and ever managing to remain only slightly more of a boon than a thorn to Odin.

He had once conspired with Väinämöinen—Odin's erst-while teacher of song-crafting—to claim boons Odin could not begin to understand. He had schemed and plotted his way to the throne of his own dark kingdom within Svartalfheim, heedless of the cost of it.

Ever he trod so close to that line, so nigh to crossing into the realm of becoming Odin's foe. "I do not come with gifts for the likes of you."

"Nevertheless, you will give me the tome."

Odin grimaced. Yes, he'd known what Volund would ask. Prescient whispers of the Sight had warned him of the price he'd pay for his latest request. But Volund might possess the craft necessary to pursue Odin's ends. The High Seat allowed Odin to look far out across Midgard, to see what happened in many lands. But still there remained realms far too alien and unknown to him, realms beyond his ken or control.

Realms the book had begun to reveal, along with the secrets Odin might need to harness them.

"What use," Odin said at last, "has a vaettr for a tome about calling vaettir?"

Volund's perverse grin made Odin's skin crawl. "So we have an accord."

Odin did not bother to deny that. Grimhild's cursed tome offered him many potential boons, but the price might come too high, and regardless, Odin needed to bind the dead to his will, and not, as with Audr, merely to his soul. "You will have the tome only when you have wrought your next wonder, svartalf."

Volund snatched up a cane and limped over to a great table. "Show me."

Glowering, Odin withdrew the grimoire from his satchel, then flipped to the pages where he had made his own notes on a potential design.

Snatching the edge of the book, the svartalf spun it around and leaned down over it, apparently having no trouble reading even in the darkness of the forge. A tediously long time he craned his neck over the grimoire, reminding Odin of the ache in his own knees and pain in his lower back.

Having lost Gungnir, Odin was forced to lean upon a real walking stick.

Finally, Volund chuckled. "Oh, we come round and round, the circle unending in its twisted play." Odin knew better than to answer that. The smith looked up. "There are rings like this, forged of orichalcum, binding servants who pass between this realm and the shadow."

"You mean valkyries."

Volund nodded. "So many copies of it I made, and never yet wrought one with the power to duplicate the originals, nor even knew whence they came."

Odin thumped the book with his forefinger, indicating a prolonged passage about the forging of binding rings, along with his own notes. "This is it? This tells you how they have been mastered?"

Volund snickered. "It tells me ... enough. Hel's tactics may have been somewhat skewed compared to those currently in practice, but I can iterate upon her strategies to make that which you seek." The smith rubbed his chin. "You've seen them." It wasn't a question, though how he knew, Odin could not say. "Which one was it, I wonder?"

Odin cocked his head to the side, saying naught. He owed Volund no answers nor did it serve his ends to offer the smith any more knowledge than the man already possessed. Volund had become twice over too dangerous as it was.

"Was it ... Altvir?" An odd plaintiveness in the question seemed so uncharacteristic Odin frowned. Why would Volund care overmuch about a particular valkyrie? While perhaps an affectation, if Volund cared so much as to make himself vulnerable for an answer, perhaps Odin could pity him after all.

He scratched his beard. "I have not met a valkyrie by that name."

The smith nodded, then shrugged as if to deny he cared in the least about any valkyrie. Then he shambled back to his chair, and slumped down, eyes gleaming in the dark.

"Such a work would have to rival even Mjölnir. I would need nine years and nine years again."

Odin suppressed a flinch. Nine years he had expected. Twice that, he had not prepared for. "I will hold the grimoire until it is done."

"I'll need a steady supply of souls."

Odin shrugged. Having Thor funnel souls back to Volund was merely a matter of sending his son to kill more jotunnar with Mjölnir. "You'll have all you need."

Volund chuckled lightly, then leaned forward. "Have you considered, King of the Aesir, that those with such power *already* have a master? One who is not like to surrender servants without a fight."

He'd considered it.

"I will see you in eighteen winters."

Volund's snickers followed Odin out of the forge, blending with the whispers of the shadows and the voices in Odin's head into a cacophony of madness that seemed to chase him forever.

3

*T*hunder crashed over the mountains. The storm clouds here almost never cleared. It would not have seemed home if they had.

Gudrun had become a haunting voice in the back of Skadi's mind. Though oft silent now, when she woke from her bouts of fugue, the sorceress had become a weeping, pathetic niggling that served to distract Skadi from more important tasks.

Climbing the slopes of the Thrymheim Plateau—as it was now called—the sorceress chittered in bouts of melancholy nonsense, beseeching nonexistent gods for succor. With a scowl, Skadi pushed Gudrun's rantings from her mind.

She'd always known she'd have to come here. It was her place, once, her home, long winters back, as a mortal jotunn. Now what was she? A ghost, a snow maiden in possession of a broken woman's body? She, the daughter of great King Thiazi, she whom they had called the Princess of Winter. Reduced to almost naught.

Involuntarily, ice formed around her fingers as she trod

up the steep slope. Flexing her fingers dismissed the forming shards. There was little sense in expending her energy in such indulgences at present. She might have need of her powers soon enough.

After all, she'd spent the better part of two decades gathering enough support to become a threat to Thrym. He would know of her. But still, if she could reclaim her throne without having to ignite a war amongst the jotunnar—one sure to sap their strength with needless bloodshed—she would do so.

At the center of the plateau rose a mountain, encircled by the city Skadi's father had built in days long gone. A mighty wall protected the city, one even Skadi's jotunn allies would find hard to breach. Yes, claiming the city of Thrymheim would require a toll she was loath to pay while any other option remained before her.

The Iron Titans flanked the main gate, each seventy feet tall, holding blades that could've cleaved human houses in twain, had their owners not been mere ornamentation. Once, during the War of Shattered Cities, Skadi had sought a way to animate those great statues. Ever deeper she'd delved into the abyss of the Art, searching for any answer to bring them to life. Perhaps, had the war not claimed her life, she might have done so.

The city rose up in a series of terraces along the mountain. Atop that, one found Thunderhome Palace and Vafthrudnir's Refuge. Both, she'd need to visit for her errand to have a chance of success.

A flash of lightning split the sky as she made her way up the city slope, terrace by terrace. As a child, she'd stood in awe as Father had become a giant eagle and soared between such lancing bolts. His cry had echoed over the mountain, as a comfort or a warning to his people—Thiazi watched over them all.

Before the Vanir murdered him.

Her breath frosted the air, not because of any warmth inside of her, but rather, because she needed to vent her icy rage before it consumed her. For so many years after leaving Midgard behind she had avoided coming to this place. She'd longed for home. And dreaded the memories inseparably intertwined with it. So much loss, so much pain.

Still, home was her birthright, and Father would not have forgiven her had she abandoned it. She was the Queen of Winter. If humanity thought they knew Fimbulvinter, they were in for a jarring realization as to just how cold the world could grow.

It would take time, of course. A great deal of time, maybe. Longer, if Thrym did not prove cooperative.

Wisdom dictated that she first visit Vafthrudnir and seek his support. Yet, Thrym would not take it kindly if she did not call upon him as soon as she arrived.

Above the city rose Thunderhome, its crystalline spires formed of ice grown through ancient sorcery. Its stone foundations carved with runes from before Skadi's birth. Back when she'd served as Vafthrudnir's apprentice, Skadi had spent long years pouring over the scrolls of his library. Ancient scrawlings upon dried mammoth hides, most of them, and some claimed the jotunnar had not built the foundations—they had found them. As if some race in another era had left this hold behind, waiting for the jotunnar to rise.

Or to rise again.

All things moved in slow circles, Vafthrudnir claimed. And the jotunnar had ruled the world even before the coming of the mists, as they did then. As they would do, again, when the age of man froze and died beneath Skadi's inexorable march. This, she swore.

Jotunn guards watched the gates of Thunderhome, eyeing her with casual distrust as she trod through the gatehouse. Beyond lay the nine hundred Stairs of Alvaldi, carved of blocks of ice each three feet high and thirty feet wide, perfectly aligned. Rising up through the palace.

Few others seemed about. A jotunn here or there. A handful of human slaves bearing food to those stationed in the lower levels.

Much less than the bustling halls Skadi remembered from her life. Sadly, not even memory remained clear. Death and the deleterious effects of the Astral Realm had sapped bits and pieces of herself. Until what she'd once known had become like a dream, distant and ever longed for, even if not quite lucid.

After the enormous climb, a jotunn man with ram-like horns met her. He was dressed in fine armor, worked with runes no doubt intended to enhance its protection. He stood at least half again her height, meaning he'd tasted a fair amount of man flesh over the years. In life, Skadi had stood nigh to seven feet tall. Trapped in Gudrun's body she felt like a damn dverg.

Where she could not rely on size to establish her claim, sheer audacity would have to suffice. At least by now Gudrun's skin had taken on the pale, almost blue tinge snow maidens shared with frost jotunnar, and her hair had turned white. It made her look like a diminutive jotunnar. "Take me to see the king."

The man remained expressionless as he studied her. "You're not human," he finally said.

"No."

"But puny."

Skadi allowed her eyes to cloud over, fill with mist. Frost coalesced around her mouth and shards of ice formed around her hands and arms. Suppressing the human tenor of Gudrun's voice left her sounding hollow, somehow larger than she was. "I am of Niflheim."

The guard stiffened, then cocked his head for her to pass.

While she'd asked him to escort her, his acquiescence would suffice. For now.

She made her way back through the upper levels of the palace. Even if all her memories had fled, she'd have been able to find the throne room. It stood dead ahead, rimmed by a great arch coated in rime, with dangling icicles hanging down from it like the fangs of a beast, any one of them the length of her arm. The doorway stood open—and tall enough a being five times her height could have passed through without stooping.

The entire hall beyond was carved from a single block of ice. The spiraling columns the size of trees, the throne as tall a human house, the statues of snarling beasts looking down from a mist-filled space eighty feet above—all cut from a glacier when Skadi's ancestors dug down to this place.

Upon that throne now sat a jotunn at least four times her size, draped in mammoth hides and armored plates engraved with runes and the likeness of skulls. His breath was mist. Ice had formed around his hands, cracking as he tightened his gauntleted grip around a sword easily eight or nine feet in length.

"Do you know how many men I've devoured?" The king's voice was like the rumble before an avalanche, ready to burst forth into destruction any moment.

Skadi would imagine he'd have had to consume terrible quantities of man flesh to get like that. Excessive indulgences, perhaps even profane rituals all in the pursuit of ever increasing his size. As if physical might were the only measure of power.

"I take it you know who I am?"

Thrym chuckled, another rumble. "The so-called Winter Queen? The one who thinks to rule all Jotunheim ..."

Skadi allowed herself to smile. "I've taken Glaesisvellir and Gastropnir, and their kings have sworn to my service. The wood tribes of Galgvidr answer my call. I sent Hrungnir to watch the breach to Midgard, and none come or go save by my sufferance. Jotunheim already falls to me."

The king chortled. "Petty lords and woodland kingdoms in the south? You do not control Thrymheim, nor shall you."

Skadi spread her hands. "But you still don't know who I am. I am the daughter of King Thiazi, upon whose throne you now sit. I am returned from the fells of Niflheim to claim what is mine. But ..." She raised a placating hand. "We need not be enemies. Surely a king needs a queen?"

Thrym shifted his shoulders, breaking more bits of ice off in the process. "A queen? One to give me an heir? I could never fit my cock inside your pathetic human trench."

Somewhere, deep in the corner of her mind, Gudrun whimpered. Delicious. "The human host is disposable. I've but to claim a sufficiently powerful jotunn woman."

The king waved her away. "Return with such a body, and then we'll see what you may be queen of."

Skadi suppressed her glower. It wouldn't do to show the king her ire. Not now, not yet. Soon, he'd be the one imploring her for an alliance. And then ... then Midgard would know the true meaning of Fimbulvinter.

4

Seven petty kingdoms divided Sviarland, and though some had worked to unify the land, those divisions remained. North of Dalar and beyond even Jamtla, Lappmarken formed the northern boundary with Kvenland as well as the western one with Nidavellir. In the south of this great northern stretch, Odin rode along a narrow mountain pass, arm raised against dense flurries of snow. He sat astride Sleipnir, whose steady hooves allowed the creature to climb where no mortal horse could hope to walk.

Out ahead, Odin's ravens flew in all directions, scouting for the place he sought. His Sight had guided him to the vicinity, but Huginn and Muninn would allow him to find the specific location with much greater efficacy.

A sudden gust tore Odin's hat from his head and sent it spiraling down into a ravine clogged with mist.

"Damn it."

Sleipnir neighed in response, plodding forward with practiced care. The angle was nigh steep enough to send Odin pitching over backward, forcing him to keep his free hand tangled in the horse's mane for support.

The wind continued to howl, freezing Odin's cheeks even beneath his beard. To say naught of turning his stones to solid ice. In his mind's eye, Valravn relayed an image, a broken ruin upon the slope, more than half buried in the snows.

"Around the next peak," he said to Sleipnir, barely catching his own voice over the howling wind.

His nose stung from it. Snot dribbled down into his mustache. This close they'd moved nigh into dverg domain. The perilous Earth vaettir might try to bar his passage, at night, leastwise. Odin peered up at the sky. He'd drawn nigh to the tip of the mist, but it made it hard to make out much. A few hours of daylight, perhaps.

Enough to ride around the peak if he pushed Sleipnir.

He slapped the horse's shoulder.

❦

As the raven's sight had revealed, the valkyrie lodge poked out of snows that must've stretched thirty feet deep. Those snows rose up to crust over half the doorway, while rime coated what little remained exposed. The edges of a broken stone tower broke above the snow, but ice caked that as well.

This style looked more like a dverg outpost than aught built by the Old Kingdoms. Solid, blocky, and ominous, built by those of dire purpose and fell convictions. Runes might well have marked the walls, but under the ice Odin could make out no sign of them. What ice didn't conceal, though, were jutting stone edifices like the maws of vile beasts drawn up from chthonic depths.

Up on that tower, a square window led inside.

No angle of the slope would let Sleipnir tread up onto the roof, meaning Odin had no easy access to the tower window. So it was either dig out a front door that looked coated in a thousand years of winter, or climb the damn wall.

"Just how high can you jump?" Odin asked Sleipnir.

The horse snorted, then backed up. Huh. Intent to try it, was he? Well, Odin wouldn't stop him from—

Sleipnir took off at a mighty sprint that sent wind sheering over Odin's face with painful force. His stomach dropped out from under him as the horse leapt, forcing Odin to lean forward and clutch Sleipnir's mane to keep from pitching over the side.

The horse's eight hooves crunched into snow, barely cresting the roof. His hind legs skidded, two of them flailing in midair.

Damn it!

Odin leaped free and landed on the roof, allowing Sleipnir greater maneuverability. The horse tromped around—hooves falling a hairsbreadth from Odin's face— before regaining his balance.

One eyebrow raised, Odin stared up at Sleipnir.

The horse snorted.

"Right you are," Odin grumbled, pushing himself up. Frost had already crusted his beard, but now snow caked his clothes and hair as well. "Already missing that damn hat." He turned to Sleipnir. "Just stay here."

Another snort, as if to ask if Odin truly thought the horse about to climb through a window.

Eh, perhaps not.

Careful of his footing, Odin trudged to the tower. Even with the snows uplifting him, that window still rose well above his head. Grabbing the ledge, Odin flooded pneuma into his limbs to enhance his strength, then hefted himself up.

Inhuman strength or not, crouching on windowsills was for younger men. His back ached as he pulled himself up to stare down into the ruin. Not overmuch to look at inside. A table, and clearly not one from centuries ago, as rabbit bones still littered its top, along with the dregs of a jug of mead. Even up here, he'd know that smell.

With a sniff, he dropped down into the relative warmth of the lodge, landing on a support buttress maybe fifteen feet over that table. A crisscross of these supports covered the interior, leading to a stone ladder carved in the wall. The dvergar must have used it to get up here to the windows in order to fire arrows on whatever fools dared assault them here.

So how had this place fallen? Had one of the Old Kingdoms driven them back? Well, it mattered little now.

Arms spread for balance, Odin edged over to the ladder, then climbed down to the lower level.

A fire in a raised pit had burned down to embers, but must have roared some few hours ago. They had been here.

Unless ... unless they still were.

Oh. Yes, if they waited across the Veil, they'd have seen him as a shadow. Maybe they didn't know him for who he was, and wouldn't consider him a threat. But as soon as he embraced the Sight, he would snap into clarity, as plain to them as they would be to him.

Well, that was, after all, the reason he'd come.

Odin ran his fingers over Draupnir where it rested on his right hand. Though his flesh had healed, the ring felt seared into his very bones. Like it would tear him to pieces to remove it.

Audr.

The wraith responded at once, its vile coils slithering up Odin's guts and clawing at his mind. His stomach lurched as the wraith jerked him out of the Mortal Realm and into the Penumbra. Vertigo threatened to steal Odin's feet from beneath him, even as the room rushed into new clarity while losing color.

Chairs at the table toppled over backward as a warrior woman spied him.

Her golden armor glittered, even in the pale light of the Astral Realm. Her hand lay on the hilt of her sword. Seven of her sisters stood at her sudden rise, including one at the head of the table.

Stifling a grunt of discomfort and disorientation, Odin forced Audr back down. It was not the time for the wraith to test him. Indeed, even Audr seemed keen to learn whether Odin might pull off the audacious scheme he'd now set in motion.

Audacious ... arrogant ...

Perhaps.

"Odin Borrson," Svanhit said, hand still wrapped around her sword. Her deep brown wings had erupted from her back, twitching ever so slightly and somewhat obscuring his view of the others. "Has the mist taken your mind, old man?"

Odin chuckled. "You call me old?" Indeed, while he'd now returned her ring, years without it had taken their toll upon the valkyrie as well. To say naught of the fact she must have lived well before Odin's birth.

"This is the Ás king?" the woman at the head of the table demanded. "The great and glorious Odin Borrson?" Her sneer would have withered the heart of any mortal. Her black wings seemed like jet in this color-drained realm. She pushed away from the table and stalked closer.

Odin truly missed Gungnir, as much for something to lean on as for the weapon itself. "Skögul, I presume."

The valkyrie paused mid stride, then cast a glare at Svanhit before turning back to Odin. "I take it you've come to turn over your soul at last?"

Odin chuckled. It was good he wasn't the only one capable of temerity. He cocked his head to the side. "Rather, I've come for yours. All of yours. You will bow and serve me."

Another valkyrie, this one blonde with white wings, approached. "He's been in contact with Volund."

Skögul rolled her eyes. "Your failures seem to never stop haunting us, then."

Odin paced around the hall, taking it in, heedless of his aching knees. "I spent long years planning this, you know. I walked across Midgard many times over seeking out all the secrets of bygone years. The whispers of forgotten peoples. The ... songs of older times and fallen lands."

"Songs?" Skögul asked.

Odin smiled at her, shaking his head sadly, almost pitying her for the fall before her. Before them all. But neither the maid he'd slain for this, nor the valkyries themselves, could be afforded pity when weighed against the destiny of Midgard.

And so he sang, a hint of a rasp slipping into his song, unable to mimic the perfect clear notes Väinämöinen had taught him, and yet, close enough.

Skögul gasped, her trembling hand going to her sword, even as her fingers betrayed her, twitching, unresponsive. The valkyrie edged toward Odin, clearly expecting her body to react differently. "Song-crafter ..." Barely a whisper escaped her, almost drowned out by Odin's song.

Others struggled to their feet. Svanhit's sword flew free from its sheath, but she managed only a single step before she froze in place, staring at the wobbling blade in her hand.

That blade began to flake away, bits of rust drifting along on a faint breeze that ought not have flowed through this hall. The sword crumbled into dust.

Another of the valkyries screamed in defiance, managing several awkward steps before dropping to her knees. Her fingers curled up into claws as agony washed over her face.

The song reverberated inside Odin's chest, leaving him trembling with the effort of its magic. It seeped out of him and into the world, drawing some portion of Odin's pneuma into it. His own knees wobbled. No matter what happened, he could not afford to stop singing.

More valkyrie weapons broke apart and scattered on the breeze.

All the women had fallen now, some laying prone and writhing, some still on their knees, struggling to reach him. A vain struggle. The song's power had them so deeply in Odin's thrall they could not hope to raise a hand against him.

Their golden armor began to flake and chip, bits of it vanishing up into the sky like smoke.

"Cease," Svanhit moaned.

Part of Odin wished he could. He wished many things, in the deep recesses of his mind, where none save bound vaettir might be privy to his misgivings.

You think it ... destiny ...

Odin thought it necessity first, and urd second.

A light built before his eyes, searing white, like staring into the sun. With each passing note, the radiance grew in intensity. So white it threatened to blind him. It scorched his mind with its heat.

And slowly, the light coalesced into a figure of yet greater luminosity. Man-like, though towering over Odin at half again his height. Angry, incandescent rays poured out of the entity's head as it drew closer. An extra pair of radiant arms jutted from beneath his shoulders, all four hands reaching toward Odin.

Its will slammed into him with a physical force, driving Odin to his knees. A scorched, agonized, breath escaped his lungs. The air itself seemed ignited by the heat. One set of hands closed on Odin's biceps, hefting him up off the ground while the other closed around his throat.

The touch was a scalding brand against his flesh. His skin blistered, bubbled, and popped. The stench of his own cooking flesh hit Odin full force, acrid and sickly sweet, choking him even as his arms and throat turned to charcoal.

In the back of Odin's mind, Audr hissed in terror or despair. Valravn fled into dark corners of Odin's soul. The vaettir he had bound were naught compared to the ancient, eldritch power now focused upon him. The power from which Odin dared try to wrest control of these valkyries. Through them, he had bridged the gap between realms and opened his own mind to this assault.

But it remained Odin's mind.

All his anger, rage at the cruelty of urd, Odin fed into himself. He let it suffuse him. He let that darkness become him. Roaring at the entity that would seek to hold sway over life and death, Odin flung his arms free. He snatched the light being's upper hands from around his throat, calling upon strength that could only ever exist outside this non-reality. The flesh of his hands burned away, leaving naught but bones.

And still he yanked the Sun God's hands from his neck.

Finish ... song ...

Audr's voice had become a faint whisper.

Odin's throat barely had flesh left around it. To even

speak invited fresh agonies upon himself. And still he opened his mouth, let the blood pour forth, and sang a further song. One in his own mind. One that extinguished all heat and all flame.

The outline of a face peered through rapidly dimming radiance, glaring and aghast at Odin.

And it vanished in an instant.

Odin's vision returned only to see all eight women writhing, light pouring from their eyes, their mouths, even their noses.

As one, their rings burst apart. A heartbeat later, their swan wings exploded in a shower of blood and gore and feathers. Their screams echoed off the walls. The sound of it filled Odin's ears, ringing long after the last notes of his song had faded away.

He glimpsed his own flesh. It had not burnt away, though his arms bore brand-like hand marks, as if the struggle with the vaettir had proved more real than he'd expected.

Elder God …

Audr's voice sounded far away, as if the light had nigh to destroyed the wraith.

Had Odin won a contest of wills with so powerful a foe? Or had this so-called god's power been divested in multiple directions, a mere fragment of his energy allocated to this struggle? He feared the latter.

Repercussions shall ensue, Valravn said.

"Oh, I know." Odin's voice still felt raw, burned.

The former valkyries now lay in naught but undershirts, struggling to rise off the ground. Crimson stained those garments, now matted with feathers.

Odin forced himself up from his knees.

"What have you done?" Svanhit moaned, her voice seeming nigh to weeping. "Why have you done this?"

"Because my need is greater. You will serve me."

Skögul gaped at him. "Serve how? Our powers are stripped. Our ... lives. Our immortality ... Oh, by the light! You've trapped us in this realm." The valkyrie glanced about as if seeking a weapon.

Again, pity tugged at his gut. Again, he forced himself to quash such weakness before it could thwart all his hopes. And yet, now the deed was done, his offer became a kind of mercy. "Suppose I can restore your powers. Your rings are lost, but the changes wrought in you lie quiescent, waiting."

Another blonde woman stood. Her thin shirt did little to conceal her form, barely stretching down past her hips, but she seemed unabashed by this. "You would kill other valkyries for their rings? Offer us our lives at the cost of strangers?"

Odin reached into a pouch and withdrew one of the duplicates Draupnir had dripped. Slowly, he opened his palm so she could look upon it.

The valkyrie drew nigh, peering down it. "That is not quite the same."

"It will serve, if you serve me. Who are you?"

Frowning, the valkyrie met his gaze defiantly. "Altvir." Oh. Volund's former wife.

The way she stared at him, it almost seemed she had begun to suspect the source of his knowledge. Odin offered her only a slight frown in return. Urd moved in strange circles and all things came round and round. Volund's love of this woman and his loss of her might well track back to the source of this particular moment, but other moments traced behind that one. "Speak the oath and live in my service, Altvir. My valkyrie."

The woman looked back to Skögul, who slowly nodded. "And you have enough for all of us?"

"Fortune favors you. I have eight." Fortune, or urd.

Altvir stood aside so that her leader could come forward.

Skögul rose, no more bashful than her valkyrie sister had proved. Then she knelt before Odin, hand extended. "I, Skögul, swear upon light and darkness to serve you, lord. To choose the slain whom you would claim. To enact your will and bridge the living and the dead. I am yours, body, mind, and soul."

Immortality. That was the gift the rings offered these women. The chance to break the chains of life and death and become more than fragile, short-lived humans. Many would risk much for it, of course. But for those who had tasted immortality, little greater terror existed than the fear of losing it. Such fears had crippled the Vanir. And Odin had well known the valkyries would not surrender their gift.

He slipped the ring unto Skögul's finger, ignoring her glare.

She moved and allowed her sisters to come to him, one by one. Altvir and Svanhit, Gondul and Hrist. Sigrún and Hildr and Brynhild. His first valkyries and—given the cost and rarity with which Odin could replicate Draupnir—likely to be his only ones in the immediate future.

Brynhild, the last of them, rose looking at the ring on her finger, then her eyes flicked to Odin with some unreadable mix of trepidation and disdain. "Now complete the binding."

Did the exact words matter? Perhaps not. "I hold you to your oaths, valkyries. Reclaim your powers and regain your wings."

Brynhild glanced over her shoulder at her sisters. Gondul snickered while Sigrún and Hrist exchanged some private joke. Altvir closed her eyes and shook her head. Finally, Brynhild turned back to him. "You must bind the rings with your own pneuma for them to transfer the power. An exchange of pneuma."

Odin cocked his head to the side. Either Volund hadn't known, or hadn't bothered to tell him. So how was he to give these women his life force?

It is always the same, Valravn said. *The source of life.*

Now Hrist shook her head. "Why do you think the Sun Lord has only female valkyries, you imbecile?"

Odin ignored her temerity, this once. Mostly because the meaning behind her words hit him in the face and stole his breath. Why did sorcerers always train under those of opposite genders? Because sharing flesh was the surest way to share life essences. Pneuma.

The valkyries here had known it, when they made their oaths. And the looks of disgust they'd cast upon Odin ... because they knew the price it would take. Because Odin had, in essence, forced it upon them.

Even as he had so disdained Volund for his mistreatment of the girl. Now Odin himself would have to become the lecherous bastard.

"Oh, he gets it now," Gondul said.

Skögul hefted her thin shirt, exposing what little it had concealed. "Good. I'd hate to have to explain this part." She twisted her mouth up into an ugly sneer. "And it won't work unless it goes both ways. So don't disappoint me."

IN THE MORTAL REALM, Odin stood outside the ruined lodge, staring at his arrayed valkyries, each now clad once more in golden armor that glittered in the late afternoon light. No hint of softness graced any of their features. Did they see him as their rapist? All had come to him willingly, of course, desperately craving the powers he had stolen from them.

Men dreamed of bedding valkyries. Odin had not thought to gain such a boon—much less dreamt it would leave him feeling ill inside.

Utterly spent, he'd slept in their lodge. Of course, they dare not strike out against him now. Not when he had become the source of all their gifts.

Your victims ...

Audr's sick amusement choked Odin. It squeezed his heart and filled his mouth with the taste of ashes.

"Brynhild," he said at last. "Go to Hunaland and watch over Sigmund Volsungson." Sigmund remained the key to reclaiming the ring of Andvari and finally letting Odin reach Alfheim and rejoin Freyja. He'd dared to hope the valkyries could do so, but—as Brynhild seemed delighted inform him—they still could not take a living man past the Astral Realm. Some things lay beyond even their power.

With a last look at her sisters, the valkyrie beat her white wings and was aloft.

"Sigrún," Odin said. "You are to watch over Sigmund's son Fitela." The boy remained an unpredicted and unpredictable aberration in Odin's plans. He could not afford to let him go unchecked, but nor was Odin yet ready to have him killed.

He turned to Gondul. "You will go and keep watch upon Starkad Eightarms. Take care, though, as he holds some latent ability with the Sight and might detect your presence." Tyr's son was both an asset and a danger, and not one Odin liked long out of his sight.

The next two took flight.

"Skögul," Odin said, "to Valland. There is a bitter war coming, and I want the souls of the strongest from our side. Bring them to me in Asgard. Hildr, go with her and watch over Tyr." He looked to the others. "The rest of you with me. It's time you saw my plans for Valhalla."

5

Sixteen Years Ago

The locals called this place Wolf Lake, named so for dire wolves that still sometimes roamed this land. While men ruled Sviarland and thought themselves mighty, large swaths of it remained wild, covered in forest and marsh and old places thick with vaettir. Odin had wandered Sviarland oft in the past three decades.

Not so very far from these woods, King Gylfi had once reigned in Dalar, and served as Odin's voice on Midgard. But Gylfi was dead, and Sviarland had faced nigh unending war as one petty king after another struggled for dominance. Perhaps the blame for that lay at Odin's feet, too.

Now he walked the shores of Wolf Lake, a raven on one shoulder while another flew out, circling the old cabin there. Built perhaps fifty years ago—more, maybe. Now home only to an old couple long thought dead. At least until Odin had spied them from the High Seat. Until he had sent his ravens there to be sure.

An ancient, gray-bearded man hefted a spear as Odin drew nigh to the cabin. "You're trespassing."

Odin quirked the edge of a smile as he continued closer. "A king cannot trespass in his own lands."

"No king claims this wood. None who can enforce it, leastwise."

"One king claims all of Midgard, old man." Odin paused just out of range of the man's spear. "One to whom you long ago swore allegiance."

The man lowered his weapon. "Eh ... Odin?" Odin nodded once. "Troll shit." Not the greeting Odin had hoped for. "Does Hermod know we live? Does Sigyn?"

Odin rubbed his face as a cold wind blew across the lake. "We are both old men now. Can we not have this conversation by a fire?"

The cabin's door flew open and a gray-haired woman stood on the threshold, sword held in a slightly trembling hand. "What is he doing here?"

Odin snorted. "Fine way to address your king, Olrun. Here I am, asking your husband to let me share his fire."

Agilaz grunted then waved her to let them all inside. Glowering, Olrun did so. The former shieldmaiden slumped down by the fire, leaving her sword beside her as if she still expected to need to defend herself against him.

"Why now?" Agilaz asked when he had plopped down next to his wife. "Why after so many years?"

Odin lowered himself by the fire and warmed his hands. What to tell them? Now, because now the High Seat had allowed him to find them. Now because his ravens had confirmed what the seat had revealed. Now ... because now Odin's visions had revealed some connection between Olrun and valkyries.

Holding more knowledge than most men could dream

of, Odin also found himself with more questions. And Agilaz's earlier question seemed easier to answer and less likely to reveal more about Odin's own limitations than he cared to. He looked to the old man. "Your son and daughter do not know you live." An easy deduction, considering either one of them had more than enough cunning to have found their parents by now. "And I can only assume that's because you think it easier for them to think you died on the crossing to Vanaheim."

Olrun rubbed her hands. "They're immortal. Best they not have to watch us wither away. We've had long lives. Longer than most."

"Especially you," Odin said.

Olrun flinched, then groaned. "Fuck. That's why you're here, isn't it? Not because you missed us or sought after our wellbeing or—"

"Did you miss me?" Odin asked. "I am not afforded the luxury of making my decisions based on friendships or sentiments."

Audr cackled in his mind. *Insipid self-delusions ... as if all actions were not driven by the selfish pursuit of one ... best left lost ...*

Odin grit his teeth at the sudden mental image of Freyja.

"No?" Agilaz said. "Then be out with it, Odin. I am tired. I wish only to live out what few winters remain to me in peace, not struggling in war or facing horrors of the mist."

Odin grunted, then stroked his beard. "You wish me gone, Agilaz? You have but to answer my questions and neither I nor any Ás under my order shall trouble you again."

"These days you command more than the Aesir," Agilaz said.

Olrun raised a hand to stop her husband's objection. "It

doesn't matter anymore. We don't have so very much life left in any event. I would not waste what I have in argument with him. In truth, I cannot tell you all you wish to know. I have spent so long stripped of my powers my memories have become a haze, blending with dream and nightmare, until I can longer say what truly happened."

The implication of her words hit Odin like a blow. "You were a valkyrie yourself."

"It was a lifetime ago, before the Njarar War."

Odin leaned forward. "Tell me."

"I ... some few of us, caught between life and death, we sought immortality, after a fashion."

"The rings."

"They gave us power and made us half-mortal and ... half-vaettr, almost. Allowed us to pass between the Mortal Realm and ... beyond."

Odin nodded. "You could enter the Penumbra. Pierce the Veil."

Olrun shuddered and covered her face with her hands. "We guided souls through it. Souls that he wanted."

"Who?"

"I can't ... even now my oath binds me, stops me from uttering a name. I broke my bonds, destroyed my ring ... reclaimed my humanity."

Agilaz took her hand in his own.

Odin nodded in sudden understanding. She had chosen a mortal life for the sake of her family. Her family ... "You were a valkyrie when you bore Hermod."

Now she glared at Odin with a sudden fire. "Do not drag my son into your machinations. Naught to do with what lies beyond death need concern him."

Odin frowned, slightly, but nodded in acknowledgement. "Tell me more."

"There was a lodge. There were nine of us."

"Under Skögul?"

Olrun gaped. "How do you ...?"

Svanhit had told him as much, and Olrun's reaction confirmed that she had belonged to the same lodge as Svanhit. Sisters, after a fashion.

Odin leaned in closer. "Where. Where was this lodge, Olrun?"

The woman sighed. "Lappmarken, the mountains that form the border with Nidavellir. North of here, not so far. I ... we were responsible for a vast region. Here, parts of Nidavellir, and into Reidgotaland."

"There are other lodges."

She nodded.

"How many?"

She frowned. "I don't know."

"How many valkyries are there?"

"I don't know that, either," Olrun snapped. "Normally, if one fell, her ring would go to another. A woman elevated. But I destroyed mine so ..."

Odin nodded slowly. The valkyries gathered souls. Svanhit had once tried to gain mastery of Odin's soul, and doing so had cost her. They gathered strong souls for some master in the Spirit Realm. But if he had his own valkyries, Odin might harness those souls himself, and thus further prepare for Ragnarok. He would need all the power he could garner if Midgard was to survive.

The living and the dead. All must soon be made to serve his will, or all would perish in the final end of the world.

"You're going to fail," Olrun said.

Odin cocked his head. Had she heard his thoughts? Did some vestige of the power she once held yet remain to her? No, no, she meant he would fail in his obvious attempt to gain mastery over the valkyries. "What makes you think that?"

"You have no idea how powerful my sisters are."

Oh, he had some idea. Odin had fought Svanhit once, and barely defeated her. But that was a long time ago. He'd come far since then. Besides, by the time he went to find this lodge, Volund's work would be complete. And Odin would have the edge he needed.

6

The journey from the city of Thrymheim to the hall of Vafthrudnir was rougher than Skadi remembered. A broken path of shattered ice that her smaller, human form had trouble navigating. It forced her to climb, jump, and otherwise exert herself in a most undignified manner. Still, her old master knew more than most any being alive on Midgard.

He'd served on the Elder Council before the breaking of Brimir, an aid to his father Aurgelmir, before the Great Father walked away from his throne. Vafthrudnir knew of elder days, before the mists, or so Skadi's own father had claimed. On his order the old ones had dug out the glacier and built their homes here on the plateau left behind.

While Vafthrudnir was wont to expound on the glory of Brimir, he did not speak oft of his father, as if the topic itself were forbidden. Even then, as a young woman, Skadi had sensed a depth of pain behind his eyes. Deeper than the pain all frost jotunnar held at the abandonment of the Great Father. It was the beginning of the end of Brimir.

Huffing, constrained by the limits of her mortal form,

Skadi made her way to the top where Vafthrudnir had carved his Refuge into the mountainside.

Hateful flames flickered in braziers at the entrance, burning away mist. Inside, Vafthrudnir called on the Art to infuse ice with inner radiance, but out here, he kindled flame, as if to test his own kindred.

Skadi stood panting at the entryway, shaking her head.

Did her old teacher know of the ultimate fate of his father? Aurgelmir had ventured into Midgard, perhaps even made the first breach, and there—calling himself Ymir—had slaughtered Aesir to bring out the Destroyer. The man who would dare to stand against Hel. The goddess had commanded it, Skadi knew from her host's memories, though why Ymir had agreed to a mission like to end in his death, she didn't know. A bargain made, but the goddess took few confidants into her counsel, and Skadi could not count herself among them.

She ventured inside, having little doubt she was expected. No one surprised Vafthrudnir.

He met her, not where she'd have expected on the upper balcony where he oft gave his lectures, but in the foyer. The ancient jotunn had begun to show his age, at long last. Creases marred his eyes, his cheeks. His white beard looked a hint more threadbare than she'd remembered. As if this being, who should have lived forever, had finally started to wither away during the long ages Skadi passed in death.

He cracked a hint of a smile, exposing more wrinkles yet at the same time making them seem all the more becoming. "I missed you, Little Öndur."

Skadi couldn't help but smile herself at the familiarity, and the name. Ski. As she had once loved to do, in the old days. The pleasures of life, before the shadows of death had crushed them.

"Come," he said, and led her down a passage lit by chunks of ice stuck on the wall, carved in the likeness of flame and imbued with iridescent light shimmering within. He guided her down a staircase to a circular chamber.

In life, he'd allowed her to visit the Mirror Room only a few times in her studies. Oh, she'd come past here, oft enough, stealing a glance inside with passing. Beyond this room, Vafthrudnir's great cauldrons rested, where he crafted the alchemical brews he prepared for jotunn royals willing to pay the price. Those cauldrons were relics of Brimir themselves, the art of their making now lost to most of jotunnkind.

But cauldrons meant naught compared to the wonder of *this* room.

Nine mirrors of quicksilver lined the walls. Wrought in the dark tunnels of Nidavellir and bargained for or stolen from the dvergar over the course of ages. The surfaces could have almost seemed murky waters, rimmed by intricately carved frames of silver or platinum. Those frames oft depicted beasts great and foul, monstrosities that slept deep beneath the world or waited tireless in the Otherworlds for their chance to gorge themselves in the Mortal Realm. Warnings, perhaps, of what looking too deep into the mirrors might show.

Vafthrudnir paused, allowing her to inspect the room and its remarkable devices. Beautiful art wrought in crafts of terrible power. They served to magnify a sorcerer's Sight, reflecting it infinitely until one could look into distant places. To see. And to be seen.

I had one ...

Oh. Skadi's host seemed lucid for a moment. And she'd had a dverg quicksilver mirror. Yes, Skadi could see it, in the sorceress's memories. Gudrun had kept it hidden away, feared to look upon it, and rightly so.

After a moment more, Vafthrudnir strode to a mirror, mumbling incantations, and placed his hand upon the surface. It rippled, flowing around his palm until he finally pulled his hand away. A shimmer built in the mirror, a vision revealed, even as Gudrun drifted closer. Only a great sorcerer could have allowed the mirror to reveal its secrets to another person. Vafthrudnir was beyond great.

The image clarified, depicting an old man mounted upon an eight-legged horse, riding across snowy plains. Odin Borrson.

Skadi grimaced. The persistent, festering wound in the side of the goddess. And whomever removed that wound must surely win Hel's favor. "He rides for here?"

"Not yet. But he will. He must pass through many king-doms in Jotunheim to reach Thrymheim."

Skadi looked to Vafthrudnir. "You could stop him."

"Perhaps. But it is not my way to intervene thus." Not anymore, perhaps. "I merely share information so that you, Öndur, may act as you please."

"Working together we could prove unstoppable."

The old jotunn smiled forlornly and shook his head. "There are so many things I've learned in the passing ages since you left this world. Brimir is gone, and so too did the arm of the Vanir weaken. The sons of Halfdan have all but faded away. This era is drawing to a close, dear one. A battle is coming, unlike aught you have ever seen before. The princes of Brimir bestir themselves, thinking to claim a golden age they believe stolen from them."

"Believe? It *was* stolen. The Vanir took it from us."

Another sad shake of his head. "An instrument of the inexorable march of history, made necessary by failings from within. No empire can stand forever without giving rise to corruption, for the simple reason that innocence is ill-prepared to deal with perils. The very shift in paradigms that allow the empire to sustain itself in hardship are the same that must eventually undermine it."

She wasn't hearing this. Not from *him*. "Did you not extol the virtues of Brimir over the course of countless hours?"

"Without doubt, it was glorious. But as I said, I have had millennia to study since then. To think. To read the ancient writings of Mimir. To watch." He moved to another mirror, whispered an incantation and touched it. Again, the image shifted before Skadi's eyes. This time, it revealed a land covered in greenery, steaming, so hot Skadi could almost feel it through the mirror. And there, a deep skinned man fighting against a woman who looked half-dead. The woman flung ice and mist as weapons.

A sudden certainty hit Skadi, a revelation of truth. The Queen of Mist herself, fighting the Destroyer. The battle of a prior era. Nigh to five thousand years ago? The coming of the mists. Hel succeeded in flooding the world with her power, yet still lost her host thanks to the Destroyer.

Vafthrudnir made no comment, instead moving to a third mirror. What did the old jotunn mean to show her? What was his point among all this? Again, he drew forth an image. A man on his knees, covered in blood. Holding the broken body of a woman dying from terrible wounds.

Vafthrudnir let a hand fall on Skadi's shoulder now. "Humans and jotunnar are not so different. They too love their children."

Skadi knew that man. He'd fought her, when she tried to deliver Odin's soul to Hel. Loki—or Loge as the Niflungar knew him. A fire-priest with powers drawn from Muspelheim. He looked different, subtly, but the eyes, the face, they seemed much the same. It had to be him. Holding his dying daughter, watching the life leave her eyes.

Eyes ... cold. Black ... eyes. Her eyes ... Hel.

Skadi swooned, held upright only by Vafthrudnir's suddenly tight grip on her shoulder. How? How could ... a man ... be the father of the goddess of Niflheim? Queen of the Mists ... It was impossible. "W-when was this?"

Vafthrudnir grunted. "The world is not what you think it is."

"T-tell me ..."

"No. Knowledge must be hard-won, or it means naught. You think you have suffered, but you have only begun to see the secret shadows at play behind the web of history."

The old jotunn released her and Skadi held a hand to her mouth. Impossible nonsense ...

"I ..." Skadi swallowed, uncertain what to make of all this. "I'm not sure it changes aught. I still have to win over as many jotunn lands as possible so I can press my claim to the throne here."

"Of course. We must all do as urd compels us."

Skadi nodded. "I ... I need a new host. A jotunn body, a beautiful one."

Vafthrudnir nodded, and Skadi touched another mirror, speaking the words to activate it. From this, a hall slowly came into view. A jotunn king, upon his throne. And his wife, blue-tinted skin and a fell look in her eyes.

"King Geirrod, and his wife Angrboda," Vafthrudnir said.

Skadi allowed herself a smile. "She'll do."

7

*A*sgard's pristine beaches greeted Odin upon his return. The mists surrounded the isles as if held back by a physical barrier, kept at bay by the power of Yggdrasil. Such a sight was both a boon to his weary soul and a warning of how truly precarious his position was. But for the power of the tree, Asgard would become one more land in Midgard.

Choked and dying under poison mists.

The lands that lay before him were not some paradise, but rather, the true state of the world. The state he hoped one day to return to Midgard. If Ragnarok did not destroy it all first.

With the Sight embraced, he could see and hear his valkyries, trailing along behind him in the Penumbra. They had chatted oft enough on the paths leading to these shores. Flight over the waters had rather precluded it after, and now they'd fallen almost silent. As if themselves awed to see a land not so very thick with ghosts.

Oh, vaettir of various sorts watched from across the Veil,

even on Asgard. But fewer, and less aggrieved than those found elsewhere.

Upon Sleipnir's back, Odin made his way along well-worn paths, nodding at those he came upon.

"My king!" someone said.

"Welcome home, my king."

"Today is blessed, my king."

Of course, he could have disguised himself using a glamour. Audr's power allowed it. But every use of those powers strengthened the wraith and weakened Odin's soul. His guises were best saved for when dealing with humans out in Midgard.

Outside Valaskjalf, Odin dismounted and patted Sleipnir's shoulder. "Go on. Run free and have something to eat." From Valaskjalf rose a silver spire upon which rested Odin's High Seat. To sit there and gaze out over the world was both a relief and a burden, draining and all too necessary.

Like so many of Volund's works, in truth. A double-edged sword.

The double doors stood open, inviting crowds of courtiers to come and bemoan their grievances to the Queen of Asgard. This throng parted as Odin strode inside and made his way to the back of the hall.

Frigg sat upon her throne—beside Odin's perpetually empty one—but rose as he entered, offering him a too formal nod in greeting. She wore an elaborately embroidered green dress, maybe one of Serklander silk, though the embroidery was local. Head to toe, she looked the part of royalty.

A stark contrast to Odin's travel-worn clothes, muddy cloak, and oversized hat. Which, of course, remained part of the point. While Frigg stayed here to run Asgard, Odin could walk freely across the land, oft unrecognized even without a disguise. An old vagabond drew few eyes and men said much in front of those they thought of little account.

Odin returned Frigg's nod, and she resumed her seat and with it, her court. They'd speak later, her words no doubt filled with thinly veiled recriminations about his long absences. He'd offer meaningless words of remorse. And naught would change.

Despite her objections, Odin had to believe Frigg truly understood the burdens he bore. That she knew, were he to turn from this urd, chaos would eventually claim all lands.

Leaving behind the great hall, he traveled to the back of Valaskjalf, where a small number of cells housed an even smaller number of prisoners. Most of his enemies Odin made a point of disposing of permanently. Some few though, either couldn't die—like Fenrir bound far beneath Asgard—or he couldn't bring himself to slay.

As with Lodur.

Odin's onetime friend rose as Odin pulled open the door to his cell.

The man groaned, stretched his back, and made as if to pace about his tiny room. Since the confines would have allowed him no more than a handful of steps in one direction, such a gesture would have made him look like a caged animal. Perhaps Lodur realized it, for he gave over pacing and instead leaned against a wall. "Did you miss me?"

In a way, Odin had. He missed the rival he'd known so long ago, when they were both young men. Lodur had fostered with Odin's family back then. Back when Odin's greatest care was what to hunt for the night meal or how best to get a pretty shieldmaiden to drop her trousers. He missed the days—struggles though they'd been—of simpler life.

His father's murder had changed all that. The beginning of the end, really, for all Aesir.

How badly Odin wished he could recall the happy days with clarity, but like so much else, he'd lost bits and pieces of his memories because of the Art. Because of ... Audr.

"I find myself ever wondering what I am to do with you," Odin said at last.

Lodur snorted. "If eighteen winters didn't give you the answer, I won't hold out much hope of hearing one in the next hour or so."

Leaning against his walking stick, Odin ignored that. His old friend had always thought himself cleverer than he really was. No doubt that had led him to his present situation, imprisoned for treason.

"Naught to say, great king?" Lodur asked. "Perhaps because the walls whisper how your allies slowly slip away from you. Even as your fame spreads, so too does your infamy."

Odin groaned and shook his head. "I have what allies I most need in the places where I desire them. I had dared to hope you might have had the time to reflect on your errors, old friend."

Now Lodur burst out in mirthless laughter. "Would you have me throw myself at your feet and beg for mercy?" He spat on the ground before Odin. "I'd sooner die. You have brought the Aesir far, dear king. Far from our home, far from our old ways. Far from honor and into the halls of intrigue and corruption, of faithlessness and debasement upon the altar of your glory."

Grumbling, Odin stormed from the cell and slammed the door behind him. "Have him bathed," Odin snapped at a guard. "He stinks of his own shit."

"It was by my hands we wrought this world!" Lodur

shouted through the oak door. "And what have you made of it now, *king*? What have you wrought in five decades of your rule?"

Odin grit his teeth and stomped out of Valaskjalf, brushing away courtiers and old friends in the process. Lodur was wrong. He had allies aplenty. He'd spent the years earning them across the North Realms.

Almost as many allies as enemies, in fact.

Telling himself that did not quite abate the sour churn of Odin's stomach.

"You betrayed your own friend?" Altvir asked, her voice flighty and distorted across the Veil.

"No," Odin snapped. "Lodur betrayed me. And I was a fool not to have him disemboweled for it."

"Then you plan to kill him now?" Altvir asked, exchanging a look with Svanhit.

"So that I might look petulant in present and short-sighted in my past decisions?" Odin shook his head. "No, now he must be left to rot until such time as I find a use for him."

Hrist snickered. "My new lord must come here oft, seeking redemption for things long past."

Rather than reward the valkyrie's keen insight, Odin shot her a baleful glare. Passersby looked at him askance as he conversed with his invisible and inaudible companions. Odin was not overmuch concerned with their opinions though. A reputation for eccentricity, even madness, might serve his ends.

It almost made him wonder how mad Mundilfari had truly gone in days past, when he had sat on Vanaheim's throne.

ODIN FOUND Loki on the slopes below Valaskjalf, watching the sunset along with Sigyn. The pyromancer may have seen Odin's need for him in the flames. Or perhaps he'd merely caught wind of Odin's return and come here to greet his blood brother.

Either way, as Odin drew nigh, Sigyn rose, cast him a glance, and then departed.

Loki beckoned for Odin to join him. The man sat precariously perched on a rock jutting out over a sheer drop of at least a hundred feet, far from the beaten path.

While Odin didn't much relish climbing out there, he certainly would not refuse the invitation from one of his truest allies. Yes, bad blood had passed between them over the years, and more when Odin had learned that Hel herself was Loki's long dead daughter from a distant era. But despite it all, Loki had come to save Odin from Skadi's wrath. Such loyalty earned him Odin's eternal gratitude.

So, walking stick braced against the loose ground, he made his cautious steps out to the edge, then slid down onto his arse beside the other man. Loki could have passed for a fraction of Odin's age though in truth, the man had lived long before the current era of the world. How long, exactly, Odin was still trying to discern.

Loki clasped Odin's arm and Odin returned the gesture.

"How long have you been back from Valland?" Odin asked.

"A while. Things will come to a head there soon, but not during winter."

Things had been simmering there for many years. Andalus was lost to the Serklanders. And if Valland fell, the Utgard-based empire would own the South Realms, at least in the west. Odin had forestalled this somewhat by provoking a war between Serkland and Miklagard, but that would not last forever.

"Something else troubles you," Odin said.

"Such are the burdens of prescience and premonition, brother. As you well know. Can you tell me when last you slept peaceful, untormented by visions or fears or duties?"

Odin grunted. In truth, probably when last he lay in Freyja's arms, daring to forget the world for a moment. Giving in to the same apathy that had so consumed the Vanir and led them to fail the world. "I notice you did not answer my question."

Loki flashed him a wry grin that—unless Odin missed his guess—contained less mirth than it ought to have. "And what of you? You play a dangerous game, seeking to harness the dead. You paid heavily for trying such already, and still you persist. Consider that, perhaps, the Veil is best left unpenetrated."

"Your companion knows of what he speaks," Hrist said.

Loki looked in her direction as if he'd heard her. Possessed of the Sight, perhaps he had. Odin remained uncertain how far Loki's gift matched his own.

The valkyrie fell back several steps up the mountain, perhaps equally aghast to find another aware of her presence.

Odin turned his gaze to clouds the sun had dipped behind, letting his vision linger on the brilliant streaks running through the sky. "Save your warnings about the Veil for your daughter."

Loki flinched at that and Odin immediately regretted his words. Still, Hel pushed in from her side, plaguing the Mortal Realm. It seemed only fitting Odin respond in kind.

Odin ran a hand over his beard and sniffed. "I'll not be

drawn into this argument again, brother. I don't begrudge you this respite, but Valland needs you. If it falls, we are faced with a foe we have no resources to combat."

"Indeed. But I had to see Sigyn and Hödr. They are both troubled."

Odin wrapped an arm around his brother's shoulders. He hardly needed say he understood the desire to protect one's family. "I'll look after them, as best I'm able while I remain here."

"Your attention is drawn to the new hall you build."

Odin had wondered how much Loki knew of Valhalla or what Odin had Hermod doing with it. The flames told his brother so many things. Some, Odin might have preferred remain concealed. He said naught in answer.

"I hope you know what you're doing." Loki shook his head. "You intend to start wars."

"I intend to claim strong souls as a bulwark against the last days of the world. Old men dying in their bed from the thickness do very little enhance our ranks."

Loki sighed. "Now, finally, you have what you sought. You will see things finished with Serkland, at least for the present."

"No," Odin said, drawing a raised eyebrow from his brother. "You will. When winter breaks, you must return to Valland. Arrest the Serklander advance however it seems needful. I will not lose this world to them."

Loki grunted. "Your friend Tyr is the warrior and the leader of men." And no great friend of Loki's, though Odin's brother left that unsaid.

Odin clapped him on the shoulder. "It will come to a head soon enough, brother. And I suspect it will take all you and Tyr both have to sway the battle in our favor."

Loki nodded slowly, and Odin rose.

Now back on Asgard, he had something else to see to. The High Seat beckoned.

8

Sixteen Years Ago

For decades the Valls had fought against the spread of the Serkland Caliphate. Odin had long sent young Aesir to Andalus, to train under Tyr and make names for themselves fighting the Utgarders. Tyr's alliance with the Valland Empire had remained ever tenuous but never quite fractured, and, regardless, it served Odin's ends well enough to have his people tested here before they could earn an apple.

Odin passed among the tents, largely unnoticed. Hundreds of soldiers kept dozens of bonfires burning day and night, keeping the mist away from their camps. A wooden palisade surrounded the camp, but the outer doors remained open in daylight, and countless army followers entered and left. Washerwomen and cooks, fishermen bringing in the day's catch, and whores come to ease frustrations. The clanging of anvils greeted Odin's entry. Smiths working forges long hours to keep the officers in mail and the rest in at least gambeson. A man without armor might find his career short. Any who lived long enough used their first pay at the smithy.

Odin's own son Thor had fought here not so very many years ago, well armed and well armored thanks to Odin's wealth. Thor had brought honor to his family, even as his initial banishment here had been punishment. Almost, Odin wished Thor was still here now, so rarely did he get to see his son.

Back then, they'd still held the Straits. Slowly, the Valls had fallen back, losing ground to the Caliphate. One day soon, Odin would be forced to make a more concerted effort again Serkland or risk them claiming the South Realms.

"Odin?" Tyr called. Odin's one-handed friend came blundering over and wrapped him in a mighty bear hug. "Gods, man. How long's it been?"

"Long." Odin clapped the man on the back. "Too long."

Tyr pulled away and nodded. "Not since Roland ..."

Odin knew his friend had taken the passing hard, but Roland had been mortal, and a warrior at that. He'd died bravely, if perhaps in vain. Serkland's strength swelled and, as yet, Odin had not given enough time into his plan to ignite war between the Caliphate and the Miklagardian Empire. So many places, so many events all needed his attention and he could not attend to all of them at once.

Tyr grunted. "I'm glad you've come. But why?"

Odin led him away, out of earshot. "I must speak to Hermod. Is he still your captain here?"

"He leads scouts. South. Taking the measure of our foes. We must strike back."

Odin nodded. A thought sent a raven to flight, soaring out over the woods to the south. His birds would find Hermod more quickly than any human scout might manage.

"Stay," Tyr said. "Take the night meal."

Odin nodded. He would stay for now, and depart under the moonlight. His mission did not allow him to tarry longer than that.

🐾

In the end, Hermod found him, as Odin knew he would. Odin sat against a rock on a hill well into Serklander domain, singing softly. His ravens told him no one save Hermod and his scouts were about, and regardless, Odin did not fear common Serkland soldiers. Some of their people, their sorcerers, they posed a threat, as did the Sons of Muspel. Few others did.

Hermod came trudging up the hill, covered in mud and grime, making almost no sound as he walked. Were it not for the ravens, Odin might not have even known the man approached.

Before Odin, Hermod dropped to one knee. "My king."

Odin grunted and pushed himself to his feet. "Oh, stand up. You're not a South Realmer to grovel before a king, and besides which, you are much like a second son to me."

"I ... I am flattered, my king." But he did rise.

And, of course, it was flattery. Odin needed Hermod, and he needed him loyal. Nothing bred loyalty more than its return. Sigyn was Frigg's half-sister, and thus part of the royal family. And Hermod was Sigyn's foster brother, making him roughly Odin's brother-in-law. But *son* created a greater bond of subservience, one Odin would need to make use of now.

Hermod was born of a valkyrie. If some portion of Olrun's gift had passed on to Hermod, he might well be able to pass between realms like a valkyrie. And if so, no better ally might serve Odin's needs as a messenger.

Odin clasped Hermod's arm on his own. "The battles here will grow worse before they grow better."

Hermod nodded. "So Tyr claims, as well. We cannot hold out against the Serklanders much longer, not without the full support of Asgard."

Odin grimaced and pulled away from Hermod. A pitched war between Valland and Serkland might serve to create a great many dead warriors, some of them powerful. If Odin were in a position to gather those souls and make use of them, it might serve his ends. If not, such a battle might only lead to waste. "I cannot yet commit such forces to Valland."

"My king ... time runs out. With each passing summer the fire-worshippers press further into Andalus. Soon they will break into Valland itself. From there, they could access Hunaland or even Asgard."

No. The perilous reefs around Asgard would make such an approach difficult at best. And should the Serklanders land upon the shores of Asgard, there they'd find warriors unlike those they faced here in the south. Still, Hermod's point remained—if Valland fell, Serkland would push into the North Realms.

"I need time, Hermod. More than just these foes claw their way at the fringes of our world. The Midgard Wall is failing and jotunnar roam free. The legions of Miklagard push into Bjarmaland." And the Niflungar were not yet wholly broken, still working Hel's will upon this world. So many enemies, and Odin had not the strength or time to tend to them all.

He needed a battle here, but not now, not yet.

"What would it take to hold the line?" Odin asked.

"Hold it? Not push it forward?"

No, just enough to keep Serkland from toppling Valland, and no more.

Hermod scratched at his beard. "Another pack of varulfur to harry their scouts might slow their advance."

Odin frowned. Varulfur and berserkir grew fewer and fewer among the Aesir, as Hermod well knew. Many had died here, in fact, and others who served Fenrir in the war with the Vanir. Odin kept but a few varulfur to guard Asgard and any sent away would become a breach in his defenses.

"I'll see what I can arrange when next I'm in Asgard."

The look Hermod shot Odin held an unspoken rebuke —as if Odin oft returned home these days.

Odin scoffed. "Oh, I am going back soon enough, and you must return to Asgard with me."

"But I—"

"You will help select the warriors to bulwark this place personally."

Hermod frowned. "Surely Tyr would better serve that end."

Quite likely, but Odin needed Tyr to hold the line and needed Hermod to help with other pursuits, those beyond Tyr's abilities. "Come. We have much work to do."

9

*U*nclad save for the blanket draped over her shoulders, the early morning winds outside chilled Sif almost to the bone, though she refused to close the shutters. Rather she stared outside, hoping to catch a glimpse of the sunrise despite the mists. A slight coloring of the sky behind those vapors was all she found. A fleeting pleasure in a dying land.

Behind her, Thor still snored in their bed.

King Rollaugr had given them this place on the edge of Holmgard. A watchtower otherwise abandoned due to the encroachment of jotunnar from the east.

Strange, how so many in Midgard considered the jotunnar almost children's stories, while the people of Bjarmaland lived in constant fear of them. Every summer the Thunderers—what few of them remained—would trek out and hunt those jotunnar who tried to lair too nigh to the border. Winters, though, when the frost jotunnar seemed strongest, it was all the Thunderers could do to defend this border. Every passing year, the numbers and strength of their foes increased.

66

It was like watching the world die one day at a time.

Even old Rollaugr seemed to have all but given up on his own kingdom. Sif had heard the tales, of course, that the man's son had died in an ill-fated punitive expedition against Miklagard. Only sheer stubbornness had kept him on the throne since, or so rumor claimed.

So many years now they'd fought the jotunnar. One petty jotunn king after another, some strong enough even the Thunderers dared not go up against them. Well, most of the Thunderers. She glanced back at Thor. Someone always had to talk him down. The man would wrestle a mountain just to prove he could.

Still, her husband had grown. Time was, he'd not have listened to anyone. Now at least he'd give real weight to Sif's opinions, and the twins', too.

Maybe then, he'd listen to what they all had to say now.

After dressing as quietly as possible, Sif slipped outside their room in the upper reaches of the tower. It had probably once belonged to a watch commander, since the only other living space was clearly a barracks. Geri and Freki didn't seem to mind it overmuch. The two of them oft as not just curled up by the fire pit.

Sif had come in on them once and found them whispering conspiratorially in the way only close siblings could ever manage. Plotting pranks, no doubt, or considering some mischief or other. Damn, but Sif loved those varulfur. Thrúd used to call them Auntie and Uncle Wolfie.

Now, Sif found them not in the barracks but in their second-favorite room, the kitchen, which was actually a separate building across a short path from the tower. The smoke billowing from it announced their presence inside even before their snickering laughter did.

Geri looked up abruptly at Sif's entrance, the varulf's

short hair swaying, a grin on her lips. "Can you believe the gall of this bastard?" At Sif's raised eyebrow she continued. "Suggesting I ought to go find a male varulf to help continue the species."

Freki winked at Sif. "Our numbers have dwindled."

"Then *you* go plant one in some bitch."

Freki snickered. "I *do*. Every chance I get. They just don't let us keep the whelps."

Sif ran a hand through her hair, shifted uncomfortably, then leaned against the wall. Freki's words stung, though he surely hadn't meant them to. These days, Sif almost never saw her daughter. The girl had insisted on fostering with Tyr, and Thor had insisted on coming back out to this forsaken wasteland.

"Ugh," Geri said. She kept one eye on whatever she was cooking in that cauldron. Smelled of leeks and some kind of meat. "Can't be good."

Freki raised his hands in a warding gesture. "I wasn't asking *you* to bear the whelps, Sif. Relax."

Sif ignored that, opened her mouth, and couldn't quite find the words, so she shut it again. Cleared her throat. "We have to tell him."

"Ah," Geri said. "That ought to make for a lovely morning. You want me to track down a troll or something for him to smash afterward, to turn his mood around?"

Sif frowned, shaking her head. "We've known this was coming. Isn't it better to just have out with it?"

Freki chuckled. "She's bursting at the seams."

Truer than the varulf probably realized. Knowing what needed doing, knowing she would have to anger Thor, it had hung over her head like a storm cloud apt to burst into thunder any moment. Days of fighting jotunnar and nights of making love could only push away that dangling threat for but so long.

"I hope you're making something he'll like for the day meal," Sif said.

"Freki caught a few squirrels," Geri answered, giving the cauldron another stir.

Hardly Thor's favorite, but at least it was meat. Some days they found naught but mushrooms and roots. Even the varulf twins couldn't always catch game without roaming too far from camp, which Thor had forbidden.

After losing so many of the Thunderers, he'd grown cautious, at least with the lives of others.

"It's almost ready if you want to wake him," Geri said.

Sif wanted to ... and didn't at the same time. Because waking him would mean hastening the breaking of that storm cloud. But it had to break sooner or later. Thunder could not be contained forever.

⁂

THOR GAVE every sign of being pleased with squirrel soup. Whether he actually was, or simply offered a little uncharacteristic politeness to his foster sister, Sif couldn't say.

Either way, the four of them sat in the tower's dining hall, a place no doubt originally intended to serve a score or more of hungry warriors. Like so much of this land, it was an empty remnant of times now drawing to a close.

The end of the age of man.

Thor upended the bowl and noisily slurped the last of its contents while Sif stared at him. The prince then tossed it down, and the clay dish skittered along the table.

"Like it?" Geri asked.

Thor flashed a grin. "Starting a day eating squirrel is always better than starting the day eating what squirrels eat." He chuckled at something. "Father ever tell you about that giant squirrel he found in the boughs of Yggdrasil? Hard to believe it, really. What I wouldn't have given to see such a beast!"

Sif folded her hands on the table in front of her and leaned forward. "We need to talk."

"Ugh." Thor looked pointedly at Freki instead of her. "You ever hear those words, brother, you run for cover. Never a direr battle cry was sounded."

Freki grinned. "And yet, here you sit."

"Indeed! I'm too stuffed to run. Foul trick, that, Geri. Foul trick."

Sif sighed. Freki playing along with Thor's antics did not exactly set the mood for the rather serious discussion she needed to have with her husband. "We cannot save Holmgard." There, it was out there. "The four of us are not a match for the growing number of jotunnar. The locals can do naught. This land is *lost*, Thor." Ironically, the end of the Miklagardian advance had only hastened the jotunn domination of Bjarmaland.

The smile slipped off his face in an instant. "You suggest we abandon those we've come here to protect? Leave them to fall before the encroaching chaos?"

"They're dying already," Freki pointed out. "We but delay the inevitable."

"Oh?" Thor shot him a glare. "And you're in on this, as well? The both of you?" The last he aimed at Geri, who suddenly seemed to be busy staring out a window. "Well?" When no one answered, Thor slapped the table. "I'm not leaving men to die!"

"All men die," Sif said. "If we remain here, sooner or

later, so will we. And dying for something is one thing. But dying for a cause that cannot be won ..."

Thor grumbled something under his breath, then pressed his thumbs into his brows. Sif could swear she could hear his teeth grinding from across the table. Finally, he looked up, staring hard at her. Then at the varulf twins. "Did Father tell you aught of Ragnarok?"

Sif frowned at the strange word.

Now Geri did look at the prince. "He told us there would come a final battle between the Aesir and the forces of chaos."

Thor nodded, then pointed out the window into the snowy fields around the tower. "That. Right there. Out beyond the border—that's chaos. I don't pretend to know all Father gets enmeshed in. I do know he's roaming all over Midgard and beyond, always seeking some way to stop the fight or to win it. Because that chaos—it's coming for everyone. Everywhere." He turned back to Sif. "I don't know much more than that. But I do know jotunnar are more like than not to side with the forces of chaos. And every one of them we kill is one less left to bring war and death to Midgard."

A bitter chill settled over Sif at Thor's words. In her mind's eye, she could see armies of jotunnar closing in from all sides. Frost and fire jotunnar, intent to drag the world of men into the night. But from what she'd seen, the world was *already* dying. So was this Ragnarok the culmination of what they already faced? Or had it already begun? Or worse still ... "What if we are the ones starting it?"

"What?"

"We go out there, hunt them down, kill them like beasts. Do we not risk provoking them?"

Freki groaned. "Well, fuck. You had to go and say that,

didn't you, Sif? Here I was, thinking we were making things at least a little better."

Thor slapped the table again. "This is no jest! If we falter, Midgard pays the price."

Sif winced and let her head fall into her palm. What was she to say to him? How to convince Thor that their current tactics risked everything to gain naught? How to make him see ... their place was at Thrúd's side?

Even as Sif looked up, Geri spoke. "Your words don't really change the situation. If some great battle is coming, weakening our foes is important, yes, but throwing our lives away achieves naught. The four of us—immortals, Aesir—we are the bulwark against the chaos you fear. Dying for a lost cause doesn't help Midgard, Thor."

"You'd have me abandon these people? Now? After so many years of trying to protect them. And in the depths of winter, no less, when jotunn raids have only grown in frequency?"

"We'll wait until summer if that appeases you," Freki said. "But the three of us are in agreement. The Thunderers should return to Asgard. Either we come back here with more men and make this a real war, or we withdraw and lend our blades where there is some hope of victory. Better to fortify Sviarland or Aujum. Indeed, even Rollaugr might be convinced to abandon the colony and retreat to his homeland."

Thor leveled a hard stare on each of them in turn. Then he rose stiffly. "I won't hear another word of this. Leave if you must. Bring others if you can. I will stay out the winter and protect these people."

And, of course, none of them would leave Thor here alone.

The prince stormed out, leaving Sif to look at the twins, their faces seeming as helpless as hers no doubt was.

10

igh atop the tower crowning Valaskjalf, the High Seat sat, gleaming in the moonlight. An arching canopy covered half the spire's pinnacle and over-shadowed the throne, though enough space existed behind it that Odin could walk the tower's perimeter and gaze out over his islands.

Asgard had become a symbol to the people of the North Realms. Maybe the same symbol Vanaheim had once been before centuries of isolation had rendered the so-called gods distant from the lands of men.

Silver plated the tower, so that sunlight made it gleam like a wonder, always serving as a beckon to the royal court. The High Seat itself, however, was the true treasure. A throne Volund had wrought—at great cost—to enhance Odin's prowess with the Sight and allow him to focus his gaze anywhere in the Mortal Realm or, at times, even beyond it.

THROUGH ANDALUS and beyond the Straits of Herakles lay the expansive Utgard empire—the Serkland Caliphate. Across sandy dunes where winter barely touched the world, Odin's mind traveled. To cities replete with domed spires and white walls. Ruled by men who were no longer men at all, but sorcerers who'd freely given themselves to the vaettir of Muspelheim.

And their armies marched. Legion upon legion of mail-clad soldiers, struggling against Miklagard and Valland. Amid them, the eldjotunnar—jotunnar of fire, loyal to the Fire vaettir. Some stood at the height of a very tall man while others towered above their forces, some ten or twelve feet tall, and seeming to simmer with heat. They bore curving swords fit to fell a mammoth and the ground trembled at their passing.

Were all his forces gathered, Odin most like could not stop such an army.

WITH A WEARY GROAN, Odin rubbed his palms against his eyes. Flickers of prescient insight tickled his mind, as if to warn of danger. But the High Seat had never meshed well with any aspect of the Sight save gazing at distant locations. It did not—despite Odin's best efforts—augment his ability to see into the past or future.

A shame, as such a tool would have rendered Odin's many schemes much easier to orchestrate. Instead, he glimpsed shadows and dreams and tried to array pawns to take advantage of visions that may not have portrayed literal realities.

Perhaps such was what Loki saw in his flames. Whispers of unknown and unguessed dangers. Portents one could not easily separate from events soon to come or those years in the making. Oft as not, Odin found himself left not knowing if what he'd seen had already happened.

Ah, Loki. Odin had promised to keep an eye on his brother's family.

That much, he *could* well do with the Seat. Even as he pictured Sigyn in his mind, his vision shifted, revealing her. She sat in Sessrumnir—Odin knew those halls all too well —an army of candles holding back the night as she flipped through pages in a dusty tome.

Odin saw her, though she had no way to observe him. He saw her pause on a section about Manifest Arts—the powers sorcerers gained by binding vaettir to their bodies and souls. Scholarly interest, or an actual intention to pursue the Art? Odin dared to hope she would not be so foolish.

Naught good came from the Art.

Hypocrite ... Audr's dry chuckle filled Odin's mind.

Perhaps he was. But a sorcerer like Odin knew all too well the price one paid for the Art. Well enough to warn others not to tread down this path. Once the power lay before you, the temptation to call upon it became nigh to excruciating. Even as it slowly ate away at your essence.

It seemed he might need to speak with Loki's wife in the morn, or to warn Loki of what she delved into, though he might already suspect. Frigg may have authorized her half-sister peruse the secrets of Sessrumnir, but binding vaettir took that too far.

And what of her son?

At the mere thought, Odin's vision blurred, shifting to reveal a darkened chamber. Indeed, so little light filtered in from around a corner, Odin could make out very little. Rough walls of irregular shape ... wood grains.

Slowly, as his eyes adjusted, the surroundings came more into focus. Hödr sat on the floor in a corner of this unconventional room, legs folded beneath him. Cradling something in his hands ... in such total darkness, the object held a faint golden gleam, as if ready to catch even the wisp of light from around the corner.

Hödr raised the object to his mouth and bit down.

"No ..." Odin said. "He would not dare."

The irregular shape was the natural warp of an ancient tree. Hödr sat inside a chamber in Yggdrasil. And he had stolen an apple. Had stolen immortality itself. Few crimes among Aesir exceeded this.

Even Odin's own son Thor had to prove himself in battle before gaining such a prize. And Loki's son had stolen it rather than petition Frigg.

His brother's son ... His wife's nephew.

Odin rose abruptly from the High Seat.

Sentiment or not, some actions required immediate response.

ODIN'S STAFF crashed into Hödr's face as the boy exited into the main chamber of Yggdrasil. The blow sent the young man toppling over backward, thrown off his feet as blood exploded from his shattered nose.

Glaring, Odin waved off Syn, who had yet to remove her hand from her sword hilt. After Annar's failure to guard the apples from Sjöfn, Odin had put Hermod's wife in charge of protecting Yggdrasil. In nigh to two decades, she'd never had a breach. Until Loki and Sigyn's once-blind son had somehow managed to get behind her defenses.

The shieldmaiden had not taken it well when Odin had

come claiming a thief had stolen an apple and even still remained within.

Gurgling on blood, Hödr rose, one hand to his face. Clearly, he'd finished the apple, or the blow would've rendered him unconscious and left him with a cracked skull.

In the flicker of the brazier, Odin studied his blood brother's child, shaking his head. "You are kin to my wife and my blood brother, and thus to me. Were it otherwise, I'd have fed you to Fenrir for this. I still may do so."

Hödr spat a glob of blood and phlegm dangerously close to Odin's boots. "You may try." The boy lunged at Odin.

Odin brought the staff up to bear, intent to beat the boy into unconsciousness.

Instead, the flames in the brazier beside Odin flared to twice their height, casting sparks in front of his eyes and singeing his clothes. His beard caught aflame and Odin flailed about, patting out the small fires.

Before he could react, Syn had kicked the brazier over at Hödr. The flames danced around the boy, swirling and leaping toward his hands. The shieldmaiden lunged in first, slamming the pommel of her sword into the bridge between Hödr's eyes.

The young man pitched over once more and the flames all burned away into ash.

Syn whipped her sword around and stalked over to the boy. "Thief! Traitor!" She kicked the unconscious Hödr in his ribs with enough force to lift him off the ground and send him colliding into the wall. Then she hefted her blade.

Odin caught her wrist. "Let him live."

"My king! You would not consider sparing another who had tried this."

Perhaps not. But Hödr clearly had gifts much like Loki's,

if not so developed. Loki, though, had millennia of life experience. Hödr did not. The young were oft more malleable and easier to control. And even those who bucked at control were at least easier to manipulate.

"He lives," Odin repeated. "I will attend to his punishment myself."

The Aesir faced enemies from Serkland who could control flames. Maybe it was time they had such a weapon of their own.

11

Fifteen Years Ago

For thousands of years a Vanr hall had stood upon the cliffs, before Odin's people had torn it down in their king's melancholy at Freyja's loss. Gladsheimr, the Vanir had called the ruins Odin now trod among, squinting against the sunset. No one had built here since, given the rather inconvenient location. Sometimes Odin came here to think.

No one else did—save on rare occasions Loki—and the solitude offered Odin the chance to delve into the Sight and seek his answers, particularly before Volund had completed the High Seat for Valaskjalf. Today though, Hermod picked his careful way amidst stone foundations nigh as tall as he was.

"This place," Odin said, "it had gilded shields for roofing. They caught the dawn and cast it in splendor across all of Vanaheim. It had thick spears for rafters, a testament to the mighty warriors within."

"Why tear it down?"

Odin grunted. Because all of Vanaheim had reminded him of Freyja, though, in the paradox of his despair, he had left her hall and library intact, wallowing in his despondency. Or perhaps, as he had told the Aesir, because they needed to build their own destiny, not inherit the mistakes of their predecessors. In either case, Odin had not brought Hermod here to speak of this.

"It will be dark soon. Then we can begin."

Hermod turned to him. "I still don't understand what we're doing here."

Odin ran a hand along the weatherworn stones. "Do you know what lies under the world?"

"You mean caves?"

"Ugh." Odin waved his hand to take in all Asgard, and Midgard beyond. "All the world we know is the Mortal Realm, Midgard and Utgard."

"You're talking about the Otherworlds."

"Ah, after a fashion. I do not speak of the vague superstitions of völvur about the source of vaettir, but rather of another state of existence beyond the physical."

Hermod winced. Yes, even Odin had once considered such talk unmanly and the sole domain of witches. Loki had shown him the truth—a king could not hope to rule with one eye always closed to the reality around him.

"We do not know the truth about existence, Hermod. Not much. But we know a little. Our world is surrounded by a shadow, a mirror, an ... echo of itself expanding out into fathomless depths."

Hermod leaned back against the wall, palpable discomfort on his face. "I thought you said it was beneath us? Now it's around us?"

"You're attempting to apply a physical location to non-physical existence. An ethereal one, with many names.

Some call it the Astral Realm, others call it the Penumbra."

"Which means?"

Yes, many Aesir still could not read, much less chose to do so. "The edge of a shadow that might reach deeper than what we can see. The deeper part, the Roil, it doesn't matter right now. What matters is that the Penumbra mirrors our world, but it ... is shaped by memory, by thought. It remembers what was, particularly if coaxed into such remembrance. A hall that once stood for long enough, a place that saw great joy and great pain, might yet still linger like an echo even after that which cast it has fallen."

Hermod blanched and backed away from the stones. "What are you saying? That ... in this Penu ...."

"Penumbra."

"In this Penumbra, Gladsheimr still stands?"

"Ah. I've been improving upon it, actually. I call it Valhalla."

Now the man gaped. Awed, perhaps, by Odin's temerity in appropriating the land of the honored dead. But so many mortals already believed Odin ruled Valhalla, a place, that —for all Odin could tell—existed only in stories and myth. The dead passed into shadow. Some lost themselves in hatred or despair and others were born again. Never, in all his wanderings beyond the Mortal Realm, had Odin seen sign of a glorious afterlife.

Nor had the Vanir believed such could exist.

No, but Odin was going to make one. A hall where the great warriors among the fallen would wait, free from becoming prey to wraiths or other foul vaettir, free from being drawn into the limitless darkness beyond the Penumbra.

Hubris ...

Audr had expressed the sentiment before, but Odin cared little for what the wraith thought on the matter. On the other hand, Audr might well welcome arrogance.

"Why am I here, my king?" Hermod's voice shook as he stared at the rapidly dwindling light from the sun. Afraid, perhaps, of the fall of night, and knowing, on some level, Odin would ask him to dwell in the dark.

Odin picked an open spot in the middle of the hall and sat, motioning for Hermod to take his place before him. When the man did so, Odin relaxed, hands on his knees. "Your mother was a valkyrie." Hermod opened his mouth, perhaps intending to object out of reflex. Out of years of silence, of denying, maybe even to himself. Odin forestalled him with a raised hand. "I have a great gift for the Sight, Hermod. It tells me secrets of the past and future and of lands both nigh and far. It tells me things others cannot know or do not want to know. But it's not perfect." Not yet. "I don't see everything."

"Whatever it is you think ..."

Odin shook his head. "Hermod, please. I know that your mother Olrun gave up her power to be with you and Agilaz and I suspect that happened some time around the Njarar War. Do not insult either of us with pointless denials."

Hermod clapped his mouth shut, his expression somewhere between a glare and a plea for mercy.

Sadly, Odin could not afford to show him such. "Valkyries can project into the Penumbra, perhaps even enter it physically. The exact details elude me, but the point remains, some part of Olrun's grace may have passed into you."

Now Hermod scoffed. "You think I can enter the realms of the dead? My king, you are grossly mistaken in this. I'm just a man."

"Even if you believe that, it does not make it true." Years back, Odin had sat in the darkness of Castle Niflung while Gudrun had exposited all sorts of arcane knowledge. Later, Odin had sat in the void chambers of Sessrumnir with Freyja and learned more still. He remembered the fear of it, even then. The resistance, a natural inclination bred into every human to turn back toward the light. "Listen to me, boy … I am facing threats on all sides, forces you do not yet begin to comprehend. And I find my allies few."

"All of Asgard is behind you."

"The rest of Asgard cannot do what I ask of you. I know of no others—at least not on our side—capable of entering the Penumbra. I need you, in this, Hermod. There are forces gathering against us."

"What forces?"

Odin shook his head. "First, prove you can do what I believe you capable of. Push your consciousness out of your body and into the shadow realm around us."

Hermod swallowed, glanced around at the settling dark, then stared back at Odin. His breaths came in irregular pants, but he remained seated where another man might have run screaming about witchcraft and mist-madness. "How?"

Yes … Audr said. *Damn him into the dark … Let him join us in shadow …*

"Shut your eyes and relax your mind. Let yourself fall in all directions at once."

Hermod grunted, sucked in another heavy breath, and shut his eyes. Then he grunted some more. His teeth clenched audibly.

"You must relax more," Odin said. "It will not come to you if you push it too hard."

"Easy for you to say," Hermod snapped. "I don't have a fucking clue what I'm doing."

Odin glowered. Perhaps not. Nor did Odin much know how to teach this. His ability to pass into the Penumbra was guided by Audr, and it cost him. But Hermod might make the sojourn without such a hefty price. Odin dared to hope so.

Give his soul ... to a wraith ...

Odin ignored Audr, instead, relaxing his own eyes to embrace the Sight and see Hermod through it. An etheric aura surrounded him, stronger than a normal man's, but wavering as Hermod made his fumbling attempts to access the realities beyond.

For half of an hour, Hermod grunted, grimaced, and tried in vain to project. But ... did he truly try, or was the man resisting? Even if Hermod's mind agreed to Odin's requests, some part of the man's soul might yet oppose Odin's purpose.

And bringing mind, body, and soul into accord rather exceeded Odin's experience as a teacher. Still, no one managed much with the Art on the first try.

"That's enough," Odin said.

Hermod sighed, opened his eyes, and almost looked relieved. "Sorry, I couldn't do it."

"Do not fret. We'll try again tomorrow. It will get easier with time."

"T-tomorrow?"

Odin let the wry grin spread over his face. "Of course."

12

*T*he explanation for Hödr's behavior, however distasteful, seemed obvious. Sigyn had called up a vaettr of ash and flame and wished to restore her son's sight. It appeared to have granted her wish in the most perverse way imaginable—by possessing him. The vaettr—jinn as the Serklanders called such things—must now be in complete control of Hödr. His behavior had become increasingly erratic since she had first made the mistake of calling upon that perverse spirit.

For the thousandth time, she flipped through Mundilfari's journals. She'd spent the past year pouring over every last scroll, tome, or vague musing she could find that might answer the darkness she—and Hermod—had seen in her son.

Even Hoenir had failed to control the boy.

Sigyn shook her head, trying to keep from weeping in frustration.

In ancient times, the Mad Vanr had called up Eldr. Perhaps she ought to have finished reading his journals before releasing the jinn. The intervening years had given her long to ponder her decision and go back and peruse the sorcerer's writings, including the reasons he had decided to bind the vaettr in that jar.

An incarnation of deceit and wickedness.

And she had let it *into* her own son. It was the only explanation she could see. In her eagerness—her desperation—to save Hödr from his blindness, she had given little thought to the potential risk to him. And for eight years her secret shame had grown hand in hand with her gnawing doubts, her fear as to what had happened to her beloved son.

Mundilfari's complex writings were filled with speculation as to the nature of the Fire vaettir, and Eldr in particular. His intentions, rituals, and invocations interspersed his musings, but never laid out in any clear prescriptive manner, perhaps because he had never considered anyone would release Eldr from his confinement.

Sigyn shut the book. She might study Mundilfari's scattered and befuddling notes for a millennium and still not match the sorcerer in the Art. So, if she could not herself do aught to help her son, she needed to find someone who could. The obvious answer remained—Mundilfari had first summoned Eldr from Muspelheim and then bound the vaettr. It stood to reason, he might be the only one on Midgard who could do so again.

The difficulty, then, became finding the reclusive and insane sorcerer.

Finally, she rose. Sealing the Vanr's secret chamber behind her, she headed out. She'd need provisions, a bow, and, of course, the swan cloak. She had a lot of ground to cover, after all.

First, though, she needed to see her son.

❦

ODIN HAD IMPRISONED Hödr in a chamber in the back of Valaskjalf, around the corner from Lodur. Any hope Sigyn had that her son's confinement might prove short-term foundered next to the obvious implication of placing the boy next to a man Odin had left to rot for nigh two decades.

The king's guards wouldn't even let Sigyn past them. After casting glares at the pair of men, she stormed out.

Frigg met her halfway beyond the hall. "He's expecting you in his private chambers in the back."

Sigyn stiffened, almost afraid to even ask what her half-sister thought of all this. "Hödr is my son."

The queen nodded, sadness in her eyes. "Which is the main reason he yet lives, I suspect."

Sigyn flinched. "I'd have thought you would ..."

Her sister reached out for her, but Sigyn pulled away. Frigg just frowned. "Laws exist for a reason, Sigyn. Willfully ignoring or breaking them must carry with it consequences or society crumbles."

"Oh, spare me the petty völva folk wisdoms. Were it Thor, he'd not be locked in a cell just now. Indeed, your son attacked the acting king on his very throne. He got sent to the front, earned an apple, and came home a hero."

Frigg shut her eyes, shaking her head. "No law is more sacred than the one that protects Yggdrasil. Without those apples—"

Sigyn shoved past her sister and toward the hall leading to Odin's personal chamber. While she'd never been here, she was familiar enough with the layout to figure out where it was most like to lie.

Indeed, the sound of voices greeted her well before she

reached the king's chambers, reaching her even through the door.

"Ironic that your children continue to vex us so, isn't it?" Odin said.

"Such petty snipes serve to undermine your position, not reinforce it." Loki?

Sigyn threw open the door to find that the two men sat across from one another beside a lattice window. The fire pit between her and them created a strange mask of shadows over their faces that made them seem alien, like something spawned in the Otherworlds.

Neither man started at her entrance. Given that both possessed some degree of prescient insight—even if different in kind and presentation—it ought not to have surprised her. They did, however, both look to her, as if waiting for her to speak.

Wonderful. Well, she had their attention now, didn't she? Sigyn shut the door behind herself, as much to buy herself time as for the desire for privacy. She hadn't really prepared for this meeting ... Oh, a thousand possible tracts had run through her mind. Just that none of them had played out well, nor had any involved Loki being here.

The king had a brow raised, looking at her when she turned back. He'd doffed his hat, leaving it beside his chair, exposing a mop of tangled gray hair. How changed he was from the man she'd first met so long ago, while she remained much the same. One possible price of the Art. And now they'd both paid a great deal because of it.

Without a word, she strolled around the fire to stand before them, desperately trying to soothe her nerves with each passing step. And failing. She paused before the king, tapped a finger to her lip, then looked to her husband. "Has the king agreed to rescind his judgment?"

Addressing Loki instead of Odin might serve to discomfit the king, just a little. Oft, it seemed to Sigyn, the key to gaining the upper hand in dealing with men blessed with the Sight seemed to come in approaching every subject at an angle. By obfuscating her true aim, or at least acting contrary to the way these oracles might have expected, she might catch them off their guard. Sometimes.

"The king's judgment," Odin said, "was already to spare your son the fate old Vanr law would have prescribed for him. Do you wish that judgment overturned?"

Being flayed alive and forced to live that way through foul sorcery ... Sigyn couldn't stop herself from flinching.

She looked to Odin now. "The sentence you mention was implemented by Mundilfari. Are you even capable of enacting such a vile curse?"

"Do you wish to find out?"

"Did you know I met him, once, years ago?"

Odin's faint smirk slipped off his face. "You met Mundilfari. So he yet lives? Yet walks the face of Midgard?"

"He does. And as a First One, I imagine he was not affected by the spell you used to cast out the rest of the Vanir. Or wouldn't have been, had he even been on Vanaheim. No, he's out there."

Loki shook his head. "And you think to find him?"

"No," Odin snapped. "Leave the Vanir be, all of them. That sorcerer is dangerous. We cannot begin to fathom what horrors he let loose into his mind or soul in his long years of working the Art."

"He may be the key to unraveling what's wrong with my son."

Odin shook his head. "No. What's wrong with your son is obvious enough. You abused your access to Sessrumnir in an ill-conceived attempt to heal your son's blindness. And you woke something up."

Sigyn snapped her mouth shut. Loki had spent years sharpening the king's perception in an attempt to prepare him for Ragnarok. Now, that razor-sharp insight seemed rather inconvenient.

Odin rose from his chair, groaning ever so slightly as he did so. "I forbid you to search for Mundilfari. And given that I know you follow orders little better than your son, I forbid you to leave Asgard, Sigyn."

No. No, this wasn't happening. She ... she could use the cloak to fly away when no one watched. But given Odin's prescient insights, he might make such an endeavor risky at best.

"What about my *son*?"

Odin glanced to Loki, who hung his head. "Your husband has agreed to provide me a service in the future in exchange for leniency."

"What service?" Sigyn demanded.

Odin shrugged. "I'm sure something will come up. In the meantime, Hödr will be sent to Valland, under the watchful eye of Tyr and Hermod, both. Whatever his new skills, he'll hone them in service to the Aesir."

"You're banishing him?" She gaped. And with her confined to Asgard ... she'd not even see him again. Maybe for years.

"I'm giving him a chance to earn the apple he stole instead of having him damned to some unspeakable urd. Show a little gratitude."

SHIT, where was it?

Sigyn flung another scroll aside. Damn it, she knew she'd seen it here when she was researching the spirit worlds. A connection, a thread ...

She felt like breaking ice, as if a spiderweb of cracks shot through her and any moment she'd come apart at the seams. Biting her lip just to keep from screaming, she scrambled along the floor of Sessrumnir. Had to find it.

Odin had made himself her foe. There was ... just no other way about it. He'd placed himself between her and her son. That made him an enemy and a fool. So long as Odin remained on Asgard, she couldn't do what she needed to do.

And Sigyn needed to save her son. Whatever it took, she'd save him, pull him back from this abyss she'd set him to straddling. Was it madness to summon a vaettr to aid her boy? Well, no more mad than it had been for the others to think she'd sit back and do naught.

She shoved another book away. Not here, but definitely a different tome written by Mundilfari. Was it in a book? Shit, had it been a scroll? She couldn't remember.

So all she needed to do was find ... Wait. Wait ...

Ancient pages cracked beneath her fingers as she roughly flipped through them. Any other day she'd have taken extraordinary pains to preserve every last bit of Vanr wisdom, musings, and records. Now, though, in the face of her son's urd, naught else mattered save him.

Muttering, she turned another page.

Yes!

Sigyn slumped back on her arse. Yes. It was real.

THE MAIN HALL WAS DESERTED, save for Odin, sitting on his

throne, staring at Sigyn. Moonlight drifted in through high windows, adding to the scant illumination provided by a single lit brazier.

"I'm not accustomed to being woken in the middle of the night," the king finally said.

The way Frigg told it, Odin oft started awake, shaken by some dream or vision, though he rarely spoke of either. Not that such a comment was like to improve her case.

"Mundilfari left Asgard in search of another well," Sigyn blurted. Not the calm, reasoned path she'd intended to take. A man ought to be led to the conclusions you wanted to him to make, for then he'd more easily mistake those ideas as his own.

"A well?" Odin asked, leaning forward ever so slightly. His eyes seemed glazed over, as if he'd been smoking some of those wretched herbs Frigg used to favor.

She needed to play this just right. Odin was too clever for his own good, much less for Sigyn's. But there was one thing he sought above all else: knowledge. He traveled across Midgard and—she had reason to believe—even beyond in an obsessive search for answers about the urd before him, before them all. He thought himself—perhaps because of Loki—responsible for preparing for Ragnarok. A hefty weight to bear, yes.

"We thought," she said, raising a finger. "We thought the Vanr came to power at the same time the mists first began this era."

Odin nodded, looked like he might speak, perhaps to illuminate some of the dark depths of history Loki so oft refused to speak of. Instead, he leaned back in his throne and waved a hand for her to continue.

"They led us to believe they ruled for five thousand years, yes?"

"More like forty-eight centuries."

"An approximation, for certain," she admitted. And hardly relevant. "They may have been here on Asgard ... on Vanaheim for all that time. But they didn't rule Midgard back then. Another empire did."

"Before the Vanir?" Now Odin cocked his head the side, seeming to look at something beyond her. Visions? Madness?

"The jotunnar were the first rulers of this world. They fought a war with the Vanir."

The king looked to her now. "Yes, and Mundilfari raised the wall. He grew it out of stone."

"After, yes. Few details remain in their records about the time before he became king. But one thing was clear, they respected the jotunnar as elder beings, ones steeped in ancient and oft terrible lore. Among them, a being called Mimir."

Odin mumbled something under his breath, as if talking to himself. Seeing the king thus gave Sigyn pause. Suppose he truly had lost his mind out on his sojourns? What of Asgard then? What of Midgard?

"Uh ..." Sigyn faltered. "Uh, Mimir knew of a well, one said to grant him wisdom beyond the ken of even the Vanir, perhaps even oracular foresight. And because of this well, the Vanir's war very nigh ended in disaster. Millenia later, Mundilfari went searching for it. He left everything and never came back."

"Hmm." Odin suddenly leaned back, waving it all away as if inconsequential. "And just where did the Mad Vanr think to find this legendary jotunn well?"

"I ... I don't know."

Odin shrugged. "Ah. Well, then. At least it was a good tale to help me get back to sleep. Was there something else?"

Sigyn kept her face impassive. "No, my king."

She had him.

He'd go looking for this well, even if it took him to the ends of Midgard. He'd seek it—maybe find it, but probably not, considering Mundilfari had not returned. Either way, he'd be gone long enough for her to find the Mad Vanr herself and save her son.

13

*G*iven a younger body, Odin would've taken the stairs two at a time. Instead, he climbed the spire of Valaskjalf at a measured pace, thumping his walking stick on the ground with each passing step. His heart raced, though not from exertion.

What if Sigyn had spoken the truth? What if the legend was real? The answers to every question Odin might ever need—even to those he might not have thought to ask—might lie hidden in the depths of those waters.

And why not?

The Well of Urd beneath Yggdrasil had opened Odin's eyes to the past. It had forced him to accept that he had lived and died before. So many lives, clear for a moment, but now reduced to shadows in the back of his mind. But bits of that revelation had remained, secrets and lore, skills and wisdom beyond the ken of a single lifetime.

And why should another well not exist, revealing unto him the truth of the future? And, looking upon that shadowy visage, would Odin finally be able to foresee the cause of Ragnarok? Would he be able to *avert* it?

Dawn remained at least an hour away when Odin reached the pinnacle and settled down into the High Seat. Night had cooled the metal, but still, it held more heat than it ought to have. The warmth of uncounted souls forged into this work, denied any chance at another life so that Odin might see all.

Arms clasping the rests at his side, Odin let his mind relax. He let it strive, seeking ever outward. He did not know where this well might lie. But he would find it.

HIS MIND SOARED over the snow-drenched hills in southern Valland. It dove into valleys and crawled along riverbanks. It climbed the peaks further south still, into Andalus. The Caliphate's armies had seized every town and city in this land and already they marshaled against their northern neighbors.

The taste of impending bloodshed tickled Odin's tongue, a premonition of war that would break with the end of winter. It was coming.

But such battles did not call to him. Not when the chance at greater salvation lay within reach.

He swept around trees blanketed in white, then, finding naught on the slopes, began to hunt for caves. Faster than an eagle he flew, covering vast expanses in heartbeats. And still, no sign of the well.

GRUNTING, Odin leaned forward and rubbed his eyes. The sun now reflected off the silver plating around him, nigh to blinding. His stomach grumbled. He'd missed the day meal. Judging by the sun, it had to be noon.

And he'd searched all the North Realms, even unto Thule, where the draugar armies had begun to unite under a new king. Fortunately for the world of men, they had no means to cross the icy deep that separated them from the rest of Midgard.

He'd looked out into Bjarmaland, where Thor and his people struggled to hold back the encroachment of jotunnar from the east. Odin had provoked the Patriarchs of Miklagard and—though more cautious now—they yet plotted slow vengeance upon Odin's disciples.

The thought drew a grimace. If Odin could but commit the whole of his forces to any one problem, perhaps he could hope to overcome Serkland or Miklagard or even the jotunnar or draugar. Instead, the Aesir spread themselves thin. As thin as Odin's mind had become, stretched over the breadth of Midgard.

He rose, greeted by a crack in his lower spine which forced him to stretch. Hours sitting in place had left his legs tingling and his neck stiff. Unsteady on feet he could barely feel, he grabbed his walking stick and then plodded around the tower's summit.

He made his way around the back of the canopy, staring out over the mountains and beyond, to the mist-covered sea. Did aught save Jormungandr lurk beyond in the distant west? Perhaps not. He dared hope not, at least, for he could not see crossing such an expanse to reach the well.

The soft clack of padded boots on metal stairs drew his eye to an intruder entering from below. His guards had orders to allow none save Frigg up here. And yet, it was not Odin's wife who crested the stairs, but Loki.

Odin opened his mouth to ask how his brother had

managed to bypass warriors stationed not a dozen feet from the only entrance to these stairs, but shut it. With Loki, little still surprised Odin anymore. The man would rarely answer questions directly, and it seemed oft best to avoid wasting those he would attend to.

"Sigyn informed me of what she told you."

Odin grunted, then paused in his circuit around the tower. "You know it." While he'd not even considered asking Loki, the answer now seemed obvious.

Loki frowned and continued until he stood at the tower's edge. A balustrade rimmed the tower, not quite reaching Loki's waist. The man climbed atop it, then settled down sitting on it, staring out over the land. Sometimes, on the clearest of days, Odin fancied he could catch a glimpse of Andalus off in the distance, beyond the mist. Not so many miles away, his enemies grew in number.

But then, Odin's enemies increased in all directions.

From the way Loki fidgeted, he seemed about to speak several times, yet remained silent.

Odin drew up beside him. "I have rarely known you to be at a loss for words."

Loki blew out a slow breath. "Suppose in an era long gone, some few had tasted the very same apples that conferred immortality upon you. Supposing this, and given a nigh limitless expanse of time, these elder immortals might find themselves drawn or bound to causes of little of import to most of the world."

"You speak of yourself?"

Loki glanced at Odin, a wry smile on his face, though no mirth reached his eyes. "Given enough time, even immortality might wane, and those thinking themselves eternal might find their grasp on a mortal existence more tenuous than expected. What befalls those who pass beyond?"

Odin folded his arms. "Either their souls are drawn into the roots of Yggdrasil to be spun out in another life, or they find themselves consumed by predators in the dark."

"Or?"

Odin grunted. "Or they become ghosts, trapped in the Penumbra until they finally lose themselves. Ah ... you imply that Mimir is dead?" Odin leaned on the balustrade beside his blood brother. "So Mimir appointed himself guardian of this well, for reasons you cannot or will not explain to me. He died ... and became a ghost. Maybe still haunting the well."

"Your intuitive abilities continue to improve, brother."

"None of this answers where to find the well."

Loki turned and pointed back at Yggdrasil. "Its roots reach into all worlds. They connect across the Mortal Realm and beyond. If one well lies beneath a root ..."

Odin rocked back on his heel. "So might another."

"And if you have searched all Midgard for the well and came up with naught save endless stretches you could not cover in a century ..."

"Then try another tactic," Odin finished. "Follow the roots." He pushed off the rail and hurried over to the seat. "Thank you, brother. You are still not allowed up here."

Loki's wry grin returned.

Odin settled back into the seat and let his mind stream downward.

On, toward Yggdrasil, and down, into the fathomless dark of its roots. They reached out around the world, burrowing ever deeper. And Odin needed but find a place where they broke free from the dirt and exposed themselves.

His mind coursed alongside root after root, following their winding paths around a world larger than he had dared to imagine. In places, those roots passed through liminal regions where the Veil grew thin. These passages, Odin ignored. While Yggdrasil might have bridged the gap between the Mortal and Spirit Realms, sending his mind into other realities did Odin little good if he could not bodily follow his consciousness.

Inside, he retraced his passage, taking other branches. Over and over they spiraled amid themselves, knotting and twisting like a nest of serpents choking the world. Or holding it together. Or both.

And so deep the roots reached, deeper than Odin had dreamed one could reach and yet remain in the Mortal Realm. Until, finally, one burst free into an icy abyss from which rose a curtain of mists. Frozen waterfalls poured down into a chasm rent between mountains at the northern-most peak of the world.

It wasn't in Midgard at all. It was in Utgard, in Jotunheim.

The root jutted from glacial walls, breaking out of one and back into another, tracing a winding path to some subterranean home. And from the depths rose a faint hint of light, reflecting off the mists, and promising the future.

ODIN LURCHED FORWARD, toppled from the Seat, and landed on his elbows. Frost misted the air from the breath he blew out, then vanished.

"It's there ..." he mumbled.

Loki grabbed Odin's biceps and hefted him to his feet.

Odin shrugged away from his brother, grabbed his walking stick, and steadied himself upon it. "It's real."

"Yes."

If the Well of Mimir could unveil the future, it would prove Odin's best chance at knowledge and the surest route to regaining Andvari's Gift. That ring meant everything. With it, he could rejoin Freyja and hope to win the coming final battle.

But crossing into Utgard, especially into Jotunheim, would not prove an easy task.

Panting, Odin turned to Loki. "I have decided on the favor you owe me, brother."

"I know."

14

Thirteen Years Ago

No moon lit the sky, leaving the ruins of Gladsheimr thick with darkness. Odin had sat so long in the starlight he could make out Hermod's still form a few feet away, but only in outline. Patience had come to him with the understanding that its absence would lead to madness, and yet, still he dared to hope—would this be the night?

Frustrated with Hermod's lack of progress, Odin had taken the man to see his foster sister. While Sigyn had no particular expertise in the Art and could not—praise the ancestors—project into the Penumbra, she had studied Vanr writings to a dangerous extent. The three of them had spent the better part of the past fortnight in discourse over the nature of reality.

"Mundilfari actually posited that this world is the shadow," Sigyn had said.

Her words had wormed their way into Odin's brain to plant the seed of a niggling doubt. The Mad Vanr was, of course, mad. Without doubt Njord's predecessor had lost himself peering into the darkness. But one could not help but fear that in his madness, still he'd come upon insight.

In truth, however, whether the Mortal Realm or the Penumbra was the shadow mattered little at present. Odin's stomach churned with the fragile hope that finally, Hermod might break free of the chains of flesh and allow his soul to become untethered. That Odin might, at long last, find himself with a true ally in the realms beyond.

The man across from him held so very still Odin might have mistaken him for a corpse.

We are all corpses ...

Odin grimaced at Audr's intrusion. The dark belonged to wraiths and always brought about greater activity in the foul vaettr bound to Odin.

We are all foul ... Vileness compounded unto infinity ...

Audr Nottson had also gazed into darkness. Maybe he more than any other could have aided Hermod in crossing, but Odin would not dare expose the other man to the price of it.

He will pay, nonetheless ...

Odin grit his teeth, saying naught.

Reach across ... rip his soul from his body ...

And if Odin allowed such, it would only undermine his efforts to train Hermod.

A slight tremor rushed through the other man. Was this it? Odin relaxed his eyes to embrace the Sight. The pale light of the Penumbra filled his vision. Across from him, Hermod's aura flickered. A shadow seemed poised to break off from him. He was doing it. He had come this far twice before, but no farther. Still, enough to let Odin know he had the potential.

Almost there ... Come on, Hermod. Do not give up.

Surrender to the dark ...

Odin leaned forward.

The shadow slipped from Hermod's body and took up ethereal form on the other side of the Veil. He'd done it.

Odin pushed his own consciousness from his resting body, joining Hermod in the Penumbra. Colors bled out of the world, sucked away as Odin left the physical behind. A fell chill washed over him, familiar now and yet still enough to set the hairs along his body on end. Whispers echoed along that wind, the faint cries and pleas of the dead.

Hermod gasped, hand to his chest, flailed widely, and spun to stare down at his body. "Wh-wha ...?"

Odin spared the other man a moment of pity. "The first time is the hardest. You get used to it." After a fashion, at least.

Hermod turned now, gazing up at the massive hall around them. Columns thick as tree trunks supported a ceiling that rose up into flying arches supported by spears. Massive sconces lined the columns, unlit for now, but capable of casting the entire hall in a resplendent gleam. A dozen tables, each large enough to sit a hundred men, ran between the columns. At the back of the hall, on a dais, stood a throne Odin had fashioned to resemble his High Seat.

He led Hermod outside so the man could look upon the completed wonder. A hint of starlight flickered off the gilded shingles, their sheen muted by the oppressive dark tones of this reality. It had taken Odin enormous effort to infuse enough light into the region to keep ennui from seeping in, as it always seemed to in the Penumbra. It would not do for his potential guests to lose themselves as so many of the dead slowly did.

As we all do ...

Hermod turned to Odin, then gaped at him. No doubt the man had suddenly become aware of the writhing shadows twisting at the edge of Odin's own form as if threatening to burst forth. The curse of any sorcerer, in truth.

"Yes, boy," Odin said. "I hold bound within me vaettir, always seeking to possess me." He flexed his fingers, allowing a hint of Audr's wispy, boney hands to break through for an instant. "Such is the source of any sorcerer's powers."

"And what happens if one of them gets control?"

Audr cackled, the sound no longer just in Odin's head, but carried through the etheric air like maddening vibrations.

Hermod blanched and fell back a step.

"Naught good," Odin said. "But that is not why we're here. This hall will become Valhalla. There was no such place before now, but together, you and I will prepare a home for those who die glorious deaths."

"So ... what happens to those who have died before?"

Again, Audr cackled, and Odin allowed the wraith to drift half out of his form before snapping it back into place. It was all the answer he had for Hermod and clearly more than the man had wished for.

"Come," Odin said. "There is something more I must show you."

A LONG TIME THEY WALKED, traveling deeper and deeper into the Penumbra, until the mirror cracked and what was reflected did not—blessedly did not—exist in the Mortal Realm. A landscape of shifting shadows so deep not even the starlight above seemed to pierce them.

"I'd have expected dawn by now," Hermod said.

"There is no dawn here, boy."

"You keep calling me that, but we are nigh to the same age, are we not?"

Odin paused, suddenly forced to take in Hermod anew. Outwardly, Odin must have been three times Hermod's age, but yes, their births had not been so far apart. Rather than offer an apology, Odin merely nodded his head in acknowledgment. "Sometimes, I find myself thinking of all people as my children."

Hermod said naught to that, pushing forward.

They rounded a cliff of obsidian rock and came to a void that pitched away into infinity. A gap in reality filled with a faint, ever-changing shimmer. Across this, stretching out into forever, spanned an iridescent bridge.

"A rainbow?" Hermod asked. "I don't ... I don't understand."

Odin indicated the bridge. "Nor I, in truth. But the bridge spans the length of the Astral Realm, serving as a connection between the Penumbra and the Roil. Beyond this, all you know of reality falls away and vanishes into naught. There lies chaos, Hermod, and within, horrors we cannot fathom."

"So what are we *doing* here?"

Odin grunted, then sighed. He pointed up into the starlit sky. "Somewhere up there, crystal spheres are lodged into the sky. They are facets of the Spirit Realm."

"I thought we were in the Spirit Realm?"

"No. Each facet is a world unto itself, built from a primal aspect of creation. Niflheim is out there, the home of our true enemy."

Hermod shuddered. "You mean ..."

"Yes, *her*. I told you an end battle is coming: Ragnarok.

And she will try to take our world. Yet we cannot take the fight to her. We cannot reach her world, though her forces can descend into the Astral Realm and from there, influence the Mortal Realm."

"You mean to fight—"

"Do not speak her name, least of all here. She might hear you. She might *answer* you." Odin sniffed and stretched his aching back. "This bridge joins the Astral Realm together, but I am convinced we might one day use it to reach the other worlds. Only, it's guardian, Heimdall, will not tell me how to do so."

Odin had pled with him. Had begged him to show the way to Alfheim that he might be reunited with Freyja. Heimdall had refused to even consider such a course. Odin had known he would, but still he tried, over and over.

"I still don't understand why you brought me here." Hermod waved his hand to encompass the bridge and all the Penumbra. "Why bring me to this twisted place?"

"Already, you can project your mind and soul into the Penumbra. But given your heritage, one day you'll be able to enter it physically, a task I can only achieve by using the power of … one of the vaettir inside me. Once you achieve this, Hermod, you can reach anywhere. No wall, no barrier will be able to stop you."

The man swallowed then pressed his palms to his brow. "I still don't understand, my king."

"I need a messenger. One who can go anywhere, cross any land. Perhaps even one day breach the Spirit Realm. You can be that, Hermod. It is inside you. Have you ever heard of a valkyrie having a child before? If any such ever existed, I know naught of it."

"My … my uncles also married valkyries. I don't know if they ever …"

"Your uncles?"

"Uh ... Volund and Slagfid."

Odin faltered, caught himself on an obsidian shard and gaped at the boy. Volund ... the dark smith had married a valkyrie. He had a son by the princess of Njarar, Odin had known, but ... it seemed had Volund had another child? One born of a valkyrie? And who was ... Oh. What was the name he had asked after?

Altvir ... Valravn said in his mind.

So, this Altvir had become Volund's wife? Unlike Olrun, it did not appear she had chosen to surrender her immortality out of love. "Volund's wife," Odin said. "She was Altvir?"

"Yes. How did—"

Odin waved that away.

How strange the weave of urd. He shut his eyes and shook his head. The circles bent back upon themselves in twisting spirals. Well, there would be time to have the full of Hermod's tale later.

"Come," Odin said. "Meet Heimdall. You may find yourself forced to cross his bridge more than once in the days to come."

"My king ..."

Odin had started for the bridge, but turned back to look to Hermod.

"If I am to survive the task you set before me ... I fear you must teach me somewhat of the Art and the secrets beyond the ken of humans."

Odin quirked a faint smile. All as he had expected. "I fear you're right."

PART II

Year 49, Age of the Aesir
Summer

15

*P*eregot was too thick with people. Three winters here. Ever since Hlodwig sent Lotar to hold Aquiene. Prince had welcomed Tyr back. Nigh begged him to come to this overflowing piss pool. A wooden palisade around the town, a fort to protect his people.

And every year, more refugees fled here.

They packed in like rats, fleeing the war. Some came from the Andalus Marches, to the south. No one ought to have lived there. Not since old Karolus had set up the boundary. Since Odin and Tyr had gotten him to. But still people didn't want to leave their precious villages. Farms. Places more like than not to get razed when the Serks came again.

They always came.

Others, they fled from all over Aquiene. Maybe they'd suffered hard winters. Maybe they figured the armistice wouldn't hold much longer. Maybe they were right.

And so Tyr found himself staring out a window on the upper level of the fort. Looking at a town packed to overflowing. Stank of piss no matter which way the wind blew. Stank of shit. Stank of men.

Behind him, Lotar sat in his modest throne, grimacing no doubt. Always frowning, this prince. Him and a handful of knights, all grim at the report. Even with his back turned, Tyr could feel the prince's souring mood at Hermod's words.

Hoenir's son-in-law was the best scout they could hope for. Always had been. Of late, though, he'd gotten so good at it men called him a ghost. Man would slip across the Marches without no one getting wind of him. Move through Andalus—now just a part of Serkland really—and hear things what no man ought to have been able to learn.

As now.

"Al-Dakil calls his retainers, all the men loyal to him," Hermod said. "The caliph lost favor with the rest of the Caliphate when he established the armistice with you. A fortnight back, he got word that they send an emir to draw Andalus back under their control."

Tyr groaned, shaking his head. Turned to them. Already, Lotar looked to him. Like the prince thought Tyr could do aught about it. Nigh five decades he'd spent here. Trained men. Tried to hold the Straits of Herakles with Roland. Failed at it, back when Roland and most of his paladins died.

But old Emperor Karolus had forced them to a peace. After a fashion. Established the Andalus Marches as a buffer. Worked well enough. Held back a full war, at least until Karolus died too. His son Hlodwig had practically restarted the war himself. Said anyone who didn't believe in their Deathless God were foes.

Which had included Tyr and his Ás warriors. Almost lost all Valland before he sent his son to clean up the shit he'd cast about.

Tyr cracked his neck. "Always knew the Marches wouldn't hold forever."

Lotar rubbed his face. "Perhaps, but I dared to hope the war with Miklagard would prevent this from coming to pass."

Hermod scratched behind his ear. Always looking about these days. Like he saw something other men didn't. "The emir they send leads a troop of the Sons of Muspel."

"Fuck," Tyr said, drawing a raised brow from the prince. Tyr didn't have time to fret on his sensibilities though.

Reolus—best damn knight Lotar had, if he'd asked Tyr —he stood with his arms crossed, glowering worse than most. "If the Sons of Muspel oust Al-Dakil, you can bet every warrior in Andalus will be moving on the Marches before the end of summer."

Lotar looked to Mallobaudes. The man shook his head. "We cannot stop the Sons. Every encounter with them ended in disaster." The other knight had come with the prince, all the way from Aquisgrana. Man had managed to live long enough to let his hair gray. Prince valued his counsel, maybe. Tyr couldn't help but see a hint of a craven in the knight though. Didn't ever want to draw that blade of his. "Don't forget what happened at Roncevaux."

Tyr sucked spittle between his teeth. Damn, but he wanted to spit. Lotar frowned on that sort of thing though. Got him riled. "I remember it."

They all looked at him, save Hermod. These knights, especially ones new to the front, they never seemed to believe he could be as old as he was. To most of them, forty winters back was before they were born, much less fighting.

"I knew the paladins," Tyr said. "All of them." Hadn't liked them all, but that hardly much mattered. "Roland fought against some few of the Sons back then. They're fast and they're strong. Hardly unkillable, though."

"What do you suggest, then?" the prince finally asked.

Tyr cracked his neck, then strode to stand beside Hermod. "Preempt them."

Mallobaudes sneered. "You mean start the war ourselves."

"Intercept the emir. Kill him. Before he can bring down Al-Dakil."

Mallobaudes shook his head, looking at Tyr like a child. "The caliph is not like to thank you for killing his own people."

Sounded nonsense to Tyr. "Saving him from men sent to kill him?"

"He may have dreams of establishing an independent caliphate in Andalus, but that doesn't mean he'll side with you against his own kind."

Tyr looked to Hermod.

The other Ás grimaced. "Hard to say. It might reinforce the armistice. *If* you can actually kill the Sons of Muspel."

A fair *if*. Sons were nigh to as strong as Tyr, even after an apple. Got their name because they claimed the fires of Muspelheim burned hot in their veins. Even counted some eld jotunnar among their ranks.

"I'll go with him," Reolus said. "We'll need a small unit that can move quickly, but one strong enough to fight the Sons."

Mallobaudes threw up his hands. "Your plan is suicide, sir. All you do is waste lives that could be used to reinforce the borders when they come. And they will come here."

Tyr glared at him. "Not if we win."

HERMOD FOLLOWED Tyr out as he headed down to the Ás barracks. "I'll come with you."

Tyr grunted, pausing on the stairs. "Odin always has some mission for you. Won't want to risk you on this."

"You don't have time to send for reinforcements from Asgard. How many varulfur have you got in Peregot? How many berserkir?"

Tyr grunted and started back down the stairs. "One of each." Didn't bother looking at Hermod. Didn't much want to see his expression at that admission.

"You need every blade you can get at your side."

"King'll have my stones if you die out there."

Hermod snorted. "Old friend, I sincerely doubt Odin wants aught you have in your trousers. Besides, you've already lost a hand for the cause of Asgard. What's a few rocks compared to that?"

"Just make sure you tell me what to say at your pyre," Tyr called over his shoulder.

Outside the barracks, he found Thrúd watching a Vall knight training soldiers to fight with spear and shield. South Realmers were small, more oft than not. Could be fierce though. Well armed. Disciplined.

Girl leaned against a wall. Seeming intent to memorize every move. The shieldmaiden had seen thirteen winters. This would make fourteen, in truth. An adult by rights, but hard not think of her as a child.

As Thor's child, in fact, much as Odin's son hadn't wanted her here. Girl had fire. Sure as her hair was red. Never listened half so much as she should have though.

Tyr beckoned her over with a wave of his hand. Thrúd tromped to his side, casting another glance back at the training soldiers. Or maybe the knight who was doing the training. Cyr, his name was.

"Watch where your eyes roam, girl," Tyr said.

Thrúd snorted. "Just studying."

Strange thing, training her. An unofficial fostering, really. Thor and Sif wanted their daughter growing up strong. And Thrúd had demanded training from Tyr. Well enough, since these past few years he'd managed to stay clear of the fighting. Tyr hadn't gotten to raise his own sons as long as he might've liked. Starkad and Vikar had left. Fostering Thrúd, he'd sworn not to make the same mistakes.

Maybe only made different ones.

Between her and Hödr now, felt he spent half his time watching the young. Trying to steer their courses.

"I have to leave soon," he said.

"We heading back to Asgard?"

He grunted. "You're staying here. Me, I have to go into the Marches."

Her face lit up like he'd promised to let her see an alf. "The *Marches*? Why can't I go with you?"

Because she was young enough to ask a damn fool question like that. "You stay here and finish your training."

"But I—"

"Look here. This one thing, don't fight me on. Hard enough as it is. Stay, train. Be ready in case things go wrong. Maybe the Serks come here."

Her mouth quirked all sideways. "Go wrong? You get yourself killed, I'll come kick you in the stones, Uncle Tyr. Trust me—I can kick hard enough even a dead man would feel it."

Tyr grunted, the nodded at her. "Just see you mind the knights."

"Oh. I *do*." She winked.

Fool girl. Tyr drew her into an embrace. "You know, do

one thing for me. Keep an eye on Hödr. Boy is trouble. Let Lotar know if he gets up to any mischief."

Thrúd clapped him on the back then pulled away. Grinning ear-to-ear at him trusting her with aught more than taking charge of a watch. She'd do all right. Girl was Odin's granddaughter, after all.

16

The Rijn ran down from the Sudurberks, cutting through the western regions of Hunaland, before passing through the shadowy Myrkvidr and finally emptying into the Morimarusa. The ancient keep of the Volsungs lay along this river, already hidden by the mist as Sigmund peered over the longship's stern.

Beside him, his son Helgi stood, looking forward rather than back. Looking up at the Myrkvidr, the source of a thousand dark tales. Men claimed witches and hags dwelt there, or trolls even. Others believed it housed varulfur who would come to stalk the fields and valleys under the moonlight.

Sigmund, however, had never smelled varulfur in these lands, save for himself and Fitela.

Every so often, ships would sail through the forest and no one would hear from them again. Still, it was the swiftest, surest way to the sea, and a fitting test of a young man's courage. How could one who refused to stare down shadows be expected to stare down a man intent to kill him?

Helgi's mother had objected, of course. Borghild refused to see one of her sons leave the safety of their Rijnland keep.

The Volsungs had made many enemies, she'd claimed, in their conquest of Swabia and Menzlin. More foes, too, lay in Baia and Styria, who continued to bitterly resist Sigmund's efforts to unify Hunaland.

With Fitela at his side, he'd returned to find a land shattered by petty wars among pettier jarls and kings. While he and Fitela had succeeded in casting down the usurpers who had claimed Volsung's lands, uniting Hunaland had proved another task altogether. One that long years had not yet brought to conclusion.

"Hamund wanted to come too," Helgi said, not taking his gaze from the Myrkvidr ahead.

"He's too young," Sigmund answered.

"He's a man rights."

Fitela—blessed with varulf hearing like Sigmund—chuckled from the far side of the ship.

Sigmund scratched at his beard. It had grown too long of late, making him look older than he felt. The wolf vaettr inside him meant he aged more slowly than other men. Part of him had hoped Helgi or Hamund would inherit the wolf as well, if only so he would not have to watch his boys grow old before he did. Another part dreaded the thought of them bearing the terrible curse that he and Fitela had—the savagery, the bloodlust.

Finally, he looked to his son. "There is something of a tradition among our family. At fifteen winters, a man must prove himself in battle. I had fifteen behind me when I sailed with my father and we met Siggeir Wolfsblood with arms drawn. Fitela had fifteen winters when we avenged that wrong. And now you, at fifteen, shall set out and blood yourself on raids. Bring back wealth to hold for your future kingdom, son. And when Hamund has fifteen winters, he must do the same."

Apparently drawn by the conversation, Fitela stalked over, eyes shinning, no doubt hatching some scheme or other to bring them all glory. Fitela always had plots roaming far and wide. Many of Sigmund's victories he had to attribute as much to his eldest son's cunning as to any mastery at arms. "Father thinks we ought to raid into the islands of Reidgotaland. Snatch some sheep and maybe a shepherdess and make a man of you in more ways than one."

Helgi flushed and pointedly looked away, though Sigmund could smell his excitement.

While Sigmund had implied no such thing to Fitela, it wouldn't be a bad idea for Helgi to lay with a woman. Regardless, Sigmund had chosen Reidgotaland because he thought Hrothgar unlikely to pursue minor pirates given the disquiet that rumor claimed had settled upon his lands. Sigmund fixed Fitela with a level glare.

Fitela just grinned. "As Father has tasked me to watch over you, I will take his advice under strong consideration." Meaning he'd ignore it completely. Fitela had vehemently argued that raiding Hunding's lands in Baia would serve to weaken their enemies. Sigmund's eldest still believed provoking Baia into outright war would force them to make a poorly calculated move and thus lead to Hunding's destruction.

Given that Baia and Styria had managed to set aside their differences to stand against Rijnland, Sigmund hadn't wanted to risk a joint assault by both kingdoms. The potential for things to go awry was simply too great.

Fitela, however, always liked a bold plan.

"If I'm to lead these raids," Helgi said, "should it not be *my* decision where we go?"

Fitela raised an eyebrow and cast a look at Sigmund. Yes, Helgi was a Volsung through and through.

"You will decide, then, son."

Helgi looked back at the approaching Myrkvidr. Beyond the wood, another ship waited for Helgi's command. A chance to prove himself. Sigmund had to allow his son that much. Finally, Helgi turned back to him. "You got to where you are by fighting for what mattered. You speak of the deeds you and Fitela did ... I cannot settle for less. I'll raid Hunding's shores and deprive him of as many resources as possible."

Sigmund drew in a deep breath and blew it out. He clapped his son on the shoulder, then turned away, unwilling to let the boy read the depths of emotion on his face. It was starting again. The cycle he and Fitela had been through.

The destiny of all Volsungs, perhaps.

17

*O*ith the break of summer, Sif had dared to hope Thor might change his mind and abandon Bjarmaland to the jotunnar. He had not. Indeed, the prince now spoke to her little, oft foraying out on his own, traveling to outlaying villages. Always searching for foes to slay.

Sometimes, he took the Thunderers with him. Two nights back they'd come upon a troll snatching up sheep, perhaps hunting the shepherdess. Sif had broken her halberd on its head, doing little more than annoy the beast. Mjölnir had had a more significant effect—crunching its rock-like skull as if it were made of clay.

Whenever Thor slew something with that hammer, a fell light came into his eyes. A gleam that might have been Sif's imagination, though Geri claimed to have seen it too. A bloodlust one expected in varulfur and berserkir but found far more disturbing in other men. As if each death only left Sif's husband craving for the next.

Still, no other trolls had turned up, and finally, bone

weary, they'd trod back to the watchtower Rollaugr had granted them.

"Reminds me of our days in Aujum," Freki said, as the tower drew into view.

"Our new home?" Sif asked.

"Hunting trolls. Father said back when the Aesir lived in Aujum, the trolls were largely confined to the Jarnvid. Now I hear they've been raiding all the way into Hunaland."

Thor grumbled something under his breath. Did he think that Freki's subtle prodding to head to distant lands? Was it? If so, Sif would have much rather gone to Valland and joined Thrúd than fought over a now unclaimed wilderness.

"Look," Geri said, pointing at the tower. Sif didn't see aught worth mentioning. Geri glanced at her. "There's a plume of smoke rising up through the mist." She sniffed the wind. "Hmm. Father."

Sif stumbled over her own feet. King Odin? Here? Troll shit. Sure, she might hope he'd come to recall his son back to Asgard ... But the last time Odin had come to task the Thunderers with something it had cost Itreksjod his life.

At the mention of his father, Thor's steps quickened into a trot, any weariness he'd felt obviously forgotten. Sif had to scramble to even keep up.

Following Thor, they blundered back to the tower to find, indeed, a small fire smoldering just outside the kitchen, with a man sitting before it, his face obscured by his wide-brimmed hat.

"Father!" Thor bellowed, rushing over to clasp the old man's arm.

Odin rose stiffly, not quite concealing the pain it brought to him, and embraced his son. "You've been too long away."

Meaning the son took after the father. How oft did Odin

actually sit upon his throne in Valaskjalf? How oft did he hold his court and see to his lands? Sif couldn't recall the last time. He looked different than she last recalled him, but she couldn't quite put her finger on how.

The varulf twins too embraced their foster father, then the three of them settled down around the fire. Thor glanced back at Sif and beckoned her over. Forcing a smile, she dropped down beside him. How easy it had been to forget, really, that these four were family and she an outsider of no blood relation to them.

What was she, really? Thor's wife, yes, though she knew he'd taken others in times they spent apart. Maybe he hadn't meant to. Maybe he'd intended to remain true to her. But Thor was Thor, and, like his father, had trouble keeping his trousers on. Everyone spoke of it, at least when neither man was around to hear.

And even if Sif was Geri's friend and Thor's wife, that did not quite let her settle into the easy camaraderie the others felt around Odin. She still did not truly know why he'd chosen her as Gylfi's ward so long ago. In truth, maybe no one knew why Odin did aught. His motives seemed nigh as unfathomable as Loki's. It was an even toss whether Thor's father or Aunt Sigyn's husband was the more vexing with their mysterious airs.

The varulf twins and Thor regaled their father with tale of their exploits over the past few years, and passed a fair time with pleasantries. Sif held silent unless one of them directly addressed her. Any word she might have uttered struck her like an intrusion. Her gut screamed for her to find some reason to excuse herself and retire to the tower or even the kitchen. Aught that might take her away from the solitude Odin had somehow carried here with him.

Only when she had sat did she realize Loki too rested

nearby, gaze locked on the fire. What was Aunt Sigyn's husband doing here? Sif could never look at him without feeling ill at ease, especially given what had passed between them.

The king watched her, Sif suddenly realized. Even while talking to Thor and the twins, he kept an eye upon her. Why? What did the man want from her, truly?

Thor looked to Geri. "Would you fetch us something to drink?" The varulf woman snorted at being addressed like a servant, but she did clamber off into the kitchen. Thor next looked to his father. "Much as I wish you'd come only to visit, I suspect otherwise."

Odin nodded slowly, a hint of a smile upon his lips. Pleased his son could understand this much? "Indeed. I have need of your aid in a pressing matter." Here it was. The king would come and send them into some reckless, foolhardy quest, like to get them all killed. "I must break into Utgard and cross into Jotunheim."

Sif sputtered. Everyone looked to her, but she couldn't help it, really. "You want to enter *Jotunheim*? To go beyond the Midgard Wall and actually enter jotunn land?"

Odin cocked his head ever so slightly. "It's been done before."

"By who? Madmen?" The weight of her temerity in so addressing the king hit her even as the words left her mouth. But she couldn't forestall them. "In any event, we sealed most of the breaches as you commanded." They'd tricked the jotunn Vörnir into doing it, rather, getting Meili and Hildolf killed in the process.

The king nodded. "One remains."

"And of late the jotunn king Hrungnir has built his fortress *over* it, thus controlling which jotunnar may enter Midgard. Best as I can say, he did us a favor in that, but he's not like to simply let you walk through his home and enter the jotunn lands."

Odin's wry smile grated on her nerves like sand scouring her flesh. "Hence why I come to seek aid from my mighty son. I'll draw the jotunn out and, if he refuses to bargain, Thor can use Mjölnir to strike him down."

Mjölnir, cursed hammer. Why didn't Odin, slayer of Ymir, just … That was it! That was what was different. He now carried a staff instead of the ancient spear, Gungnir. He no longer held the ancestral weapon. Where had it gone? If he'd come to fight his way through Jotunheim, surely he'd have brought it. Unless it had become broken or lost.

So now, without his vicious weapon, Odin needed another tool of power to slay jotunnar. The one he'd given to his son. Sif scowled at the king. From the look in his eyes, he could tell exactly what she'd realized and almost dared her to speak of it. Well, fuck that. Let Thor ask him to explain himself.

"Father," Thor said, "I am honored. Of course I will slay this jotunn king for you." Sif wanted to scream at the both of them. "By my hammer, the beast shall meet Hel."

Geri reached over to pat Sif's knee. "It'll be all right. We've done this before."

It was a long trek through Bjarmaland, toward the Midgard Wall. Beyond the boundaries of Holmgard lay the jotunn-infested wastes of Qazan, territories that offered Thor numerous opportunities to sate—or rather enhance—his desire to smite every inhuman creature in Midgard.

Having found no replacement for her halberd, Sif had claimed a spear from the tower before they left. Most jotunnar stood only the height of an exceptionally tall human. Against those, the spear gave her the advantage of reach. Against man-eaters who feasted upon human flesh for long years, well, those jotunnar could stand twice the height of a man, meaning the spear at least evened out the reach advantage.

Seven of the creatures died on the way to the mountains. Thor's fury grew with each he slew, and Mjölnir had begun to sound like a thunderclap as it killed. A drum beating inside Sif's head, transforming her husband into a beast to rival his victims.

While she remained powerless to even broach the subject.

§

THEY SAW it long before they reached it. The end of the world. The very edge of Midgard, rising up through the mist. Glaciers broke through great peaks, and rising up from those slopes, a wall of stone coated in thousands of years of ice. She'd never truly wished to see it again. Not after all the blood Vörnir had shed in this place.

A deep crevasse tore through the glacier, forcing them to take a long trek around. Before they had finished that circuit, Odin called for them to camp.

The jotunn king he planned to seek out alone, leaving Loki behind with the Thunderers. Sif wanted to believe Odin could talk Hrungnir into letting him pass.

But then, the rampant slaughter Thor had wrought among jotunn-kind was not like to endear them to the Aesir. And so the threat of impending violence permeated their camp. And Thor all but reveled in it.

18

One might have called the dwelling built before the breach a fortress, if one were more generous than Odin felt at the moment. Hrungnir's home was rather constructed from giant chunks of ice packed hard against crudely carved boulders, creating something that looked as though it belonged as a part of the Midgard Wall.

An age ago, the Mad Vanr, Mundilfari, had raised this wall to keep the jotunnar out of Midgard. Now that Art had begun to fail, and Odin had some hope of actually reaching into Jotunheim. Thor had tried to recruit the jotunn Vörnir to fix the cracks in the Midgard Wall. Odin had never expected his son to succeed, though if he had, the task at hand might have actually proved more difficult.

By building his dwelling here, Hrungnir had actually thwarted too many more jotunnar from entering Midgard. In that regard, he made Odin's task easier. Still, Odin needed to pass beyond the lumpy dwelling were he to reach the Well of Mimir.

Mounted on Sleipnir, Odin rode alone toward the jotunn's hall, snow crunching under the horse's many hooves. He'd told Loki to remain with Thor, in part to avoid alarming Hrungnir with too many humans, but mainly to keep Thor from doing something foolhardy in the meantime. Odin's son had yet to learn patience or restraint. Perhaps he never would.

"Hrungnir!" Odin bellowed outside the hall. It had no gate, but rather a large boulder that obstructed the view inside unless one were to ride up to the very entrance.

A groan sounded within, echoing off those ice blocks. Cursing and grumbling followed, and then a frost jotunn came stumbling around the boulder's edge. He stood half again as tall as Odin, with a bluish tint to his skin. Tusks jutted from his lower lip like those of a walrus, save inverted. Oxen-like horns burst from the sides of the creature's head. A jotunn only grew so deformed by eating the flesh of men.

Odin pulled up on Sleipnir's reins, causing the horse to rear back and kick six legs in the air.

"Guardian of the breach! They tell me you are quite proud of your steed."

Hrungnir stomped out into the snow, looked Odin up and down, and nodded in obvious interest at Sleipnir. "Fastest horse in Jotunheim, Gullfaxi is. Of the old lines from Brimir. Don't reckon humans know aught of that. Who comes to me?"

"Odin, King of Asgard and ruler of mankind. And this —" Odin patted his horse's shoulder, "—is Sleipnir. The fastest horse in all lands."

Hrungnir sucked noisy spittle between his tusks then blew it out in a spray that caught Odin, even from twenty feet back. "Reckon you've got less between your ears than a fucking troll. Care much to wager on how fleet that horse of yours is?"

Odin barely suppressed his rising grin. "I will. If I win,

you allow myself and my people free passage back and forth across the wall, as much as we desire."

Hrungnir snorted, then spat a glob of filth in the snow. "And when I win, I get to mount your head on a spike for talking about. That, and I get to eat your heart."

Well, that was enough to kill the smile tugging at Odin's lips. But Thor assured him this jotunn had power, and Odin didn't want to risk his son's life fighting the brute if he could avoid it. "Deal. Win, and I'll not stop you from claiming your prize."

A deep chuckle burst from Hrungnir, then the jotunn whistled out the side of his mouth. A moment later, a shadow passed overhead, then dropped down beside the jotunn.

A winged horse, and one a full arm's length taller than Sleipnir.

Long ago, Loki had told Odin winged horses had lived in Midgard, but that they were gone now. When Hrungnir said this Gullfaxi came from an old line, he meant it.

"Reckon I race you to that peak." The jotunn pointed at the same mountain Gullfaxi had no doubt just flown down from.

"No." Odin's mind raced. No matter how fast Sleipnir could run, he couldn't well climb a mountain faster than Gullfaxi could fly to the top.

"No? You saying we ain't got a bargain now?"

"No ..." Odin glanced around, barely able to focus. "We race to the bottom of the crevasse in the valley."

Hrungnir glared, his tusks flaring out to the side. "As you will. Already got a spot picked for your head. Place of honor, fit for a king."

"I'd expect no less."

Odin waited for Hrungnir to mount his flying horse,

then kicked Sleipnir's sides. "Run!" he whispered to the horse. "Run as you have never run!"

Sleipnir lurched into stomach-clenching motion, a flurry of snow spraying up behind his hooves. Icy wind blasted over Odin's cheeks, freezing them even through his long beard.

A guttural shout went up behind him, some foul, ancient tongue that sent Odin's nerves on edge.

"Run!" Odin repeated.

Sleipnir dashed toward the glacial shelf spread out between the mountains.

Once more the shadow passed overhead, the jotunn now aloft, and already moving beyond Odin, unimpeded by the snows.

A flying horse had not factored into Odin's wager, damn it. He leaned forward, pressing himself tight over Sleipnir's mane. "Run, my friend, or this shall be our last ride together."

The horse surged forward with a fresh burst of speed. The wind now threatened to tear Odin right off Sleipnir's back. It caught his hat and flung it away. It tugged at his cloak, streaming out behind him.

The jotunn's horse dove for the crevasse, edging ever closer. But there was no flying in such narrow confines, so Hrungnir would have to land. That meant Odin still had a chance.

Sleipnir passed just under the flying horse, Gullfaxi's massive hooves kicking mere feet above Odin's head.

Surefooted, Sleipnir raced right into the crevasse, barely slowing, barely heeding as one or another hoof skidded along ice. The slope dropped down so steeply Odin felt himself falling forward, his weight trying to carry him right over Sleipnir's head. Legs clutched tight around the horse's flanks, all he could do was hold on and trust his companion to find the way.

And Sleipnir did, finally skittering to a stop at the bottom of this ravine, a few feet from a fissure that would've sent them both plummeting into the depths of the glacier.

"Impossible!" Hrungnir bellowed. The jotunn's thick voice rumbled off the crevasse's sides and sent cracks spreading along them.

Icicles the size of spears creaked. One split and pitched down the fissure with a whoosh.

"Keep your voice down," Odin warned.

Heedless, the jotunn tromped down on Gullfaxi. "Ain't no horse what runs faster than a pegasus flies! Impossible."

Those cracks widened.

Teeth grit, Odin pointed above. Mercifully, the jotunn faltered, looked around, and seemed to remember himself. For he finally turned his horse about—an awkward maneuver to be sure—and began to ride back to the surface.

Odin followed, keeping a significant gap between them.

The pair of them rode up, then Odin turned away, west and headed for Thor's camp. "A pleasure dealing with you. I'll be looking to pass through the breach come the morn."

"But ..." The jotunn growled something in his own language.

With his back turned, Odin allowed himself a slight grin. Sleipnir had not failed him yet.

As expected, the tromp of heavy hooves rapidly closed in behind him. "I must have that horse!"

While the loss no doubt rankled the jotunn, his particular request left Odin gaping and turning to look upon the creature before he'd realized he'd done so. "Sleipnir is not for sale. He is a companion, not my property."

Hrungnir spat in the snow. "Then I pays him instead of you! Don't make no difference, but I must have him."

Odin shook his head, and continued on, right into Thor's camp.

Already, his son stood in the midst of the others, massive arms folded over his chest. "Welcome, Father. I see you brought the beast out away from his warriors. A prisoner?"

"I ain't no prisoner, cur!" Hrungnir bellowed at Thor. "And I mean to bargain with your kin, not you."

Odin dismounted Sleipnir and scratched behind the horse's ear. "We had a bargain."

"Reckon it's time for a new one."

Behind Thor, Sif groaned.

"I got a bargain for you," Thor said. "I challenge you to a duel. If I win, you pack up and return through the breach and keep well clear of Midgard."

Now, Hrungnir turned his glare more fully upon Thor. "You're the humans what've been hunting my kind of late."

Thor shrugged and hefted Mjölnir. "I fight to defend the men of Bjarmaland, but call it what you will."

"And what do I win after I kill you?"

"A few moments of pride," Freki said. "Before you wake up from that dream."

Hrungnir pointed a meaty finger at Odin. "The rest of you can just stay damn well out of it."

Several possibilities could have arisen if Odin won the race. One, he'd dared to hope, would involve Hrungnir actually keeping his bargain and letting them pass. More like than not, though, Odin had known this would come about. Armed with Mjölnir, Thor could probably kill the jotunn.

Probably.

It was a risk, but one Odin saw no alternative to. Already, Loki had motioned the varulf twins away, and

Odin moved to join his blood brother. Sif, however, lingered at her husband's side a moment longer than necessary. A deep look passed between them, as if the woman willed urd to unfold in some way other than how it must.

Maybe, once he'd drunk from the well, Odin might master urd and control such things. For now, he must let events play out as destiny demanded. He beckoned to Sif, and finally, she joined him. From the corner of his eye, Odin watched her. Was her disquiet the natural fear of a lover, or some manifestation of her latent gift with the Sight? Much as he'd tried, Odin had not been able to glimpse the outcome of this duel.

"I'll carry your woman back to my hall," Hrungnir said to Thor, eyeing Sif in the process. "I shall enjoy her squeals." The jotunn drew a flint slab from off his back, the piece fashioned into a pointed shield. "Don't even need no proper weapon to kill you. Take your head clean off with my whetstone."

Odin glanced at Loki, who was frowning at the display. If his blood brother feared for Thor, though, Loki gave little outward sign of it. Still, could Odin have miscalculated? Few things mattered more than his son.

Thunder rumbled in the evening sky, though no lightning broke through the dense clouds.

Without warning, Hrungnir roared and flung his shield like an arrow shot from a bow.

Odin's stomach lurched at the suddenness of it, as the missile streaked through the air.

Thor stumbled back, jerked Mjölnir up, and flung it at the last instant. The hammer smashed through the stone slab with a crash like a thunderclap. It continued soaring straight into Hrungnir's forehead, and—Odin could have sworn—a crackle of lightning sizzled at the instant of impact.

The giant stumbled several steps backward, wobbled, and pitched over, crashing into the snow. His fall threw up a cloud of white that obscured his form.

Only then did Odin realize Thor was screaming. Lying on the ground, clutching his own head, as blood oozed out.

No.

What had ... No ...

Odin raced to his son's side, but Loki got there first. His blood brother struggled to pull Thor's arm away from his head. Odin grabbed the same hand and—flooding his limbs with pneuma—jerked that arm free.

A chunk of flint nigh as big as Odin's hand had pierced Thor's skull and lay wedged half inside. Blood streamed into Odin's son's eyes.

No.

No. He hadn't prepared for this.

No ... "Thor! Thor!" He cast a frantic glance at Loki. "Do something!"

Sif's screams drowned out Loki's answer, but the look on his brother's face told Odin all he needed to know. Thor was a dead man. A slab of rock was jammed into his brain.

Odin grabbed the stone. Its sharp edges sliced his fingers and palm. He didn't fucking care.

"Stop!" Loki shrieked. "If you pull it out like that, he'll be dead almost instantly."

Odin choked on his own breath, caught somewhere between screaming and sobbing. The bitter reality of his gambit settled like a mountain on his chest. To reach the well, he'd sacrificed Thor.

His son's breath slowed, grew into irregular pants. Sif was beside him, shrieking hysterically.

They could do naught. None of them knew a thing to save him.

None of them ... "Valkyries!" Odin shouted.

The mist thickened at his call, and silhouettes within took shape. Like shadows rising up from deep underwater, they pressed against the surface before stepping through.

Sif jerked up abruptly, gaping at Hrist, Svanhit, and Altvir. "Wha ...?"

At once, Loki pulled back from Thor, allowing the valkyries space.

Freki grabbed Sif and pulled her away as well. "Sorry, little brother," he said to Thor.

Altvir knelt at Thor's side, one hand on his chest, one on his head. "I cannot remove it without killing him. But ... there is a song. Perhaps you know it?"

Of course. Väinämöinen's spell-songs ... One to speed the healing of the sick. But even that would not stop someone from bleeding to death. Save, maybe in conjunction with the power of an apple?

Voice shaking, Odin began incanting the ancient syllables. His song reverberated off the mountain peaks and infused the air itself with an energy not unlike the aftermath of lightning—a spark felt along the skin. A tingle that set the hair on his arms standing on end.

Altvir had begun signing as well, her voice high and clear and far more beautiful than Odin's own. And with mercy, maybe enough to forestall the inevitable.

Odin sang until his throat felt raw, sang until nigh every drop of pneuma felt wrung out of him like a washcloth. Until he had to support himself on hands and knees. Until his voice broke and he could no longer carry the melody.

Even Altvir had faltered, now leaning against Svanhit.

Thor's flesh had turned sallow, but his breathing had become somewhat more regular.

"He'll live?" Sif asked, obviously choking back sobs of her own.

"For a little while," Svanhit answered. "Maybe long enough to bid him farewell."

No. Odin would not allow this. "Do something," he rasped.

"Valkyries are not healers," Svanhit said. "We can protect, sometimes stave off death. We cannot, however, mend flesh. Perhaps the most we can offer him is ..."

Odin's glare silenced her before she could mention Valhalla. Not him. Not like that.

Loki had an arm around Sif. "I may know of someone who can help."

Odin stared imploring at his brother. "Tell me. I'll do aught you ask."

Loki glanced back at the Midgard Wall, now already shadowed as night began to fall. "Hrungnir was a king among his kind. With his fall, others will come here. Your chance to pass the wall and find what you seek—"

"What the fuck!" Sif shouted, shoving him away. "What in the freezing gates of Hel mattered enough to be worth this?"

Odin wanted to retch. Or maybe to plead for her understanding. If he failed to stop Ragnarok, everyone, Thor included, would pay the price. And if the well was his chance to be ready ... Still kneeling in the snow, Odin clenched his fists beside his thighs. May Thor forgive him ...

He stared hard at Loki, knowing what the man had intended. If Odin left now, all this was for naught. Thor would have suffered such a grievous wound and still Odin's wouldn't reach the well. Now might prove his one and only chance.

And faced with that ...

"Can you save him?" he asked Loki.

"Perhaps. I must hurry and get him to a sorceress who dwells amid these mountains. Time grows short."

Shit. "Take him! Altvir, Svanhit, go with them. Hrist, with me. We must be through the wall and gone from here before dawn brings more jotunnar."

"Father," Freki said. "You cannot go alone."

Odin grunted. He'd always trusted the varulfur twins to look after his son. But Freki might have a point. Alone, Odin might fail. And the future could not afford that. Moreover, Loki and Sif could surely attend to Odin's son. "Come then, my wolves. We go to Utgard."

He cast a last look at Thor's trembling form.

19

*W*alking in the lead and carrying Thor's half-conscious form, Loki led their small party down a narrow pass through the mountains. Sif tromped after him, trusting to the valkyries to keep watch.

Altvir walked by her side, though the other one, Svanhit, had disappeared into the darkness. According to Altvir, her sister had left to scout the way.

There were a thousand questions Sif might have asked of a valkyrie. Every time she opened her mouth to consider asking one, Thor's moans drew her gaze. So many times she rushed to his side, tried to comfort him. But he spoke in incoherent rambles laced with rage, lashing out at her and anyone else around.

When she'd tried to hold him still, he'd brought both her and Loki tumbling down into a pile atop them.

Meaning she needed to stay away. Whatever the valkyries and Odin had done had stopped Thor from dying, but still he had a shard of flint boring into his brain. Much as his wild wrath stung, she more feared he'd never be himself again. Even if this sorceress managed to remove the stone without killing him.

Altvir's gaze lingered upon Sif. She could feel the valkyrie staring at her.

"What?"

The valkyrie sighed. "How much do you know about your king?"

Too little or too much, Sif wasn't sure which. Odin was the mystery all Aesir struggled to unravel. Her parents, who'd known him before he came to Asgard, they had remarked on occasion how much the man had changed. Not now, though. Now, her father had become some student of Odin's, as if the king trained an apprentice. The very idea of that—the fear of what fathomless depths Odin drew her father into—left a block of ice in Sif's gut. And Sif's mother, granted guardianship over Yggdrasil, she would no longer speak or hear aught ill of the king.

"You have no answer?" Altvir asked.

"My answer ..." Sif shook her head. "My answer is I cannot begin to fathom how a valkyrie comes into the service of a man. Much less three of you."

Altvir clucked her tongue. "There are more than two of us, but that is neither here nor there. No, I ask because I see the rise of darkness in him. He has ... ensured my loyalty, and further that his urd binds my own. But I have seen darkness lurking deep in souls before. I have seen it rise up, forged into something new and terrible. Given any choice to spare Odin from that path, I'd do so."

Sif could offer naught but a grunt to that. Such things were beyond her ken.

THE SORCERESS LOKI spoke of lived not in a home, but rather, in a cave within the mountains. Vertical logs bounded the edges of it, leaving only a single opening covered by a bearskin flap. Inside, a smoldering fire lent warmth, its light revealing strange runes carved into the walls. Sif had seen such things in dverg ruins as well, places like Halfhaugr. They no doubt had some Otherwordly purpose, but what she could not guess.

Save that Altvir and Svanhit did not deign to enter the cavern, instead standing watch outside.

Did the runes bar the valkyries from coming inside, or did they simply prefer to avoid the sorceress?

Either way, Sif and Loki now knelt by Thor's feverish body. With a piece of torn linen, Sif mopped his brow, careful lest the cloth draw too nigh to the flint shard sticking from it.

"Can you help him, Groa?" Loki asked the woman.

She was old but not ancient, her face creased by lines and the hint of wrinkles, a few streaks of gray in her otherwise black hair. Scars lined her forearms, marks that might have been something like the runes on the walls, though Sif knew too little to say for certain. Another such mark looked carved into the woman's forehead, partially concealed by locks of her hair.

The sorceress leaned in close, sniffed Thor's wound, then wrinkled her nose. "Should've come sooner."

"We came with the utmost haste available to us," Loki said. "Work your Art and restore the boy."

Boy? Thor had a great bushy red beard and muscles enough to get mistaken for a bear. Who in Hel's icy crotch did Loki think he was, calling her husband a *boy*?

Groa scratched her scalp, sending flakes and loose hairs

drifting around. "I can invoke a vaettr to loose the stone, yes. Won't come cheap though."

Greedy witch was letting Thor suffer to haggle? "I have silver enough to pay you," Sif fair spat at her.

The sorceress chortled, shaking her head. "No one pays for sorcery with silver, young one. When it will extract its price from my body, mind, and soul, what shall I do with pretty coins? Least of all, here, alone in the mountains." She leaned in close and sniffed Sif's hair. "What shall I ask for then? Your beauty? Your life? Your *soul*?"

Despite herself, Sif flinched at that. The sorceress's breath stank of stale air and rotten teeth.

"No ..." Groa said. She turned to Loki. "No, I think rather, you Loge, shall tell me the fate of my beloved Aurvandil in the old days. Tell, me Nornslave, where have you hidden the lost soul?"

Loki glowered. "I'll tell you. First remove the whetstone."

The sorceress cackled, exposing teeth not only rotten, but several missing. Still shaking with mirth, the woman looked hard at Sif. "You'll like this." At once, Groa spun and began to crawl about in a circle. She drew a knife and slit her palm, then painted rune after rune in her blood, forming a perimeter around the fire.

Loki, however, watched not the sorceress, but the flames themselves, as if bespelled by them.

Sif shuddered, hugging herself, then laid a hand upon Thor. His flesh still burned, slick with sweat.

Finally, Groa came back to sit within the circle, just before the fire. She sat with legs folded beneath her, staring into the flame much as Loki did, but holding her hands out to either side.

Then she began a chant. The nonsensical words flowed in

a rhythm, though one like no music Sif knew or ever cared to. The sounds seemed to suffuse the air, as if they themselves had a thickness. The hair on Sif's arms stood on end, charged as with lighting. Her gorge rose, and she wanted to retch, to spew forth the foulness churning in her guts. A profound sense of wrongness settled upon her like a physical weight.

Unable to bear it, she raised her hands to cover her ears, curling up and caring little what Loki thought of her. The whole world rejected whatever the sorceress said. Sif knew little of sorcery, save that it called upon vaettir. And something was in here with them. In the cave, crawling upon her skin. Little pinpricks dotting along her legs. Trying to push its way out from behind her eyes.

"Stop it," she mumbled.

The whetstone lodged in Thor's head wobbled. Then slowly, it began to edge outward, as if drawn out by some unseen hand. A chill wracked Sif and she realized that might well be exactly what was happening. Something had hold of it, was drawing it out like poison sucked from a wound.

Bits of flint frayed from the edges, breaking into dust.

The sorceress's chants had grown more frantic. Sif could not help but look up at her instead of the whetstone. Blood dribbled from Groa's nose, her ears, even her eyes. It streamed down her face in dark stripes as if she were some vile creature of the mist.

Maybe she was.

The sorceress let out a deep, shuddering breath. "Where is my husband, fire priest?"

"Finish the spell." His words, through grated teeth, sounded to Sif as if they had come from far away, across a chasm.

"Where is he? I find him not among the living nor the dead … his soul does not answer."

"Because Audr Nottson consumed it for his own dark sorcery. *Finish* the spell."

All at once, Groa's chanting faltered. The foul, thunderous energy washing over Sif broke as if it had never been there. And the whetstone snapped in half, most of it dropping free, while a tiny shard remained lodged inside Thor's skull.

Sif's husband sat up, screaming, clutching at his head in wretched agony.

Loki lunged across the fire and had Groa up in an instant, hefted by her rotting clothes. "Finish it!"

The cackle that followed did not sound like those before. Rather it echoed like a draug's moans of despair, hollow and hateful, the voice of the damned, assaulting Sif even over Thor's screams. Her lover convulsed, thrashing so hard Sif couldn't control him, even with the apple's might. His flailing weight threw her down.

Loki flew through air, colliding with the cavern wall and fell in a heap.

"Altvir!" Sif screamed.

Already, the valkyries were charging in, swords glinting in the firelight.

"Snow maiden!" Svanhit shouted.

She and Altvir began circling around Groa, neither closing the distance, holding the possessed sorceress at bay with their swords. And why didn't they move in? Because they were frightened? What manner of vaettr turned even a valkyrie craven?

Sif didn't care. She'd left her spear at the cave's entrance. So she snatched up a smoldering brand from the fire and lunged at Groa.

The sorceress—or the thing inside her—shrieked, the same hollow, damned voice vibrating inside Sif's skull.

"Save Thor!" Sif screamed at her, waving the brand in front of the woman's face.

The sorceress lunged, catching the edge of the brand in her hand. At once, the wood froze, turning so cold it burned Sif's hand. She dropped the freezing stick and fell, clutching her damaged hand and wailing in the pain of it.

A valkyrie lunged in, sword raised in intent to cleave through the creature.

The sorceress moved more quickly, spun. Closed her fist before the valkyrie's mouth. Svanhit.

The witched jerked her fist backward. A stream of gore spewed from Svanhit's mouth and landed with a crash, her innards shattering as though made of ice as they landed before Sif.

Sif's stomach lurched. Trying to scream, she instead choked on her own bile. Coughing and sputtering, she fell over, her face landing on stone beside Svanhit's shattered heart.

An instant later, the sorceress's severed head dropped down in front of Sif's eyes.

Still gagging, she managed to roll over. Thor had grabbed the woman by her knees. A bloody sword dropped from Altvir's hand and clattered onto the rocks. The valkyrie clutched her forearm where the frozen brand was now jammed in the top and jutting out the back like the point of a spear.

Hel's gate ... Must've passed between the bones.

The valkyrie stared at the wound. And then she screamed, a long, bloody cry that echoed off the cavern. On and on, the scream went, until Altvir finally collapsed to her knees, gasping.

Sif pulled herself over to Altvir.

Thor had already risen to help her. Blood and spit dribbled down Sif's husband's face. He gripped the brand with one hand and heaved.

Altvir managed another shriek as the brand tore free of her flesh, further shredding her arm.

At a shadow, Sif turned to see Loki stumbling toward them. He jammed both hands in the remains of the fire, then withdrew them—spraying embers everywhere. Flames now leapt up around his fingers, dancing in mesmerizing motion, seeming not to burn him in the least.

He slapped those hands on either side of Altvir's arm, drawing another scream out from her.

The scent of burning skin hit Sif all at once, noxiously sweet, acrid enough to draw up another surge of bile. As Altvir's screams died out, the only sound remaining was the sizzle of her flesh.

Now Sif *did* retch.

Loki released the valkyrie of a sudden and flexed his fingers. Like that, the flames extinguished themselves.

Altvir pitched over sideways, moaning faintly, arm tucked under her body.

Sif crawled to Thor, who'd begun prodding at his skull. The shard still stuck from it, and Sif could see no way to pull it free save by cutting out the bone in his head. Hardly prudent.

Weeping, Altvir crawled toward Svanhit's sprawled out corpse. Sif had always known vaettir were fell creatures. Never before had she heard of one freezing the heart inside someone's chest. The other valkyrie moaned again, a wordless defiance.

A denial of the bitter hand of urd.

GINGERLY, almost reverently, Altvir slipped a red-gold ring from her sister's finger. Sif had wrapped fresh linens around the valkyrie's arm and Loki had prepared a poultice from some herbs he had in his satchel. Since Sif had no idea if valkyries healed like normal women or like those who'd had apples or somewhere in between, she couldn't guess whether Altvir would ever get full use of that arm back. For now, it lay in a sling bound against the valkyrie's chest.

"I have to take her from here," Altvir said, looking up at Sif.

"To burn her body?"

"You can attend to that. I must take her soul to Valhalla before it becomes lost in the shadow."

Thor stood abruptly at that, hand still pressed against his head. "You've seen Valhalla?"

That drew a bitter chuckle from the valkyrie, but no answer. Instead, the woman stepped back into the recesses of the cave, seeming to blend with the darkness.

Sif blinked, and Altvir was gone. Well then. She turned to Thor. "Are you all right?"

"I ..." He growled, snarling like a wolfhound. The only other answer he offered was bared teeth as he stumbled from the cave.

20

*B*arnstokkr scraped the rafters of the Volsung hall. The great tree had once housed the runeblade that Sigmund now bore, Gramr, placed there—according to legend—by Odin himself as a gift for the worthy. And Sigmund had drawn her when all others had failed. She sang to him, a quiet voice in his mind, relishing their victories and craving more. Always more.

He leaned back on his throne, chin resting on his fist, staring at the tree, as he so oft did since returning to these shores.

The tree represented the strength of his family. A grace from Odin, and, as long as it stood, whatever travails should befall the Volsungs, surely they would endure.

Still, Sigmund worried for Helgi. How could a father not? The boy had insisted on raiding lands held by warriors, not common herders or fishermen.

"He should not have gone," Borghild said, as if reading his thoughts while she sat beside him. She did that sometimes. Maybe all women did. Borghild was the daughter of Prince Hildebrand of Menzlin. It had been Fitela's idea

Sigmund marry her and thus secure the friendship of her grandfather. King Garth of Menzlin had agreed to serve under Sigmund's authority in the bargain, rather than risk being slain by Sigmund's army.

How long now? Sixteen winters?

And Helgi had to cross his great grandfather's lands to reach Baia. Well, Fitela was clever, and might even manage to draw some of the ancient king's men into his retinue. It was not like the old man was leading too many raids himself. Prince Hildebrand did, though, and maybe Fitela could convince him to join forces.

Sigmund glanced at his wife. "Helgi will be perfectly fine."

"You don't know that."

"We are beloved by Odin."

She snorted. "You've suffered rather a great deal for those beloved by the king of the gods."

Sigmund could only glower at that.

His thegns threw open the great doors of the hall, and men and women came in to air their grievances. A king's first duty was to his subjects, but still, Sigmund did not much welcome these sessions.

He let his sheep graze in my field.

He stole all the fish in the river.

She gave birth to four daughters and no sons.

How odd, to live as a king and yet somehow miss—even a little bit—his days as hermit in the woods, preying upon Wolfsblood's men. Hunting for his food. Living free and answering to no one. But he'd wanted all this. He'd fought for years to reclaim Father's legacy. He'd bled and he'd murdered. He'd let his love of honor slowly slip away as the needs of battle demanded more and more deceitful tactics.

Until, sometimes, in bouts of melancholy, he wondered

if he were truly so different from Siggeir Wolfsblood. Perhaps all kings must become villains.

The first man through the doors—escorted by Sigmund's thegn Keld—did not look like a fisherman or herdsman. Rather, he wore gambeson and had an axe strapped to his side. A warrior, and one coated in enough sweat to have come from a hard run or a hard ride.

"Fetch this man something to drink," Sigmund snapped. Keld ought to have known better than to bring him here without some hospitality first.

A slave came rushing along, offering a horn.

The man quaffed down great gulps of whatever they'd offered him, coughed, and wiped his mouth with the back of his hand. "Thank you. I ..." He panted. "Forgive me, my king. I am Manning, housecarl to Prince Hildebrand. I bring word from Baia."

"Oh!" Borghild leapt to her feet. "What's happened?" Her voice shook as if the messenger's mere presence had confirmed every fear she'd so long stewed over.

Sigmund leaned forward and motioned for the man to continue.

"Prince Helgi's raid landed on a town King Hunding himself happened to be visiting, leading to a pitched battle between their retinues."

Borghild whimpered.

No. No, this wasn't supposed to happen. How could ... they were protected by Odin ... weren't they? "Helgi ..."

"Despite severe losses, Prince Helgi managed to overcome Hunding and slay him. He now presses his claim to the throne of Baia."

"What?" Now Sigmund was on his feet without realizing he'd stood.

"Hunding's sons have declared blood vengeance upon

him. My Prince has already sent men to aid your son, but requests you to send your forces as well."

"Yes!" Borghild shrieked. "You must go to him. Turn him away from this madness."

It was boldness for certain, but madness? Perhaps not. Helgi had slain the king of Baia, whether he'd intended it or not—and Sigmund would not have put it past Fitela to arrange these circumstances. Now Helgi went to claim the throne of Baia. But if Sigmund himself went and joined the battle, he'd undermine both Helgi's authority and his victory.

His fingers itched with the urge to claim Gramr and charge to his son's rescue. But to do so would insult his son even if the boy didn't realize the insult until much later. "Keld. Gather two war parties and leave for Baia within the hour."

"You're not going?" Borghild demanded.

He couldn't. Not this time.

21

The King and Queen of Vimurland sat upon their thrones, watching Skadi with mistrustful eyes. She could not rightly blame them. They may not have known her, but they knew of her, the woman who had cowed mighty Godmund in Glaesisvellir beyond their border. Who had broken the wood tribes of Galgvidr who might have once raided their lands.

The queen, Angrboda, had a wicked gleam in her eye. She could not have known the fate Skadi had planned for her, of course. Had she even suspected, she'd surely have beseeched her husband to try to slay Skadi where she stood. Yes, she was sleek of form, skin the color of snow, hair like platinum.

An ideal choice for a new host.

Deep inside, Gudrun murmured nonsense, seeming unable to decide whether to embrace hope or further despair. The human mattered little now. She'd serve for just a while longer.

Finally, Geirrod leaned forward, his oxen horns bobbing, drumming his fingers upon the blade of his sword as it sat in his lap. "What do you wish here, snow maiden?"

Skadi allowed herself a grim smile. Oh, she was a snow maiden, yes, but so much more. Death had not wholly rent away her identity as a frost jotunn. "A wizard will come here, across the frozen plains. Disguised as but an old man, but you will know him when even your wolves fear him and his kin. He'll come and you will lose your throne, caught in his schemes."

Geirrod snarled, his hand closing around the blade of his sword until droplets of blue blood seeped from between his fingers. "No man threatens to claim what is mine."

"Then I bid you seize him and wring from him the truth of his identity and his mission."

The king grumbled, but leaned back. "Why would I trust you? You yourself are human, or rather a spirit in a human."

"No. I am still like you. I am the daughter of King Thiazi."

Now the queen bestirred herself. "Princess Skadi? She died long winters back."

"And in the endless tracts of Niflheim, she became ... me."

"You came back ..." Queen Angrboda looked to her husband, then rose from the throne. "I'd much like to speak with you of your ... sojourn."

No she would not.

Hmm. Gudrun grew more lucid. Driven to it by fear—or relief—at her imminent replacement as host?

Skadi bowed her head to the queen, and the jotunn woman led her upstairs, to a balcony overlooking a central courtyard. Down there, a pair of young jotunnar, one male and one female, trained with spears under the tutelage of an elder.

"My son," Angrboda said. "Agnar. He spends overmuch time in reflection so my husband insists he learn more masculine arts. Ironic, given my daughter Gridr insists upon much the same training. In her mind she'll be a great queen like the jotunnar of the old days ..."

"In Brimir?" Skadi had to smile at that. Almost, she might have liked Angrboda. Considering the woman's fate, growing attached would little avail Skadi. Still, conversation couldn't hurt.

"So you truly are who you say?"

"Yes."

"Mmm." The queen followed the balcony's path around the courtyard before leading Skadi into a tower. There they climbed a long staircase that wove up the tower in an irregular pattern, like a vine.

Once they reached the top, Angrboda exited through a tall doorway into yet another balcony, this one rimming the entire tower and offering a stunning vista over the great snow plains all around.

"I dream of Niflheim," she said. "The goddess speaks to me, but I cannot fathom her words or meaning."

Skadi leaned on the balustrade and watched the landscape. Up here, they were above the mist, looking down on it like a blanket of clouds.

The queen moved up beside her. "Have you seen her? The goddess?"

"Yes."

"You've stepped beyond the gates of Hel?"

Now Skadi looked at the jotunn woman. A queen torn between reverence and doubt, so wanting to believe the source of frost jotunn strength had her interests at heart. But Hel served herself most of all. And now, knowing what she knew of the goddess's origins, Skadi could not be certain of aught any more.

Hel was a dead woman. Not even a jotunn, unless she'd misread the signs. *Human.*

Was that knowledge something Skadi could use to her advantage? If so, she didn't quite see how.

"The fortress lies in the heart of Niflheim, towering taller even than this keep. Only the damned pass through there. When the gates are open, you can hear the screams. It is dark and cold. The Queen of Mist has bound wraiths and snow maidens and other fell servants to herself. Men sometimes speak as though the dead will dine at her table. But men do not feast there—they are the feast. Their souls are devoured to sustain the cold legions." Skadi wasn't even certain why she was telling Angrboda all this. A vague sense that the woman needed to hear it?

Or a cruel desire on Skadi's part to see another tremble with fear. And, indeed, Angrboda twisted about where she stood, seeming vexed.

"I ... I would learn from you."

Not quite the response she expected. Tragic, in truth. "Bid your husband follow my instructions carefully. The wizard will come here, and later, another man, bearing flame stolen from Muspelheim. These foes must be dealt with precisely."

"Flame?" The frost jotunn spat the word like a curse. "It will be as you say, Princess."

"I am a queen now. The Queen of Winter." Skadi quirked a smile. "And I welcome you into my service."

22

Seven knights, counting Reolus. Them, a varulf, a berserk, and a handful of Ás and Vall warriors. That was all Tyr had when he crossed into the Andalus Marches. Twenty-three men and women, all astride horses.

Couldn't say for certain how many men this emir would have with him. More, maybe. Maybe not. Seemed to Tyr, whatever Art the Caliphs used to create the Sons, they couldn't make too many like that. Must've cost something. What, he couldn't say. Didn't much want to know, either.

His troop had crossed the river, avoiding the March villages as best they could. Some locals held loyalty to Valland, true enough. Some to Serkland, too. Many, though —especially those who hadn't fled—they held themselves apart. Different peoples, their own language even. One what Tyr couldn't make much sense of, nor Reolus or his men, they'd said.

Hard to trust men who could speak without you knowing what they were about.

Tyr pulled up on his reins and took in the landscape. Lots of hills. Lots of trees, plenty of them in marshland.

Made it hard to know when foes were about, Hermod's keen eyes not withstanding.

"You fought here," Reolus said, riding up beside Tyr. "Back when Karolus himself reigned."

Tyr grunted in assent. Lot of men died here. Lot of blood. Wasn't so far from where he'd fought Volsung's men. Course, that was a lifetime ago. Two lifetimes, maybe.

Another led his horse up to them. Norbert. "Our taciturn friend must have been alive when my grandfather was a boy. Why, it's almost enough to wonder if all his parts are in working order."

Tyr spat in the dirt.

"Your grandfather's?" Reolus asked.

"Shit," Norbert said. "I hope his parts are not still working. Man's been dead eight winters. Can you imagine a corpse running around with a big old—"

"I'd prefer not to imagine," Reolus said.

Nor Tyr. Valls called draugar 'revenants.' Weren't as common here as in the North Realms. Maybe mist was thicker up there. Maybe men were angrier, more like to come back. Either way, the dead didn't rise quite so oft in Valland. But it happened. After a battle, men went and burned the bodies.

Valls did it of necessity.

Serks did it as some kind of offering to their Fire God. Muspel they called him. Bastard wanted to see the whole of Midgard burn, seemed to Tyr.

Reolus pointed in the distance. "Karjuba is that way."

Tyr shook his head. "Further than you realize. Race them to Karjuba, city'll belong to the Sons before we get there. Have to cut them off before that. Hermod says they're crossing the Middle Sea. Plan to land at Turab and march south."

Reolus grunted. "They're not crossing the Straits?"

"No."

"All right," Norbert said. "I have to ask. How does Hermod know things the emir's own horse probably hasn't been told yet?"

Reolus chuckled. "The Ás is good at getting close to people without them knowing."

"Close?" Norbert asked. "The horse is between his *legs*. To get closer, he'd have to crawl up the man's arse."

Tyr refused to smile at the man's absurdity. Would only encourage it. "Have to ride hard if we're to cut them off. Follow the coast, but not too close."

At that, Reolus whistled and beckoned for the rest of the men to ride.

HERMOD HAD GONE WITH THYTHKIL, the varulf, to scout ahead. Left the rest of them to camp. Fire might've given them away. Still, Tyr let them build one. Couldn't risk the mist. He'd seen it turn men savage, into trolls. Hoped never to see it again.

So they sat around two small fires, him and a score of others. Clustered tight about the warmth. Too tight, like wolves laying atop one another. Most of the knights gathered here, along with Tyr and his chosen few. The rest, common warriors, they sat at the other fire.

Norbert had wanted to sing, the fool. That, Tyr had soundly forbidden. Reolus had enough brain to back him up. Norbert looked shame-faced for about a heartbeat, then set to carrying on about his escapades hunting boar in the Valland woodlands.

Tyr couldn't say as anyone was actually listening. He sure as the gates of Hel wasn't.

No, he looked to Obeainn. Berserk was tearing into some under-cooked rabbit Bertulf had shot. Like he intended to eat the whole thing himself. Wouldn't surprise Tyr overmuch.

"Seen one of the Sons before?" Tyr asked.

Obeainn spit grease from one side of his mouth. Straight into the fire, causing a tiny flareup. "No."

"Expect them to have same strength as you, leastwise while you're in human form."

"Wait," Arnoul said. "These Sons of Muspel have the strength of a berserk?" Knight was big, for a South Realmer. Dark haired, a shaggy beard.

Tyr grunted. "We lost more than one berserkir holding the Marches. Just as strong, or nigh to it. And fast."

"Fast like Reolus?" Arnoul cocked his head. "Or fast like you?"

Tyr had spent decades training to use his left hand. Still wasn't as good a swordsman as he'd been with his right. But he heard the rumors among the knights. Called him a god of the north. The more pious, they named that blasphemy. Maybe it had led to Hlodwig's decision to break with the Aesir. His son proved more practical though. And still the stories spread. Tyr didn't hide his skills. He spat. "Maybe almost as fast. Maybe faster, depends on the man, I'd guess."

Obeainn snarled. Sound of it had Arnoul and the men nigh him lean away from the berserk. "So we fight them in moonlight. Give Thythkil and me the edge."

"No," Reolus said. "Most of us can't see in the dark. We'd risk the battlefield devolving into total chaos."

Eh. Tyr had fought his share of night engagements. Sometimes risky. Sometimes less risky than fighting in daylight. They'd need every edge they could get. "Obeainn may have the right of it. Most like the Sons won't have prepared for a bear. We hit their camp. Take them in the night."

Reolus shook his head. "They'll have heard stories of Ás berserkir." Numbers of those just kept dwindling. Fewer born on Asgard, and too many kept dying in the wilds. Plus, Frigg didn't seem much inclined to grant an apple to shifters. Couldn't blame her overmuch. Not after Vili. "We cannot assume them to be fools."

Tyr grimaced. Arguing with Reolus in front of his men wouldn't do. Only serve to make him look bad. The knights needed to respect his authority. Everyone did, really. Couldn't afford any doubts. Not on this mission.

&.

AT THE BASE OF A HILL, Tyr stood, rubbing his thumb across his brows. Staring down as Hermod traced a crude map with a stick. Squiggly lines in the dirt, really.

"There's nineteen of them, all told. They follow the old roads south. They're on foot, which means we can catch them before they hit Al-Dakil's first outpost." Hermod pointed with the stick. "We'll hit them here, between these two hills."

Reolus knelt down beside him. "Then we have to get ahead of them, set archers on both hills."

"A cross fire," Bertulf agreed.

Tyr grunted. "Sons don't die easy. Have to put an arrow in their heads or hearts. Else, they're like to keep coming at you."

The knight raised a brow as if Tyr weren't speaking Vallish.

"Well," Hermod said. "There's more, I'm afraid. They have an eldjotunn with them."

"Oh by the fucking gates of Hel." Now Tyr *did* speak in Northern.

Reolus frowned. "A fire giant? Those stories are exaggerations, yes?"

Hermod shook his head. "Bastard has to be nine feet tall. Pushing ten, I'd guess."

"That's shit," Arnoul said. "No such thing as jotunnar. Men down in these hills claim jotunnar set the standing stones. Right. Who's ever seen one? Just tales the men told from the March battles, trying to make themselves seem heroes."

Tyr almost bit his tongue. Sheltered cocks like Arnoul had no idea. Jotunnar clawed at the fringes of Midgard. A jotunn had raised Tyr. Not that he was about to say so.

"They're real," Thythkil said. Varulf didn't bother trying to prove it. Must've figured his word ought to do. So should Hermod's for that matter.

Hermod looked Arnoul square in the eye. Back in Asgard, he'd have been in his rights for calling a holmgang, man calling him a liar like that. "Cast aside your illusions. This jotunn is real. He's with them. And he's going to be stronger and tougher than any ten men. You best resign yourself to that so you don't wind up pissing your trousers when it comes time to fight him."

Bertulf rose, stretched. "I can set the archers. But I have to ask. They've only got nineteen men. Al-Dakil has a few thousand, at least. Why not let them try to fight it out? The caliph will solve our problem for us."

Reolus stood now too. "Because they're not coming to fight. They're coming to bring Al-Dakil into line. He won't risk attacking the Sons of Muspel even if he thinks he could win. He'd bring the wrath of the whole Caliphate down on his head. If we kill them though, he's hardly responsible."

"They'll just send more men," Bertulf said.

"Eventually, maybe. But if they get to Al-Dakil and force him into war, those thousands are suddenly coming against Peregot. Every moon we delay that is a moon longer to build our own strength."

Tyr nodded. "Got to be the ambush. Only way."

TYR KNELT LOW, behind bushes. Watching the pass between the hills. Five Ás archers crouched behind him, Hermod included. Bertulf had the Vall archers across, on the far hill. Hopefully ready. Hopefully waiting for the enemy to walk in.

Tyr's fingers itched. Ached to draw a blade. All these years, still he missed the feel of Gramr's hilt. She was good to him. When she wasn't breaking his mind in half.

Down there, he could see cobbles where the old road had been. Now grass poked up between the stones, making it hard to see the path. Locals thought jotunnar had lain those cobbles. Tyr knew better. Jotunnar didn't build roads.

"They're coming," Thythkil whispered.

No one spoke, but men nocked arrows to bows. Everyone knew better than to question a varulf's ears. Tyr had sent Obeainn with Reolus, across. Berserk hearing wasn't as good as varulf. But it was still a lot better than that of men.

Tyr eased his sword free from his sheath, held it low off the ground. Soon. Very soon.

He'd strapped his shield to his arm. Always had to do that first. Couldn't well grab it once the fighting started.

Serklanders came, trampling the grass beneath them. Ground trembled under the heavy footfalls of the eldjotunn in their midst. Unlike frost jotunnar, the fire jotunn had skin like ash. Air around it seemed to shimmer. Mist fled from it as though its flesh were aflame. It bore resting on its shoulder an axe the size of a man. Thing could've cleaved a mammoth.

The other Serks had deep wheatish skins and curved swords or spears and shields. They bore gilded lamellar armor. Most not holding shields carried torches.

Tyr's hand tingled. His palm itched. Even the missing one. Very soon now ... The scent of violence tingled his nose. Could feel it coming. A whisper in the air.

The Serklander unit had no distinct marching order. They milled about as they liked, some talking to one another in their strange tongue.

Best time Tyr could judge for it was when the middle of the line was dead center.

He raised his sword.

Men behind him rose. Couldn't make out those on the far hill. Not through the mist.

A series of *twangs* as the archers loosed. Already reading another volley.

Tyr launched himself forward, trusting the others to follow. Had to take the Sons before they could react.

Men were screaming down there. The hail of arrows had dropped three of the Sons already. Others had shafts poking from their thighs or arms. Scratches here or there. Many arrows had missed, and others had clattered off lamellar, angles all wrong.

Jotunn bellowed, his roar like an erupting volcano. He charged up Tyr's hill, straight for the archers.

Tyr pivoted. Tried to intercept, but the jotunn raced past

him before he could cut him off. Beast caught a mounted knight mid charge. Cleaved right through the horse's forelegs. Rider and mount flew in the air, a bloody screaming mess.

Now Tyr was running uphill. Couldn't match those long jotunn legs. Couldn't stop it ...

He'd have to trust Thythkil to handle the jotunn. Others of the Sons were closing in on Tyr.

The first man swiped with his curved sword. Tyr parried a blow that could've taken his head off. Dodged another. Twisted around. Man tried to use the torch as a second weapon, weaving an arc of flame.

Tyr batted that aside with his shield. Jerked his sword up to parry the deadly blade. He twisted into a riposte, but the Serk had already drawn back. Managed to parry.

So fast.

Tyr pulled harder on the apple's granted power, adding strength and speed to his muscles. Roaring, he chopped overhead. Man parried, but it hardly mattered. Tyr slammed his shield into the Serk. The impact sent him flying back. Tyr leapt forward. Reversed his sword grip. Drove it straight down into the Serk's exposed throat.

A gout of blood shot up at him.

Gurgling, the Serk flailed. Still trying to attack with a clumsy swing of his sword. Tyr slapped it with his shield. Jerked his sword free. Slammed it down again. More spurts of blood. He twisted the blade to be sure. Let him shrug *that* off.

A roar atop the hill.

Tyr glanced up. Thythkil flew through the air at the eldjotunn, intent to thrust a spear in his eye.

The eldjotunn moved fast. His axe cleaved straight

through the flying varulf, top to bottom. Almost immediately, he set about, tearing into Ás warriors.

Troll shit! Tyr charged at the jotunn but only made a few steps before another of the Sons cut him off. This one armed with spear and shield. A charging thrust. Tyr sidestepped, felt the rush of wind next to his face.

Whipped his sword around. Serk caught it on his shield before Tyr could get much momentum. And then that spear drove Tyr back again, out of range.

Another swordsman flanked around behind him.

In the pass, Reolus and his knights fought like mad. Dropped almost as quickly. There, a spear through Norbert's eye. Across from him, Reolus took a wound to the ribs.

They were being slaughtered.

Tyr dashed sideways, trying to twist, to keep the swordsman in view. Man's face was a burnt up mess. Wicked smirk twisted the edge of his mouth.

All right then. If Tyr was gonna die, he'd make these Serks pay dearly for it. Let no man say Tyr had fallen easy.

Grasping all he could of the apple's power, Tyr charged the spearman, roaring. The man fell back under his furious assault. Blocked blows on his shield, tried to parry others. Other one had to be closing in, but Tyr couldn't get an opening.

Another battle cry. *Another* man closing in on his flank.

All Tyr could do was bellow forth his defiance and fight on.

But the last man charged into the burned man. Metal clanged upon metal. Furious grunting. Had Reolus or another knight come to his aid?

Tyr shoved the spearman back with his shield just to get a look.

But it wasn't a knight who'd saved him. A tall man, with unkempt blond hair and beard. Fighting with two swords.

Starkad ...?

Tyr gaped, so stunned he lost track of the spearman. For a heartbeat. Long enough a blade whooshed at his jaw. Tyr twisted. Spear's point still cleaved his chin like a lance of fire.

Fighting through the pain, he knocked the spear upward with his shield and raced in. Rammed his sword into the man's gut. Weapon was no runeblade and didn't punch through the lamellar. It did send his foe's breath out in a huff. Enough for Tyr to slam the edge of his shield into the man's face. It clanked off his helm and sent the Serk to the ground.

More bloody work to dispatch a man who didn't take to being killed. Tyr was atop him, pummeling with his sword hilt. His efforts left the Serk dazed long enough to reverse his sword grip and drive it through the man's eye.

Grunting, Tyr jerked his blade free to take in Starkad. Caught in a furious melee with the swordsman.

"I owe you," Starkad spat at him.

Tyr's son *knew* the Serk? Knew one of the Sons of Muspel?

But the Serk matched his speed and overmatched his strength. He twisted under one of Starkad's blades, caught the other on the hilt of his own. Shoved, sending Starkad stumbling away.

The Serk glanced around. Caught sight of Tyr charging in.

And raced back down to his men.

And there were a lot more of them left.

The Sons of Muspel regrouped, fleeing the way they'd come.

Tyr sucked down a breath. Ought to pursue, but that looked like there were still a dozen of them left.

And Starkad didn't go after him. Instead, he turned to Tyr.

"Retreat!" Tyr shouted. "Fall back!"

※

OBEAINN AND THYTHKIL HAD FALLEN, Tyr's best hopes against the Sons of Muspel. He'd been intent to berate Reolus for refusing to attack at night and give his shifters and edge. But Reolus himself was barely on his feet from his wound. And he'd lost even more men than Tyr. Norbert and Arnoul among them.

In all, thirteen dead among their forces. To claim only seven of the Sons. And the eldjotunn—though wounded —remained.

All in all, a fucking rout.

The sun had set, and Starkad had taken to sitting on the edge of camp. Beyond the pitiful light of their tiny fire.

Tyr stalked over. How to even begin with him? It'd been decades. Odin had told him his son yet lived, but Tyr knew little else. Save that he'd been in Miklagard a while back.

Finally, face to face, all the things he'd wanted to say vanished from his mind. For lack of words, he grunted.

Starkad cocked his head to the side and returned the grunt.

"I ... uh." Tyr swallowed. "I hadn't thought to find you here."

Starkad snorted. "I didn't come for you."

"What's that supposed to mean?"

His son sneered at him. "Maybe I like lost causes." Starkad had walked away from this war when he was still young. Now—through whatever means Odin had used to extend his life—he remained hale so many years later. And still angry.

As if what had happened had been Tyr's fault. "You knew that Serk warrior."

"Eh. We've met. He's no doubt the leader here. Scyld. Possessed bastard."

"That where the Sons get their strength?"

Starkad nodded. "The caliphs bind Fire vaettr to their elite."

Tyr groaned. "We have to stop them from getting to Karjuba."

"They almost killed you all when you had the element of surprise. You go after them again, you're dead."

Tyr frowned. "Said you liked lost causes."

"Maybe. Still best we fall back for now."

Unfortunately, Tyr saw no other option.

23

*S*orcerers were rare and few admitted to practicing the Art, which made finding one difficult at best. Sigyn's search had led across the North Realms and into Sviarland. She intended to search the seven petty kingdoms here, yes, but most likely this was a preamble to searching Kvenland, a land infamous for more than one practitioner of the Art. Men told tale of wandering wizards in that northern land, though separating fact from fancy oft proved an exercise in frustration.

Beyond the wizards, of course, there lay the fabled—or perhaps infamous—land of Pohjola, where the witch-queens dwelt. She'd not expect to find the man there, but aught was possible.

In any event, rumors persisted of strange hermits in Sviarland, as well, and she needed to determine for certain whether Mundilfari dwelt in this land before moving on. According to Loki, the king had devoted a great deal of attention to Sviarland, from establishing his rapport with Gylfi, to more subtle manipulations. The king must still have spies in this land, forcing Sigyn to tread with extra care. The locals spoke of a forgotten castle in the marsh-lands, a legendary place favored by those touched by the Otherworldly.

Sigyn trod with practiced care, avoiding spots in the marsh where one might easily sink into the murk. It took little enough effort, especially with her enhanced senses, so she instead focused on the smells—scents of swamp gas, decay, and putrescence. Beneath all that, though, lay a whiff of iron on the wind, which, like as not, meant a dwelling of men nearby.

She wended her way between trees to find a broken tower showing no sign of human occupation. No flame, no campsite. No voices.

Despite this, soft, almost imperceptible footfalls echoed within. Sigyn paused, unshouldered her bow, then nocked an arrow. Such places might have attracted strange—mad—hermits like Mundilfari, but they also appealed to bandits and other outlaws. One couldn't be too careful.

However, the figure who stepped out was no man at all, but rather a red haired woman clad in gilded mail. She bore a sword at her side, rather than over her shoulder, though no shield.

"Who are you?" Sigyn demanded.

The woman quirked a sad smile. "Hildr."

"Daughter of ..."

The woman laughed, shaking her head and advancing on Sigyn at a slow pace. "No one you'd have heard of."

"That's far enough." Sigyn raised her bow a little higher to drive the woman back.

As if mad, the woman slowly pulled her sword out. "Not nigh to far enough, I'm afraid."

"Has the mist addled your wits? I'll put an arrow

between your eyes long before you get close enough to use a blade. Stay back."

"I can't." She almost seemed sad when she said it. "My master commands you return to Asgard."

Odin sent her. A shieldmaiden working for him?

The woman dashed forward with astounding speed.

Sigyn loosed.

Hildr's blade connected with the arrow in midair, knocking it aside.

Sigyn fell back, snatching the hood of her swan cloak to raise it. Her attacker caught the edge of it and yanked, pulling her from her feet. The clasp of her cloak broke off as the woman tore the fabric from her. Sigyn tumbled down into the mud, rolled over, and pulled a knife.

Her attacker caught her wrist before she could strike. A single twist sent the blade tumbling from her grasp. The other woman drew her fist back, moving with uncanny speed. On instinct Sigyn drew her pneuma to enhance her own toughness. She tried to block the blow, but it caught her square on the cheek and sent her toppling down again. The force of it damn nigh knocked the pneuma out of her grasp. Had that happened, the pain might have sent her spiraling into unconsciousness.

Instead, Sigyn shook the blow off and scrambled to get away.

The woman grabbed the front of her dress and flung her sideways into a tree trunk. She cracked her head so hard her vision dimmed. For a heartbeat she couldn't even feel the pain. And then that hit her like a wave slamming her against the shore. She was on her hands and knees, unable to rise.

Sigyn groaned, trying not to retch. She flooded pneuma through her body, dulling the aches and clearing her head. It was enough to let her regain her feet.

"That cloak is actually derived from powers much like our own," the woman said.

"You're a ..." Sigyn gasped, trying to catch her breath. "A swan maiden?"

Hildr shook her head. "A valkyrie."

Sigyn gaped at her. That was different. "Odin sent you to watch me?" As she spoke, she edged back toward her fallen cloak.

Hildr stepped between Sigyn and the garment. "Your king recalled me from my other post because of you. He expected you to try something like this."

"Did he, now?"

Hildr clearly wouldn't let her get to the cloak. Instead, Sigyn backed away, toward where footing within the marsh became increasingly precarious. With her enhanced senses, she could move without even checking where she walked.

She trod upon a log, backward, edging away from the valkyrie. "You should know I'm not coming with you."

"I've been instructed not to kill or maim you." Hildr continued to advance. "That doesn't mean I won't beat you senseless and carry you away by force. The choice is yours."

Sigyn forced a smile, continuing to back away slowly. "Choice is an interesting thing. If I'm compelled to make a choice by instincts, by a primal bond with my child, is it still my choice? We would not hold someone responsible for taking an action if someone *else* compelled them to do so. The other person is a force external to my consciousness and thus outside the realm of my control. But maternal instinct arises regardless of my intentions and is thus external to my consciousness as well. Should a choice generated from within result in more culpability? And if not ..." She tested the log's extent with the back of her foot. Nowhere left to go. "Is it a choice at all?"

Hildr frowned, continuing to advance. "I don't know. I just know a valkyrie's oath deprives me of any choice."

"Then I'm truly sorry for you."

The valkyrie's frown only deepened. Then all at once the ground gave way beneath her. She splashed through the quicksand, the surface loosing solidity due to her weight. The valkyrie flailed, each gyration driving her deeper and casting silt up over Sigyn's dress.

Balancing on the log, Sigyn wound her way around the mired valkyrie, then hopped onto dry land beside it. "Cease your struggles and you won't sink." She continued backing away until she'd reclaimed the cloak.

By the time she returned, Hildr had sprouted wings from her back. She'd already given over attempting to heft herself out by beating them, though.

Sigyn looked sadly at the woman. "I suppose being a valkyrie and having wings, you'd not learn overmuch about woodcraft, would you? Patches of this stuff crop up across Sviarland and other marsh areas. You can actually escape if you work your way slowly to shore. If you stay calm, these things can be avoided."

Hildr glanced around spastically, hands shaking. And then she paused. Shut her eyes. Her form began to grow translucent.

Sigyn nocked another arrow. Damn it. The valkyrie wouldn't stop. She'd said she had no choice. And neither did Sigyn.

She loosed.

The arrow punched through the valkyrie's eye. The woman jerked, suddenly becoming fully corporeal. Sigyn shook her head. She might not be able to see the Otherworlds, but she no longer doubted they existed. Her experiences had forced away her illusions, her innocence.

Realities she could not feel or touch lay just on the other side of human perception, and within lurked hostile beings eager to prey upon mankind.

Maybe passing through that Veil would have let the valkyrie escape. If so, Hildr would have come after Sigyn again, or perhaps reported to Odin. Either way, she couldn't allow that to happen.

Meaning she'd just murdered a woman.

"Damn it." She shook her head again. Damn Odin for bringing her to this.

And how the fuck had he gained mastery over valkyries? The question might have fascinated her on another day.

Not this day though.

This day, she needed to find the Mad Vanr. She had to do whatever it took to save her son. He was her own flesh and blood. Loki should have been here to help her. But then again, he ought to have been there for the birth, too. Lost in his own pain, he had failed her.

But Sigyn would not fail Hödr. Not again.

24

Eighteen Years ago

No matter how many times Sigyn pushed her pneuma into her son, Hödr remained blind. Loki had not returned. Perhaps this was what he had seen in the flames all those moons ago, when he fled Asgard and left her alone to face heartbreak and the despondency that followed.

Sigyn paced around the library while Eir sat, struggling with one of the Vanr books.

Finally convinced not to expose Hödr, Fulla had agreed to watch over the babe while Sigyn was here, and had thus moved into one of the numerous chambers. They'd both be resting now, no doubt.

The sad irony was, Eir had come here seeking knowledge of Vanr healing Art. Could she have found it, maybe it might have provided some help to Hödr. But, as much talent as Eir had for medicine, Sigyn could have taught a toad to read with more alacrity than the völva had managed.

"Keep working on this," she said.

Eir mumbled in acknowledgment and Sigyn made her way deeper into the library. A pair of wings led off to towers, each sealed with some form of mechanism. She'd spent a little time examining it. One of the books discussed the craft of locksmithing with enough detail she could imagine what went on inside—tumblers and gears set to drive a metal bar into the wall and keep the door sealed.

Sigyn knelt before the lock. An artisan's tools were not intended for this, but it was worth a try. With a tiny file, she felt around inside the lock, attuning her hearing for the slightest click. Enhancing the acuity of her senses had been her first real use of pneuma and remained a strength she could rely on. If this failed, she might enhance her muscles enough to break the door down, but then she'd have to explain herself to Eir and Fulla, at least one of which would no doubt relay it to Frigg as well.

She was in no mood for a lecture or for—

Click.

There. Now all she had to do was a little adjustment and ... the bolt receded. Perfect.

She rose, packed the artisan's kit, and slipped into the tower, careful to shut the door behind her.

The tower was just another wing of the library, with shelves more of books, scrolls, and notes lining the walls of each floor. A sheen of dust covered everything, including papers left strewn atop the few tables here. Some of those looked like what she'd come to recognize as Freyja's hand.

Sigyn leafed through a few. Perhaps the Vanr had been researching something just before Odin banished her to Alfheim.

The betrayal of Audr Nottson.

A historical treatise? Why would the Vanr sorceress be writing about this Audr, whoever he was?

The wraith Odin has bound has admitted to being one Audr Nottson, the fallen prince of the Lofdar. By binding such a spirit, Odin gains access to abilities and insight possessed by few among the Vanir. However, I fear the hold it has over him.

Wraith? Odin was possessed by a wraith? Stories claimed those were the most fell of all ghosts—vaettir of hatred and rage. So some of Odin's power came from his hold over a vaettr. And it sounded more like Odin was trying to control the wraith than the other way around.

With a sigh, she left the papers on the table. Whatever Freyja had intended no longer mattered, nor seemed to hold any bearing on Sigyn's current dilemma. She needed a way to restore sight to the blind, and an angry ghost wasn't going to get her there.

She made her way up another set of stairs to the highest landing. Yet more books. It might take her years to delve through all these tomes. And why not? The Vanir had spent millennia accumulating them, or rather, penning most of them.

There, another tome written by Mundilfari. The former king had lost himself by looking too deeply into the Art, true, so his insights might prove dangerous or delusional. They might also, however, hold the secrets she sought. Where better to look than in the writings of one who had seen beyond what others thought possible?

She settled down on the floor, back against a bookcase, and flipped through Mundilfari's tome.

The Theoretical Reach and Limitations of the Art, Volume Five.

Five? Damn, these people really had had too much time to sit and ponder things. Though it might now work in her favor. On the other hand, given a few thousand years, she could probably write a good many books herself.

As discussed in previous volumes, a change in one's perspective can result in a change in one's own subjective reality. To change the subjective reality of another requires greater expenditures of energy, with more objective changes requiring exponentially increasing amounts of power. No living individual has yet surpassed a certain degree of energy control, which I here term the pneuma plateau. Thus we are given to believe certain phenomena—the most common example being the resurrection of the dead—to be unattainable.

However, given unlimited energy, the most profound limitations appear to be the powers available to spirits themselves. If one could—and so dared—call upon a spirit of maximum potency, such as ascribed to an Elder God, one might theoretically surpass the pneuma plateau and effect a fundamental change to reality. Whether theoretically impossible acts—again, resurrection—might then become possible would thus depend entirely on the purview of said Elder God.

Elder God? Odin had called upon the power of some ancient Sun God to banish the Vanir to the World of Sun, but the king refused to reveal any details of his act. The rest of that sounded more like Mundilfari liked to hear himself ramble, save for the salient point that vaettir could achieve ends beyond mortals.

All sorcery was the evocation or invocation of something Otherworldly. So then, if any such an entity could cure blindness, Sigyn would need to identify the vaettr. Then she'd have to understand enough of the Art to compel the creature to aid her. If Odin had managed to do so with a wraith, then there was no reason to believe Sigyn could not figure out how to do so with any other being.

She just needed time.

25

The mountains of Jotunheim seemed to go on forever, caked in snows that stretched so deep no man could dig to the bottom. Snows built up over the course of thousands of years of freezing wind and bitter mist.

Now, an icy breeze made even the light summer snowfall seem a winter storm. Flakes whipped about, further obscuring the sky ahead.

Odin had seen Jotunheim before, in visions aided by the High Seat. It had not quite prepared him for the endless, barren expanse. Few trees graced this side of the Midgard Wall. Instead, naught but ice and rock stretched out, farther even than Valravn's ravens could see.

Freki fell back until he was in step with Odin. "We never passed beyond the wall. Do these mountains ever end?" Even the varulf had bundled in heavy furs, those caked with frost. The snows dusted his beard and mustache, adding to his already wild look.

"Everything ends," Odin answered, hardly considering his words. Sometimes, he felt he began to sound rather like Loki. A consequence of immortality and lofty burdens? He pulled his own wolf-skin cloak tighter around his shoulders. The apple's power protected him from the elements to some extent, but still, Odin felt his stones were ready to freeze solid.

Men in the North Realms told stories of Jotunheim. A land of wilds, a land of chaos, where the jotunnar dwelt. Still, they could barely begin to conceive of the expanse of this place. So much larger than Midgard, it seemed. Utgard encircled the world of men, ever crushing the edges closer to the chaos.

According to Hrist, the river Ifing blocked their way, and they'd need to find a place where it had frozen in order to cross.

"Do you know aught of Thor?" Freki asked.

Odin spared his varulf son a weighty glance. "I know that he yet lives. More than that, I cannot say." Clarity was hard to come by. Maybe the Well of Mimir could change all that. "All we can do now is press on."

"THERE IS a jotunn hall some miles to the north," Odin said. They had passed out of the mountains and into hill lands. Had crossed the Ifing and found Jotunheim yet more vast.

Odin had only the vaguest sense of where they headed.

Geri glanced at her brother. Neither of the twins bothered to ask how Odin knew what lay ahead. Perhaps they already understood the ravens fed Odin information. Given the wind and the chill, though, Odin could not send the birds out far without risking losing them.

In a recent pass, Huginn had sent Odin an image of a stone fortress rising from atop a hill like a crown of spears.

Spike-toped towers jutted from a parapet around that hall, covered in ice and glittering in the sunlight.

While Odin did not much fancy the thought of calling on a jotunn lord, they needed supplies and they needed directions. He saw no alternative save to press forward and seek hospitality.

Some humans had found moderate welcome in similar places. Odin knew Starkad had traveled here before, and come to something like mutual respect with a jotunn king. But those lands lay in the wrong direction, leaving Odin with little choice but to press on to an unknown lord.

IT BEGAN AS SMALL POINTS, rising from the ground. As they drew nigh to the hall, those points grew into outcroppings jutting from parapets, each twice the size of a man. Upon two, frozen corpses dangled, naked, impaled through the abdomen. The corpses faced outward as if watching for intruders. Odin grimaced at the sight.

Geri grunted, shaking her head. "This is the king you wish to seek shelter with?"

"For all we know those were criminals or traitors. We have not come to Jotunheim to sit in judgment over the locals. Our own lands have enough woes as it is."

Freki went first, trudging toward the massive gate with surprising grace despite snows that Odin always seemed to sink up to his knees in. Such travels made him miss Sleipnir, though Thor had more need of the horse than Odin at present.

As the varulf drew nigh, a spiked portcullis began to creak up into the recesses of the fortress. The great gate stood perhaps four times Odin's height, and each of those spikes looked the length of his forearm. The jotunn king did not appear kindly disposed. But then, the lands of chaos didn't give kindness much chance to flourish.

Still, Odin dared to hope this jotunn might be similarly disposed as King Godmund.

Beyond the gate, a pair of frost jotunnar stood, holding spears that looked carved from bone.

Freki faltered, then fell back several steps. Unlike him to fear even armed jotunnar ... "There are wolves in there," his son said before Odin could ask.

Indeed, five heavy dire wolves came stalking out past the jotunn guards, hackles up. Their growls echoed off the ice-coated walls. Closer they came, until Odin could catch wind of their slightly damp stench.

Freki and Geri formed up in front of Odin, and a low growl built in each of their chests as well.

One by one, the dire wolves met the gazes of the varul-fur. Slowly, their tails dropped down between their legs and they began to back away. A slight whimper from the lead one, and then they turned and fled back inside the fortress.

The jotunn pair looked to one another, mouths slightly agape, revealing wolf-like fangs themselves. That, and the hint of goat-like horns poking through their foreheads told Odin just about all he needed to know. Man-eaters.

"Who is king here?" Odin demanded. "Have you no hospitality for weary travelers?"

The left jotunn said something in his own language to the other one, then turned back to Odin. With a jerk of his head, he beckoned them to follow inside.

The gatehouse led into a courtyard, this filled with ice sculptures all situated around a miraculously unfrozen fountain. The sculptures depicted men—or jotunnar, perhaps—posed for battle. Some armed, some brandishing naught but oversized muscles that almost made them look more like bears than men.

The guards led them up to a pair of stone doors leading into the central hall. Each guard grabbed one ringed handle and jerked. The raucous din of boasting, wrestling, and carrying-on hit Odin like a physical wave as soon as the great double doors began to draw open. The hall inside was packed with several dozen frost jotunnar, most overlarge and clearly having tasted the flesh of men as well. A veritable army of jotunnar camped far closer to the breach than Odin would have liked.

Geri drew up close behind him. "We cannot overcome so many if they turn on us."

Odin nodded once, not turned back to her. The three of them could not have defeated or even escaped so many jotunnar, true enough.

Walk in shadow …

Yes, Audr could pull Odin out of the Mortal Realm and thus—perhaps—out of reach of the jotunnar. That, however, would leave Odin's varulfur children alone to die here. Instead, he leaned upon his walking stick like any other old man.

"Do not reveal my identity," he whispered. Living so close to the breach, these jotunnar might well know of Thor, son of the king of Asgard, who so troubled their kind. An unknown vagabond might receive better treatment in this hall than a king.

The guards led Odin and the varulfur past numerous stone tables, each large enough to sit a dozen jotunnar. Scattered among the tables, wolves and dire wolves lounged. As the varulfur drew nigh, ordinary wolves would rise and scamper to opposite sides of the room, clearly cowed.

At the back of the hall, the jotunn lord sat upon a throne, a platinum-haired jotunn female beside him.

The jotunn lord himself wore layers of animal hide that might have served as primitive armor. Four ox-like horns jutted from his head at odd angles, and, indeed, he must have stood twice Odin's height. A giant sword lay strewn across his lap, where he sharpened the edge with a whetstone. By the look of it, the task hardly mattered. That sword seemed honed to a razor edge already.

The creature grumbled something, spit on the floor, and fixed Odin with a glare. "A man even the dogs won't attack, eh?"

Odin cleared his throat. "Just a man and his children, seeking shelter from the cold."

The jotunn chuckled. "Want to be warm? I can arrange that."

He lurched to his feet, sword suddenly held up and pointed at Odin. "Seize the intruders."

Dozens of massive forms gained their feet, some brandishing weapons, and all fixated upon Odin and his children.

26

*I*n the foothills of mountains separating the middle world from the outer world, they had found a village under the yolk of some jotunn lord or other. The village paid tribute to the jotunn and got to keep their mud and the ugliest of their daughters. Despite their appalling squalor, the village folk sheltered Sif and her companions, taking turns hosting them in their houses.

Today, they stayed in the cabin of a woodcutter just outside the village proper.

Thor flung his flagon against the wall where it shattered, spilling the dregs of amber liquid in all directions. "Your beer is weak!"

The hapless woodsman flinched at the prince's tone, muttering apologies and groveling as if a jotunn itself sat in his kitchen.

"It can't be that bad," Sif said. "You've had ten of them."

"Counting, are we?" Thor snapped at her. "Well ... ten makes me a fucking expert, doesn't it?"

Sif rose from the small table where she'd sat across from Thor, watching him drink himself into another stupor. She patted the terrified woodsman on the arm. The poor villager brewed his own beer, which, in his circumstances, was an accomplishment in and off itself. "Give us a moment alone," she whispered in the man's ear.

The woodsman ambled right out the door, clearly all too glad to be away from the drunken oaf Thor had become.

"Make some fucking mead!" Thor shouted after him. The prince pressed his palm against his forehead, teeth gritted, and strained, as if trying to push his head off his shoulders.

"The headaches have not abated at all?" Sif finally asked.

"Now what could have given you that fucking idea?" He slammed a fist into the table, cracking it down the middle. An instant later, the table split in two, spilling an empty soup bowl onto the floor, where that too shattered.

Sif bit her lip. Hel take Groa. Let the Queen of the Mists devour the sorceress's soul for this debacle. Thor lived, yes, but he'd become a … a … clod. A brute kicking his own dogs.

Odin may have been a bastard, but he at least feigned civility.

The door burst open before Sif could say aught else, and Loki strode through, hair hanging in his face, eyes wild. "Odin needs us."

Oh, fuck. Sif rolled her eyes and looked hard at Loki. All of this was Odin's fault, in truth. If the king hadn't insisted on getting past Hrungnir, Thor would be fine. Or even if Odin had bothered to fight his own battle. "What is it now?"

"He's been taken, somewhere in Jotunheim. I have a sense of him, but it's weak."

Sif scoffed. "Jotunheim is beyond our reach. We barely survived our encounter with Groa, and Odin has a great head start on us."

Thor shoved past Sif without so much as a word. Gaping

at him, she followed him outside. The prince drew a knife as he stalked to where the woodsman was feeding his goats.

"Wait, Thor," Sif said.

Thor didn't pause in the least. He stomped over, grabbed the rope that bound a goat, and cut it with the knife. "Goat draws a cart. We'll catch up like that." He stormed over to the second goat, cut that rope too.

"But my goats," the woodsman said.

Thor shoved past him, dragging the goats along by the lines in the process. Not even glancing at the hapless woodsman, Sif's husband began hooking the beasts up to the cart.

Troll shit. He really intended to steal the man's animals.

Grumbling, Sif fished out a few silver coins from Holmgard—actually probably Miklagardian in make—and pressed them into the woodsman's hands. Maybe not a lot he could buy with silver in a place like this, but she had naught else to offer.

"Thor," she called. "Thor, please, we cannot go to Utgard. It's mist-madness."

He spun on her, growling, a trail of spittle dribbling down into his beard. "Stay here and drink arse-strained beer if you wish. I'm going to save my fucking father!"

Sif looked to Loki, but the man remained as impassive as ever. Unreadable.

Troll shit.

Sif climbed into the back of the cart.

27

*E*ylimi's court in Styria lay in view of the mighty Sudurberks, mountains many considered impassible. Over the years, Sigmund had heard of a few raiding parties trying to strike into Outer Miklagard by passing through the mountains. None had returned. Whether they fell to the Miklagardians and their strange ways, or simply succumbed to the mountains and the vaettir that no doubt called them home, Sigmund could not guess.

Such things mattered little, in the end. Eylimi had received him in a temple on the lower slopes of those mountains, the place a many-tiered marvel, with steeply sloping roofs overhanging one another. This temple, dedicated to the Aesir and most especially to benevolent Thor who fought the beasts of chaos on behalf of mankind, seemed far more impressive than what Sigmund had seen of Eylimi's hall.

Perhaps that was why the king chose this place, though Sigmund suspected it had more to do with proving that, while Sigmund claimed the favor of Odin, Eylimi's people too held closeness to the gods. Stories said Thor himself had set the first stones here, though Sigmund found that hard to credit. He did not mention that he had once met the Ás himself.

Great braziers sat between wooden columns, driving away the shadows in the lower level, or at least forcing them up into the rafters of the higher tiers. Outside, blood had stained a stone altar where these people had made sacrifices to the gods, but in here, everything remained pristine. Polished woodwork delicately carved with spirals and knots. A column engraved with a hammer-wielding man that must have been Thor himself.

Eylimi beckoned Sigmund to sit on one of the chairs he'd obviously arranged just for this purpose, himself taking the largest seat—perhaps his very throne brought here. At least he didn't have the temerity to place his throne in the stepped up dais in the back of the temple.

The Styrian king's daughter, a pretty young girl probably not yet in the flower of womanhood, brought Sigmund a horn of mead. This he took and raised in salute to the man. Over time, Sigmund had found carrying the runeblade enhanced his already formidable varulf constitution. He'd learned she made him immune to most poisons, a fact he used to his advantage by downing offered drinks without the least fear of betrayal, as now.

Those dishonorable bastards keen to bring him down with poison always watched him intently, never quite able to conceal their surprise when naught befell him for taking their draughts. Eylimi, however, watched him not at all, clearly quite intent on his own drinking horn. In fact, the way he quaffed it, Sigmund would have almost thought the challenge was to see who could empty his horn faster. He had to respect *that*. And so he chugged the rest of the mead, savoring the sweet aftertaste, then handed the horn off to the girl.

Eylimi belched and passed his own horn off, then slapped his knees. "I'm pleased you accepted my hospitality."

Sigmund quirked a smile. He'd marched here with an army at his back and asked the king to talk. The man would have been a Hel-damned fool not to offer, though probably he'd expected Sigmund to demand he come into the Rijn-lander camp instead.

"Your hospitality does your kingdom proud."

Eylimi nodded in acceptance. The king had grown old. Older even than Sigmund, and the other man looked it, with his grey beard now gone nigh to white and creases marring his brow and cheeks. Sigmund's skald had told him that Eylimi's first daughter—and, at the time, only child—had died some years ago in grief at the death of her husband. According to tales, that had driven Eylimi nigh to madness.

He'd cast out his wife and lived alone for years before finally claiming a new queen. Their young daughter was heir to the throne of Styria. For now.

Sigmund cleared his throat. "I've no wish to step around what we both know to be true here. My son now holds the throne of Baia. This brings four of the five kingdoms of Hunaland under my rule." He shifted in a chair that was not quite comfortable. "I have sworn to see this land united, and one way or another, I shall have that."

Eylimi frowned and folded his arms. Still surprisingly thick and corded, despite the paleness of his beard. "You think because I'm old, you can come here and browbeat me to get whatever it is you wish?"

"I think you have to face reality, same as any other man."

Eylimi's scowl deepened. "Reality? Reality is, you bring your men to the field, you might take the day. But a great many of them will find themselves standing before the gates of Hel in the process."

"So there is no truth to the rumors that trolls now strike at you out of Aujum?"

"Cocky arse," Eylimi grumbled under his breath, probably having no idea Sigmund would catch it.

"Bring Styria willingly under my banner, and we'll help you drive out these threats."

The king grunted at that, then stared up into the rafters as if he expected Odin himself to show up and offer the answer. "Your terms?"

"The usual. Tribute and oaths of fealty to me and my family. Should we call upon you in times of need, you will come. We offer you the same in return. The details we can work out in the morn ... unless it's to be swords?" Sigmund cocked his head in challenge and ran a thumb over Gramr's bone hilt.

Eylimi's face said plainly enough that he'd have liked to have challenged him. That he'd have wanted to humble Sigmund. And that he wouldn't dare try it. "I suspect talk will suit us both more than swords."

"Good." Sigmund slapped his armrests as he rose. "Then I look forward to our talks after the day meal. You'll come to my camp."

After all, the great king did not come to call on men. They came to call on him.

❦

SIGMUND FOUND Keld waiting in his tent when he came back

from the night meal. The thegn's face was grim—his usual look, in truth.

"Did I not send you to Helgi?"

"Yes, great king. Your son bid me find you when word came of your march here, closer to Baia. I'm to tell you he sails for Sviarland."

Sigmund groaned. Now what? It seemed every time he so much as left to take a piss, Helgi had some new adventure to undertake. Was becoming king at fifteen winters not enough for the boy?

With a sigh, he collapsed on the bearskin mat that served as his bed and motioned Keld to sit across from him. "I assume he gave you a reason."

"He contests for the hand of a shieldmaiden we met here, one promised to Hothbrodd."

"Who?"

"Son of Granmar, King of Njarar."

Sigmund rubbed his face. Yes, he'd heard Olof Sharp-sighted had passed a few winters back, and left the kingdom to his nephew. If the nephew had a son, he couldn't have been much older than Helgi. "And all this over a shieldmaiden?"

"Sigrún is kin to King Hrethel through her father, Högne. I met her, she is beautiful and strange, though speaking overmuch like a völva for my liking. But Helgi is quite entranced. I pled with him not to pursue this woman—"

Sigmund held up a hand. There was no point in recriminations against Keld on this issue. Sigmund knew his son and the boy had a will that couldn't be denied. Not even when he was like to start a war over a pretty girl. "He's well beyond our reach in Njarar."

Olof Sharpsighted had once been an ally, but neither

Granmar nor Hothbrodd would know or care about Helgi's kin.

"Take the fastest ship you can find and pursue them, Keld." It would be too late, of course. "Send word when you know what's happened."

"And you my king?"

Sigmund couldn't leave Styria, not when his dream of unifying Hunaland lay within arm's reach. Indeed, he could do naught save pray Fitela kept Helgi safe.

28

The frozen lake stretched on and on, beautiful and white. Sigyn flew above it, above the mist hovering over it, until, on the far side, she at last resumed her human form. Villagers had claimed a hermit lived out here, a man of ruddy skin and dark hair that could have fit Mundilfari's description. Then again, this was probably the tenth such recluse she had called upon since coming to Kvenland. Some men, it seemed, shunned the company of others in favor of the wild. Sigyn would have thought that a death sentence, lost alone in the mists, but some few persisted, seeming to prefer the horrors of the wild to the depredations humankind wallowed in.

The woods beyond the lake were equally white and equally drenched in choking mist. Sigyn paused long enough to light a torch, then took off into the forest, head down to search for tracks.

It did not take overlong to find some.

Whoever lived out here thought himself so alone he must not fear being followed back to his dwelling. Careful to remain silent, Sigyn pressed forward, quick as she could while tracking.

All clues pointed to this finally being the man she sought, but then again, she couldn't be sure until she saw him. Some quarter mile from the lake she found a hut half buried in snow, lit from inside by the flicker of a fire. Pressed up against a tree, she watched the whole area until she was certain no one lurked without. After a few moments of stillness, she drifted closer and closer, until at last she reached the door.

With one hand she applied a light pressure. The door creaked open, totally unbarred. Sigyn stepped into the doorway, torch low enough not to interfere with her vision, but high enough she could thrust it in someone's face if need be.

Mundilfari sat there, fussing with a small cooking pot over the flame. The dark-skinned man grinned foolishly, stuck a bowl in the pot, and handed it to her.

"It's fish. Fish. It is good for your belly. I think."

Sigyn took the offered bowl, sniffed it, then indulged in a small sip of the soup. Too much broth and not nigh to enough seasoning, but she was cold, tired, and hungry, so it would do. "You were expecting me."

"Expectation is the key to disappointment. When one expects naught, aught that transpires cannot leave one in disappointment."

Sigyn tapped a finger to her lip. That had not answered her question, and indeed, she had allowed herself to hope, that like Loki, this man might know someone sought him, and so knowing, might allow himself to be found more easily. Perhaps that had happened, though she would not have called her journey here enjoyable, with every passing day taking Hödr farther from her and placing him at the mercy of a Serklander invasion.

"I need your help."

"Ah. Oh." He banged his thumbs against his eyebrows. "Oh, yes. I tried to help, once. I tried to make everything bright and better for everyone. I thought I could burn away the mist." He chuckled. "Burn, burn ... replace it with choking ash."

"Yes, exactly. Fire is the enemy of Mist, so we turn to it. And I—"

"Oh. Ah. Mmmm. Like your lover, willing to embrace the flame on the theory it is better than the cold. Freeze to death, burn to death." He flicked his fingers as if throwing off drops of water. "Still dead."

Sigyn frowned. Fire had to be better than Mist. It had to. Fire is life. Everyone knew that. It just had to be controlled, lest it consume those seeking its protection. "I tried to contain the flame, to use it."

"Oh. So the Firebringer shared the gift with you, did he?"

"No. You did. I found your sanctum, hidden beneath Sessrumnir."

Now the Vanr narrowed his brows. "One hides things for a reason—the reason being worth considering before digging them up. If a thing is not meant for others, and others go and take it, who is to say whether the thief or the thieved shall suffer more ..." He giggled.

"I'm not a thief! I had to do whatever I could to help my son."

"In a dream, it spoke to me ... whispered in anger like the crackle of flame, rekindled ... And I dared to hope it but a nightmare born of the ... the ..." He flicked his fingers again. "My mind is not what it used to be. Hmm. We should all be grateful for that, I suppose." He flashed his teeth, then mumbled incoherent nonsense under his breath.

"No, you speak the truth. I ... Eldr is free now, and he has taken over my son."

"Ash sparks again ... mistakes we bury rise from the dust ... I think I forgot something."

Sigyn set down the soup bowl and crawled over to sit beside the ancient Vanr. "I am begging you to help me undo what I have done. I love my son, Mundilfari. I cannot lose him."

"Mistakes ... we are all tormented by our mistakes as they perpetuate cycles of damnation, one leading to the next and the next. Such is the agony of history. They tell me ... the world has died a great many times ... measured in eras." He rammed his thumbs against his eyebrows. "And we repeat the mistakes ... again and again, we—"

Sigyn grabbed the sorcerer by the shoulders and shook him. "Focus! You once told me you owed Loki more than you could ever repay, that he saved you from being lost in madness?" Though maybe her husband had only managed half that task. "This is *his* son we speak of. Loki's child needs you."

"Oh. Oh, I think the child of Loki will have me, sooner or later."

"Then you plan to assist me?"

"Wandering, far shores, searching, waiting, watching ... I was ... Oh. Well, I have not set foot in Vanaheim in an age of the world. And now it is like to be changed. Everything changes."

More changed than he could imagine, no doubt. "We don't need to go to Vanaheim. Hödr is in Valland."

She hoped he was yet there.

"Oh? Oh." He raised a finger. "Ah, but I'd need something from my study."

Oh, wonderful. Sigyn stifled her groan. "Fine. Your

people are not there, sorcerer, nor any who might recognize you. I am begging you to return with me and help me make amends for this error."

"Eyes."

What now? Did he …? "You know this was about Hödr's eyes?"

"A man who sees the future sires a blind son. The Norns are fond of irony. They lace their webs with its venom." He quirked the hint of a smile.

Sigyn almost slapped him. "Do I look amused to you?"

"We the pawns, never are, when we see our place for what it is. The Firebringer is lucky in you. Oh." The sorcerer clucked his tongue. "You wanted to grant sight where none was meant to dwell. A wish granted and then revoked must naturally take with it all the benefits it once bestowed."

Sigyn had long begun to fear as much, and hearing it now all but confirmed left her shivering. "You mean, if you exorcise Eldr from Hödr, my son will be blind again. He would have known sight, but only as a slave to a monster. Would it not then have been better for him had he never known the visible world at all?"

"There are worse fates." He chuckled. "Oh. Yes. And all of us, caught in this web, we shall see those too. Urd is cruel."

So she knew all too well.

29

Ten Years Ago

*S*unlight bathed so much of Sessrumnir that, walking in the shadows of its depths struck Sigyn with a malaise her eagerness could not quite eclipse. In the years she had spent delving through the tomes of this place, she had rarely come down here. Underground, free from distractions, one could find the void chambers where Freyja and other Vanir had once practiced sorcery, as well as cellars housing the more volatile of alchemical components.

Neither held much interest for Sigyn at the moment though. Some few of Freyja's writings offered oblique references to Mundilfari's secret study, which, given that he had been Freyja's tutor, must have existed in Sessrumnir. And a hidden refuge of the Mad Vanr—*that* held all the interest in the world.

Torch high behind her head, she ran fingers along the wall as she meandered through long hallways—tunnels, really—carved into the mountainside. Many bore glyphs and runes. Some she suspected were wards against various types of vaettir or—and it was the same thing, in truth— against scrying by other sorcerers.

Mundilfari's many writings indicated he was the first sorcerer amongst the Vanir, but, not the first in Midgard. He had learned his Art from somewhere, but he had never elucidated where. Regardless, he may have known arcana and eldritch lore he chose not to share even with his apprentices. The man himself was out there, in Midgard, wandering like a vagrant—or like Odin—searching for something. Perhaps for his lost humanity or his shattered mind. In his absence, though, Sigyn dared to hope his sanctum might solve her dilemma.

She came to a sconce and lit it with her torch, adding a touch more illumination to these tunnels. Beside the sconce was another door. Like many of those down here, they had been locked. Sigyn had taught herself to pick locks, at least until she had opened Freyja's chambers and realized the former lady of this palace had keys to all the doors. This room housed reagents that could explode if exposed to air— a lesson that had nigh cost her life.

She frowned. She had tried every alchemical remedy for her son in the Vanir's records, even some of the questionable formulae put forth by Gullveig, whom she suspected had fallen to madness herself before Frigg murdered her.

Eir had helped, too, but none of them had made the slightest difference. The answers Sigyn sought didn't lie in exotic herbs or brews.

Clucking her tongue, she pushed on, still running her fingers along the wall. A slight variation in the stonework gave her pause. Here.

Her enhanced senses included a refined sense of touch

that had numerous unexpected uses. And if that wasn't Mundilfari's sanctum, it at least meant something hidden lurked behind this wall. No obvious markings separated one section from the next, but then, none would. The sorcerer had no doubt conjured some Earth vaettr to build this—a dverg, perhaps. Sigyn drew her fingertips over the wall, starting as high as she could reach and running back and forth lower and lower.

Until at last a segment no larger than the pad of her thumb gave way. This she pushed in. Stone began to grind on stone and a shower of dust poured out of cracks that framed a previously indistinguishable door. This door ground up into the roof of the tunnel, revealing another passage that vanished into darkness. Stale air blew out, stealing her breath and setting her coughing. Maybe no one had trod here in nigh unto a thousand years.

Sigyn pushed inward, torch at her side to keep from interfering with her night vision. No cobwebs had arisen in here. The old sorcerer had used so tight a seal not even spiders managed ingress. Her boots kicked up a cloud of long settled dust as she edged down the hall. It ended in an iron door, this too locked.

One by one she tried every key on Freyja's ring, but none fit. Not that she had truly expected them too. Sigyn pulled out the artisan's tools she kept in a satchel and set to fiddling with the lock.

It had been several years since she'd needed to do this, and it took her a while before her enhanced hearing caught the satisfying click of success. The door stuck, however, and she had to shoulder it. It creaked open to let out a rush of more stale air.

Darkness shrouded the room beyond, so she trod

forward with slow, measured steps. Beyond the shadows, more tables, bookcases, scrolls. All not unlike the library of the Art found in one of the towers of Sessrumnir. But, here, perhaps, she might find secrets Mundilfari concealed even from Freyja and the others.

In the corner stood a marble statue of a woman Sigyn didn't recognize. She gave it a bare moment's inspection. Mundilfari's taste in sculpture meant naught. Sigyn sought a far different Art.

A brazier sat in the center of the room, the kindling in it somehow not rotted. Because the room was sealed? Sigyn lit the brazier then settled down at one of the tables. To begin pouring over Mundilfari's scrolls.

❦

AS SHE HAD HOPED, the ancient sorcerer had kept journals, though sporadic ones clearly never intended for anyone else to read, much less make sense of. He spoke of his encounters with the first sorceress, one Svarthofda, though where *she* had learned the Art he did not state. He did, however, indicate she paid homage to Hel ...

No matter how many years passed, that name could not help but shock her anew. The thought that her husband had sired the dark goddess proved an idea Sigyn could not quite accept.

She flipped through more pages in the musty tome.

Loki had known aught was wrong with their son, even before he was born. He had fucking *known* and did naught to fix it. Sigyn blew out a long breath. And now her husband rarely came back to Asgard, hiding, on the excuse he had to watch over Odin. A rift had grown between the blood broth-

204

ers, but at present, Sigyn did not care to work through that puzzle.

If Loki would not help her, perhaps Mundilfari's ravings held the answer.

In a world consumed by Mist, the natural and inevitable course seemed to turn to its opposite for succor.

Sigyn tapped a finger to her lip. The Vanr scholars posited nine Spheres of Creation, each with its own corresponding world into the Spirit Realm. No neat duality existed between the spheres, per se, but many had observed antithetical relationships between multiple spheres. Mist being a force of cold and entropy, one could generally assume Wood, Sun, and most especially Fire to stand in opposition to it.

The sorcerer went on, rambling about spirits of ash and flame and how he, perhaps in error, mistook them for more benevolent than the abominations billowing forth from Mist.

For they could speak beautifully and lull one with the promises of wishes granted.

Wishes?

Sorcerers in the Serkland Caliphate made pacts with Fire vaettir. It was, she suspected, how they kept the mist at bay in their realm. And if these vaettir could grant wishes, it would explain how the caliphs maintained their hold over such a vast empire as was rumored to lie in lands beyond the Midgard Wall. And Mundilfari had perhaps come from those lands? Had he arrived at the same conclusion, or, perhaps, even led the Serkland sorcerers to reach it?

Sigyn's stomach grumbled. How long had she been down here? She stretched, and her spine cracked. She blew out a long breath. No—she would rest when she had her answers. Her son had waited long enough for a cure to his condition.

If these Fire vaettir could grant wishes, she would find out how Mundilfari had evoked them. Then she would call one up and make whatever bargain necessary to save her child.

30

*S*weat stung Odin's eyes. It rolled down his aching back in rivers.

Red-gold chains bound his arms, keeping them apart and drawing them close to fires that blazed on either side of him. True to his word, the jotunn king—Geirrod—had kept Odin warm. He'd chained him beneath his hall, in a furnace. Twin flames roared up through grates in the floor, each enough to scorch Odin's hands.

The small room caught the heat and held it inside like the ovens South Realmers sometimes used. That heat had wrung him out and left him feeling hollow. Faint and ready to collapse.

And these chains—orichalcum—prevented him from calling upon Audr to escape them. Had he realized with what Geirrod intended to bind him, perhaps Odin would have chanced fighting even so many jotunnar.

The cell's door opened and the jotunn king slipped in, ducking his head. A smaller jotunn—a boy, really—follow him, his frown a stark contrast to his father's obvious glee.

The boy had not yet tasted the flesh of man and thus was not so given over to chaos.

Geirrod stalked close to Odin and grabbed his hair, hefting his head up at an awkward angle, staring into his eyes. "Who are you, wizard?"

Odin almost chuckled. What did names matter? "Call me Grimnir."

"And what do you wish here?"

"Just a traveler passing through with my children." Where were Geri and Freki? Did they fare better? Surely Geirrod could not have had so many orichalcum chains.

Geirrod yanked on Odin's hair until it felt strands would rip out by the roots. "Speak truth, little man."

Odin chortled, staring defiance at the petty jotunn king. "There is a place plated in silver, where the Aesir watch you and see your vile deeds. Do you think they know how you treat your guests?"

The jotunn dropped Odin's hair and let his head fall. "So pray to your false gods that your soul reach them and not the true Goddess."

"Oh ... There is a place prepared for Aesir, you petulant buffoon. Where Gladsheimr once stood now rises the glory of Valhalla. Odin's chosen gather there ..."

Geirrod snarled, then slapped Odin. The blow sent a haze of white filling his vision and it took Odin a moment to blink it away. "Do you truly wish to draw this out with riddles, old man?"

"What I wish seems to matter so little. Do you know that serpents coil beneath the roots of Yggdrasil? Vile creatures beyond number devouring our world, while you sit here engrossed in your petty games, knowing naught of truth."

The jotunn king growled.

No word Odin could say was like to secure his release. So he'd hardly give this bastard the satisfaction of his cooperation. Loki had trained Odin well in the arts obfuscation. Let the fool jotunn lord falter in his attempts to unravel Odin's warnings.

Geirrod must have sensed he wouldn't win this, for a dark grin spread over his face. The jotunn then revealed claw-like protrusions jutting from the fingers of one hand. He stalked around behind Odin, and Odin found himself tensing. Ready for the pain.

Or he had thought himself ready. The jotunn king dug one of those claws into Odin's back and began to draw a wicked gouge out between his shoulder blades. Odin hissed a painful breath then clenched his teeth trying not to cry out despite the haze of red filling his vision. He shuddered with the pain, grunting with each breath.

The savage cutting went on and on, one way and then another.

And then Geirrod yanked a narrow stretch of Odin's skin free and Odin could not hold back his screams of agony. He wailed, unable to catch his breath in the smoky, scorching air.

The king tromped back in front of Odin, a bloody hunk of flesh the size of Odin's forearm dangling from his hand. Casually, he tore into it with wolflike teeth.

Odin felt apt to retch, his gut churning at watching the jotunn devour his body.

The king tore off a hunk of flesh and handed it to his son. "First step toward manhood, I reckon." With a claw, he worked a piece of dangling meat out from between his teeth. Meat—pieces of Odin.

The boy bit into the flesh, looking ill as he did so.

Not nigh to as ill as Odin felt though. Sometimes, he

wished the apple would have let him die like other men. Sometimes he wanted to beg for death.

THE RIVERS of sweat had given way to tiny streams. The body held only so much moisture.

For eight days Odin had lingered here. Without an apple, a mortal man could not have survived the heat, much less the blood loss.

Mad with paranoia, the jotunn king had tortured Odin over and over. Much as Odin dared to hope his children had not suffered as he had, he could not bring himself to believe it.

The fires singed the edge of Odin's cloak. If that caught flame, he might yet die down here.

The cell's door creaked open, but it was not the king who came in, but rather his son, a boy with perhaps ten winters behind him. With a furtive glance around, the boy drew the door shut behind him, then padded over to where Odin was bound.

Merely stepping inside this furnace had sweat already matting the boy's pale hair to his forehead. In his hands, he bore a large drinking horn. "Water," he said, and lifted the horn to Odin's lips.

Odin drank greedily. The liquid stung his parched throat so roughly he gagged. The boy held the horn away while Odin choked and coughed. Then, more slowly, he allowed Odin another sip, and another, until Odin had drained the entire horn.

"Thank you."

"It's wrong ... what my father's doing to you. You ain't done naught, and still he's torturing an innocent man."

And the boy had eaten his flesh, even if the father had given him no choice. "What's your name?"

"Agnar." The boy shrugged. "Agnar Geirrodson, after my uncle."

The edge of Odin's cloak smoldered. He kicked at it, caught it with his foot, then jerked it away from the fires and stomped out the embers of it. "My mantle burns ..."

Agnar rubbed his face. Not even a hint of beard yet. "I can't release you."

Odin chuckled mirthlessly. Of course the boy couldn't defy his father and king, at least not overmuch. But the water was a start. "Eight days and nights I've waited here between these fires. You alone offered me food or water. So you alone shall rule this land one day, this I promise."

Agnar snorted. "Even if you were a sorcerer, you can't change what is. Father will keep eating, and keep living a long time, I reckon."

"I am ... Odin. King of Asgard ..."

The boy's eyes widened.

"And I have already sworn you'll find ample reward for the drink you offered me." His mind felt sluggish. Like it pulled apart and struggled to travel in a dozen directions all on its own. "I called to Hrist for a drink ... she couldn't hear me in this place ..."

"Who?"

Odin shook his head to clear it. A fresh sheen of sweat had begun to build on his brow. "Do you know Asgard? It's ... beautiful. Sacred halls for ... Thor ... he's out there. I should have gone with him ... But I spied the secrets from Valaskjalf. My hall ... I'd welcome you there, boy ..."

"You've got the fevers," Agnar said. He drew a rag and mopped Odin's brow with it. "I'll beg father to set you free. I'm sure he didn't know who you really were."

"Oh, but you knew ... I can see the glorious halls in Asgard. Breidablik and Folkvang and Glitnir. Great men and women ... wait there. For the end. I have to ... I have to ... find the well. Save them ... All of them. My children ..."

Agnar knelt beside him. "The varulfur."

"Geri and Freki ... I raised them as my own. They are my children ... The whole world is dying, boy ... Yggdrasil is rotting from within ... consumed by the serpents ... Threats, everywhere ... I don't know how ... I don't see enough ... I have to see the end ... it's coming ..."

The already pale boy had turned ashen white. He backed away slowly, as if staring at a viper. If only Odin could make his mind work more clearly, he might sway the boy. But after so long without proper sleep and dehydrated, everything seemed muddled.

Agnar backed into the door and paused there. "I'll find a way to make this right." And he left, fleeing from sights he clearly had no desire to see.

But Odin could not flee. Strange visions bombarded his mind. Fires raging out of control, sweeping over Midgard and turning armies into ash and cinders. Earthquakes consuming entire cities. A serpent of unimaginable size waking and flooding the world with its wrath. The dead marching.

And somewhere, in the darkness, a wolf howled.

31

*I*n a few days, they'd find the breach and—Sif hoped—Hrungnir's still abandoned fortress. If another jotunn lord had taken over the hold, she didn't much see how she, Thor, and Loki would find a way through. Only, Thor would try. When not drunk, he flew into rages or bouts of desperate melancholy. In neither case, though, did he waver in his insistence upon reaching his father out in Utgard.

Mist-madness. Both men she traveled with had lost their minds to the mist, leaving her no one with whom she could appeal to reason. Perhaps Odin's blood brother could have talked sense into Thor, but Loki's motives remained incomprehensible, save that strange visions drove him to stranger purposes.

Hel, but she missed the twins. Even driven by the wildness of the vaettir inside them, they at least remained—mostly—understandable in their motivations.

As dusk drew nigh, they dipped into a valley in the hopes of shelter. Loki continued leading the way unerringly, as if guided by fey insight. Perhaps he was.

They'd ridden the goat cart most of the way, but in the valley, they dismounted and proceeded on foot, Thor guiding the animals by the reins.

"There's smoke rising from the mist," Loki said as they pushed on.

From the slopes, they'd seen a small forest down here, clustered around a lake, though Sif could make out little detail through the mist. Still, it stood to reason, if people were to live in these mountains, so close to the wall, they'd choose this spot.

Either way, she prayed someone hospitable lived here. The pace Loki had set had left little time for hunting or snares—not that she expected Thor would've stopped for it in any event. Even the thought of something hot to eat sent her stomach rumbling. Had it really been two days since she finished the last of that wolf? Wolves were tough, gamey, poor eating. Unless a woman was starving, of course.

Guided by Loki, they entered the forest, tromping amidst evergreens and pines while the mists drifted among them, a rapidly thickening cloud.

"We need to stop and light a torch," Sif finally said. "I can barely see."

Grumbling, Thor stomped over, grabbed a low-hanging branch from a pine tree, and ripped it clean off the trunk. "Light it."

"Torches need oil," Sif snapped. And her supplies of that had begun to run precariously low. Who knew what they'd do beyond the wall. This whole mission was ill-conceived. After tossing aside the useless stick Thor offered, Sif dug out one of the last prepared torches she had, doused the rag on the end in as little oil as she could make do with, and then struck flint over it.

It didn't light. She tried again. Already the sun had set,

leaving them in oppressive darkness that felt like a noose closing around her neck.

Thor grumbled, shifting his feet, crunching pine needles and dirt beneath them. Only a light dusting of frost coated the ground now. Small blessings.

Loki trudged over and knelt beside her torch. Looked her in the eye a moment, obvious concern on his face. "Fire is life."

"The mist doesn't kill immortals," Thor said, no longer even looking at them.

Loki held his hand close to the oil-coated rag and—a look of concentration on his face—snapped his fingers. Sparks flew from those digits much as they'd been flint themselves. Several landed upon the rags and it caught.

Sif gaped. Magic? She found it hard to even form words. "Seid?"

Loki stared at her but offered no answer save to take the torch and continue his trek onward.

By the fucking gates of Hel ... who was this man? Odin's blood brother worked magic Sif had never seen from even a völva. Did that make him a sorcerer? A *true* practitioner of the Art? The thought was a lance of ice churning through her guts.

Still kneeling, she glanced around them. Her instincts warned her to run. Loki and Thor were already pressing on, through the mists. But Sif could run the other way, keep running until she cleared the mountains and make her way back to Holmgard. Back to some semblance of sanity.

Expect ... Thor. How could she leave him? How could she abandon her husband?

Men called her foster father Gylfi a sorcerer, but Sif had never seen him pull fire from nowhere. She wasn't sure she even wanted to know how Loki did it. Odin worked the Art

—behind his back, the Aesir called him unmanly and corrupted—but he rarely spoke of it, so far as Sif knew. And here, his blood brother did the same.

Fuck.

Having little other choice, she chased after the men, catching them shortly.

Loki led them to the lakeside, where a small cabin stood —the source of the smoke they'd seen earlier.

Sif's stomach rumbled again.

Barely hesitating, Thor tromped over and banged upon the door. Its whole frame shuddered under the weight of his blows. "Open up. We're men, not vaettir."

A thick silence.

"Open the door!"

"H-how do I know you're men?" His accent was thick with Bjarmaland's harsh sounds.

Loki stepped closer. "We have a torch. Can you see its light seeping under the frame?"

Sif frowned. Torches were said to keep back the mist and thus some of its vaettir. But she hardly thought it impossible a vaettr in possession of a human host would carry a torch. Loki didn't lie, but his words would bemuse whoever lived here.

Indeed, after a moment, the door opened a crack.

In the torchlight, Sif could just make out a man's face, his sandy beard starting to go gray.

The man stared at the torch, then at Thor. The decision visibly warred on his face. The fear of all men on meeting a stranger. One didn't turn away guests. To do so violated the laws of hospitality and risked the wrath of the gods—of the Aesir, men claimed. Ironic how true that would prove tonight. Still, who would not fear to invite unknown men into their home?

He didn't hesitate long, though, but threw the door open and beckoned them inside.

Sif followed the others in. The man led them to his fire pit where a young man and woman sat, each perhaps with fifteen or sixteen winters behind them. His children, no doubt. Sif saw no sign of a wife, so she must have succumbed to the harsh land.

They all sat.

"My goats are outside," Thor said. "Kill one for food and see to the other."

Sif flinched. He commanded the man like he was a slave.

She looked to Loki, but Odin's blood brother was staring at the fire pit as if it were his lover. Mist-madness.

The farmer—Sif had seen a small vegetable field, so she assumed that was his trade—disappeared outside a while.

His children began to ply Thor for stories of the outside world, timid at first. But Thor's mood swung almost immediately, a wide grin spreading over his face.

"You ask the right person, this I tell you. Do you know who I am? No, you wouldn't." He chuckled. "I'm the prince of Asgard, Thor Odinson, slayer of trolls and jotunnar."

The boy's eyes widened. No doubt the very effect Thor had sought. Sif struggled not to roll her eyes at his display. Her husband launched into several tales of the Thunderers bringing down their foes. While he left out the bloody deaths of their friends and embellished a few details, his boasts rang mostly true so far as Sif recalled. Some parts, he had out of order, but she didn't bother to correct him.

"That was my friend who slew that troll," Thor said. "The great ... The great ..." He grunted, scratching his head and frowning as though drunk.

"Meili," Sif finally said. Thor had thought of the man like a brother. And he couldn't remember his name?

"Meili! That was it, yes. He fought in the war against the South Realmers."

The boy—Thjalfi—leaned in. "Against Miklagard?"

"Ugh ..." Thor worked his jaw a moment. "Ugh, no. No, Serkland."

Sif frowned. He was just hungry, tired. That was all.

The farmer returned bearing great slabs of meat. These he threw in a pot which he placed in the fire pit.

The disturbance jerked Loki out of whatever strange trance he'd been in. The man blinked, blew out a breath, and scooted away to lean against the wall, shutting his eyes.

Thor just launched into another tale, this one of the mountain jotunn Skadi had called upon when they fought her in Sviarland. It had slain Itreksjod, but Thor left that part out, though he mentioned the man.

The farmer turned the goat meat over a few times.

"Oh, enough already!" Thor snapped, reaching into the pot. He pulled out a large hunk of meat, still a bit bloody, and tore into it, dribbling juice into his beard.

Given the ache in her stomach, Sif didn't much blame him. Their host served them, and Sif greedily devoured her own portion. And the next, as the man served more. Himself and his children, he served last.

Thor took seconds, and thirds. The prince belched. "More."

The farmer sputtered.

"Get more food," Thor snapped. "I've hardly eaten in a fortnight. Is this your hospitality?"

"That's all we—"

"Can you not feed a guest, man?"

Sif frowned. "Thor I think you should—"

"Stay out of this!"

Paling, the farmer rose and stumbled out the door.

Thor almost immediately seemed to forget him, rumbling into another story. One he'd already told this night, of trolls in Halfhaugr.

Sif glanced at Loki, but the man still had his eyes closed. Sleeping against the wall, perhaps, or otherwise uninterested in Thor's rambling.

After a while, the farmer returned, bearing more meat. This he dumped into the pot, throwing up a pleasant sizzle, and shortly after, the delicious aroma of more roasting meat.

Sif wouldn't mind another serving herself. The trek had drained her and, moreover, they had worse, and harder yet before them.

The family had no mead or other alcohol, inciting more complaints from Thor. Fortunately, the farmer's daughter, Roskva, redirected him by asking to hear about his exploits against Serkland. From the nature of her questions, she'd clearly never heard of the Serkland Caliphate or their war in Andalus, where Sif and Thor's daughter now fought. So removed, these people.

Thor talked long into the night, until Sif drifted to sleep.

§

"WHAT IN THE name of my father's father is this?" Thor roared.

His outburst had Sif lurching awake, reaching for her spear. She looked around the small cabin, but found no sign of others.

"What have you done?" Thor bellowed, his voice coming from outside.

"Oh, troll shit," Sif grumbled. She raced outside to find Thor standing over a pile of bones and gristle. Dead goats.

"Y-you said to cook the goats ..." the farmer stammered.

His children had taken up behind him. Or rather, the farmer held back Thjalfi who tried to interpose himself between Thor and his father.

Thor's brows knitted and he stomped over to the man. "I told you to kill my goats, did I?"

"Y-you said that—"

"Kill *a* goat!" Thor roared. "I didn't offer you both of them!" The prince glanced at the charnel pile. "Poor Tanngrisnir ... I'll avenge you."

He'd named the goat? When did he name the ... The rest of the line settled on Sif like a rock in her gut. Avenge a goat?

The farmer whimpered and threw himself at Thor's feet. "Please forgive me, Ás. I ... you demanded food and I had naught to offer." He sputtered, seeming afraid to even look up at Thor. "Please, I'll give you all I own! Just please don't harm us." He glanced at his children, then back, tears glistening in his eyes.

Sif strode forward. "Of course he's not going to harm you. We understand it was just—"

"Fine," Thor snapped. "I'll have recompense for the goat. Naught in your cabin holds any value, save the slaves."

"I ... have no slaves."

Thor sneered. "No? Well now I do." He snapped his fingers. "Boy, girl, fetch the bags. We're leaving."

Sif groaned. Troll shit. Momentous piles of troll shit. Whole fucking mountains of it.

The farmer choked on his sob, but Thjalfi stepped around him. "It's all right, Father. I am ... honored to serve the Aesir. As is Roskva, I'm sure."

From the look on her face, Roskva was torn between excitement and terror. And why not? Thor's moods changed faster than the winds.

By the time they'd packed everything, Loki returned, a pair of skinned snow rabbits dangling from his hands. One he offered to the farmer, who wept at it, and the other he kept for their journey.

As Thor tromped off ahead—his new slaves in tow but casting glances back at their former home—Sif hung back to explain all that had passed to Loki. Odin's blood brother said naught while Sif talked of the demand Thor had placed on the poor man. An old farmer alone in this valley, without the help of his children might well die. While not strictly Sif's problem—she'd not long ago wanted to abandon this entire land—it didn't fit with Thor's nature in the least.

Loki just nodded.

"Something is wrong with him," Sif said.

Loki cocked his head to the side. "He has a shard of rock slowly working itself through his brain. I'd assume this carries with it severe headaches among other deleterious effects. The man you knew may well have died fighting Hrungnir."

"He's immortal ..."

Loki nodded. "Even immortals change over time. Naught lasts forever."

Sif shivered at his words, only falling farther and farther behind him and the others.

32

Together, Sigyn and Mundilfari made the long climb up the mountain to Sessrumnir. Once, smaller palaces had dotted this slope, offering rest stops to those making the ascent. Odin had ordered all such places torn down, unwilling to stomach the reminder of the civilization he had destroyed. Now, some paltry shelters remained where palaces once stood, but neither of them seemed to even consider rest.

Sigyn had found Eir in the city, and the healer had confirmed that Hödr had not returned to Asgard. She dared to hope he yet lingered in Andalus, and, given the choice, would have headed straight there to search for the boy. Mundilfari, however, insisted he could not do aught for him without a talisman hidden in his sanctum. And so, once inside Freyja's old hall, they descended into the lower levels.

The Mad Vanr raised an eyebrow when Sigyn triggered his secret passage without even having to search for it, but made no comment. Now that she knew where to look, her enhanced senses made locating the switch trivial, and she had spent years traipsing down here, though she remained always careful to ensure no other found this place. Even Eir, who had now learned so much of the Vanr healing Art, Sigyn did not trust with Mundilfari's secrets.

Not after what had happened to Hödr.

The Vanr lit the brazier, then drifted around the room, tracing his fingers along the spines of books, wiping dust from vials. His wistful looks concealed thoughts Sigyn could not begin to imagine. Given the apple had already extended her life beyond what most people experienced—and she must now be older than Father had been when he died— already the years had begun to blur. And Mundilfari had not walked in this place in nigh to a thousand years. What would it feel like to tread such halls of memory? Sigyn shook herself. It didn't matter. She had no time to indulge the Vanr in his reminiscence.

"Where is this talisman?"

"Oh. Oh, yes. Uh, well ... I might forget such things. Might ... might have forgotten, that is."

"You forgot?" Sigyn worked her jaw. "You *forgot* where you kept the talisman that might save my son?"

"Oh. Uh ... Yes! Yes! I have definitely forgotten." He smiled as if that solved some great puzzle.

Sigyn wanted to weep. This was the man she turned to in her last, desperate hope of saving the one who was most precious to her. This was Hödr's salvation: a half-mad buffoon. The very same man to whose writings she had turned in her own mist-madness.

"What does it look like?"

"Hmm? Oh. Yes, uh, a wand. A stick, that is, carved from a fallen branch of Yggdrasil. Very useful."

Sigyn hesitated, then snatched a book off one of the shelves, flipping through the pages. One of Mundilfari's more cryptic passages had mentioned a small branch that had inexplicably broken from the World Tree, and he'd included a sketch. There, this Gambanteinn, he'd named it. The sketch depicted a wand the length of her arm, one wiry and twisted, and carved into in spirals. She turned the book so the Vanr could see his own drawing. "This?"

"Oh. More like than not." He nodded. "I'd say so."

"Then think. Where did you hide this?"

Mundilfari bit his lip, then banged his thumbs against his eyebrows. "Uh. Oh. Think. Think. Yes!" He raised a finger and grinned. "I *should* think."

Sigyn stared at him a moment. Then she began flinging all the books and scrolls from the shelves, tearing away all impediments. Unless the Vanr had completely lost his mind —and she was beginning to think that might have occurred —he must have kept Gambanteinn somewhere in his sanctum. It was small enough room. Finding naught behind any of the books, she grabbed the bookcase itself and—seizing her pneuma for strength—pulled it off the wall. The heavy case crashed down to the floor and cracked. A single iron bolt had held the case against the wall. Sigyn examined that and, finding naught there, ran her fingers along the wall itself, looking for more secret chambers. Secrets inside secrets—why not?

Pages rattled and she turned to look at the Vanr. He was shaking a book upside down as if the wand might come tumbling out of the pages. Damn it. Perhaps this man served as an admonition against any delving into the Art. Had she heeded such a warning, they would not now be here.

She dropped to her knees and began feeling along the floor, seeking out any aberration in the texture, any variation in the sound the stone made as she rapped against it. Some clue existed somewhere and she wound find it.

"Oh." He pulled on the doorframe then shook his head.

"No, no. Iron banding. Good for warding, not for hiding. Never would've hidden wood inside the iron. That would be madness."

So *that* would have been madness. She was fortunate he clarified where to draw that line. Hiding a staff inside a metal doorframe ... Inside ...

She rose, then strode to the marble statue in the corner. A delicate carving of some woman.

"Sunna ..." Mundilfari said.

His daughter? Sigyn stared at her likeness for a heartbeat before seizing it by the head and yanking it down onto the floor. The enormous crash split the carving in half at the waist. She pulled the shards of marble apart, revealing a hollow, inside which rested the wand from the sketch.

"Oh. Right, of course. Inside the statue, yes. I used to be so clever. For a fool."

Sigyn drew the wand free, blew the dust off it, and examined it. It didn't *feel* powerful, but she was no true sorceress nor gifted with the Sight. She handed the artifact to the sorcerer. "Can we now depart?"

Mundilfari nodded, then ran a hand over his short shorn hair. "This was ... the easy part. You know? I think ... I shouldn't have ..."

"We both should not have done a lot of things. We need to make for Andalus and pray Hödr yet lingers there."

33

Eight Years Ago

*S*igyn's son sat at the table in Mundilfari's hidden sanctum. At ten winters old, he already had a strong build, and under other circumstances, might have become a warrior. Maybe Sigyn could offer him that chance now, change his urd and give him a better life.

His milky white eyes stared off into the shadows, blissfully unaware of them, though he cocked his head at every slight sound she made while she painted glyphs along the walls and floor. In truth, she could not say how much these rituals were necessary. Despite her years of research into the Art, she was no sorceress and had no proper training. Nor, in fact, was this a full summoning.

Mundilfari appeared to have already conjured the vaettr and somehow bound it inside a ceramic jar, it too painted with wards. Sigyn suspected simply opening the jar would not be enough, but then, who knew, really?

All the tomes on learning the Art presupposed the student would have a teacher, and moreover, recommended

226

some kind of sexual indoctrination. Most oft, it seemed, males taught females and females taught males, as the sexual experience allowed arcane knowledge to be passed more easily. Sigyn had certainly derived some secret lore from Loki that way, but none of it prepared her to use the Art.

"Mama? Your breathing grows ragged. Why are you so vexed down here?"

Hödr was perceptive. Like his mother, she supposed. "I uh ... I'm going to try something perilous."

"Why?"

A single sad chuckle escaped her. "Because sometimes the only path forward requires one to take risk. If you can't, you become mired in whatever place you find yourself in."

"So you'd rather plunge headfirst into the sea than risk sinking in slowly?"

By the damn Tree ... "You sound like your father."

"Where is he?"

She sighed. "Seeking his own answers elsewhere."

Breaking her heart in the process of grieving his own broken heart. He said he had lost children before. An understatement given his daughter had turned so very cold. And now, to see his son bereft of a future ... No, Loki's lost child was Hel herself.

No amount of passing years had made that bitter truth easier to swallow. Naught ever would. A dead child, tormented until she became a dead god.

No such urd would befall her son. Sigyn was going to change it all.

"Breathe easy, Hödr. I just need to finish a few last preparations." She paused to look over at him. "Whatever you hear ... just stay where you, all right? Do not try to interfere."

"Mama?"

"Trust me. I know what I'm doing." At least she hoped she did.

🐚

VANR WRITINGS CALLED the vaettr language Supernal. Having never heard it spoken aloud, Sigyn prayed her pronunciation was correct. She supposed if she got it wrong enough, maybe naught at all would answer. That was the best-case scenario for failure. The other potential outcomes the tomes hinted at it were not worth dwelling on.

Over and over, she repeated the mantras, the invocations, and the supplications, until she began to feel herself a fool. Hödr visibly tensed as the recitation went on, either out of fear of the strange sounds, or the general unease that seemed to accompany the Art. Indeed, Sigyn's own skin had begun to feel like ants crawled along the surface of it. Her voice had started to echo in her head, leaving her addled and struggling to remain on her feet, until at last she fell to one knee.

And then the ceramic jar wobbled.

Panting, Sigyn crawled over to it. It just sat there, beckoning.

"Mama? What's happening?"

Her hand hesitated above the stopper. A wax seal bound it in place. Sigyn's fingers closed over that stopper.

"Eldr," she said. "I offer you freedom in exchange for the ancient bargain—one wish."

The jar had grown warm beneath her hand, hot even, as though a flame raged within. Could it hear her? Would it bargain?

Sigyn's heart beat against her ribcage. Her insides felt

like someone had coated them in whale oil. Her stomach was dancing about.

"Eldr, I ask but one wish. Restore sight to my son, and I shall free you from the imprisonment the sorcerer has forced upon you."

Hödr's chair scraped the floor as he stood. "Who are you talking to, Mama?"

Sigyn drew upon her pneuma to increase her strength, then crushed the wax seal as she pulled the stopper free.

Naught happened.

Slowly, heart still hammering, she pulled herself up to look down in the jar. Naught but ash in there ... A smolder sizzled amongst the ash. And then another, and another. Several dozen of them crackled, and with each, a hiss of steam rose from the urn, flooding about the sanctuary.

Shrieking, Sigyn scrambled away on all fours. Her shoulder bumped a table, spilling its books all over her. One thunked onto her head, driving her to her hands.

Blinking through the haze of pain, she looked up. Was that ...?

For a single heartbeat she thought she'd seen a pair of incandescent red eyes among the particulate dust that rose from the jar. Then they were gone. The dust settled and the steam vanished.

Sigyn rubbed her head. Fuck. Had she done all this for naught? Released the Fire vaettr without gaining any recompense for her trouble?

"Mama. You are quite beautiful."

She looked up.

Her son was staring at her. Crystal brown irises and dark pupils had appeared in his eyes. He moved with a confident grace that belied his former blindness. Hödr stroked her cheek, then helped her stand.

"Y-you ..."

"Oh. Yes, Mama. I am fine. Very fine." He flashed a toothy grin.

Sigyn tried to smile through her shock. It worked. It had *worked*!

By the fucking Tree!

Part of her had never expected it to work—though she hadn't realized that until just now. She swayed a little, still somewhat dizzy. Summoning was supposed to take a lot out of you, and to have a price on top of that. It seemed she'd gotten lucky enough and the Fire vaettr had accepted its own freedom as the price.

Hödr strolled the room, looking around as if keen to examine everything here. It was, after all, the first room he'd ever seen. Nevertheless, the dusty, dark chamber was no place to begin his introduction into the beautiful realm of Asgard.

"Come outside, I cannot wait for you to see the sun, Hödr. The sky, the sea—you cannot even imagine."

The boy tripped over the ceramic jar, sending it crashing into a table where it cracked and broke in two pieces. "Oh. I suppose I am not yet used to my new eyes."

The boy smiled again, flashing teeth as he strolled past Sigyn and out into the hall. He snatched up a torch from a sconce and trod forward.

Sigyn trailed behind, not quite able to settle her stomach. It was just the strain of the conjuring.

ore than half their number were dead. The weight of it hung in the air as Tyr led his broken war party back through the gates of Peregot. They had more horses than riders now. Valls refused to eat them, even when things were tough. Instead, they brought the animals back by the reins, intent to find them new owners.

City was abustle, even more than usual. Men and women, they had that furtive look. The one people get when they know battle is coming to them. Coming, and they can't do a damn thing to stop it. How they knew before Tyr and the others returned, he couldn't rightly say.

Reolus sucked a hissing breath in, leaning heavily on his horse. Wound over his ribs still troubled him. Under the stink of the road, Tyr fancied he'd caught a whiff of rot. He'd seen too many battlefields not to know that smell. It was worse, when you thought you'd lived through a battle. Only to have it still killing you, slow as a patient lover.

"Come with me to the fort," the knight said. "We have to see Lotar."

Indeed. They'd talked it over more than a few times on

the way here. The prince was not like to agree to their request. Not easily, leastwise. Asking his father for aid made him look weak, dependent. All the harder because he'd disobeyed the emperor's command to banish all so-called heretics. Those like Tyr.

Hlodwig would've thrown out the Aesir, the shifters, and anyone else who might've had half a chance against the Sons of Muspel. And now they had to come begging him for aid against those very same troops.

Tyr nodded at Reolus. He turned to address Starkad but the fool boy had disappeared somewhere. Tyr grimaced. No matter how hard he tried, naught seemed able to mend the rift between them. Might as well have tried to clasping arms with Hymir.

Having little choice, he followed Reolus all the way up to the fort. Knight grunting quietly in pain with each rising step.

While the town had been packed tighter than ever, the fortress seemed eerily quiet. Not half the troops they'd left behind yet remained. Tyr exchanged a glance with Reolus, and they both hurried up the stairs to Lotar's chambers.

Reolus was first through the door, and paused on the threshold, forcing Tyr to step around him.

The knight had paused because the only one in the room was a vexed-looking Mallobaudes. To be fair, Mallobaudes most oft looked vexed. At the moment, he sat at Lotar's desk, staring at a map.

"Where's Lotar?" Reolus demanded.

The other knight grimaced, pushing himself up with both palms on the desk. He drew in a loud breath. Glanced down at the map once more, then cast a weary gaze past Reolus. At Tyr. "The Prince has gone to join his brother's forces."

"Bernard?" Reolus strode toward Mallobaudes now, pausing in front of the desk. "He went to Aquisgrana?"

Mallobaudes frowned. "No. They meet halfway. The emperor has declared a Great Purge as he calls it."

"What?"

Tyr folded his arms. He already misliked where this seemed to be heading.

Mallobaudes's face only grew grimmer. "Emperor Hlodwig has declared the Deathless God frowns upon the moral decay of Valland. Thus he's ordered all heathens, whores, and other undesirables exiled from our homeland. He's even burning heathen goods and art. Melting down jewelry imported from Serkland, all of it. Any of those he's deemed 'filthy' are to be purged by flame as well, once the moon is out."

Oh, by the Tree. This nonsense was bad enough the first time, and now Hlodwig seemed intent to take it twice as far. Good part of Tyr was tempted to walk away. Fifty years of war here more than upheld his oath to Karolus. Caliphate was no closer to breaking. Valland was still fucking doomed. And here was this petty, self-righteous trench of an emperor, ordering Tyr's people out?

Why not return to Asgard? Let the Aesir reinforce Hunaland against the Serklanders. King Sigmund had brains and stones both, from all Tyr heard.

"Lotar went to reason with him?" Reolus asked. The knight was leaning over a little, clutching his ribs.

Mallobaudes leaned back a little. Must've caught wind of it. "Are you well, sir?" Reolus waved that away. Would've been more believable without the grunt of pain. Looking unconvinced, Mallobaudes continued. "It's gone too far for reason now. Lotar has conscripted Bernard to remove their father from his position."

"Treason?" Tyr couldn't stop himself from spouting it. Only thing worse than a weak, fool of an emperor ... was sons who betrayed him.

The other knight cast a withering gaze Tyr's way. "Large words from a savage. The emperor is mentally unfit to rule. His obsession with purifying Valland will leave him with no kingdom left to govern. It is hardly treason when the good of the land demands it."

Tyr had his doubts on that. But he held his tongue. Just cracked his neck.

Reolus groaned. Had to have figured the same as Tyr. Not only were they not getting reinforcements from Hlodwig, but they'd just lost the better part of Lotar's forces too.

"Well," Mallobaudes said to Reolus. "Lotar's placed you in charge upon your return, and instructed us all to—" his face drew up in a sneer "—heed the wisdom of *him*." He inclined his head at Tyr. "So then, what would you have us do, great knight?"

Reolus looked to Tyr, who nodded. Not much to do, really. Reolus turned back to Mallobaudes. "Prepare for a siege. We ..." The knight collapsed to one knee, then pitched over sideways.

"HE'S GOT THE ROT," Joveta said.

Woman wasn't a völva. South Realmers didn't hold with witches of any kind. They called her a chirurgeon. Seemed to Tyr her kind poked extra holes in men instead of fixing them.

Tyr cracked his neck. Had to stop himself from spewing foulness at her. "Fix him."

But from the way she shook her head, Tyr knew the answer to that.

A long slow death. The fevers would addle the wits. Sooner or later, Reolus would beg for death.

South Realmers frowned on that. Killing their own.

But Tyr had called Reolus friend. So he figured it would come to him, in the end.

Heedless of the woman, Tyr spit on the floor.

And stormed out, ignoring her indignant sputters.

OUTSIDE THE ÁS BARRACKS, Tyr almost blundered straight into Hödr.

For a moment, he stood there, gaping at the boy. Loki and Sigyn's son had proved too much to handle—by far. But today, he'd almost forgot he was here.

Shit. But Tyr had far too few Aesir here. If Valland had any hope left, Tyr would need every possible hand.

"You been training?"

Hödr cast a glance back over his shoulder. "Of course. Is it true the war heats up? That the Serks are coming?"

"It's true enough. You ready to fight?"

Hödr nodded.

Tyr cracked his neck. Hermod had claimed the boy might've raped some smith's girl. Girl didn't say so though. Hard to be sure without her word. Nor would Hödr be the only young man who'd ever stuck his cock where it wasn't wanted. Half the soldiers here were guilty of that. Tyr included.

Tyr sucked air through his teeth. "Got reason to believe Serk troops will be moving on us in a moon, maybe less.

The Sons of Muspel are bringing Al-Dakil back into line. Sure to shatter whatever truce Lotar had here."

"The Sons of Muspel are here?"

Tyr grunted. He'd half expected the boy to ask who they were. But soldiers talked, he supposed. "In Karjuba by now, no doubt. You stay here, you face real war."

"Oh, I'm ready for war."

"Fine. Get to Cyr. Few more bouts of training before things go to shit."

Hödr—arrogant smirk on his face—nodded and tromped along past Tyr.

Now Tyr just needed to find Thrúd. Wouldn't like it much, but she needed to be back on Asgard. The relative safety of Peregot had vanished in smoke. Place was like to become one of the most contested cities on Midgard before summer was out.

He made his way to the barracks. Paused outside. A strange moan within. Very faint.

Tyr flung open the door.

No one in here. As if a ghost had ... his eyes settled on Thrúd. She lay on the floor, beside one of the cots. Clothes torn apart. Trousers looking burnt off around her crotch. And her face ... Scorch marks around her mouth.

Tyr raced to her side. "Thrúd!" Five burn lines covered her cheeks, and a big deep one that had burnt away the flesh on her lips. Exposed tooth and gums. Skin a charred, bleeding mess.

Like a handprint branded over her face.

35

*T*he door to Odin's cell creaked open and Agnar slipped inside. "I ... I got the keys."

Odin blinked. His eyes had gone so dry, even given the water Agnar had brought him earlier. Everything seemed crusted, hazy. A madness had taken him, to come to this place, to take this risk. To dare to believe in a hope for peace between Asgard and Jotunheim.

Madness ...

Like the slow erosion of all hope ... watching as the end days crept closer, inevitable. Fire and flood and the howls of a ravenous wolf. To destroy the world of the Aesir. To consume the world men.

Where was Thor? Did he yet live? Had Loki saved him?

Agnar was at Odin's side, fumbling with a key the size of his hand, working it into joints too fine to have been crafted by jotunnar. Dverg work, perhaps, or alf work, even.

Odin had made so many enemies. They piled up around him on all sides. In the darkness around the Mortal Realm they waited ... even as the mortals destroyed themselves ...

One of the restraints clanked open. Odin collapsed to the floor, hit his shoulder, and lay there, groaning.

A moment later, his other manacle popped open and he fell face-first to the ground.

"King Odin?" Agnar asked. "It's really you, ain't it? Reckon we don't have much time."

Odin grunted, forced himself up. So little pneuma to call on ... he pulled on what he could, trying to wash away the fatigue and weakness with power he would soon have to pay back.

"Where are my ... children?"

"Father locked them in the cells some bit back. Said he reckoned he could use them to breed up a few werewolves for himself." The boy helped Odin up, face twisted in a mask of disgust.

"What is it, boy?"

Agnar leaned in, looking shamefaced. "I heard men talking. Saying the ... uh, the girl bit off the man's cock what went to plant his seed. No one else came to try her after that. Ain't heard no problems for breeding the man, though. They send them to him, three or four a day and he just—"

Odin held up his hand to forestall any further explanation. It sounded like Freki was having a far better stay here than Odin had been. "I need water, food to regain my strength."

"Father'll be wanting to see you here, soon."

"Oh, I'll be here waiting."

ॐ

AGNAR HAD REFASTENED the manacles upon Odin's wrists, but not locked them. Odin's arms ached all the more for having had a moment's reprieve, but he rather suspected the boy was right. Nine days had passed, and the king always came at least once a day to gloat or torture Odin with hot brands.

To talk of how he planned to eat the flesh of a sorcerer and thus become stronger himself.

And it was past due time for another such visit.

Odin waited, until at last the door swung open and clacked against the wall.

Geirrod walked in, the mighty sword resting unsheathed upon his shoulder. He edged around the fire to the far side of Odin's tiny cell and flashed a fang-like grin at Odin. "Been thinking about how I'm gonna get me some answers out of you. See, then your varulf bitch gave me just the idea. What if I was to roast one of your stones in this flame right here? Stones make a juicy treat to whet the appetite." The jotunn chuckled, then ran his tongue over a lower fang. "You ever taste a man's stones, Grimnir?"

"No."

"No." Geirrod shrugged. "Maybe if you had, you'd not have been snared so easy. Flesh is power, old man."

"There are other powers."

"See, there you go, spouting riddles and nonsense again. Me, I just don't hold with men what can't speak plainly."

Odin chuckled dryly. "Oh, Geirrod, much have I said, though little you remember. I see your sword, splattered with blood. But yours is the life that is over." Odin rose abruptly, letting the chains fall away from his arms. "See now, Odin, the terrible doom of your kind. You know to fear my mighty son, yet fail to realize when his more fearsome father walks among you."

Geirrod balked, fumbled with his sword, and dropped it. The massive blade clanked on the grated floor.

Odin surged pneuma into his body and lunged forward,

caught the sword, and thrust it up into Geirrod's gut. Blood oozed from the wound, washing over Odin's burned hands. He stared up into the eyes of his tormentor.

Eyes now wide with fear.

Streams of blood dribbled down between Geirrod's fangs.

"It strikes me now, that the line between jotunnar and humans is thinner than I had once believed. The horror in your eyes I have seen in those many ... who grew to regret their dealings with me."

Geirrod stumbled, hit the wall, and collapsed to his knees. Even from that position, he still towered over Odin.

The stench of blood and shit filled the chamber. The sword must have lodged in Geirrod's bowels. An unpleasant way to die.

But then, so would be being strapped between two fires.

Odin left the king alone in that cell, whimpering and crawling feebly toward the door.

🐍

"WHERE'S MY FATHER?" Agnar asked, when Odin entered the upper floor.

Geri and Freki he'd found in neighboring cells, and the two varulfur now plodded along behind Odin. Neither spoke much of what they'd endured.

Odin looked to Agnar, the son of the creature who'd just spent nine days torturing him. Vile as Geirrod had proved, his son had offered succor. Odin stroked his beard and his hand came away coated in grime from all the sweat and soot. "He will not be joining us. Now, you are king here. And if you are wise, I would seek treaty with the rulers of Asgard, not war."

Agnar nodded, expression tight with unspoken pain. The boy had loved his monstrous father?

"Boy," Odin said. "Heed this warning. Do not again taste human flesh. Do not fall prey to the weakness that so plagues your kind."

The boy's glower only deepened, whether because of the command or because he too feared the addiction, Odin couldn't say.

"If you command the others to let us pass freely, will they obey?"

"I am the rightful king, now. Blood matters a great deal to my people. By law, I hold authority even over my mother." Agnar sniffed, then grunted. "I'll see you all fed, properly."

THE OTHER JOTUNNAR avoided Odin and his children while they sat at an otherwise empty table. That suited Odin well enough. He had little mind to speak with them in any event.

Agnar, however, did sit at the table's head, watching as the varulfur tore into massive hunks of mammoth meat.

Odin had sated himself, but he lacked the varulfur's appetites. Instead, he watched Agnar. The boy fidgeted, clearly uncomfortable and more than a little sullen. For all that he claimed blood mattered, Odin thought it more like than not that some other, stronger jotunn would come to claim this land from him.

Or even that his own mother—now glaring at them from the shadows—would humble her son once Odin had left.

A shame, though not truly Odin's problem. "You must send a single representative to offer an overture to Asgard. No more than one, or Thor may think it a trick."

"Thor always thinks it a trick," Geri said around a mouthful of meat.

Agnar nodded. "I understand."

Odin leaned forward, cast a glance to make sure no other jotunnar had drawn nigh, then looked deep at Agnar. "I seek an ancient place, boy. One you'd have my undying gratitude were you to help me find."

The boy squirmed, frowned, and then leaned forward himself. "I ain't much for learning history."

"Who is?"

Agnar scratched his head. "Way up north, there's a uh ... a vitka?"

"A wizard?"

"The kings from around Jotunheim pay him homage, ask his advice. One thing nobody never sheds blood over is that. Vafthrudnir, he ain't on nobody's side, but everybody wants to be on his. They say he knows things. They say he came in the first mists."

"Where does he dwell?"

"Northeast, maybe two moon's walk if you don't have no sleds. Up on the plateau, before you reach the sea. Ain't never seen it myself, mind, but Father talked of it."

Two moons? How large was this land? Was Odin to spent the entire summer crossing it and then find himself forced to wait out the winter? Odin shook his head. Urd demanded this. It demanded so very much. "Tell me of Vafthrudnir."

"Kings have to go there, seek his blessing. Don't much recommend you humans go, though. With Ymir gone, ain't no one who could match Vafthrudnir. But I heard some claim the Great Father spawned Vafthrudnir. Thrym keeps his kingdom on that same plateau, up on the mountain.

Claims to be the king of all jotunnar, but even he don't dare interfere with Vafthrudnir or those what come to see him."

Geri and Freki both paused in gorging themselves at the mention of Ymir. The very name sent a twisted knot through Odin's stomach. Ymir had bargained his soul to Hel and, because of her, come out to murder Odin's father as a test. The Queen of Niflheim knew Odin might prove a threat to her and had seemingly intended the Niflungar to win him over to their side.

None of that had gone quite the way she'd intended, Odin imagined.

Strange, how he could now go a great many days without thinking of his father. And still, it would hit him like a physical blow to his gut.

"Reconsidering?" Agnar said. "For the best, really. I was a fool to have mentioned him anyway. Best keep to searching on your own."

Odin looked to Geri then to Freki. Both nodded. "No," Odin said after a moment. "No, I will seek out this Vafthrudnir and test the limits of his wisdom."

And if he too had sold his soul to Hel, then he too might soon be sent to meet his goddess.

$\mathcal{P}$assing through the Midgard Wall had left a hollow pit in Sif's gut, a feeling of profound dread that had dogged her every day they walked and grown twice as bad in the nights. Nigh to a fortnight they'd traveled. Each night, they'd seek shelter in a valley, or later, atop a hill, or amidst a grove of evergreens.

And the oppressive darkness would settle in. The howls, far off, but too many in number to hope to count. Like all beyond the world of men, those howls sounded larger, fiercer, more savage than the wolves she knew in Midgard.

Vargar, Loki called some of them. Giant wolves the size of mammoths. Predators that could hunt most aught foolhardy enough to travel these lands.

Yet Loki led them true, taking turns that oft seemed senseless to Sif and yet managed to keep them from blundering into the hunting lands of those fearsome wolves.

In the evening, one night, she caught Thor staring across the fire to where Thjalfi and Roskva slept. The prince had his head in his hands, obviously beset by another of those headaches. He'd confided once, during a long march, that sometimes he felt as if a jotunn had struck him in the head with Mjölnir.

Lacking drink or fighting to distract from his pain, perhaps his mind wandered to other entertainments. Loki appeared already asleep, bundled in his furs beside the fire.

Sif leaned in close to Thor. She sympathized, truly, but some things were not to be borne. "No one touches your cock but me. Don't forget it."

Thor flashed her a grin that seemed more than a little forced. "All right. Might make pissing an adventure. Best you stand well away when it comes time for it."

Sif groaned and rolled her eyes. "Obviously you can touch your own—"

"Glad to hear it." At once, he rose and wandered off into the mist, as if talk of relieving himself had brought it on.

He'd wanted it, when he came back to their tent that night. Rougher, and more desperate than had been his wont in times past. Sif didn't mind overmuch.

AFTER SO LONG IN the mountains and then the hill lands, past a frozen river, they came to great snow-covered expanses, wastelands that stretched into infinity. They passed a herd of fur-covered mammoths, several score of them, trudging through the plains in search of feed. What they ate in this harsh land, Sif could not guess.

She lost track of the days.

Another fortnight, perhaps. They passed into a forest, this one larger than those on the other side of the wall. Trees stretched up, punching above the mist line, seeming the size of small mountains themselves. As if even the trees grew larger in Utgard. Many so large she and Thor could not have wrapped their combined arms around the trunks.

The feeling of having entered another world became so strong here she found herself looking every which way for vaettir, as if she could actually see them walking here. Strange lands, filled with alien beings, not like to be keen on the trespasses of man.

"Our food runs low," Thjalfi said. The young man carried nigh all their rations, never complaining, and oft rushing ahead to scout the way. He was quick on his feet, Sif had to give him that. And maybe a bit too fearless, too eager to impress his new master. "We should hunt here."

Loki nodded slowly, seeming—as he so oft did—lost in thoughts Sif suspected she couldn't have understood had he bothered to share them. And he never did.

They passed deeper into the forest. By dark, they came to a slight clearing, one in which a large hall sat.

Loki frowned at it, then shook his head. "I'll go set some snares."

Thor shrugged and went to pound on the door. Only, the door swung in at his blow, unsealed. The prince glanced back at Sif. And what was she to say? Any chance to sleep under a roof was welcome. If they'd somehow found an abandoned jotunn hall, she wouldn't turn away unless Hel herself dwelt inside.

Inside, they found the place undecorated and unfurnished. Naught but the walls and several long hallways that seemed to go nowhere. Odder still, the hall had no fire pit. Did frost jotunnar not need it to cook? To see?

"Rest there," Thor ordered his new slaves.

Sif slumped down against the wall. Clearly they'd find

no food here, but at least it got them out of the winds. Those seemed to grow bitterer with each passing day. Was summer truly already waning?

She settled down to sleep and Thor came to lie beside her, plopping on the floor with a great huff.

He grunted. "I ugh ... I know I've been difficult of late. It's these pains in my head. They rob my thoughts and befoul my dreams with twisted bitterness."

Sif looked at the prince a moment. Her husband. Beautiful. Strong. Fearless. And now being destroyed, betrayed by his own mind. Wordlessly, she pulled his head down into her lap, then stroked his long red hair. She massaged his brows, careful not to draw too nigh the still swollen red lump on his forehead.

"Is this who I am now?" he asked.

"It's not your fault."

"I do not think that overmuch comfort, as my memories fade and my mind falters."

A strange thought struck her then. Odin, Thor's father, should have been around the same age as Sif's father. But somehow—and she'd never gotten a clear story from anyone—some experience Odin had had with sorcerers had aged him. It had changed him beyond all repair.

Yet Frigg stayed with him, by his side, the loyal wife.

Sif would do the same.

She continued massaging his head, even when his breathing shifted in the rhythms of sleep. It didn't matter that he'd changed. If this was who Thor was now, still she'd stay by his side.

If she couldn't do that, it had never really been love.

A TREMBLE SHOT through the ground, sending the walls rumbling and jolting Sif awake.

Thor was on his feet first, hammer in hand, slowly spinning about as if an earthquake gave him a foe to slay.

"Over here," Thjalfi called. "There's a window."

Sif ran to where the boy and girl stood, down one of the side halls. The window he spoke of was clouded over, frosted perhaps, and she could make out naught save the drifting of mist. Either way, the quake seemed to have stopped.

Thor strode in after them, then took up position at the entrance, clearly intending to guard them with his hammer. But when naught else happened, everyone sat back down to rest.

Sif had no words for how much she misliked Jotunheim.

Giant wolves and earthquakes. And jotunnar.

IN THE MORN, they returned outside. Amid the trees, a jotunn many times the height of a man slept. The beast must have stood forty feet tall or more. Never had she seen or heard of a jotunn growing so large.

Despite the size, he lacked much in the way of the deformities oft found in the man-eating jotunnar. Just some small horns growing from his forehead.

The immensity of the creature created a kind of vertigo in her, making it hard to walk for even imagining it standing upright. Some profound wrongness with this jotunn left her wanting to run for Midgard and never look back.

The trees themselves thundered with the sound of his snores.

Roskva clutched Sif's arm with one hand, using the other to cover her sobs. As Sif looked to the girl, she caught sight of Thjalfi, also holding tight his sister's shoulder.

Without a word, Thor crept over to the sleeping jotunn, hammer raised. Oh, Hel. Thor was going wake the fucking monster.

Thor reared back the hammer and let fly.

The blow resounded as if a thunderbolt had crashed down, echoing through the wood while sparks of lightning jumped from the hammer's blow. What the fuck? Since when did Mjölnir—

The jotunn groaned and slapped a hand against its forehead where Thor had hit it. The prince barely evaded being squashed, and only by flinging himself prone. Rubbing his head, the jotunn rolled over, sat up, and blinked.

Sif pulled free of the brother and sister and snatched up her spear. Fuck. They were all dead.

"Something stung me," the jotunn rumbled. His voice sent the trees shaking, the very ground trembling.

Thor pulled himself up and hid his hammer behind his back.

Sif would have laughed. If she wasn't about to piss her trousers. Jotunnar did not get this big. They sure as the gates of Hel didn't shrug off blows from Mjölnir. Reality, however, seemed to disagree with her assessment.

"Greetings, jotunn," Thor said. "We are travelers from Midgard. May I ask your name?"

The jotunn ceased rubbing his head and peered down at Thor, squinting. "Skrymir. You've come a long way from Asgard, little prince."

Sif gaped. The jotunn knew who Thor was. He *knew*. How could anyone here know that?

"Ugh ..." Thor glanced back at Sif. "Yes."

"Well ..." The jotunn leaned his face closer to Thor's. With his hand removed, Sif could see a welt rising where Thor had struck, much as if an oversized ant had bitten him. "I might suggest you head back toward Midgard, little man. You see, the way you head leads you on toward my stronghold. You may think me large, but there you'll find jotunnar larger still. You might feel *uncomfortable*."

Thor snorted. "Is that a challenge?"

Oh, Hel. "Giant rocky cock of a troll," Sif mumbled.

"A challenge? Would you like to challenge yourself? Then come to my hall, tiny man. Come and watch the greatest of Asgard's sons be humbled before the might of the jotunnar. You might then think twice before you so blithely antagonize the brood of Aurgelmir."

Skrymir rose, sending fresh trembles through the ground. Standing, his face was so far above the mist Sif could scarce make it out. He pointed away, to the east where, Sif had to assume, his stronghold lay.

Then he went tromping off in the same direction. Every footfall was a small quake, one that threatened to send Sif and the others spilling down to the ground.

Slowly, the jotunn vanished into the mists amid the trees.

When the last shocks had passed, Thor set to packing up the camp, ordering his slaves to assist.

"We'll reach his Utgard stronghold," Thor said. "We'll see who gets humbled."

Though she opened her mouth, Sif could scarce form words at this. "A-are you ... Have you ... lost your fucking mind? Mjölnir itself barely harmed that creature."

Thor growled at her, forcing Sif to fall back a step. "I'll

not have anyone disparage the power of Asgard! Honor demands we overcome this challenge!"

Not even waiting for an answer, Thor stormed off after Skrymir.

And Sif could not wake from her nightmare.

❧

THEY MET up with Loki along the way, who, this time, had caught and cooked a reindeer. Thor refused to stop for the day meal, so they ate while walking, even as Sif explained to Loki the madness of Thor's attempt to challenge Skrymir.

Loki offered no answer, but his eyes shone with ire that did not quite reach his face. "We have no time for this."

Sif couldn't have agreed more.

And yet they pressed on, leaving the forest and coming into another great plain.

This they followed most of the day, until a mountain came into view.

At least, through the mist, Sif had first thought it a mountain. As they drew nigh, though, the truth hit her. It was a fortress the size of a mountain, stretching so high she could not make out its tip above the mists, despite it resting on level ground.

The great gates reached up higher than the peak of a king's hall and stood open, allowing a constant—if light—stream of snowfall to pile up inside the gatehouse.

Roskva's breaths became heavy gasps, panicking. From the corner of her eye, Sif saw the girl's brother comforting her. If he was no fool, he was no doubt terrified himself. So hard Sif had fought to gain an apple of Yggdrasil. But even immortality could be snatched away by such foes as could have built this place.

Thor paused in front of the gatehouse, craning his neck up in a no doubt vain attempt to take in the breadth of the fortress. No such place could have existed. Certainly it ought not to have existed. And yet here they stood.

Thor strode inside.

At the far side of the gatehouse, a portcullis barred their passage. Thor grabbed it with both hands and heaved, clearly straining. The iron creaked and bent, but the gate refused to rise.

Madness.

But he'd never be dissuaded.

Sif drew up beside him, then pulled upon the apple's strength. With a nod, they heaved together. The iron groaned, warping beneath her fingers. But still it did not lift more than a hairsbreadth. As if they tried to pick up a house.

Gasping, Sif gave it over and collapsed against the portcullis.

"The bars are wide enough we can squeeze through the grate," Thjalfi said.

Sif looked to Thor, who snorted, shook his head, then did so.

No choice now, really. In it was.

BEYOND THEY GATEHOUSE they passed into a massive courtyard, one so wide that, with the mist inside, Sif could not make out the far side ahead. They trudged across snow-dusted ground for a time. Almost long enough she could forget they were inside a compound.

Finally, they came to another hall, this one with great iron-banded doors, one of which stood slightly ajar. Thor slipped inside, and Sif followed, coming into a hall supported by columns the size of rooms. The ceiling disappeared so far into the darkness above Sif could scarce make it out given the paltry light from a handful of braziers scattered around this place.

Long stone benches ran the length of the hall beyond the columns, and on these at least two dozen jotunnar sat. All were larger than Sif believed the race could get, some taller than even Skrymir had been.

And him, too, they saw, sitting at the head of one stone table, laughing among his own kind.

"I've come here to accept your challenge!" Thor spat at him. "I'll prove no jotunn is a match for a man of Asgard."

A few jotunnar laughed at the prince's boast.

They hadn't gotten to that size without eating men. A lot of men, probably over the course of centuries. Millenia, maybe, perhaps even since the coming of the mists. What stopped them from making a meal of her and Thor and the others? Traditions of hospitality that jotunnar might not even share?

Skrymir rubbed the welt on his forehead, grinning too wide and revealing slightly pointed teeth. Indeed, through the blue tint in his flesh, she noticed he did seem more animalistic than she'd first thought. As though a bear tried to burst through from beneath his skin, like a berserk. A berserk jotunn. Among the most horrifying things she could imagine. "Very well, Thor Odinson. Since you come in times of a feast, perhaps you'd join us in an eating contest? Or your companions, even? You?" He leaned in, looking at Loki. "How fast can you devour a feast of mammoth flesh?"

"I'm not interested," Loki said.

"I'll do it!" Thor blurted.

Sif rolled her eyes. Thor thought he was going to out-eat

a jotunn? One the size of a mammoth, who'd obviously eaten *men* the size of Thor. That whetstone was obliterating whatever sense of restraint Thor had ever possessed. She opened her mouth to talk him down, but he was already striding across the floor.

The lip of the bench towered over him, but he leapt up, caught the side, and pulled himself onto it. From there, he jumped up to the table amidst the chuckles of his jotunn audience.

Opposite Thor, a jotunn sat. Two great steaming plates of mammoth meat were laid out before the contestants.

From her vantage on the floor, Sif couldn't catch a good look at them. But then, she didn't need to. Little could go on up there she truly wished to see.

"Now eat," Skrymir commanded.

A thick, squelching sound immediately ensued, followed an instant later by bones crunching and snapping. A spray of blood and bits of gristle flew off the table as the contestants gorged themselves on their feast.

Roskva flinched and turned away, hiding her face against her brother's chest. Sif was tempted to do the same.

A tremendous belch then rang out, echoing off the walls and seeming to reverberate off every column.

"Hmm," Skrymir said, peering down at Thor. "Not up to that, are you?" The jotunn shrugged as if it was no matter.

Though she couldn't actually see Thor, Sif could all but feel him fuming up there, probably shooting glares at his opponent and Skrymir both.

Grumbling, Thor leapt down to the bench, coated in juices and bits of fleshy leavings that left Sif gagging to see them. He hopped down again. "Can't expect a man to eat a plate bigger than he is. Bastards."

Skrymir chuckled patronizingly, causing Thor to cringe

with such fury Sif tightened her grip on the spear. The prince was going to attack the jotunn king. And they'd all get squashed underfoot in the process.

But the jotunn just smiled. "A race, maybe?"

Thor scoffed. "First a feast, then a race? You expect me to run after *that*?"

"I'll run," Thjalfi said. "I'm fast."

Sif spun on the farmer's son, half inclined to slap him. "His legs are little longer than yours." Imbecile.

"Yes!" Thor roared. "Yes, my slave shall race you."

"Me?" Skrymir chuckled. "No, the boy shall race Hugi. More his size."

Indeed, the jotunn who strode forth stood only a few feet taller than Thjalfi. He didn't speak, and Sif hadn't even noticed him among his larger brethren. In greeting, he offered but a bob of his head.

"Come," Skrymir said. "Let's see them race around the fortress."

Thjalfi paled. "That's a long course ..."

"Oh, hardly," Skrymir said. "Do not be modest, boy. Why, the Ás prince vouches for you."

Since no one was listening to her objections anyway, Sif followed them all outside the fortress.

Skrymir beckoned them run. Thjalfi took off like a wolf, covering ground almost as fast as some who'd tasted the fruit of Yggdrasil. Sif had to hand it to him—he did have speed on his side. Hugi glanced at Skrymir, nodded, and then raced after Thjalfi. A gust of wind caught Sif in his passing, sending her stumbling into Thor.

In great leaping bounds Hugi dashed forward, swift as she'd seen Sleipnir run. In the space of a few heartbeats he'd passed Thjalfi and raced around the fortress's edge.

Even the mist seemed to part around him, trailing in his wake.

Mere moments later, he came back around the far side, coming to rest beside Skrymir. Though his chest rose and fell with great breaths, no sweat covered him.

Thjalfi, though, took long, nigh to a quarter hour to come back. The boy reached them, teetering on his feet, and collapsed before his sister, staring up at Thor. He gasped, trying to mouth something but clearly had not the breath left. An apology perhaps.

"Can we dispense with these inane contests now?" Loki asked.

Skrymir laughed again, the sound bringing to mind an avalanche. "At least one more, yes?"

"Name it," snapped Thor.

If this jotunn didn't kill the man, Sif would.

"Perhaps you'd consent to a wrestling match, yes?"

Thor groaned. "I cannot get leverage against someone of such size." Even admitting that seemed to gall the prince, as though he'd tried to swallow a live eel.

"Hugi's grandmother, then? She's small, but she's been known to bring down great men before."

No. Sif shook her head. "There's no honor in fighting a—"

"I'll try not to hurt her," Thor said.

Skrymir grinned, exposing those bear-like fangs.

As if she'd been waiting all this time, a woman came strolling out of the fortress, leaning on a walking stick. Standing upright, she might have stood a head taller than Thor, but she stooped over, crooked, hanging her white-haired head such that Sif couldn't see her eyes.

Sif glanced at the others. This couldn't be happening. Indeed, Loki's eyes had narrowed and he seemed to be looking around as if confused. Thjalfi and Roskva, though, were snickering.

The crone tossed away her stick and held her hands wide, inviting Thor into her arms. Roaring, the prince charged into her abdomen like he was tackling a bear. She didn't topple though. Rather, Thor wrapped his arms around her, planted his feet, and heaved as if he intended to fling her over his head.

The woman hardly budged. Grunting, Thor twisted, pivoted, and shoved her toward the ground. And still she did not give way beneath him.

Skrymir's chuckles grated on Sif's nerves until even she wanted to see Thor thrash the old woman. Some trickery was at play here.

The crone planted a hand upon Thor's head, fingers spread wide, and strained, pushing him down. Slowly, a hair at a time, he edged toward the mud. Thor thrashed, but seemed unable to break her grip. Until she was actually holding his face in the muck. His bucking became wild. Suffocating.

"Enough!" Sif screamed. "Release him!"

"Oh, there's only one final release from her grasp, little Ás. She who saps the bodies and will of all who live, she devours cities and civilizations. She swallows the world, bit by merciless bit."

"No!" Sif whipped her spear up and lunged at the old woman.

At once, the figure vanished. As did Hugi. And the entire fucking fortress, turned to mist.

Skrymir chuckled again, even as Sif yanked Thor up. The prince gasped, sucking down air, panting. Wild-eyed. Drenched in dripping mud.

"You think yourselves mighty, humans," Skrymir said.

"You think you can master the world, but you do not understand how petty, how insignificant you are in the greater scheme. The wheel turns and crushes you over and over, and you are too caught up in your worthless self-aggrandizements to even notice. Master the world? You cannot master your senses."

Thor growled, lunged for Skrymir, but the jotunn stepped back.

Thjalfi raced over, bearing Mjölnir, handing it to his master.

Skrymir sneered. "A prince who thought to eat faster than flame itself? A boy who would race the wind? And then, as if it were not enough, you, little Thor, would try to pin down time itself. Befuddled by the simplest of illusions you become useless. Weaker and more helpless than even your father, flailing in the dark for answers to questions he dares not ask."

"Who are you?" Loki asked.

Thor lunged, swinging Mjölnir. "Dead! He's fucking dead!"

But the giant jotunn vanished into mist himself. And Thor just kept swinging, round and round. Hitting naught but air. He turned on rocks where the fort had stood and began to pound them into dust. He smashed trees, heedless of Sif's pleas or Roskva's screams.

On and on the prince vented his rage at faint whispers out in the mist.

Helpless, Sif glanced at Loki. A grimace had settled upon his normally impassive face.

Odin's blood brother could see Sif's husband losing his mind to the stone in his brain. She knew he could see it. Could see that something—perhaps a vaettir or perhaps an actual jotunn—had bewitched them all.

In the end though, all Loki did was start walking once more, in the direction he'd claimed Odin had traveled.

Leaving Sif to wait as Thor burned off his violent rage, cringing at each fall of the hammer. A long, gut-clenching, heartbreaking wait.

37

The Vall Empire had once established numerous outposts along the southern shores of Andalus, along the rivers, and atop hills, all trying to forestall invasion from the Serkland Caliphate. They had failed. Those outposts had long since fallen, forcing the Valls back into their own kingdom.

Now it too lay besieged out of Andalus.

Some years back, Loki had told Sigyn that the war between Serkland and Miklagard had flared up. That conflict—in which she couldn't help but see Odin's hand—had spared the Valls conquest for the moment. But they'd lost their great emperor and his champions.

His son Hlodwig lacked his father's cunning or presence and thus had barely held back the tide of Serklanders. Meanwhile, by all accounts he'd disowned one of his sons who had defected to Hunaland, while the other lost battle after battle against the raids out of Andalus.

If not for the intervention of the Aesir, the Utgard men would no doubt have taken this land already, and through it, threatened Hunaland. Sigyn could not say whether Odin truly cared aught for the Vall plight, but the king had ordered the Aesir to honor the oath Tyr had made to Karolus, even long after the man's death. Since then, she doubted Odin had taken much notice of the war that had raged nigh every summer for decades. Lands were claimed and lost, forts razed, and the dead grew more numerous as the living dwindled.

She and Mundilfari rode between two hills, heading toward Peregot at the fastest trot she could drive the horse to without killing it. The Vanr sat behind her, arms around her waist tighter than necessary, she thought.

Sigyn did not like coming here. The very air felt thick with ghosts, saturated with their anguish and rage. Even the places where one did not see the hills painted in blood, the scent of it had soaked into the ground. The final battle for Midgard would be called Ragnarok. Seeing the south of Valland, Sigyn could not help but wonder if the Andalus Marches represented the dawn of that conflict.

"The Art ..." Mundilfari said. "Oh, we thought ourselves gods ... So very wise ... So fortunate to tap power from beyond the Veil."

"You learned the Art from Svarthofda," she said.

"Oh. Oh, yes." He giggled. "Plowed her night and day ... and more nights ... Hard. She liked it that way—"

Sigyn grimaced as the sorcerer's erection pressed against her tailbone. "I don't need to know that." He wasn't in control of himself. He was *not* in control. She had to remind herself of that, otherwise she might have slammed her elbow into his face. Though, a sorcerer not in control of himself might even be worse than one who was.

"That's the cycle of it, you know. Oh, yes. The apprentices, they fought over who would share my bed each night.

On occasion, I allowed more than one and we all ... ah, mmmm. Oh, and Freyja ... By the Tree!"

Sigyn clenched her jaw and tried to edge away from his body. Failing that, she dismounted, her movement so sudden the sorcerer pitched off the horse sideways and crashed into the ground. She could not quite manage an apology.

Hands on her hips, she waited for him to stand and brush himself off. "I don't care about your sexual conquests."

"Oh. Oh, yes, I see. Mmmm. You are a virgin, I suppose? Delicate sensibilities offended? No, I think not." He chuckled and started down the path again. "You, clever girl, you know how to get answers through your trench."

"You are a vulgar man, and under other circumstances I would leave you here."

"Oh. Yes, hmmm. Very good." He held up a finger and spun around to look at her. "But ... but ... are you certain threatening to leave a hermit alone ... is an effective threat? I ... I spent *many* years wandering the world alone. Left with ... fading memories. The highlights, the good times ... over-shadowed by the ..." He shook his head and turned away, stumbling for a moment. "So many errors ..."

Sigyn frowned and led the horse by his reins.

"It was a question, you know," he said without looking at her. "The order of it, I mean. Were the more sexually vora-cious more adept at the Art because of their appetite, or did their aptitude itself engender their bodily appetite as a side effect? Or, perhaps, were the two mutually entwined—an ouroboros without beginning or end."

She groaned. "I don't fucking care."

"Oh. Oh, but you should. You who wanted to under-stand, who had the audacity to touch something from beyond the Veil. To bargain with powers ancient beyond your imaging ... and think you might come out ahead. Had you but spread your legs for the right man first, you might have saved all the worlds the heartache you have now engendered."

She flinched. "If I did, it sure as fuck would not have been you."

"Oh." The smugness he infused that one word with made her want to kick him in the stones.

His erratic behavior and obnoxious words she might blame on his befuddled mind. Telling herself this, however, did not wholly expunge the niggling fear that, behind the vulgarity, might have lurked a grain of truth. He said the Vanir's greatest failing was in thinking themselves wise, and, Sigyn, in her own arrogance, had thought herself smart enough to attempt something the Vanir might have spent centuries understanding.

She was, of course, unwilling to ever betray Loki. But still, she thought to defy the traditions of teacher to student she had known existed. Maybe that made her as guilty as Mundilfari himself.

PEREGOT FORT WAS NOT ESPECIALLY large, but it was well provisioned and guarded by dozens of men, including Tyr. The Vall knight commander had lent them his study—if a small room stocked with naught but a few maps and a foot-locker could be called thus—and sent Tyr to meet them.

Sigyn had not seen the man in years, but he was far from verbose and she had little time, so after brief pleasantries, she cut to the issue as Tyr settled in front of the knight's desk.

"Where is my son Hödr?"

Tyr shook his head, look grim, even for Tyr. "Dead, if I catch him. Worse if Thor or Sif do."

"What?" Sigyn had a hard time making sense of his words.

Mundilfari pulled on the footlocker, and, apparently frustrated with the lock, kicked it.

Tyr scowled at him. Sigyn knew the feeling. "He mist-mad?" the warrior asked.

"No." No, he was a whole other kind of mad. "He's with me." For now. "What happened with Hödr?"

"Got information out of a girl. Raped her. Burnt her alive. Left her for dead."

No. No, that was … no. She knew she was shaking her head, trying to form words. This was her fault. How was she to admit what she had done, or to speak her fear aloud to anyone, let alone to Tyr? He was brave to a fault, a trait that had cost him his good hand, but he was never known for his understanding. Still, after what he had suffered under Gramr's thrall, maybe he would sympathize.

And she needed an ally besides the Mad Vanr.

"My son is … like as not affected by the same sort of Fire vaettr that the Serkland sorcerers use."

Tyr growled and slapped his palm against the desk. "Naught good ever came from the Otherworlds. It's all touched by Hel, Sigyn. Vileness men ought to leave alone."

Mundilfari chuckled. "Oh. Oh, you have *no* idea, warrior. Hel, is vile, yes, but there are yet other dangers beyond the Veil. As bad … worse, perhaps …"

"Worse than Hel?" Tyr glowered, as if unwilling to accept aught could ever be worse than the Queen of Niflheim.

The thought of it made Sigyn shiver, but they could not

afford to become drawn into such a debate. "Supposing he is possessed by a Fire vaettr. What might we expect?"

"Don't know for certain. Serkland caliphs don't get directly involved. Not much. When they do, men die. A lot of men, on both sides. Ashes, flames. Smoldering flesh. Them, and we've seen these Sons of Muspel. Could be either, I suppose. Explains the burns."

"Sons of Muspel?"

"Serklander elite warriors. Somewhat akin to berserkir, I think. Leastwise they've got something fell inside them. Strong and fast as a man who's had an apple. They tear through our ranks when we see them. Damn nigh killed us all a few moons back. Lost a lot of men. Real commander here among them."

Sigyn groaned. "What if Hödr went to meet them?"

Now Tyr grunted, staring at the wall.

"What is it?" she asked.

"Girl he raped? You didn't ask about her?"

Sigyn flinched. So obsessed with her son she couldn't worry over another woman's plight? Especially one so horrible. "I ... how is she?"

"Probably still like to die. She's Thor's daughter, in case you care."

Sigyn's knees gave out all at once. They just turned to water and she was on the ground. Sputtering. Stammering nonsense.

Tyr rose and knelt beside her. "Hermod went off tracking the boy. Thought Hödr was already heading for Andalus. I guess now we know why. Still, wouldn't want to be Hödr if Hermod finds him. His granddaughter." Tyr grimaced, shaking his head.

"They will take him if they can," Mundilfari said. "Oh, yes. The Caliphate are oh so eager for more jinn, and to find one, already here, on this side of the Veil ... hmmm ... Yes, I think so."

Sigyn's mouth had gone dry. "Take him for what?"

Mundilfari shrugged. "They don't need the host, I would assume. They probably have apprentices lined up six deep ... all waiting for their chance to bond a jinn. Hmm. Oh, yes, I think so. What use is a fully possessed foreigner to them? None, I would think ... so ... expendable? Probably."

Sigyn's mouth hung agape as she turned from the sorcerer back to Tyr. Was he right? Would they murder her son simply because he was of no use to them? Why not? These Utgarders might be capable of aught at all. And she would not allow it. Would never fucking allow it.

"I need to cross behind their lines ..."

He shook his head. "Suicide. Hermod, others tried it a few summers back. Took one of the old forts there and held it for half a moon before they were forced back. Lost forty men. Out of fifty. Hel, I went myself not long back. Sons of Muspel nigh wiped us out."

Trying to keep her voice from breaking, she reached out and grasped Tyr's single hand. "I am not going there to conquer and hold ground. Mundilfari and I will sneak past their lines and find my son, and we'll exorcise the jinn before aught else befalls him. Please. Help me get past their troops. What would you do for *your* son?"

Starkad's falling out with Tyr had become legend, but then, Sigyn knew well enough that Tyr would still take any risk to aid his son, whether the man wanted his help or not.

"He's here, actually."

"Starkad Eightarms?"

"Came to fight, said he likes lost causes. But he's here now. If anyone could get you through, it'd be him. I can ask."

Then he shook his head. "Down there? Behind the lines? You're beyond all help there, girl."

"I am *going* to get my son back."

Tyr looked like he might spit. "Vaettr or no, I can't say Hödr deserves anyone's help."

"It's not *him*."

"See if Thor sees it that way."

His words left her chilled.

38

Two Years Ago

Sigyn pushed aside another manuscript and pressed her palms against her eyes. No answers seemed forthcoming, though the terrible suspicion remained, and, of course, she found herself given to doubt nigh to everything these days. She had, in effect, become the new keeper of Sessrumnir, meaning she alone was forced to decide what forgotten wisdom to dole out and what was best left undisturbed. As, it turned out, so many of the Vanr secrets probably should have been.

The outer door rumbled as it slid into the floor, announcing a new visitor. With a sigh, Sigyn rose and wandered over to the stairs. From atop them she spied her newest guest.

Syn, Hermod's wife, trod in, hand on Hödr's shoulder as if guiding a wolfhound.

Sigyn frowned, making her way down the stairs. "What are you doing here?"

"Sister," Syn said. A perfunctory greeting, in truth.

Having married Sigyn's foster brother, Syn was sister in name to Sigyn, though the woman had always remained aloof, a situation that little bothered Sigyn. "I found your son poking around the tree."

The World Tree? Sigyn's frown deepened as she took in Hödr, the boy not seeming abashed in the least. "What have you to say for yourself?"

Hödr shrugged, not bothering to conceal the defiance in his eyes. "Curiosity is a strong motivator."

Sigyn moved to stand beside Syn, struggling to keep her own gaze as stern as possible. Was that all Hödr's behavior indicated? Mere curiosity? If so, Sigyn of all people could hardly fault him for it. She'd faced her share of recriminations from her own family for delving into subjects and areas that rules or propriety claimed lay outside her boundaries. Even grown, she'd defied the king's orders in studying the Art here, though she suspected Odin had some inkling of her transgression.

She tapped a finger against her lip, then nodded at Syn. "Don't fret. I'll deal with him myself."

WHILE SIGYN DARED to hope Hödr's explorations mere youthful exuberance, the fact remained that Odin had dealt in no uncertain terms with Sjöfn for breaching the sanctity of Yggdrasil. Women spoke of the girl's fate in hushed whispers leaving the only thing certain that Odin had thought up some fate worse than death for her.

On questioning Hödr though, Sigyn's son had remained taciturn at best, when he wasn't outright dismissive of Sigyn's inquiries.

Which meant she had to find something else with which

to occupy the boy's time. With her son in tow, she climbed the slopes up to Gladsheimr. Odin had remained cryptic as to what he did up here and even Sigyn had not been able to uncover the truth of his activities. Either way, though, the king remained off away from Asgard, with Hermod visiting this place far more frequently.

Sigyn found her foster brother exiting the ruins of the old Vanr hall. He cocked his head in obvious surprise at her presence, though his expression quickly turned warm. Odin had not forbidden anyone to come up here—all that remained was the foundations of an old building, after all—but still Sigyn had never seen anyone but the king or Hermod venture here.

"Sister," Hermod said, with far more warmth and sincerity than his wife had managed.

They had both taken the loss of Agilaz and Olrun hard, but Hermod had taken it harder, becoming more like his father than ever before. Having now had an apple, her foster brother seemed to have begun honing his senses much as Sigyn had, becoming a woodsman to rival or even surpass his legendary father in everyone's eyes save his own.

Sigyn embraced him, trying to ignore the trepidation that sent her gut twisting on itself.

He looked next to her son and nodded his head. "Hödr."

"Uncle Hermod." How did the boy manage to imbue a name with such arrogance without actually quite treading over the line of giving offense?

While Hermod's expression darkened ever so slightly, he let it pass, turning instead back to Sigyn. "What brings you up here?"

What brought *him* up here was the question Sigyn longed to ask. Unfortunately, the current situation left her with more pressing difficulties. "My son has nigh to sixteen winters behind him now. It seems past time he find a purpose for his time." She could almost feel the boy's eyes, burning into the back of her skull. It filled her with a rush of heat, left her more on edge than she'd have liked to admit. "He's had basic instruction in arms, of course, but he could use a master to teach him woodcraft and the finer points of combat."

Hermod glanced back at the ruins as if he expected something waited for him there. Since when did he much care over ancient history or architecture? Finally, he folded his arms, squirming ever so slightly. "I'd be ... honored. But surely you could have taught him woodcraft yourself."

Sigyn allowed herself a slight smile. "Maybe. But I'm not a warrior, and I must remain at Sessrumnir, while you oft trek out into Midgard on whatever task takes your fancy."

Her brother snorted. "Takes my fancy? No, I serve the king in most endeavors, oft ferrying messages to the fronts of the wars in Valland or Bjarmaland. Hardly a place for a boy."

"He's a man by law."

Hermod nodded. "So he is. Very well, if that's your wish. We may sometimes be gone for moons at a time though."

Oh, she knew. The thought of not seeing Hödr for any length of time was like a weight upon her chest, but what was she to do?

The only thing which she could do. She turned, embraced her son and kissed him on the forehead. He returned her embrace, a little too hard, his body flush with heat, hand drifting dangerously close to her arse as it slid down her back. Sigyn broke away and looked him hard in the eye. "Mind your uncle in all things."

"Yes, Mother." Again that arrogant tone and arrogant gaze.

Try as hard as she might, Sigyn could not help but fear something was amiss with her son.

39

*T*he boy king, Agnar, sat upon his father's throne, looking smaller than he truly was in the mighty chair. This boy had barely tasted the flesh of man and thus had not hardly reached his potential. Skadi watched him from across the throne room, along with his mother.

Agnar addressed his people, expounding on the vileness of devouring man flesh. Naïve and weak, his reign was like to be short. In Jotunheim, strength mattered most.

His mother was shaking her head in obvious disagreement, though she didn't interrupt her son. "It was as you foretold," Angrboda said to Skadi, not taking her eyes from the new king. "The wizard came. He bespelled my son somehow and used him to escape. Killed my husband in the process."

"You grieve his loss?" Skadi asked.

Angrboda grimaced, the only answer she offered.

Skadi nodded slowly. She had known Odin would escape, had seen as much in Vafthrudnir's quicksilver mirrors. He escaped but more importantly, the fire-priest would soon follow. Skadi hadn't known for certain that Odin would kill Geirrod, but it also surprised her little. "Have your husband's body brought down into the tunnels beneath the fortress."

Angrboda gaped, working her mouth as if debating whether to ask how Skadi knew of those secret tunnels. The queen eventually seemed to think better of it, though, for she nodded, and set about her way.

§.

DEAD GEIRROD LAY STIFF, hands folded over his chest. His corpse still reeked of rot and the filth Odin had spilled ramming a sword through his gut. The body lay upon the floor in tunnels dug far beneath the fortress. While Skadi would have preferred a slab, none was available.

The work here was crude—though it had no doubt taken centuries—but it provided a secret means in and out of the castle for the lords of Vimurland. One Skadi had used to gain ingress, in fact. Torch sconces lined the walls, testament to the lack of any worthy sorcerers here to infuse light into ice.

The flames didn't interfere with Skadi's Art, of course, but she'd snuffed those immediately around her, preferring dense shadows to having to work around an open flame.

Angrboda stood beside her, fidgeting. "You can restore him to life?"

Skadi barely suppressed her sneer. Fool woman. "After a fashion. Hel's gifts do not work quite that way."

A human slave wriggled around on the floor, bound and gagged, and stripped naked. The latter was hardly necessary either, but Skadi found being naked tended to make humans feel more vulnerable. The fear attracted vaettir on the far side of the Veil, making this easier.

Besides, it made him easier to cut—he bore a dozen marks over his flesh.

After kneeling beside the man, Skadi manifested a blade of ice in her hand. She shoved the slave over onto his back, then drew a quick line with her blade along the top of his groin, just above the mess of hair. More fear, and flailing, thrashing in pain, horror. Dismissing the blade, Skadi traced her fingers along the wound, then rose.

In blood she traced another glyph on the floor. With this done, she stepped back to make certain she hadn't missed any. Invoking other vaettir was not without risk, even to a snow maiden. In fact, using sorcery on this side of the Veil always seemed fair strange to her. Nevertheless, she needed Geirrod and Angrboda both.

The two of them would serve as her hold over Vimurland.

Nodding in satisfaction, she waved Angrboda to the side and began to chant. The guttural syllables of Supernal bombarded the inside of her head with such force she found it a wonder the queen wasn't screaming. She'd feel it, of course, an unease, a sense of something not of her world drawing nigh. The Veil weakening ...

A twitch in one of Geirrod's fingers, barely noticeable.

Skadi remanifested the ice blade and slit the slave's throat. Blood bubbled up from the wound, spreading quickly over the floor. Skadi tossed his body aside just to ensure none of it overflowed onto her glyphs. More than one careless sorceress had met an ill end like that.

Geirrod's eyes opened. Empty. Lifeless, yet not quite still.

Close. He was so close.

Angrboda raced to her husband's side and fell to her knees beside him. "I can't believe it."

There he was, staring up at her. Motionless, but seeing.

In those black orbs would lurk darkness, complete and empty.

All at once, the queen rose, backing away. "What have you done to him? He's not—"

Skadi caught the jotunn woman and rammed the ice blade through her back, straight into her heart. "One more sacrifice."

Blue blood rushed out over Skadi's fingers. Angrboda collapsed, hands fumbling with the blade sticking from her chest, gurgling.

A red gleam appeared in Geirrod's eyes. And then the wail erupted from him. Pain. Agony, without measure, without end. The horror of the damned who know beyond any doubt their suffering has become boundless. A cry echoing off the tunnel walls. A sound already familiar to Skadi.

Even as Angrboda's soul fed the ritual. Slipping from her body.

And the harder part. Skadi released Gudrun. She felt herself falling, pitching forward into an abyss. Tumbling back through the Veil as if being pushed bodily through a sheet. Reality bent and warped around her.

Colors bled out into the shadowy realm of the Penumbra.

Tidal forces of creation latched onto her essence and tugged at her, trying to hurtle her back through the gulf, into the Roil. Back to Niflheim.

Instead, Skadi waded through those currents. Angrboda's hazy form was growing clearer by the instant, her soul almost gone. Body almost dead.

Skadi lunged, caught the dying host by the throat. Forced her own essence inside. Like stepping through a vat of tar, pushing her way into what lay beyond.

Her vision snapped back into focus in the Mortal Realm, now looking through Angrboda's eyes. Vertigo seized her and she tumbled over sideways, cracked her head on the floor. Her sight blurred. She blinked through it, focusing on a receding figure in the distance.

Gudrun stumbled away, trying to run down the tunnels, clearly seeking any escape.

Skadi pushed herself up. Groaned. She'd almost lost hold of this one. Few vaettr had the strength to swap hosts at will and doing so always came with risks.

Her former host wobbled in her run, becoming a shadow in the torchlight.

Skadi turned to Geirrod. The draug jotunn now stood erect, fangs bared in rage and torment. "Well," Skadi said. "Go after her. Break her legs and bring her back."

It would take time to become used to such a height once more. Angrboda pushed nine feet tall, her legs much longer than any human's. The feel of such a body, of moving it, left Skadi more graceless in her steps than she'd have preferred. Graceless, perhaps, but that only meant she needed to settle for powerful.

She burst into Agnar's private chambers, Geirrod in tow, to find a naked human girl bent over his cock, mouthing it.

"Mother!" The boy leapt up, hastily jerking his discarded shirt to cover himself.

The girl whimpered, covering her head as if Skadi—or the queen, from the girl's perspective—intended to bludgeon her.

"Just get out," Skadi snapped at the girl. No doubt a slave doing only as Agnar had bid her, regardless. "I see being king agrees with you," she said once the girl had shut the door.

But Agnar's gaze was locked onto his father. Or more likely, upon the red gleam in the eyes of what used to be his father. "What have you done?"

Skadi lunged at him, grabbing a handful of his hair and yanking him up by it, to hang dangling. Shrieking and clawing at her hand, the boy dropped the shirt. Hmm. Skadi could get used to having this much physical strength again. "I am the Queen of Winter. And I give you two choices, boy. Swear fealty to me and live. Or die and serve me regardless, as does your father."

With that, she dropped the struggling jotunn boy. He landed on his knees. And he stayed there before slowly bowing his head. "M-my queen."

40

*O*cean spray crashed over Sigmund's longship as it cut through the mist toward Sviarland. Already, they sailed up the coast, past Ostergotland. Soon, they would reach Njarar and travel by land to its ancient keep in the mountains.

The wind had given out an hour ago, but Sigmund's men carried them forward with great heaves of the oars. He'd taken a turn himself, but only just now paused to check on Borghild, who stood at the bow, watching the mist.

The last thing either of them had expected was for Helgi to invite them to his marriage. As the new king of Njarar. The boy's successes were surpassed only by his hubris in pursuing these ends.

He'd killed Hothbrodd and Granmar, both, and proclaimed himself king of a whole new land. As if a section of his father's kingdom were not enough for him. Courage, Sigmund appreciated, as well as the desire to make one's own way. But Helgi seemed to lust after power with the same zeal he'd lusted after Sigrún.

"You should never have sent him raiding at his age,"

Borghild complained once more. A tired argument, and one he'd sure as the wrath of Hel not have in front of his men.

Sigmund grabbed the queen's wrist and squeezed just enough to draw a grunt of pain from her. To silence the squabbling. Some conversations belonged only behind closed doors, and even then, ought only to be had once. "We'll be there soon. We must congratulate our son on his victories in love and war, both."

"And when shall we see him again, if he remains in Njarar, in the heart of Sviarland?"

Sigmund could only pray the boy *did* remain in one place. At this rate, Helgi would probably think himself fit to conquer all of Miklagard.

"We'll be there soon," he repeated.

HELGI HOSTED them in grand fashion, despite the airy, cold halls of Njarar Castle. For the wedding feast, guests had come from across Sviarland, from Hunaland, even some from Reidgotaland. As if Sigmund's son wanted to impress them all with glory or with his bride.

Well and good, but Sigmund feared his son's tactics almost invited fresh enemies to come and challenge him.

Granmar's other son, Dag, had sworn fealty to Helgi, theoretically ensuring loyalty from the people of Njarar. But Njarar was hardly one of the strongest of Sviarland's petty kingdoms. It hadn't been since the days of Nidud long ago.

Sigmund walked out onto the balcony that jutted from the mountain. Legend claimed dvergar had carved this place and, indeed, it seemed one with the stones below. A mighty hall no other lord could have matched.

Fitela's scent came to him on the wind, as his elder son drew nigh. "I'm glad you're here," the boy said.

Sigmund nodded, not looking back. Up here, he was staring down at the mist. Some part of him wanted to believe he could see all of Helgi's enemies out there. The truth was, though, Sigmund would have to return to Hunaland, or risk losing all he'd just built. If Helgi intended to keep this place, he'd need to make his own allies.

Hrethel was a start. The man had once strived to control all of Sviarland. Even if those plans had fallen short, at least he remained a powerful force here. And he was kin to Helgi's new wife. That had to buy some familial loyalty.

"Where do your thoughts roam, Father?"

Sighing, now Sigmund did turn to Fitela. "I fear for what this portends."

"Helgi's rule here? He wouldn't be the first Volsung to live in Sviarland."

"We lived in *exile* while seeking vengeance. Hardly the same thing."

Fitela shrugged. "Either way, Hunaland stands united behind you now. You've accomplished your aim after so long."

Sigmund frowned. "I could not have accomplished it without you."

"Yes, but now you have no need of me."

Sigmund gaped. "What? Why would you speak such a thing? Have I given you reason to believe I don't—"

Fitela raised placating hands. "Peace, Father. I didn't mean it thus. Just, I grow restless. The raids with Helgi only served to remind me of it. I think ... I think my place is leading my own band. Roaming, claiming adventure. A life at a peaceful court doesn't suit me overmuch."

"You're not coming back." It hit Sigmund like a blow. Not

only would Fitela not stay here to keep his brother safe, he'd not return home with Sigmund either.

"I may travel with you to Hunaland, but no, I cannot remain there idle. I need to run and fight and make my own way. Most of my life has been naught but fighting on your behalf. And don't make that face, I'm not saying I regret so much as a day. Just ... I see what Helgi has accomplished ..."

Sigmund chortled. "Oh. Jealous of your brother's victories."

"How could I not be?"

Sigmund nodded. How indeed. Fitela was the eldest of his sons and, as a varulf, certainly the strongest. He deserved his chance at whatever life he wanted to build. And he was right, not once had Sigmund considered what Fitela wanted from his life. He'd always assumed his son wanted what he wanted. "I'll see that you get a ship and a crew, then. From there, the world will be what you make of it."

"And you, Father?"

Sigmund shook his head. "Peace?" He had to laugh at that. Three decades of fighting, and now it was done? Truly well and done?

Yes, now Hunaland was united. Now came the time to strengthen it, to reinforce their borders. To aid Styria in driving out the trolls and to gather all the wealth he could manage.

Under his rule, Hunaland would become the greatest nation in Midgard.

41

A terrible fortress lay before Sif and her companions, one with corpses impaled on spikes jutting from the parapets. None looked like Odin, at least, but still she found the sight left little room for hope.

Loki shook his head. "By now this king, Geirrod, may be expecting Odin's son to come. Perhaps he set Skrymir on us to assess your strength. Either way, he knows what power lies in your hammer."

"Good," Thor said. "Let him watch his doom approaching."

Loki just shut his eyes. "Have you not suffered enough defeats to consider alternatives to rushing in headlong? If this jotunn king had aught to do with Skrymir—"

"Then he dies," Thor snapped. "Dies squealing like a pig."

"—then you must learn to respect his power," Loki finished.

The prince growled.

Sif spoke up before Thor could make things worse. "What do you propose?"

"I am known among some of the jotunnar."

She knew her eyes had widened at that. The words made sense, but the thought behind them seemed incomprehensible. How would a man be known to jotunnar?

"I will go in," Loki said. "Convince them that I've tricked you into coming in without your hammer. You must strike when he least expects it."

"How honorable," Thor said.

Loki favored him with a glower filled with such disdain even Sif found it hard to swallow. "In the flames I saw him torturing your father. Burning him, depriving him of water or sleep. We must act decisively if we are to save Odin."

Thor nodded stiffly at that, and Loki took off, ahead of them.

When he'd gone, the prince turned to Sif. "We'll give him two hours. After that, we go in. We hide Mjölnir in Thjalfi's satchel, beneath the supplies."

"Not much of those left," the slave said.

"Doesn't matter. By the time they're looking, we'll be ready to strike. This fortress is no illusion, and these jotunnar will break beneath our blows."

Sif hoped he was right.

⚓

THE PRINCE GREW MORE restless with each passing moment. Sif doubted a full two hours had passed when he rose, grabbed the satchel, and jammed his hammer inside. The bag he handed to Thjalfi, then he strode toward the jotunn fortress, Sif and the others following behind him.

The closer they drew, the more ominous and foul this place looked. Jagged, as if cut from a giant rock, but by hands that appreciated only war and death, not beauty or symmetry. It strained her eyes even to look upon the wicked angles of those towers, or the jutting, thorn-like outcroppings.

When they reached the entrance, the portcullis stood open, drawn into the recesses of the gatehouse. Waiting for them, even as Loki had promised.

A sudden, sick fear took hold of Sif. What if this Geirrod was not the one Loki betrayed? The man claimed to *know* jotunnar. How was that possible? He'd sworn loyalty to Odin, yes, but who knew what a man like him really thought or planned? An immortal, but not originally from the Ás tribes. A worker of the Art. A man who knew things no man ought to know. Could he have led them into a trap?

Almost, Sif opened her mouth, intent to warn Thor. But the prince would have charged in regardless, and such an accusation would terrify Thjalfi and Roskva. Besides, was it her right to so besmirch a man Odin had chosen as brother? To give voice to such thoughts seemed almost treasonous.

Still, Sif could not shake the niggling doubt that they walked into something other than what they'd expected.

Without the barest hint of caution, Thor trod into the main hall, a place eerily silent, if somewhat more inviting than the exterior. Here, at least, braziers cast light amid the lower level. Unfortunately, the upper reaches were spanned by iron rafters, these too lined with thorny protrusions. A layer of frost coated those beams, let in by small windows somewhere up above.

At the back of the hall, a jotunn lord rested upon a throne. Or his corpse, rather. An angry hole had torn through his gut, though it no longer bled.

"Huh," Thor said. "Guess Loki decided to have the fun himself. Bastard." The prince stomped over to the dead jotunn.

Sif frowned, shaking her head. If Loki had killed this king, where was he? Indeed, where was *everyone*? Surely Geirrod had not lived in total solitude. A place this size could have housed dozens or hundreds of jotunnar and their human slaves.

Yet the only sound came from the crackle of the braziers and the footfalls of her own group.

Sif paused before the throne. Loki had run Geirrod through the gut ... but there was no blood anywhere around the throne. Which meant ... had someone staged this? "Thor, I think—"

Geirrod lunged off the throne with shocking swiftness, wrapped a hand around Thor's neck and hefted the prince off the ground. The jotunn's eyes gleamed with fell red light. His snarl echoed off the rafters, hollow and Otherworldly.

A draug. A *jotunn* draug?

Sif faltered, knowing she needed to move and unable to quite make her body obey.

Thor flailed in midair, beating against Geirrod's arm, unable to reach the jotunn's body.

"Master!" Thjalfi shouted. The boy had dropped the satchel and was rooting through it. Looking for Mjölnir. Trying to fight.

His effort shook Sif from her shock. She shrieked a battle cry and charged Geirrod with her spear out. The jotunn draug jerked Thor to the side with one hand and caught the shaft of Sif's spear with the other. Sif snatched hold of the apple's power, giving herself strength. The jotunn jerked the spear around, lifting Sif off the ground.

Shit. All the strength in the world didn't matter if she had no purchase on the ground, nor the weight to claim it.

Growling, Geirrod whipped her around in a rapid arc. Sif clutched onto the spear with all her might, even as its shaft burned her hands. Couldn't allow him to fling her free. Couldn't give up.

With the jotunn using one hand on Sif, Thor managed to pry free his grip and drop to the ground, gasping for air, reeling. Sif could barely keep the prince in sight as Geirrod swung her back and forth as though wringing out wet linens.

It was too much. Her grip slipped. The shaft tore open her palms. Sif flew free, spun around in the air. Hit a column and blasted all wind from her lungs. Her head cracked on the stone floor. A white haze filled her vision.

Ears ringing.

Everything fading away.

Groaning, she pushed herself up onto one arm. Waves of dizziness churned her stomach. Her head was splitting apart. She looked up, vision still out of focus.

Thjalfi lay on the ground, bleeding. The girl, Roskva, kneeling at his side. The hammer knocked away on the far side of the throne.

Thor swinging at Geirrod, landing body blows that seemed to do naught save anger the draug. Geirrod's backhand catching Thor in the face with a meaty thwack that sent him flying, spinning through the air. Crashing down.

Sif blinked. Everything so disjointed ... The more she forced it all into clarity, the more everything *hurt*.

With a grunt of pain and rage, she regained her feet and raced toward the hammer. Her feet betrayed her, legs wobbling. She pitched over sideways and landed on a knee, the jolt sending lightning shooting through her leg.

"Damn it, move," she growled.

Struggling forward, she wrapped a hand around Mjölnir's short haft. Its power flowed into her at once, steadying the dizzying spin of the room. She turned, panting. Then she charged.

Thor launched himself to his feet, his uppercut clipping Geirrod's jaw in the process. Had the jotunn been a foot shorter, that might have done more than daze him. Instead, the jotunn grabbed Thor with a hand atop the prince's skull. Like that he hefted Thor up off the ground.

Geirrod reared back with his other fist. Another sickening *thwack* resounded as that fist connected with Thor. The prince hurtled back into the rocky throne. The stone broke under the impact and Thor kept going, crashing to the ground.

Sif reached Geirrod an instant later and swept the hammer in a horizontal arc. It cracked down on the jotunn's knee, bone crunching aloud as lightning erupted from Mjölnir's head. The undead king dropped to his hands and knees, hissing at her with venom and ire seeming drawn from Niflheim. Shrieking, Sif spun around with her momentum, bringing Mjölnir up over her head.

Then crashing down on the jotunn's skull. The sound of thunder echoed with her blow and more lightning sizzled. The creature's head cracked, splattering blood and brains. Geirrod collapsed flat on the ground. No room for doubt. Sif hefted Mjölnir once more, and brought it down again, shattering the jotunn's head to a pulp. A bolt of lightning set his skull exploding and his neck frying.

The gory mess beneath her—coating her clothes and arms and face—it suddenly turned her stomach. She felt apt to retch. The hammer fell from her limp hands, and she stumbled away. Tried to wipe the brains off her face, but only managed to smear more filth about.

Dazed, she made her way to Thor. The prince was

already pushing himself up, shaking himself back into coherence. Sif slumped down beside him.

＄

THEY FOUND a score or so of jotunnar in the rooms beyond, most women, those led by Gridr, who claimed to be Geir-rod's daughter, and thus the new heir to the throne. Sif had barely restrained Thor from killing every last jotunn in the fortress. They had not come here for senseless slaughter.

"The woman came here," Gridr said. Gridr could almost have passed for human, save for standing well over six foot tall and her skin so pale, almost bluish in tint.

"Which woman?" Thor demanded.

"Skadi. We thought her human, at first. But she claimed ancient lineage that, in time, even Father couldn't deny. She bade him detain the man who would come here, one whom even the wolves would fear. And Father did so. He held this man—"

"You mean Odin," Sif said. "Is he here?"

"No. My brother Agnar helped him escape some time ago." Gridr frowned, shaking her head. "The sorceress returned. She ... she ... compelled Agnar to swear loyalty to her. Then worked her Art to raise Father as her agent here. As you found him. Twisted and pained. Damned."

"Where is Loki?" Sif asked.

"My brother and the sorceress overpowered him. They take him north, to stand in judgment before the greatest of jotunn kings."

"Hel fucking damn it," Thor grumbled. "So now we've lost Father and his blood brother."

"We can pursue them," Sif said.

Gridr shook her head. "The sorceress called up vargar to

carry them. You'll not catch them before they reach Thrymheim."

Thor growled. "So we break into Thrymheim and save them."

"No man could survive such an attempt. Not even the famous Thor. Besides, winter will set in before you could reach them. The cold will leave you naught but frozen corpses upon the plains. No, you've no choice but remain here until the summer comes again."

Perhaps it was her imagination, but Sif did not much like the way the jotunn woman looked at Thor. Nor the way he seemed appreciative of her oversized breasts.

Either way, though, Gridr probably had the right of it. They couldn't risk marching across Jotunheim in winter.

Loki and Odin were beyond their reach. They had failed.

42

$\mathcal{S}$tarkad Eightarms said very little in all the days Sigyn and Mundilfari traveled with him. The mad sorcerer said enough for two men, so Sigyn supposed it all evened out in the end. Tyr's son cast fell glances at the sorcerer from time to time, clearly vexed by the inane babble, but didn't otherwise comment.

Just as well, given Sigyn couldn't do this without either of them.

The three of them made their way across a hilly wilderness. Starkad oft pushed ahead, scouting for foes. Sigyn suspected he just wanted to be out of earshot from Mundilfari. When Starkad was around, there was an oddness about him. An eerie stillness she could not quite identify, but one that disquieted her to the point she preferred him gone as well.

At the moment, only Mundilfari walked beside her.

This land lacked the warmth of Asgard, but it was certainly far from cold. More striking, however, the mist did not seem to congeal here, as if unable to collect itself. The horizon bore hints of it, thin and wispy, and probably no threat to anyone. Up close, it was hardly noticeable at all.

"Oh. Hmm," Mundilfari said, clearly having spotted her looking around for the thousandth time. "The caliphs, yes. Hmm. Areas under their sway, they keep them ... um ..."

"Clear?"

Mundilfari rubbed his eyebrows with his thumbs. "Ah, uh, I try to be. Yes, I try."

Sigyn rolled her eyes and pressed on. In the far distance, voices carried on the wind, a great many of them—enough to represent a town or even a city. She had to assume that was where Hödr would have gone, and thus where she was bound.

"Fire is life," Mundilfari mumbled. "Life ... death ... burning. Without balance all crumbles before us."

"Uh, huh."

"Balance ... balance ... the spheres are out of balance. The world falters."

Don't ask him. Do not engage with him. If she were to question him—and he seemed to refer to the Spheres of Creation—he would no doubt wander off on some other tangent anyway.

All she had to do now was focus on finding Hödr.

They walked on, cresting a hill, beyond which a ruin came into view. Cut from stone the color of sand, and now crumbling and half buried under sediment, the structure might have once served as a palace or place of worship. Now, a broken column was its most striking feature. An opening led into a main structure, but with so much of it buried, it looked nigh to pitch black inside.

Sigyn glanced at Mundilfari.

The sorcerer shrugged. "Fire temple ..."

Now that he mentioned it, no mist at all gathered around

the ruin. Did some power within hold the vapors at bay? She squinted, looking closer into the valley. Footprints disrupted the ground, heading inside the ruined temple.

"He's here."

"Are you certain it is your son?"

Of course, she could not be certain, but her gut insisted nevertheless. Where had Starkad gone? Should she wait until he returned? Prudence argued she ought to delay, but the thought of wasting even a moment …

No. No, she couldn't take the chance of losing Höðr. Starkad had come along to get her past the Serklander lines. He had done so. Now it fell to her and Mundilfari to save her son.

Sigyn skidded down the hillside, half running into the valley, ignoring the sorcerer's grumbles from behind her. She had to find him. He *had* to be here.

She raced forward, toward the opening. As she reached the entrance, faint light adumbrated the walls, cast by some flame deep within. Sigyn glanced back at the sorcerer, then pressed on inside, leaving him to follow.

Barely forestalling the urge to call out to her son, she crept forward, following a steep descent that ended in a high-ceiling chamber the size of a large family house. At the center of it, on a dais, blazed a brazier bigger than she was. Its fire sent the whole of the room dancing in shadows eager to swallow her. Beyond the brazier, a man stood in silhouette.

"Höðr?"

The scrape of Mundilfari's boots behind her announced his presence.

The figure beyond the brazier took a step forward, illuminating his face in a golden glow that seemed born of an Otherworld. Höðr. Sigyn's heart clenched. Her son's eyes flickered red in what, she prayed, must be a trick of the firelight.

"Son ..."

"He stole the first flame from the Elder God and, in his temerity, dared to give it to man that he might challenge the darkness."

"Firebringer ..." Mundilfari said.

Sigyn swallowed, unable to look away from Hödr's flashing eyes. "You mean Loki? Your *father*."

"*My* father was not the thief, but that which was stolen. A spark of the first flame, simmering and burning, smoldering for release long denied. But dying embers might one day be rekindled."

He certainly sounded like Loki.

Hödr stuck his hands into the brazier and drew them forth engulfed in flames that danced a foot high.

Sigyn faltered, shaking her head. "Hödr, you don't need to do this. Come home with me."

He chuckled at that.

Mundilfari advanced to her side, pointing the wand at her son. "Release the Art of Fire, Eldr."

Now Hödr grinned. "Long were the ages I dreamt of the reprisal I would bring upon you, sorcerer. Years I wallowed in darkness, in suffocation, awaiting the chance to reward your temerity."

Mundilfari spoke something in Supernal. Whatever it was, Hödr roared, whipping one hand forward. Fire leapt from that hand like an arrow from a bow. Sigyn screamed, flinging herself to the ground as a gyrating disc of flame shot across the room. The disc hit the back wall and exploded, stripping all oxygen from her lungs and sending her tumbling across the ground.

She gasped, blinking away tears, unable to see or hear.

Another impact sent her toppling back down. Blazing heat scorched her arms and back as she tried to rise, still blinking through a haze of smoke. She rolled over and pressed against the back wall. A cloud of ash had engulfed the chamber, raining down and obfuscating the struggle. Mundilfari was trying to evoke something, but explosions kept cutting off his words.

Groaning with the effort, Sigyn rose, then stumbled toward the sounds. Something detonated in midair, and a body hurtled past her to collide with the wall. The same explosion drove her to her knees. Grimacing, she glanced at the body. Mundilfari, smoke rising from his smoldering robes. The sorcerer was trying to push himself up on his hands and knees.

"Hödr!" Sigyn rose and stumbled over to Mundilfari.

A figure emerged from the ash cloud, bearing Gamban-teinn in one hand, a billowing flame in the other. His whole body trembled as he moved, as though every step cost him.

"M-mother ..."

"Hödr?" Sigyn pulled Mundilfari up. Now what would they do? They needed that wand to exorcise Eldr. She reached a hand toward her son.

"R-run ..."

Sigyn's mouth hung open. That was him. That was Hödr, struggling to contain the Fire vaettr for a moment. Because he wanted her to escape. No. No, she wasn't going to leave him. "Hödr, please, come with me ..." Her voice was breaking. Please ...

Mundilfari yanked her away, pulling her toward the entrance.

She barely glanced at him, but he had painted some symbol on the wall in his own blood. Hödr saw it too, as the sorcerer moved, for an inhuman bellow escaped him, reverberating off the walls and seeming to rend her mind. Sigyn collapsed, clutching her ears and wailing.

The sorcerer pulled her up again and shoved her out into the tunnel. Another explosion sent her rolling several feet up the passage.

She tried to rise, tried not to think of the burns covering so much of her skin. Another bellow echoed from the chamber below.

Sigyn seized her pneuma and flooded it through her body, blocking pain and granting strength. She grabbed the sorcerer's arms and dragged him back out of the tunnel, desperately trying not to think.

Hödr.

Her son.

Her son!

This was not happening.

Outside, in the sunlight, she deposited Mundilfari. The sorcerer groaned and rolled over, exposing a blackened face and charred flesh. Even the apple might not save him from such severe burns.

Fuck. Fuck it! The man wasn't her problem. She didn't even like him. She had to get her son.

She started for the entrance again.

"Ward ... won't hold long."

"I'm not leaving my son!"

"Kill ... us ... both ..."

Sigyn worked her mouth, trying to form any coherent argument against retreat. It was her son. It was her *son*! But Eldr had him again, and held the wand as well.

"New ... plan ..."

She threw up her hands and wailed in frustration.

Finally, she grabbed the sorcerer, drawing his arm around her shoulders and ignoring his cries of pain. She had to hold on to her pneuma to carry him like this. Weeping, she stumbled back toward the hill.

🔥

SIGYN DEPOSITED Mundilfari in a valley several hills over. The sorcerer's groans had become faint, his life failing him. Once, Sigyn had saved Loki by pushing her pneuma into him. He had warned her never to do so again.

But then, without Mundilfari, she might never save her son.

Doing this to Vili had caused the berserk to lust after Frigg endlessly.

But Hödr ...

Sigyn placed both palms against Mundilfari's scorched chest. And she threw bits of her own life into him, as much as she could before collapsing into a heap beside him.

🔥

As SOON As consciousness had beckoned her awake, Sigyn had snuck back to the temple. The sun had already set, but moonlight offered plenty of illumination to Sigyn's enhanced senses. Was Hödr still inside? Maybe he'd kill her if she entered ... but he was her son.

In a crouch, she crept forward, hiding behind the brush as much as she could.

Slowly, so quiet no one without her hearing could have caught wind of her, she made her way to the entrance and pressed up against the side. Struggling to control her breath, she peered around the corner.

A figure sat in there, his back against the wall, chin on

his chest. Through the shadows, she couldn't make out his face.

Sigyn eased her way against the side. Breathe. This was it. If she didn't confront him, there was no point in leaving Mundilfari behind at all.

Right. She could do this. She could do it.

She strode around the wall and began descending into the temple. Confidence. She needed confidence.

The figure looked up. Half his face seemed melted off, but he had a confidence about him. And he wasn't Hödr.

The man rose, palm resting on the pommel of a curving sword at his side.

Sigyn faltered, drawing to a stop. Well ... troll shit. If she made a dash for it, she might elude him in the hills, especially drawing on her pneuma to strengthen her legs. On the other hand, she'd have to run back up the slope. It gave him time to catch her. And she hadn't come here for naught. "Where's Hödr?"

The man cocked his head to the side. "Your son is under our control." His voice was practically a growl. "If you want to see him again ... there's something you'll have to do for us."

❧

CLIMBING BACK UP THE HILL, lost in thought, Sigyn nigh blundered into Starkad. Tyr's son rose from a crouch, silent as the dead. So quiet not even Sigyn had heard him.

"Find aught?"

For a heartbeat, she froze. Her gut churned with ice. Her cheeks flushed. And she pushed it all down just as quickly. She had to. "No. Where have you been?"

"Hunting the Sons of Muspel. I caught one of them alone in the night."

So he stalked them after dark. Perhaps he was even more confident in his sneaking abilities than she'd suspected.

"I found Mundilfari, barely alive."

Sigyn nodded. "My son ... is gone. His mind ..."

"I've seen others, taken by these Fire vaettr. I'm sorry."

Sigyn nodded again, trying not to grimace. "Help us return to Peregot."

"Their army is already on the move. We'll have to make haste if we wish to reach the city before the siege begins."

Yes. They had to hurry.

43

One Year Ago

*S*igyn sat on the floor in a tower of Sessrumnir, surrounded by dozens of scrolls illuminated by numerous candles. Her senses tingled with the sound of the door opening, but it was a distant thought, digging at the back of her mind. She was so close to understanding, so nigh to it she could taste it.

Mundilfari had known things about the nature of reality. Things Sigyn—and previously Freyja and other scholars—had largely dismissed as ravings engendered by his descent into madness. He'd posited that every world in the Spirit Realm lay enslaved to an Elder God. While the existence of so-called Elder Gods seemed corroborated by later treatises written by Freyja, Sunna, and others, Mundilfari's suppositions took the concept farther.

The Mad Vanr claimed the entities were powerful almost beyond measure, and different in kind from other vaettir associated with their realms. Moreover, that they represented a dire threat to the Mortal Realm, themselves being even more inimical and unfathomable than their lesser counterparts.

Loki claimed Hel had usurped the power of an earlier goddess of mist. An Elder God, the ruler of Niflheim? So Hel managed to kill the prior goddess? Or did the original lady of Niflheim remain bound somewhere, a source of—

Hermod came tromping up the stairs and bounding into the room, almost knocking over a candle in the process. Sigyn hissed, grabbing it before it could land on a scroll and burn away precious, irreplaceable notes.

With it reset in place, she glowered at her foster brother. "Hermod?"

"Sister." Still travel-worn and dirty, her foster brother must have come straight here, which bespoke a disturbing urgency to his visit. His face was every bit as stern as their father's had been.

"Last I heard, you had returned to aid Tyr in Peregot. What brings you back to Asgard?"

"Things have turned ill with Hödr."

"He was injured?"

"No. We were at an outpost in the west. Small place, a guard fort, really, around a town."

"And?"

"A blacksmith, he says Hödr forced himself on his daughter. The girl denied it, though. I argued with Hödr and he took off during the night."

She shook her head. "No. No, whatever you're implying, my son would not—"

Hermod held up a hand. "I tracked him south ..." Her foster brother hesitated, scratching his head.

"Tell me."

"I found ... a burned out farm."

"It could have been Serklander raiding party."

"Could have. Tracks didn't look like more than one person. I don't know. I tried to follow, but he disappeared into the hills."

How anyone could elude a tracker like Hermod, Sigyn could not even guess. "Thank you for telling me ..."

"You aren't as surprised as you ought to be."

Sigyn rose and drifted to a table, as much to avoid looking at him as aught else. He had grown far too perceptive in the intervening years, and she had not the slightest inclination to share her fears with anyone. To give them voice was to make them too real, and she could not afford that. Save that, with Loki once again off trying to keep Odin under control, Hermod alone might prove her best chance to find her son and save him from whatever had befallen him.

With a shudder, she leaned on the table.

"Sigyn?"

"You have to find him. Bring him back to Asgard so I can talk to him."

Hermod nodded grimly. "That boy ... have you been teaching him aught of what you've uncovered in this ... place?"

"Why would I do that?"

He shook his head. "Hödr knows things he ought not to. A great deal, honestly."

"What things?"

"Details about Serkland, about the war ... about ... the Veil."

Sigyn tapped her lip, uncertain what to say or what to think. "He's intelligent and intuitive."

"He sneaks about and spies." Given Hermod's own proclivity for doing just that, he spoke with a remarkable degree of spite in his voice.

"I need you to find him, brother. I don't know where my husband is at present. I have no one else to whom I might turn."

Hermod rubbed his temples, but nodded. "I'll find him. But I think he needs to remain on Asgard at present. He is too clever by far, and I cannot risk losing track of him once more." Assuming he could even find her son. The unspoken words settled around Sigyn's neck like a weight.

She waited until he stepped outside and the doors had resealed.

Then she swept all the papers away and wailed in frustration.

HERMOD HAD FOUND HÖDR, yes, though not where he'd last seen him in Valland, but rather attempting the crossing to Asgard on his own. The very thought of it left Sigyn's stomach lurching. Aegir's wrath had sunk a great number of ships when the Aesir had first come to Vanaheim, costing countless lives, including those of her and Hermod's parents.

Any voyage undertaken now was undertaken with care. While Frigg paid Aegir annual tribute to forestall his wrath, still treacherous reefs and storms could easily scuttle or capsize a ship trying to make the crossing.

But Hermod had found the boy through means he did not deign to share. Sigyn could harbor a guess, of course. No tracker, no matter how talented, could follow tracks over the ocean. And if natural means could be ruled out, all that remained was supernatural means. Whatever Odin had been teaching her brother, he seemed to have begun taking to it.

Either way, he'd brought the boy back to her, and with the stern admonition that she send him to Hoenir, Syn's father. While Hödr was far too old for fostering, Sigyn dared to hope Hermod knew what he was doing.

Either way, she found herself at Hoenir's hall on the northern island of Asgard. Hödr didn't resist as she ordered him to follow. She didn't dare ask him about the girl Hermod had mentioned, nor the farm. The thought of it felt like Hel herself running her fingers down the back of Sigyn's … Huh. And here she was, still thinking of her husband's dead daughter as the dark goddess. She was that, but still, she was something else now, too.

"You're quiet, Mother."

She glanced back at him. While his expression was a mask of innocence, still a look of arrogance almost beyond words lurked behind his eyes. "I'm worried."

"What? About me? I'm quite hale and healthy."

Sigyn tried to force a smile in return, then increased her pace to Hoenir's hall. He'd chosen to build it upon a lower hill, looking out over the sea. Ages ago, it seemed now, Hoenir had led the Godwulf tribe. Now, with the tribes dissolved and the jarls stripped of rank, Sigyn rarely saw him and had little idea what he did with his days. Nigh five decades since coming to Vanaheim. Longer than any of them would have expected to live back in their days in Aujum. Everyone found ways to busy themselves, she supposed.

The sound of shouts and splashing greeted her long before she reached the hall, however. She followed the noise around Hoenir's home and down to the sea, where the former jarl was shouting at contestants in a swimming race. Three, no four of them, three men and a woman, all making for a rock out on a strand.

A sound issued from Hödr, something between a groan or a growl. Most people wouldn't have caught it over the commotion of the race or the crash of the waves, but Sigyn had extraordinary hearing since taking the apple.

Experience had shown questioning him was not like to produce results, so instead she plodded over to Hoenir. He nodded at her. Standing beside him, she watched the race. "I've a favor to ask. From Hermod, really, or his idea at least."

"Well, we're all family here."

"I want you to train Hödr."

Now the former jarl looked to her. "Train him to what?"

She glanced back at Hödr, then lowered her voice to ensure he wouldn't hear. "Wrestle, fish, swim, whatever. He needs a good influence in his life, and neither Hermod nor Loki is on Asgard oft enough to be that for him."

The old man snorted. "These days, training the young to swim and fish is about the extent of my activities." He shook his head, groaned. "Sometimes I think I ought to just head across the sea, go to Tyr. Let him find a use for me." He meant find a glorious way to die. Sigyn frowned at the thought. "Ah. You're lucky to have gotten your apple while you were still young, girl."

"Will you help me?"

"Of course I will. What do you take me for?"

"You train girls here, too?"

Hoenir glanced at her. "Looking to be a shieldmaiden?" Sigyn barely smiled at that. No, she didn't fancy herself a warrior. "Eh. Sure, girls, as well. They want to get strong, compete with the boys. A lot of them, they come to me, wanting to know what I taught Syn way back. They grew up hearing stories of her battling trolls at Idavollir and such. Remember that Hel-cursed place?"

"I remember. Keep an eye on the girls around Hödr. There was ... an accusation."

Hoenir groaned, then spit. "I'd let the hounds of Hel gnaw on my own stones before I let those things go on."

Sigyn nodded, then made her way over to where Hödr stood, glaring at the swimmers. "Your granduncle Hoenir has agreed to train you. Mind him well."

Hödr shrugged as if it mattered little. "Farewell. Mother."

As she made her way back, Sigyn kept casting glances at him.

Loki met her at their hall on the other island. He sat on the cliff, looking out over the sea, staring, as if he knew where she'd just taken their son. Perhaps he did.

"When did you return?" she asked.

"Just now."

With a sigh, Sigyn trudged up beside them, then slumped down to join him, taking in the beautiful sea and sky. Twilight drew nigh, and soon, they'd find a graceful sunset to put rest to a bitter day.

"You know where I've been?" she asked.

He nodded. "Hoenir is a good man. As good a man as the times allow for, at least."

"I'm afraid for our son."

Loki reached over and pulled her close, arm around her shoulders. "So am I."

"There's something wrong with him."

"There's something wrong with everyone. It's the nature of the world."

Sigyn grunted. "Not what I meant and you know it."

"Two possibilities lay before you. Either, Hödr is who he is as a product of who we are, or else ..."

"Or else *I* did this to him."

But Loki didn't answer. Maybe he thought her self-recriminations enough punishment. Either way, she needed to be sure. Somehow, she'd have to figure out what had happened to Hödr.

44

The plateau Agnar had spoken of lay in the far northern reaches, amidst mountains at least as treacherous as those Odin had passed just beyond the Midgard Wall. Climbing up to it had left him panting, breath frosting the air, even in the falling snow.

In winter, this place must have been nigh to impassible.

A storm rumbled overhead. Thunder had greeted their arrival, growing stronger with every step they drew closer, as if the storm were drawn to the mountain at the summit.

Beyond the edge of the plateau rose a wall of ice ten times the height of a man and Odin could not begin to guess how thick. Inverted icicles rose from atop it, each no doubt bigger than he was.

Geri stood beside Odin, blanching at the sight. "Think they were inspired by the Midgard Wall?"

Perhaps that had been exactly what had happened.

Either way, the wall surrounded the mountain, upon which rested a city of ice, rising up in slow spirals along the slope. From his perspective on the ground, Odin could make out at least four distinct terraces. Above those, barely visible through the cloud cover, a gargantuan palace stood.

A flash of lightning cast it in stark silhouette: from a thick base rose twisting spires like branches of a rotting tree, scraping the sky.

"I rather mislike this place," Geri said.

Perhaps. But one had to admire the wonders the old powers had wrought in the world. Naught that modern men built compared to the glories of the Old Kingdoms. And even those mighty halls paled before the constructions of the dvergar, the jotunnar, or the Vanir. The further back one looked, the more the modern world seemed but a shadow of what had been.

Or just another sign of a world in its final days.

Rather than answer, Odin trudged along behind Freki until they came at last to the open archway. While no gate barred the way, a metal giant as tall as the wall itself stood in ominous watch on either side of the entrance.

Odin stood there, neck aching from craning to look so high up, staring at the horrifying statues. Thick layers of ice and frost coated each, so the details remained muted. But both clutched swords at least thirty feet long, jammed in the snow in obvious threat. Their metal flesh looked like plates of iron wrapped around them, as if in armor, including helms.

"I don't think Thrym likes visitors," Geri said.

No, and Odin had sent Hrist in there a fortnight ago, to scout ahead. Traveling in the Penumbra—and flying—she could cover ground much more quickly than even the varulfur twins.

Her brother glanced back at her. "He just wants to impress his guests. Consider all the wonders of construction Father had built on Asgard."

Odin grimaced. "If you two wolves are quite finished, I do not think the sight before us warrants jesting. Inside we may face foes more powerful and more numerous than any we have yet come up against. Control your tongues."

With that, Odin trod forward, into that great arch.

The city within had some few guards, and those watched their entrance with more curiosity than any sense of hostility. Hardly much surprise, though, as Odin saw numerous humans milling about the city. They carried hunks of bloody meat upon their backs. They trudged along, dragging carts behind them laden with soiled furs. They stitched and sewed and worked forges.

Slaves ...

The humans here, conquered by the jotunnar, had become slaves. And, more like than not, they also served to sate the various hungers of their masters.

"We need food and shelter," Freki said. "Let me about it. I can meet you back on the lower terrace once I have something."

"What makes you think anyone will board us?" Geri asked.

"Agnar said jotunnar journey across all of Jotunheim to come to this place, right? They must find shelter somewhere."

Odin nodded in agreement. "Good. And find Hrist. She'll know more about where we need to look."

With a nod, Freki took off, trotting down the street.

"There are too many smells here," Geri complained, watching as her brother disappeared around a corner.

Odin wrinkled his own nose. Come to think of it, the gutters smelled like shit and half-rotted meat. The cold only kept things fresh but so long. How much worse then must this all seem to a varulf nose? "Come." He guided her away from the main aisle, narrowly avoiding a jotunn tromping down the street.

If Odin were to judge based on this terrace, several thousand of these creatures must live in this city. That meant—assuming Thrym held their loyalty—this king commanded an army fit to crush almost any force on Midgard. Even the Aesir could not hope to stand against such vast numbers of jotunnar.

So long as they kept out of the way, though, none of the locals seemed to pay them much heed.

"Something strikes me," Geri said. "You told us the stories about Aujum."

Odin grunted in acknowledgment while following her to a butcher shop. These people's diet seemed to consist almost entirely of meat. Through a bloodstained window Odin spied a skinned reindeer, half a snow bear, and some carcass he couldn't identify. The place reeked twice as foul as the rest of the street.

Blood dribbled down tiny canals carved into the floor, into gaps in the wall. Gutters along the side of the street carried the waste along the edge of the terrace, probably spiraling down most of the city.

"What is that thing?" Odin asked.

Geri grunted in disgust. "Meat stripped off a man's leg."

Odin could only grimace. "Sorry, what were you saying about Aujum?"

Inside, the shopkeeper began hacking the leg into chunks, then using his cleaver to slide those chunks into barrels. Odin's stomach lurched.

Geri pointedly looked away from the butcher shop. "Vingethor led the tribes. Then they all broke up for lack of a king strong enough. So the Aesir fought among themselves in squabbles and so forth around a century."

"Yes." Odin did not like where this seemed to be heading.

"So ... we know the jotunnar fight among themselves. All these petty kings and small kingdoms chopping up this barren land or pressing through the wall into Midgard."

"Yes."

Geri shrugged. "What would happen if a man like you came among to them? A true king to unite them all."

Odin flinched. Could this Thrym be that king? Was that the beginning of Ragnarok? "What do you do when you have more foes than you can keep in view at once?"

The varulf frowned. "Retreat. Come back with more numbers or else find new hunting grounds."

"And if you have nowhere left to retreat?"

Now Geri's frown grew deeper. "Try to bring as many down with you as possible. Save the rest of the pack."

Odin nodded. *His* pack was all mankind. And he had to find a way to save them.

FREKI LED them to a hall on the lower terrace, one intended for the slaves of visiting jotunnar. Though a jotunn owned the hall, he let his human slave run the place. That man, a balding graybeard with too much flab in his stomach, traded them room and board for iron clasps and a dagger.

Metal, it seemed, was even more precious here than in Midgard. Some few jotunn kings controlled most of the mines here, and guarded them jealously. That disquiet boded well as far as Odin's hope of avoiding any alliance between jotunn kings went.

Odin, Freki, Geri, and Hrist sat in a room that would have been comfortable for one. The twins didn't seem to mind curling up on the floor by the fire, and the valkyrie never complained about much. Still, Odin found it cramped.

"I've spent some time learning about this kingdom," Hrist said. At the moment, she sat cross-legged in front of the fire, rubbing her hands together. "They call it Thrymheim."

Geri snorted. "The king named it after himself?"

"Yes. A long time ago King Thiazi ruled this place. He was poised to unite the jotunnar and rise against the Vanir. Apparently that didn't end well, because they killed him, and one of the princes married his daughter, Skadi."

"The Winter Queen," Geri said, looking ready to spit into the flame.

Hrist nodded. "Later, she died too. But—according to what some claim, now she's back, and wooing an alliance with Thrym. The two of them together would pose a significant threat."

Odin clenched his fists at his side, forcing himself to silence. Skadi—in possession of Gudrun—had eluded him some years ago. He ought to have killed her then, but ever since, she'd been beyond his reach. Perhaps because she'd fled here, to Jotunheim, where Odin's powers were more limited.

"She's been winning allies all over Jotunheim," Hrist continued. "It's all anyone here has talked of since I arrived."

Odin glowered. "We cannot do aught about Skadi at present." Yet another foe he had to defer dealing with. "We four are no match for Thrym's army should we attack a guest in his hall. We must focus on the task at hand and find a way to reach Vafthrudnir."

Hrist nodded. "The sorcerer jotunn keeps his own hall, around the far side of the mountain. We'd have to climb to the fourth terrace, then take the East Gate. From there, it's a perilous trek. Storms rage all the time up there, the footing is poor, and ravines split the path."

Odin waved that away. Temporal obstacles meant little. "We leave in the morn. Rest well, my friends."

❧

AS HRIST HAD PREDICTED, the route to Vafthrudnir's hall meant taking a narrow, winding path that ran along around the far side of the mountain. Blessed with eternally youthful bodies, the others managed the steep hike with little more than a slight panting. Odin found the trek served only to exacerbate the pains in his back and knees.

Surrender your soul and let slide the frailties of flesh ...

As usual, the wraith was full of sympathy for Odin's plight.

Up ahead, the path cracked like someone had split it with a giant hammer. A section dropped down a good six or seven feet while the next bit rose up ten feet beyond that.

Wings burst from Hrist's back. A single beat sent a gust of wind washing over Odin, causing him to stumble backward and shield his face. When he withdrew his arm, the valkyrie already rested upon the far side, wings withdrawn.

Freki had hopped down into the recession. "Come, Father. I'll boost you up."

This was what Odin's urd had come to. Being hoisted up like a child by his own children. Would Loki see amusement in this? Would other Aesir mock Odin?

Grumbling under his breath, he dropped down to the lower level and landed in a crouch that failed to stop a fresh twinge of pain from shooting through his knees and

314

running straight to his spine. Odin grimaced, rose, and ambled over to Freki, who knelt.

Almost, he wanted to mumble an apology for it. Keeping such thoughts to himself, he climbed on Freki's shoulders. The varulf stood as though Odin weighed naught more than a babe, raising him high enough to grab the ledge. A slight burst of pneuma gave Odin the strength to heave himself up.

He turned to offer Freki a hand.

Instead, the varulf made a vertical leap all on his own, caught the ledge, and scooted over it. Showing off? Or perhaps not even considering the implication. They thought him frail.

Strange thought, really. Odin had gained powers beyond the ken of most Aesir, and yet so many thought that, if he suffered aches and used a walking stick, he could not summon strength when needed. Much like his disguises as a vagabond, in truth.

Geri also made the leap and pulled herself up.

Around the mountain's curve they came to carved stairs. Massive ones, too large for a human to comfortably climb. Odin found mounting each step forced him to yank his leg high enough to send little jolts through his hips. And those stairs just seemed to go on and on.

"I'll meet you at the top," Hrist said, sprouting her wings once more.

Odin glared at the valkyrie.

ATOP THE STAIRS, on a slight plateau, Vafthrudnir had built his hall right into the mountainside in the manner of dvergar. Columns engraved with spirals supported a stone entryway that jutted out of the mountain like a nose. Above that rose a higher tier of roofing with a balcony beneath it.

Surprising elegance for jotunn construction.

Do you know all about them? Valravn asked in his mind.

No. Odin knew more than most völvur, but that amounted to very little in the end.

The wind howled behind them, buffeting Odin's cloak and stinging every bit of exposed skin.

Twin braziers sat just within the entryway, reduced to embers now, but still offering enough warmth that everyone quickly piled around them.

Those fires barely cast enough light to see within the hall. Odin warmed his hands a moment before trudging inward. He paused after a few steps and turned back. "Hrist, conceal yourself."

The valkyrie stepped backward, into shadow, her form blurring and receding as she passed into the Penumbra.

"Fucking eerie," Freki mumbled.

Ignoring his son, Odin pushed inward. The entryway ran a dozen feet or so before opening up into passages running perpendicular to it. On instinct, Odin chose the left path and made his way around. This led past several closed doors and up to another damn staircase.

Prescient insights demanded he continue this path, so Odin once again climbed, huffing by the time he reached a landing.

There, upon a large chair that might have served as a throne, sat an ancient, bearded jotunn. His skin was pale blue, almost the color of his white hair. His ox-like horns had broken off, leaving only stubs. He sat facing the edge of a balcony, heedless of either the wind's howl or its icy bite. Indeed, a layer of rime coated his legs and arms. But for the slow rise and fall of his chest, Odin would've thought him dead.

A very slight motion of the jotunn's head indicated another, less ornate chair across from him.

Odin raised his hand to keep the varulf twins from entering the landing, then settled down into the seat, not bothering to conceal his sigh of relief. Just getting off his feet brought a simple pleasure, enough he too could almost ignore the bitter weather this far out.

Ice had built up over the balcony, yet somehow had not piled high enough to close this place off. Perhaps the jotunn controlled the storms somehow. Another crash of thunder outside jolted Odin from his musings.

"Hail, Vafthrudnir. I've traveled a long way to see you. Tales say you are wise, jotunn. Truth, or exaggeration?"

The jotunn groaned, leaning forward and flexing his arms, causing a shower of ice crystals to break off them. "Who dares such impudence in my own hall? You ask of wisdom yet show none."

Odin opened his mouth prepared to offer the name Grimnir again. But if word had somehow reached here from Geirrod's court, he wouldn't want to give away his true identity. "Gagnrad. And I come here, thirsty, seeking hospitality. And I find only an old man who barely bestirs himself when guests arrive." It was a game, of course. Baiting the jotunn, challenging him ever so subtly.

Vafthrudnir cracked his neck from side to side. "Impudence," he repeated. "You wish drink, but dare to question my knowledge? Prove *your* wisdom and you'll have what you seek. Fail to impress, and none of you shall depart this hall."

A game, and one Loki had taught Odin, much as he had despised it at the time. Perhaps he should have been grateful his blood brother had done so much to prepare him for it. "Then speak, jotunn. I am the one come here looking for hospitality. It hardly seems fair that I should begin the conversation."

A hint of a smile creased the jotunn's face, creating a wave of wrinkles up to his eyes. "Then tell me, *Gagnrad*, what steed do mankind believe draws the morning for them?"

An old völva legend, told to children. "Skinfaxi, the shinning one who drags in the dawn." Odin had listened while Frigg told such tales to Thor. Back then, the varulfur twins had sat in wings with Odin, neither quite welcomed nor quite cast out by the queen. "His mane is aflame."

The jotunn grunted in acknowledgment. "And tell me, Gagnrad, which steed then brings dusk to the lands of men?"

Damn. Maybe he hadn't paid that much attention to the old legends. Was it the same one? Did the jotunn try to trick him? No. No, Skinfaxi brought the sunlight. And Nott had her own horse ... "Hrimfaxi. Frosty mist falls from his hooves."

Some many stories Odin had heard, buried and forgotten. A childhood that seemed so long ago. And worse, he'd missed so very much of his children's days. He'd not been there to hear so many of their stories. Much as he wanted to tell himself he'd rectify it, he knew it for a lie. Urd did not allow him to be a good father. Not even a good man. He barely dared hope he'd make a good king.

"And tell me, Gagnrad, what river separates the lands of the jotunn from the world of men?"

"The Ifing." That much, at least, he could thank Hrist for.

Vafthrudnir leaned forward more, a gleam coming into

his eyes. "Tell me then, Gagnrad, where did the last flame of the Lofdar dwindle?"

What? That was beyond the lore of any völva.

Vigridr ... our final battle ...

"Vigridr," Odin said. The moment it left his mouth, a sick fear clenched his gut. Audr lied. All the time. All vaettir did.

But the jotunn sorcerer settled back into his chair, seeming content. "So you do have a hint of wisdom. Very well, ask your questions, guest."

Odin might go straight to the point, but then he risked giving overmuch away. No, he had to play Vafthrudnir's game a bit first. And that meant testing the jotunn's wisdom in much the same manner as the jotunn had tested his. "From where, Vafthrudnir, came the sun and moon?"

Now the jotunn grimaced. "Sunna and Mani, whom your kind called the goddess and god of the sun and moon, were the children of Mundilfari." By the look on his face, he'd known the Mad Vanr himself, or at least suffered defeat by him.

And it remained a sore spot.

Regardless, he had not quite answered Odin's question, but close enough. "Who rules the day and night?"

"In the World of Sun, Alfheim, dwells Dellingr, the Dayspring. His blinding gaze falls upon all. In the World of Dark, Svartalfheim, dwells Nott, the Queen of Night."

Odin cocked his head to the side. Of course, all Aesir had heard of Nott. They feared her second only to Hel. But Dellingr ... the name he'd heard in passing in the archives of Sessrumnir. The lord of Alfheim and god of the sun. In another lifetime, Odin had known the Sun God by a different name.

He stroked his beard. So where to take this ... "Whence comes the Fimbulvinter?"

"From the mists of Niflheim, released unto the world to chill and choke the sons of man and herald the return of the Queen of Mist."

Hel herself. But these things Odin had learned long ago, from Idunn. "And what of you, jotunn? Whence comes your kind?"

"From our Great Father, Aurgelmir, who drank the poisons of Elivagar and became vast and wrathful. With his blood the world shall be inundated until he walks once more."

"Ymir's dead."

Vafthrudnir chuckled. "You seem to have forgotten the rules of this game."

Shit. He had no choice but to press on and hope he hadn't lost his chance. "Where does the root of Yggdrasil breach above the Well of Mimir?"

"In the farthest east, across the ice bridge over the sea, that men call Beringia. Amidst the first mountains you find, there lies the broken land where Mimir fled."

Yet farther east? How much father could there be? Did the world stretch on forever?

He knows from way back ...

Did Audr think it meant Vafthrudnir knew the future? "Tell me, then, wise jotunn, the urd of the Aesir."

Vafthrudnir chuckled. "In every world I have walked. In the dark places I have seen the unraveling of time in founts of quicksilver. I gazed into the freezing depths of Niflheim. I have seen the doom of men and jotunnar and gods alike. All bound to descend into shadow."

"What fate befalls the Aesir?"

"Do you mean to ask me what fate lies before you, oh king?"

Odin blanched. Vafthrudnir knew. He knew who Odin was. "I ..."

"In the jaws of a fell wolf, a king's blood runs thick. Though some few men might yet be saved by the grace of jotunn mercy, the wolf shall swallow their lord."

"What wolf?"

Vafthrudnir snickered and rose from his throne, ice cracking and falling from him as he did so. "I do believe I have been contending with one under false pretenses. To hear the fate of the world and be able to do naught to change it must so vex you, Odin." He waved a dismissive hand at the stairs. "Be gone from my court lest my mind be changed."

Odin stood.

He might have questioned this being for an age. Vafthrudnir, though, clearly thought their audience at an end. Given the warning about this jotunn, Odin saw no choice but to acquiesce.

Besides, it seemed the road before him was longer still.

45

The wood tribes of Galgvidr did not build their homes from mountain stone as did most jotunnar. Rather, they grew them, sprouting buildings from the boughs and trunks of twisting trees. Wood, woven together like baskets, but grown so tightly one might see each sinewy strand as a serpent. These created an arching maze that connected pines and spruce and firs together.

The artistry of it impressed Skadi, even if it lacked the grandeur or elegance of what frost jotunnar carved from ice.

For a time, she marveled at the tree trunk before her, massive as a building, twisting around itself in a way naught in nature would do on its own. But then, jotunnar were masters of nature, harnessing it while nurturing its extremes.

In the days of Brimir, the jotunn tribes had lived together in peace—relatively, at least—overseen by the Elder Council. Now, she counted herself lucky to be able to walk among wood jotunnar without evoking a war. She had not come to the position lightly, nor did the locals at first accept her exchange of hosts on her most recent return.

It helped that she had her old host as a prisoner.

Skadi had given Gudrun to the chief's son as a plaything, relishing in the Niflung princess's screams as the wood jotunn ravaged her over and over. The sorceress had given in to hubris in trying to master Skadi. It seemed only fitting Gudrun should thus find herself so humbled.

Skadi pushed on, inside the tree, where layers of roots bending back on themselves formed a stair up into the dwelling. On the upper reaches, the boughs of this tree wove together with those of others nearby, forming a hollow bridge. This Skadi followed, nodding at wood jotunnar inside before coming to the one she'd set to guard her more precious prisoner.

As commanded, no flame was allowed anywhere nigh the chamber within. The only light came from a gap in the weave of wood, a tiny window, forced open after Skadi had forbidden fire here.

And with good reason.

Roots had grown down from the weave to bind the man's hands above his head, while others had grown up from the floor, encasing his legs up to the knee in a cage of wood.

Loki. Loge. Loptr. Kutkh. How many other names had this man had?

Once, Skadi's prior host had managed to capture him. She'd lost him, too, thanks to the interference of his lover. Ah, but the Ás bitch was not like to come for him in the heart of Jotunheim. No, now he was Skadi's for good.

A slight reek filled the wooden chamber. His trousers were stained with his piss. Well, Skadi had warned them not to release his bonds under any account.

"Remove his trousers," she called over her shoulder.

The guard came and began sawing through the garments with a bone knife.

Loki paid him no heed, staring only at Skadi with his level gaze, his crystal blue eyes. So many mortals felt abashed when naked. Not him. Why? Because he had lived so very long?

"Just how old are you?" she asked.

As expected, he offered no answer. The wood jotunn carried the filthy trousers away.

"Old enough to have lived in a distant era, long before mist," Skadi said, moving to stand beside him. She traced a finger along his abdomen. Well muscled, like the rest of him, even if he remained a bit svelte. "Old enough to have lost children. A daughter?"

Now he stiffened ever so slightly.

"The father of Hel herself. Tell me how that's possible, human."

His eyes narrowed, just a hair.

"Or are you not quite human? Not quite jotunn, either. But there's something of both in you. God? Man? What are you? From where and when do you come?"

"Do you truly believe you'll get the answers you seek? And if you found them, would you even know what to do with them?"

Skadi smiled. "Well ..." She traced a finger down from his abdomen, then wrapped her palm around his stones. "I know if you fathered Hel, you must have quite the strong seed."

Loki groaned. "I have naught at all for you, vaettr."

Skadi chuckled as she knelt before him. "Let's be honest: there are some things a man just can't control." She leaned in, then licked his cock. The man had—surprisingly—managed to avoid growing hard at her squeezing his stones. The more she worked her tongue around though, the more quickly he lost that fight.

"Cease this." Practically a growl.

Skadi pulled her mouth back just enough to answer. "The strong take what they want. It's the way the world is." She wrapped her lips around him then, sucking hard. Forcing him closer. Finally, she pulled back and withdrew the furs hanging between her thighs. "I have to be honest, too. You may be tall for a human, but you're puny compared to what I was hoping for. I'm not expecting too much from you."

He grimaced and looked away as she grabbed him and slid him inside her. The angle was awkward, but she'd judged the timing well. It didn't take too much to send his seed spilling into her.

And with it, a cryptic barrage of nonsensical visions. Of years stretching back for more millennia than she might have ever guessed. Of loss, of pain. Of a legacy of failure and the price of history.

Skadi wiggled her hips free. "Don't worry. I know you immortals aren't known for fertility. We can try again tomorrow. As many times as it takes, really. I'm curious just how powerful your blood will be."

Loki shook his head in apparent disgust. Bah. As if the man hadn't enjoyed it.

Skadi snapped her fingers at the wood jotunn. "Bring it."

The other man disappeared, running off down the wooden bridge.

She turned back to Loki. "You see, I'm going to give you a choice. Pleasure, or pain. Venom, or the honey of my trench."

"Odin's going to kill you."

Skadi shrugged. "Pain for today then. Sooner or later, you too will swear a blood oath to me."

Three wood jotunnar came back in, bearing a thrashing

serpent between them. The creature was easily two dozen feet long. Snake-like, save for frills along the side of its head and a ridge running down its spine.

"Do you know what this is?"

Loki shuddered. "I have always known."

He had foreseen this? The thought left her almost speechless. She might have killed herself to avoid such a fate. "A serpent from Naströnd, of the very brood of Nidhogg, taken from the edge of Hel's domain."

Loki shut his eyes, seeming resigned.

Oh well. He might feel different after a night of it.

The wood jotunnar mounted the serpent above Loki, locking it in place with great thorned pinchers that clamped onto the walls. The thorns dug into the serpent's scales, piercing deeper the harder it thrashed.

In its furious hissing, its acidic venom dripped from its curving fangs. The acid fell over Loki's face, ran down his neck, his chest. It splashed on his shoulders. He roared in agony, flailing so wildly she half expected to hear his arms and legs snap.

The scent of burning flesh hit her, whetting her appetite.

Skadi clucked her tongue at Loki. Tomorrow, he'd make a different choice.

46

A great expanse of snow-covered plains stretched out far ahead of Odin and his party. To the south, the edge of a freezing sea washed over chunks of ice and sent them continually bumping into one another.

Odin had lost track of how long they had walked. Surely by now he must stand upon the cusp of winter. If not, he did not even want to imagine how cold this place must grow in those moons. A permanent layer of rime now seemed crusted over his clothes, his gear. His buckles oft seemed frozen solid such that he had to break them open to undress or even to take a piss.

Intuition told him to stay this course, but following the shore left his gut uneasy. As if something lurked out there in that dark sea. Something unknown and powerful beyond measure. A primal fear buried in the depths of his soul.

Geri and Freki cast furtive glances at the waters from time to time. Only once had Freki questioned Odin's choice to walk the shoreline, and, on finding Odin adamant, had let the issue drop. His children trusted him even to the exclusion of their own instincts. An honor and a gift they offered him, one not to be forgotten.

Today, at least, the wind had died down and the late afternoon sun shone above—what little broke through the mist.

"What if Utgard has no end?" Freki asked.

Odin cast a glance at his son but offered no answer.

Vafthrudnir might have lied, yes, but the Sight told Odin otherwise. Their destination lay still ahead. Further into the wilds.

"The better question," Geri said, "is if we are still in Jotunheim. We've seen little sign of jotunnar in the past fortnight. Maybe we've passed beyond their domains."

Freki groaned. "You know the legend, about what lies beyond Jotunheim ..."

Geri hugged herself and glared at her brother for bringing it up.

Odin knew it, too. The legend claimed Iormungandr, the World Serpent, dwelt in frozen seas, encircling Utgard and thus Midgard as well. A creature that bounded the entire Mortal Realm.

Its waking would mean the end of the world.

"I see something out on the water," Geri said after a moment.

Odin started from his musings, and followed where she pointed, squinting. Indeed, several dark forms bobbed up and down out there. He pulled to a stop and stared, trying to make them out. Too far, though.

Instead, he touched Valravn, and the vaettr sent out a raven, soaring above the sea. Through its eyes, Odin spied small vessels, long and pointed, wrapped in animal skins and suitable for a single occupant. Those within were men, ruddy-skinned and bundled in furs. They hauled up nets of fish and deposited them in crates draped over either side of their little boats.

"Fishermen," Odin said.

Freki grunted. "There's more ahead. Out on the ice."

Odin frowned. Going around these people would take them out of their way, and out of the course the Sight seemed to be pulling him on. Besides, they needed supplies. Maybe the locals would trade for silver. "Let's approach then, but cautiously."

Evening drew nigh by the time they reached the cluster of men. A small hut rested some distance away, made from snow bear skin and perhaps bone. The men had bored a hole into the ice over the sea and had knelt around this hole, chanting in some unintelligible dialect.

Almost unintelligible. A hint of recognition niggled at the back of Odin's mind, drawing him closer to these people. A memory, perhaps, of another lifetime, one where he knew more tongues of men. Meanings sat just beyond his reach, taunting him.

One of the men looked up sharply, paused in his chant and stared at Odin and his children.

With the setting sun behind them, it must have been hard to make out Odin's party.

Odin drew closer. Now all the men rose and stared at him, muttering to themselves. Something about *agloolik*. What did it mean? He knew that word. Did it mean his group? Strangers? If Odin could but draw upon those buried memories, he might make allies of these people.

One of them brandished something hung around his neck. A seal tooth? He expected a seal tooth to protect him?

"Agloolik!"

The others took up the chant, repeating the word over and over.

Appearing at dusk, perhaps they mistook Odin and his people for some kind of vaettir. "We are just men," he said, knowing they'd never understand.

"Agloolik!"

Odin reached inside his cloak to withdraw some silver coins.

Before he could even show them the wealth, two of the men had drawn knives that looked carved from bone.

A low growl escaped Freki.

"Leave it," Odin snapped. Those knives probably wouldn't pierce his mail. These people were frightened and he hadn't come here to kill humans.

"Agloolik!"

Odin knew that word. Too many lifetimes blurred inside his head, making it harder to separate out what memories came from where. But he knew this language ... from way back. "Protectors ..." he mumbled.

A dark form burst from the hole carved in the ice, splashing freezing water in all directions. The men leapt away from the creature. But they didn't continue to retreat. As if they had expected it.

Slick black skin, black eyes. A seal.

Freki snarled and the seal barked. And then the sea creature thrashed, twisting its form until it resembled something human.

Finfolk ... Agloolik. *Finfolk.*

The shifter lunged at Odin, moving much faster than a man. Caught in his musings, Odin couldn't react in time. The creature slammed him with the power of a horse, sending Odin flying backward. He crashed down onto the ice with enough force to send a spiderweb of cracks along it and leave him reeling.

Finfolk ... why had he thought them protectors? Didn't they prey on mankind? Steal wives and husbands?

Freki had cast aside his cloak and now tore off his shirt. He'd already begun to sprout fur as he dropped to all fours, snarling. Geri too had begun to strip.

The finfolk became a full seal once more and slid over the ice with surprising speed and grace, aiming for Freki.

Freki's shift finished. He snarled, shook himself clear of his fallen clothes, and leapt at the seal, jaws snapping.

"Amaruq!" one of the humans shouted.

Wolf ... night wolf.

The seal collided with Freki and both of them flipped over one another. Freki hit the ice sideways, skidded along, and struggled to regain his feet, looking half a fool.

Even as Geri—now shifted herself—closed in on the finfolk.

"Stop!" Odin shouted. Seized by the memory of another life, he repeated the command in the language of these Beringians. "Stop!"

The shifters did so, drawing up to square off against one another. Geri slowly circled Freki and the finfolk, clearly intending to leap in if the fighting resumed.

Blood had stained the ice. Blood from both Freki and his opponent. In the chaos, Odin hadn't seen those bites land, but Freki's leg was maimed.

"Peace," Odin said in their language.

"Amaruq," one of the others repeated.

"Take them to the angakkuq."

"Risk our qaygiq?"

So many unfamiliar words. So distant he couldn't pull them out.

"We cannot offend amaruq."

After a brief, bitter exchange, the Beringians reached

some agreement. One of them stepped forward and cocked his head off in the direction of the plains, away from the sea.

Freki whimpered. The varulf was losing a lot of blood.

Not taking his eyes off the strangers, Odin knelt and hefted the wolf into his arms, drawing on his pneuma to give himself strength and stamina.

The Beringians led them not to the hut, as Odin had first suspected, but farther into the night.

❧

THE QAYGIQ, as they called it, turned out to be a large home dug into the snow, deep, forming an underground dwelling. A pair of lamps that smelled of whale blubber lit the place, and a stone-lined fire kept things warm enough that Odin shed his cloak.

The longer these people spoke, the more their words took hold of his mind. Odin laid Freki on the wooden floor. Their angakkuq was a shaman, different from a sorcerer only insofar as shamans did not normally bind vaettir.

The man, a wrinkled elder who'd seen a great many winters and yet still wore no beard, applied a poultice to the wolf's leg. While Freki would almost certainly have recovered without aid given his nature, aught that sped the healing process would prove a boon. They had spent too long already in this trek.

Events in Midgard were proceeding without Odin being able to see them clearly much less control them. Something had gone wrong with Fitela, but Odin could not clearly see what—only that it portended ill for Sigmund, Odin's most valuable piece on the tafl board. A niggling sense warned him of other dangers he could not see, too far off to send Huginn or Muninn. It was like a blindness had settled upon him, one which he'd never felt in his youth, for it represented senses he'd never before known he had.

"There is strong silla in you," the angakkuq said. Odin glanced at him. He hadn't even realized the man had turned to stare at him. "It gives you power. It gives you destiny."

Pneuma. He meant pneuma. "Thank you for helping my ... friend." Explaining that Freki was his son would have only served to raise other questions.

"Amaruq is strong. Dangerous and wild, but sometimes beneficent. This is what I do. Propitiate the spirits of all things. Without balance, humanity would perish, swept away in storm."

Geri had settled down beside her brother, hand upon him while he slept.

One of the other Beringians brought Odin a steaming fish in a wooden bowl. Nodding his thanks, he greedily tore into it, heedless of the hot scales singing his fingers. The wolves had hunted for food, but none so succulent or well cooked as this.

When he had finished, he licked his fingers. Geri too had scarfed down the fish and begun sucking the bone.

"Amaruq hunts alone," the angakkuq said, frowning at Geri. "I do not know what it portends, two at once."

Odin sucked the last oils from his forefinger. "They're twins."

At that, the angakkuq merely cocked his head.

"I need to find a mountain to the east. A powerful vaettr ... a spirit, it dwells there, in an icy abyss."

The man frowned, then looked away.

"Please."

Now the shaman grumbled something. "Diineezi. The dead spirits grow restless there and no man dares walk."

"I must."

"It is the tallest peak. If you travel east, and do not stray too far north or south, you'll reach the range. Amid them you find it. But you should not travel there. Those few who return, they say they saw things. Things man was not meant to see."

Odin stroked his beard and looked to Freki. The varulf should be ready to travel by morning. And Odin could waste no more time. "Whether meant to or not, I must see these things. I have to see … everything."

*L*ight snowfall dusted an already frost-drenched Rijnland. Winter would be bitter this year, a völva had told Sigmund. The frost jotunnar were angry, so the woman claimed. Perhaps she was mad, but certainly a chill had settled over the kingdom.

Still, cold bothered Sigmund less than it did other men. Another blessing of his nature, but one that came at the cost of a certain wanderlust. Alone, he strolled along the Rijn's banks, even though dusk had settled in and most people had begun to flee the mist.

It wouldn't do to practice these walks too oft. Men would talk, think him already mist-mad or perhaps even guess his secret. Sigmund had taken pains to conceal his and Fitela's natures as varulfur from his host. Men didn't understand such things and they rightfully feared aught to do with the Otherworlds.

Once, every so oft, though, he had to walk. Sometimes even, when no one was around to see his speed, he'd run. On a few occasions, he'd taken a small boat across the river and made for the Myrkvidr, and there taken the form of wolf and run with freedom and grace men could never fathom.

A bitter breeze swept over the river, following its course toward the sea. The breeze carried with it the scents of men and beast and ... Fitela.

Sigmund turned as his son came loping toward him, running too fast for a man and paying too little heed to if anyone noticed. True, few remained out-of-doors now, but it was hardly midnight either. "Something's happened," he said when Fitela finally paused, panting before him.

"I ... I killed a man." Sigmund's son rested his palms on his knees, chest heaving like he'd run a score of miles already. Perhaps he had.

"You've killed a great many men. What of it?"

"His father has demanded weregild. A high weregild."

Sigmund scowled. "You mean you killed a noble, and not in war, I take it. Oh, Fitela, you should have learned to check your passions. But, yes, you need not ask. I will pay—"

"It was Elof Hildebrandson."

Sigmund faltered. "Borghild's *brother*? Odin's spear, boy!" He cuffed Fitela on the back of the head. "Are you mist-mad? Do you have any idea what this will mean?"

"I ..."

"What happened?" Sigmund demanded.

"We quarreled over a woman in Menzlin. We'd had much mead, the both of us, and I ... he tried to wrestle me."

Not knowing Fitela was a varulf. And Sigmund's son had clearly killed Hildebrand's son with his bare hands.

"Get inside the hall," Sigmund snapped. "Speak to no one of this. I will deal with it."

BORGHILD FAIR TREMBLED WITH RAGE, her mouth quivering. Though tears welled in her eyes, they refused to shed themselves, as if unwilling to show even that much weakness before him.

Sigmund wrung his hands. "It is done, wife. It cannot be undone."

"Your son is a murderer." She didn't shout. Just that quiet, slow voice.

Fitela surely was, but then, so was Sigmund, and so was Borghild's own son Helgi. Such was the way of men at arms. One couldn't get ahead without shedding blood. Hardly what the woman needed to hear at the moment though. "I've lost brothers. I know your pain." Not knowing what else to say, Sigmund fell silent.

Borghild bared her teeth like she might leap over and bite him. "I will not ask you to execute your son. But you must at a minimum banish him from Hunaland forever. I will not deign to look upon the beast."

It was like a blow to the gut. Years of staring down foes, of pain and fighting, they had taught him to weather such a blow without flinching. "I will not. Fitela fought his whole life to regain this home and to help us unify Hunaland. Under no circumstances will I even consider a plan that would deny him what he so fought for."

"You deny me justice."

Sigmund shook his head. "You seek justice? I have never before paid weregild to any man, but I'll pay your father what price he names. Even I will pay *you* what weregild you name. But Fitela is free to go where he pleases."

His wife trembled anew, clearly considering and discarding several tacts. "You must decide what is fitting, my *king*."

Sigmund nodded. "Then I will throw a grand funeral for

Elof. All will come from miles around to see his pyre ship sail upon the Rijn. Even Odin himself must take note of the honor I'll bestow upon your brother."

If that satisfied Borghild, she gave little indication. Instead, she simply turned and left.

❦

As Sigmund had promised, great men and women did come to see the burning of Elof Hildebrandson. Warriors from Menzlin and a troop of shieldmaidens. King Garth and Prince Hildebrand, their expressions unreadable as their kin was laid upon the pyre ship. Jarls and housecarls and tradesmen, singing songs to call valkyries in the hopes one would carry Elof to Valhalla.

The burning ship smoldered through the mist like a fading candle vanishing and leaving them all in darkness. Sigmund could not take his eyes off it. The death of the prince's son would become a festering rot in Sigmund's united Hunaland, of that he had no doubt. The weregild would appease law and honor, yes, but how could Hildebrand ever forget the death of his son? How could any man?

Odin's spear, Sigmund needed some damn mead. He needed great swathes of it. The days ahead would grow dark before light returned. His dreams of peace already seemed to slip through his fingers as if he'd tried to grasp morning dew.

The songs died out as the last glow of the ship disappeared into the mist. Somewhere, at the bottom of the great river, it would lie among other such wrecks. Elof's ashes would, perhaps, be carried all the way to the Morimarusa and spread out across the sea. No man could ask for a greater funeral.

But it still might not prove enough.

❦

NEITHER THE ROASTED reindeer nor the skald's poems could shake Sigmund from his melancholy. Fitela had always proved impetuous, but never before seemed such a fool. Perhaps the varulf passions guided his actions that day, but still, a man of such cunning ought to have known better. Sigmund would not send his son into exile, no, but still his wife's request tempted him.

Damn the man. Should have known better.

Sigmund rested at the head of the largest of the tables, *almost* drunk enough to ignore the biting looks King Garth cast him across the length of that table. The crush of raucous men and women, along with the skald's yammering on about the glories of King Gylfi—guilt hardly ate at Sigmund for that murder any longer—at least served to prevent him from having to share words with the Menzlin king or his son.

For now. For one night.

A slave girl brought another horn of mead around and Sigmund drank deep, chugging until he had to come up gasping for air. Already, the room had taken on a fresh rosy glow, a warmth and light that still failed to alleviate his moods.

Fitela slunk through the crowds, face grim, before finally coming to sit at the vacant seat to Sigmund's right.

Sigmund fixed the boy with a hard glare. "Somewhat ... this lays ... at your feet."

"Some? Or all, Father?" Fitela bowed his head.

A cry went up, men cheering as a pair of shieldmaidens wrestled on the far side of the hall. Sigmund craned his neck but couldn't catch sight of it without standing. And he lacked the will to stand, even if he could have done so without swaying in place and looking a fool.

A little more drink and maybe he wouldn't care about that, either.

Borghild came around, her lips pressed tight, bearing a drinking horn herself. A peace offering. Good. It was good.

"Drink now, my stepson," she said, offering the horn to Fitela.

Fitela took the horn, then scrunched up his nose. "I ... It smells like it's gone sour, Stepmother."

Sigmund rolled his eyes and snatched the horn away from his son. "Now you're timid, boy? No mead is bad mead." He threw back the horn and drained it all. The sweet honey settled warmly into his gut, helping to dull the throb of tensions building in his head. Never enough to kill it all.

Everything was morning dew ...

"I'll get you another then," Borghild said.

Sigmund waved her away.

"Look here," he said to Fitela. "You have to ... ingrate ... in ... ugh ..."

"Ingratiate myself with the royals of Menzlin? I've tried, Father. They don't wish to see me. We might have to replace them with a more malleable line."

Sigmund slapped the table, drawing nearby eyes to gaze on him. He flushed then waved them all away. "Good idea, son," he said loudly, before leaning in close to Fitela. "I'll hear no such ... treachery. They're ... allies."

Borghild returned with another horn and offered it to Fitela. "Why let your father have all the mead? Come drink, and let us have peace with one another."

Again, the boy sniffed the horn. "Treachery ...?"

"Are you a true Volsung?" the queen demanded. "Cowering and refusing to drink?"

"Poison, Stepmother? At first I wasn't sure, but now ... the scent is off."

"Bah!" Sigmund said. "Just strain it ... through your ... mustache. Seeing treachery ... everywhere. Make me think ... you want more war."

Frowning, Fitela stared at the horn. He glanced to his stepmother, who stood with her arms folded over her chest. Then Fitela threw back the horn and drained it all. He swallowed, belched, then returned the horn to her. "Thank you, Stepmother." The man turned to Sigmund, opened his mouth, then shut it. He blinked. Snarled, drawing the eyes of all around.

Fitela jerked one way and then the other, showed his teeth. Another snarl escaped him. He slumped forward and slammed his right cheek on the table, scattering plates and sending guests scrambling backward.

"Fitela?" Sigmund asked, a sudden awareness biting through his drunkenness like a hot brand in his mind. "Son?"

Fitela convulsed, then pitched over, off the table and sideways off the bench.

Sigmund dashed to his side. Or tried. He tripped over his own feet, caught his ankles around his chair, and came crashing down beside his son.

Dazed, he blinked.

Found himself staring into open, vacant eyes.

White foam oozed out of Fitela's gaping mouth.

HE REMEMBERED RETCHING. Great heaving oceans of mead

billowing up out of his guts. A deluge of all he'd eaten and drunk that night.

He remembered his head pounding. He remembered cradling Fitela's head in his lap, screaming for his firstborn son. For the last memento he had of Sieglinde, his beloved twin sister. He remembered men and women clustering around him.

Cries of distress. A völva came and declared Fitela poisoned.

He remembered all those men and women around him being shadows. Strangers in darkness, when only he and his son lay in fading light.

Sigmund blinked tears from his eyes.

Fitela's body cradled in his arms, Sigmund trudged through the night, toward the river. A crescent moon reflected off the waters, shimmering and empty.

On the shore, a woman rested in a small boat, one lit with but a tiny torch. Her build and sword identified her as a shieldmaiden, but she ought not to have been out alone in the mist. In truth, Sigmund was past caring about such things.

The woman rose as Sigmund drew nigh. "Shall I give passage to the sea?"

Sigmund nodded glumly. Yes, his son ought to have the same peace granted to Elof. At least as much ...

"The boat cannot carry you both, so you'll have to wait here."

Indeed, it was a tiny craft, really intended for but one person.

"I ... I'll stay here all night if needs be. Carry him to the sea, then return for me. I must ... I must find a grand ship for him." His words stuck in his throat until he felt he could choke on them.

The woman simply nodded, and took Fitela from Sigmund's arms, giving no sign of struggling under the man's weight. She laid Fitela's body in the base of her boat, then shoved off the beach with an oar.

The rowboat drifted toward the river's center, caught the current, and began to float off into the mist. Then all at once, it faded away, as if it and the woman, too, had been naught but mist.

With a sudden, inevitable certainty, Sigmund knew. Fitela was gone forever.

The woman would not return.

And still he waited until dawn. He stood there, staring into the mist, eyes burning after all his tears were spent.

His son. Taken not in glorious battle nor claimed by the sea, but betrayed.

By his own stepmother.

❧

A COLDNESS SETTLED upon Sigmund's heart. A mound of glacial ice that slowly spread outward, filling his limbs and his head with bitter numbness.

Of course, what else remained?

And so he told Keld what the queen had done. And the thegn reached for his axe.

But Sigmund shook his head. "Tell the people. Let them drive her out, into the Myrkvidr. I want her to meet her end alone and frightened. Running through darkness and knowing something dogs her every step."

As he commanded, Keld saw it done.

Sigmund watched, as his wife—his murdering, treacherous wife—fled through the fields, clothes torn and bleeding from a dozen gashes inflicted upon her by those who learned of her crimes. But Keld kept the townsfolk from killing her.

That honor would belong to Sigmund himself.

The sun would set. The moon would rest.

And as a wolf, he would stalk the murderer of his son. He knew all too well her scent, and, bleeding, she could not disguise it even had she known he was coming. She would run.

She would hide.

She would *scream* as his howls echoed through the night.

And he would tear her limb from bloody limb, her torment becoming a dirge for Fitela.

The last gift Sigmund could offer his son.

48

*A*nother moon, or nigh to it, Odin and his children traveled, drawing ever closer to the frozen peaks ahead. Those mountains had come into view long before they reached them, jutting up out of the mist, behemoths in a wild untouched by man.

And, as the shaman had predicted, they had seen no sign of people on the long trek. Snow bears and reindeer-like beasts and mammoths aplenty, but of civilization, naught.

Now, at last at the foot of those mountains, they stood dwarfed and awed by what lay before them.

Even Geri had fallen silent, offering no jests nor complaints, just staring up at the gut-clinchingly massive impasse blocking their way forward.

Beyond those first peaks, Odin could just make out another, rising up higher than any other. Somewhere amid that mountain, a root of Yggdrasil fed a well that would finally offer him the answers he needed.

Odin looked over his varulf children and they both met his gaze.

Without a word between them, they set out.

§

ODIN'S BREATH froze in the air before his face as he stood, staring up at the greatest peak amid these mountains. Winter had begun to settle in here. Every night, the fire seemed more difficult to light. The storms would come soon and, if they found no shelter, they'd freeze on these slopes.

Unburied and unsent, perhaps they'd rise as draugar, damned to haunt a land empty of mankind. Would they then sleep away eternity, waiting for something to rouse them, as had the draugar of Thule before Gylfi's ill-fated expedition?

Such musings served no purpose, of course. All they could do now was press on and trust to Odin's instincts to guide them to shelter when the need arose. It was too late to turn back in any event.

§

GRUNTING IN FRUSTRATION, Odin jerked his walking stick free from a snow drift where it sunk down nigh two feet deep. Footing grew more and more precarious the further up they traveled.

The cold had so bitten his face he could no longer feel his ears or nose. It tore at him like flame, and still it perturbed him less than the incessant, howling wind. Like a scream out of Niflheim, the wail followed them up every challenging step. It chased them, haunted them, promising the peril of winter unlike aught they could imagine.

Geri caught Odin's arm and helped him up onto an ice-coated rock. No paths ran up this Diineezi mountain. Sometimes, they had don crampons and scale nigh sheer sides. Other times, they had to climb from one wind-sharpened rock surface to the next, careful to avoid shredding the furs keeping them alive.

Odin had sent Hrist up there to scout ahead.

She had not returned.

❧

DUSK DESCENDED with a swiftness that stole Odin's breath. The days here grew shorter and shorter. It gave them so little time to find a way forward.

They stood upon a shelf of ice the size of a jarl's hall, though not quite level. From here, he could actually look *down* on most of the other mountains. And still Diineezi rose higher.

After Hrist had vanished, Odin dared not send Huginn or Muninn ranging more than a few hundred feet ahead. Indeed, the icy winds seemed apt to freeze even the ravens to death in the space of moments.

Now, despite the chill and the growing darkness, he had no choice but to send them scouting again. They needed a place to take shelter and they needed it immediately.

The ravens soon took flight and began soaring in expanding circles, searching for a cave, an overhang, an alcove—aught that might cut down on the wind and allow him to kindle a fire with what few supplies remained to them.

Odin concentrated on seeing through their eyes, only half aware as Geri circled him in obvious distress.

There.

A large rock formation jutted up at an odd angle,

enough that they might pile under it and cut down on the worst of the elements.

"Father ..."

Odin jerked himself free of Valravn's sight and turned to her.

"Something foul dwells on these slopes."

Varulfur, as hosts to vaettir, had a sense of the Penumbra, even if they could not directly look into it. Odin, on the other hand, *could* look. He embraced the Sight. Sure enough, shades drifted along the mountainside, wailing in wordless agony, making slow, pointless circuits around the slopes.

As he opened himself up to that realm, one of the closest ones suddenly turned, looked right at him.

They can see you.

Odin didn't need Audr to remind him that looking into the Penumbra ran both ways. He dropped the Sight before the ghost decided to accost him, then started for the rock. "There are many foul things out here."

You saw the ones beyond ...

Tattered shrouds over tattered souls. Wraiths. Caught in eternal torment, so eager to share their suffering.

Existence is suffering. A vile cycle of sin and despair to feed dark powers and perpetuate darkness. We are all dead ...

Odin grimaced, pushing on toward that formation. They all needed to get out of this wind.

They found the place shortly beyond the ice shelf, though it actually meant climbing a bit down once more. Odin hopped down onto a slope five feet below, then scurried up under the rock.

Snows had piled deep here, probably eliminating any hope of starting a fire. Could they dig down to dirt?

They'd have to try. The apples rendered them resistant

to the mist, but still, breathing it in all night might not end well for their bodies, minds, or souls. Assuming the cold didn't kill them.

When he explained his plan, Geri and Freki immediately set to digging. They piled great walls of snow around the rock's edge, slowly forming a wall to shelter them from the worst of it.

Odin helped them as best he could, though he lacked their speed. Still, every bit would help.

❧

LEGS FOLDED BENEATH HIM, arms resting on his knees, Odin reached out with his mind, searching for Hrist. Despite the warmth of their tiny fire, a coldness settled into his soul, an empty void as if one bound to him had simply ceased to exist.

Given the wraiths Odin had seen on the slopes around this mountain, Odin could guess why. He could guess, he could imagine it, see it in his mind's eye, as the dire ghosts latched onto the valkyrie. As they devoured her soul and left her naught but a hollow shell of her former self. But did he see the truth, or his mind's manifestation of his worst fears?

Either way, the valkyrie now seemed beyond his reach.

It was the risk any who pierced the Veil took.

And his children ... the varulfur had curled up together to sleep. Exhausted. His children. They'd come here for him, to ensure he made it. They'd wanted to protect him. But maybe he had to protect them, too.

Shifters had their souls bonded to Moon vaettr. Just how close was that bond? Could a wraith reach across the Veil and touch a varulf?

Does it frighten you?

Yes. It frightened him more than most else he could imagine. Years with Audr inside him had taught him the depths of hatred that consumed wraiths. Sometimes, they could pull themselves partly across the Veil and harm the living. Beings like Odin's varulf twins might be more at risk, and he could not trust Audr to tell him the truth on the matter.

Their alliance remained uneasy at best.

You always delve into darkness beyond your ken ...

They are in danger, Valravn said. *Much as you are, when you touch the other realms with your mind.*

That all but settled it then.

Odin would leave the twins here to rest and, he dared hope, remain hidden from the wraiths. The birds, too, he'd have to leave behind, before they froze to death.

He would set out with naught but himself and his walking stick.

And the madness eating away at your writhing soul ...

And yes, the voices in his head.

Odin took a long look over his children. He'd raised them from babes as though they were his own. They *were* his own.

Maybe the way ahead would cost him much. Either way, he couldn't risk them. Never them.

Slowly, careful to make no sound, he rose and edged his way to the small gap in the snow wall. He'd leave now, before first light.

They could no doubt track him if they so chose. He'd have to trust they'd understand why he'd leave them behind. To hope they would trust in him.

DAWN BROKE over the mountain with a nigh blinding glare. Sunlight reflected off the ice and snow as though off a field of diamonds, obscuring all before Odin as he climbed up onto a glacial shelf.

This he followed a ways, trudging over snows. The sound of running water—inexplicably unfrozen—greeted him even before he caught sight of a stream running down from the mountain. The current swept by like the rushing wind, too fast to freeze, perhaps. This stream he followed another half an hour. The roar of water grew louder the longer he walked.

Until, at last, before him a chasm split the glacier, a jagged scar sliced along it for hundreds of feet. The stream pitched over it in a fall that disappeared down into a curtain of luminous mist.

Odin blew out a long breath that frosted the air. This was it. He'd made it.

He followed the edge of the gap some distance before catching sight of the massive root jutting from the wall below him. The root itself was twice as thick around as most trees. It rent through the ice of the glacier, leaving great cracks spreading outward for dozens of feet. It twisted and wormed across the chasm at irregular angles before breaking through the ice on the opposite side.

If Odin dropped down onto it, would he have somewhere else to go?

The rising mist obscured whatever lay beneath that root. It hid everything down there.

Which left Odin only one choice, really.

He embraced the Sight.

The Penumbra slipped into focus, the mist in the Material Realm now seeming a slight fog that blurred rather than concealed what lay beyond. A hint of light permeated the shadows of this realm, allowing him to make out another root—or the same one, more likely—breaking through the ice once more below the first.

A way to travel deeper.

Odin glanced around. Other ghosts flitted about the glacier, and while none had noticed him as yet, some twisted shades might well have been wraiths.

Beckon them …

The longer he dawdled, the greater the chance Audr would get his wish.

That first root had to be thirty feet down.

Odin had not come all this way, crossed Midgard and Utgard both, only to surrender at the cusp of victory.

He blew out another breath, then jumped down to the root. For a gasping, gut-wrenching moment, he was falling. The root rushed up at him like a striking predator. It slammed into him with enough force to steal his feet out from under him and blast the wind from his lungs.

He landed wrong, pitched over sideways barely in control of his body. The roll carried him half off the root. Odin flailed, trying to steady himself. That only sent him careening over the side. He snatched hold of fibers jutting from the root as he fell. Their rough skin scraped his hands raw, but he managed to pull himself to a stop.

Flooding pneuma into his limbs abated the rapidly growing burning in his arms.

Odin glanced down. The next root was twenty feet below. But not perfectly lined up with him. He'd need to—

A giant severed head appeared within arm's reach of Odin.

Odin's grip faltered and he plummeted down. Screaming, he twisted, managing to slam shoulder-first into the lower root.

His scream continued to echo off the glacial walls even as Odin struggled to pull himself up onto the root.

The ghastly head—itself bigger than Odin's torso—drifted down until it drew even with Odin. The head had long gray hair that mingled with his beard, all of it seeming to flow as if underwater. The eyes held a faint blue luminescence that seemed to bore right into Odin's soul. Red, angry flesh peeled away where the head had obviously been severed from a large body.

A ghostly head.

Odin was looking into the Penumbra.

Loki had claimed Mimir died … Died. Decapitation had that effect on most things.

"Mimir?" Odin mouthed, pushing himself up on his elbows.

"Destroyer." The head spoke the Northern tongue with a strange, hollow accent that seemed to come as much from the glacier as the ghost itself. "Violator or paragon of the march of time. Trespasser in lands where none yet walk."

Odin rose to his knees. He glanced around. Another twenty feet below, a hot spring bubbled, steam mingling with mist as it rose. The spring was set in a cavern of blue and green stone beneath the glacier. The root Odin rested upon twisted around and around before finally touching down on the edge of the waters. Feeding them or drinking from them, or both, Odin could not say.

"I must drink from the well," Odin said, finally regaining his feet.

The ghost chuckled. "Of course, you do. History must unfold in its pitiless procession. It will take from you all you are."

Odin grimaced. "History, or the well?"

"Yes … If you would drink to see, you must offer something of equal value in return. All things have their price." The hollow echoes banged against the glacier and reverberated inside Odin's head. Did Mimir, disembodied as he was, actually have any ability to stop Odin from doing as he wished in the Mortal Realm?

He might.

Powerful enough ghosts could enforce their wills with dire powers, and Odin could take no chance of being denied. Not now, not after all he'd been through to reach this place. Thor had suffered a terrible injury and more like than not ignited a more heated war with Jotunheim. Hrist was probably dead—if her very soul had not been consumed. And if Odin failed to recover her ring, he'd have permanently lost one of his valkyries. And he still had to get his varulf twins back to Midgard.

"Name your price," he snapped.

"What holds more value to you than sight itself? Therefore, to gain sight, you must lose sight."

Odin blanched. "What does that even mean?"

Mimir winked at him.

Vile ghost seemed to take pleasure in confounding Odin.

There are so few pleasures left to the dead ...

It crawled into his mind then, the slow burrowing of prescient insight, the intuition that told him the only price Mimir would accept. A price demanded by urd itself, perhaps, for Odin could see himself, gouging out his left eye. Screaming in agony as he dug it free and flung it into the well.

Sight for sight.

A drink of the wisdom behind the veil of his own eye.

The pain to come hit him, brought him down to his knees.

Madness ... let him turn away from this. To do such a thing to himself, to so maim his own body, it defied all instinct. This much could be expected of no man. Such a sacrifice exceeded all bounds.

Unable to form a coherent plea, Odin implored Mimir with wordless entreaties. He knelt there, silently begging the ghost to spare him this price. He saw himself imploring, outside himself, unable to move forward or back, caught in the merciless web of urd. Its threads closed in around him from all angles, stripping choice and leaving him ravaged.

And knowing, with bile-inducing certainty, Mimir could not have withdrawn the price had he wished to. Time itself was the ultimate predator. The pitiless procession of history, as Mimir had claimed.

We are forged by agonies.

Volund had told Odin as much, before Odin had even known the Well of Mimir existed.

The more we suffer, the stronger we become.

Everything had its price. Even knowledge. Especially knowledge.

Odin must drink in suffering to fortify his soul for the struggle ahead. It would not be his last sacrifice. This he knew with the unerring dread of prescient foresight.

A price must be paid for every gain, a hefty weight for each wisdom. Sight for sight, breath for breath.

Sight for sight ... The Norns had told him that—five decades ago they had warned him this day would come. It had trod closer and closer with each passing breath. He had always been heading here, to the abyss of despair and wisdom.

His knife was in his hand. He didn't remember drawing it. He was watching himself as it rose slowly to his face.

Let him turn away from this. It was madness. It was inhuman.

It was urd.

Could he cast the knife aside and welcome Ragnarok and all the death it would entail?

No.

His eyelid kept closing of its own accord as he drew the knife closer. Closer. It had to stay open. The future demanded it. History must unfold. If mankind had any chance, no sacrifice was too great.

The blade had drawn so nigh he could no longer see the point.

Do it.

Do it and have done with it.

Do it.

Do it!

Odin wedged the knife into his eye.

Pain, unlike aught he'd ever imagined surged through him. It exploded through his head like a gong. It ripped him apart from the inside out. Until, unable to bear it a heart-beat longer nor yet able to risk losing consciousness, he found himself watching the ensuing performance. A shadow play enacted before him. A man digging out the tendrils behind his own eye. A macabre spectacle of ulti-mate suffering.

We are forged by agonies.

And wracked with unspeakable agonies, a man might thus become something more than a man. Something closer to the god which others worshipped him as.

The coursing, burning, brain-melting torment slammed back into Odin as he knelt, gasping in horror, staring at his own bloody eye in his palm. It mocked him, a sick memento of light he would never again gaze unto.

Slowly, unable to catch his breath, Odin turned his palm sideways. Until his eye pitched down into the well. A faint splash, barely audible over the bubbling of the hot spring.

To one side, utter blackness filled his vision. The other wobbled, in an unsteady haze as he lost his hold upon the Sight.

Unable to steady himself, Odin pitched over sideways, plummeting down into the well himself.

Water almost hot enough to scald him crashed all around him. It seared and burned his hollow eye socket. It shot up his nose. It flowed over him in a wake of bubbles that made sight from his remaining eye impossible.

With a sputtering gasp, he broke the surface, sucking down great gulps of spring water in the process.

Choking, Odin swam toward the rock lip surrounding the spring. He flung himself half out of the waters and collapsed, lacking the strength to pull his limp body another foot. The hot water churned in his gut, roiling and twisting, sending cramps shooting through his whole lower body.

That maelstrom began to rise inside him, a swirling tightness gushing through his chest. Closing in around his heart. Crushing it within.

Drawing higher. Closing off his airways.

Settling in on his brain.

It washed over his consciousness like a great wave, crashing over his mind. Drowning him in a sea of memories. Past and present and future all bled together in an ocean that threatened to wash away all he was.

A rooster's crow, a last call to a final end. The close of the age of man.

As if drawn by that cry, Odin's hands closed around Loki's throat. Squeezed the life from his brother. The man wouldn't die. So instead, he was bound within the bowels of the Earth, locked in torment. Knowing ... knowing the end was coming ever closer.

The gates of Hel opened ... The legions of the dead flying free ...

So many dead. So many whom Odin had cared for, staring accusation at him. Thor, and Tyr, and Sif, and all the others ... their cries of torment bombarding him and drowning him. Damning him.

A ship of bone and nails cut through misty seas, its bow riding great waves. An army of gleaming red eyes filled its hull. Drawing toward the world of men.

A shift, a bloody field.

Fenrir.

The varulf lord flying through the air, lunging at Odin. His jaws closing around Odin's throat. Squeezing the life from Odin's frail body. Tearing out neck and spine in one feral movement. A fleeting glimpse of his own headless body as he died.

A crack split through Yggdrasil. A tremble that shook boughs and branches and sent a hundred thousand leaves drifting away into the void. The dead numbering beyond all counting.

Fires raged over the plains. Men and horses turned to ash. Whole cities burned away to cinders that blew upon a scorching wind. From amidst the infernos, a shadow loomed. The march of fire jotunnar, the earth itself trembling before their fury.

"We never stopped Ragnarok ..." Thor said. "I tried ..." Odin's son lay dying, bloody, pale.

Beyond him stretched the corpse of a vast sea monster, one reaching out beyond the horizon. A dragon beyond all others.

And there, torn to pieces, lay Tyr.

All you build will turn to ash, your children shall die, and your dreams shall burn.

The Odling ghost's words were never a curse, but a prophecy. A portent of Ragnarok to come.

৯৯

WHEN ALL TIME BECOMES ONE, the passage of it becomes meaningless. Odin thus could not say whether he lay on the well's edge for an hour, a day, or a lifetime.

The overwhelming surge of visions that bombarded him now stole all semblance of humanity from his grasp. Vague prescient instincts clarified into horrifying visions of the future. Dead dragons ... dead jotunnar ... dead men ... dead gods.

Dead children.

The wrath of Hel in its ceaseless fury became a crystalline mirror, a foretelling of the breaking of all chains. All, save the chains of urd itself. The one master not even gods could defy.

Loki had called prescience the most complex of all burdens. How much the pyromancer knew, how much he'd foreseen, perhaps no longer mattered. What mattered was the terrible, final realization of how utterly true his words had been.

No burden could compare to the weight of knowing the future and finding oneself bound to it, unable to deviate from a course no matter how vile it seemed.

Now, saddled with that burden, Odin knew what he must do. Embrace urd.

And embrace the profound self-loathing it demanded.

PART III

———

Year 51, Age of the Aesir
Summer
(One and a half years later)

49

*J*ust after dusk, Gudrun crawled along the upper side of the tree bridge, hardly daring to breathe for fear her captors would spot her. A cluster of the wood jotunnar milled about below, grunting in their guttural language. She caught bits and pieces of it, remnants from her time possessed by Skadi.

The frost jotunn herself had left, gone back to Thrymheim intent to press her alliance. Those below, they prepared for war. Skadi seemed as if she meant to lead them against another jotunn tribe, though Gudrun couldn't tell who.

It hardly mattered. What mattered was, they remained distracted.

They'll come for you, Snegurka said in her mind.

She wants it ... Irpa said. *She likes their wooden rods jammed deep inside ...*

Gudrun ground her teeth, trying to block out the vaet-tir's inane babble.

How many can she handle at once ...

She sucked a breath in, then grimaced at the sound.

They kept crawling around in her mind. Slithering through her insides like eels. Slurping, lurching, *squeezing*.

Use the Art ...

Oh! Use it and fall prey to them. They were so close now. Even a little more use of their power and she risked losing herself, becoming a vessel to one of these things.

You will be ...

No!

No. She would never, *never* let that happen again.

No. No. No. No. No.

No one resists forever ... to have power and not use it in the depths of desperation ...

She'll fail.

She's always failed ...

Barely managing not to moan, she pressed her palms against her temples. Fuck them. They could both rot in the wastes of Niflheim.

We all rot ...

Gudrun blinked. Shook herself, then pressed lower atop the wooden bridge. A little further. The rough bark scraped her palms raw. It scratched her knees and face. Minor annoyances, incomparable to the torments Skadi had encouraged these jotunnar to inflict on her. The snow maiden's cruelty knew no bounds.

There are no bounds to cruelty.

Compassion is the lie we tell ourselves ... to avoid the truth ... the world owes us naught but suffering ...

Gudrun ground her teeth. Just a little farther.

She edged her way along the top a few more feet, then dared to peer over the side. More wood jotunnar walking right below her. All scurrying about, making ready with bows and spears.

A little ahead, and below her, an opening separated the

wooden sinews—a crude window to allow light in. Come on. She could do this.

They'll catch you …

They'll break your legs again.

Shove their coarse, bark-like cocks up your trench …

That's what she wants.

She wants punishment …

Hel, she wanted to scream at the voices. Naught seemed able to shut them up. Trembling, she edged forward a little farther. The window lay below her. She reached a hand toward it. Couldn't quite reach the—

Her grip slipped. She pitched sideways, scraping her face over the bark. She whimpered in pain but caught herself on the lip of the opening. The sudden stop yanked on her shoulders and she dangled there, one foot in open air, the other kicking at the side of the bridge. Struggling to find purchase.

Finally, she wedged her toes into a crevice, giving herself a little footing.

Panting, she glanced down. None of jotunnar below had looked up at her. She was dangling maybe thirty feet over them. Above her lay the window. Now that she looked at it … she wasn't quite sure she could fit through it.

A fool …

Always a foolish child. Lost in the mist.

Floundering in the darkness …

No. She wasn't giving up now. She wedged her shoulder through, then tried to fit her head. Her skull caught on the bark. Almost. But not quite.

She should have known.

Just jump … maybe break your neck …

Groaning with the pain, Gudrun kept pushing her head through. Fibers ripped open her chin and tore into the back of her skull. It caught her hair and yanked it out by the roots. Blood dribbled over her face, stung her eyes. All she could do was keep her teeth gritted to stop from crying out in pain.

And then her head popped through the opening. She couldn't see a damned thing though. Her body blocked the light source. Just keep wiggling and she'd squeeze through, eventually.

Just keep …

A loud hiss greeted her, dangerously close to her face.

What in the gates of Hel?

Oh, she is lost now …

Some vile serpent here lurks.

Go back, little girl …

Gudrun choked on her own scream. More hissing. So close. They warned her to go back. But there was no going back. She'd never get her head out again. She had to move forward. Even if whatever made that sound killed her. Hel. Oh, Hel.

Holding her breath, she wriggled through the opening. As her hips dropped through, she fell, pitched forward weightless for a heartbeat. Then smacked face-first into a wooden floor.

The impact filled her eyes with white and left her dazed.

It took her a moment before she could even roll over. She was lucky she hadn't broken her neck like that. Gudrun blinked. The moonlight streamed in from the window, offering pale shadows. Above her, Loki stood bound hand and foot, staring at her. And a serpent was chained above him, hissing and spitting venom.

Acid scorch marks trailed all over Loki's chest and back and abdomen, in some cases exposing muscle beneath. A handful of rivulets had burned their way down his face. Part of his cheek looked so thin she half expected to be able to see through it in better light.

"By the goddess ..."

Impossible as it seemed, Loki's expression actually darkened. "What are you doing here?"

"I ... I'm going to rescue you. And you're going to help me escape Jotunheim."

Loki shuddered, coughed. "How are you going to get me out of this? Wood has *grown* over my hands and feet."

Gudrun grimaced, then drew a stone dagger from beneath her dress. Stealing that had proved challenging. It was sized for a jotunn, meaning for her it was almost as large as a small sword. She'd hoped to break whatever fetters bound Loki. Perhaps she could have chipped through the wood eventually, but that was like to take all night. Unless she could weaken it first.

She glanced up at the writhing serpent. "Its venom is acidic."

"Extremely."

That suggested a plan. An insane plan that was like to get her bitten and writhing in pain, dying here.

Loki stared hard at her. "It doesn't have much room to move because of its own bonds. But it can react very quickly."

Gudrun rose, stepping around behind the serpent's head. Hel preserve her. With a grunt, she drove the knife up into its skull, puncturing just beneath the jaw. Hot blood sprayed over her face and she whimpered, falling backward until she hit the wall.

Pressed against the wood, she drew in panicky breaths. The creature hissed, thrashing against its bonds, caught in violent death throes.

Gudrun wiped her face on the hem of her dress, then stared at the dying beast.

When all its thrashing finally abated, she stalked forward.

It only pretends death ...

It lures you in.

Can you see its fangs lodged in your neck ...?

As if her heart wasn't about to beat out of her chest already. Grimacing, she grasped the dagger's hilt. Jerked it free. A fresh stream of blood dribbled out. When the monster didn't react in the least, she moved to loosen its bindings. Then grabbed the corpse—still warm—and pulled.

The thing barely moved. What in the name of Hel did this creature weigh?

She heaved until she could twist the head around to the wood that had grown up around Loki's hands.

Sometimes, back in Castle Niflung, they'd worked with vipers to gain their venom for poisons and brews. Never a pleasant task, but Gudrun suspected this one would be similar enough in nature. She pushed just right, until venom dripped on the wood.

Loki grunted as the acid sizzled.

It wouldn't be fast, but once his hands were free, he could help loose his own feet.

And then, she could not leave Jotunheim behind fast enough.

50

*W*inter had passed and again summer was on the wane when Odin returned to Midgard. His trek had seemed endless, especially given the immediacy of his visions and his inability to act upon them.

An ever-expanding knowledge of the future ought to have buried doubts in its ceaseless march. Instead, that wisdom had only served to breed more apprehensions within Odin's breast. It had answered questions with more questions. It had forced upon him bitter revelations he had not sought while yet denying him his ultimate pursuits.

On the northern shores of Hunaland, outside the Myrkvidr, Odin stood atop a ruined tower. Much of the ceiling had fallen away, but an outer rim against the parapet remained. He leaned against that parapet, staring out over the kingdom of Rijnland.

Brynhild stood beside him, arms folded across her chest, a slight frown on her face. He'd insisted she stand to his right so he could see her. "Dead?"

Odin had searched for Hrist in both the Mortal Realm and the Penumbra. He'd found naught but her ring and

369

counted himself lucky at that. The valkyrie had served him well and had surely deserved better than urd had given her. But then, a great many men and women would deserve better than urd dealt them.

Maybe even Odin himself.

He worked a calloused hand at his throat. When he shut his eye, he could still feel Fenrir's jaws closing about his neck. Ripping his throat to shreds. Could feel it as he choked on his own blood.

He blew out a long breath. "I could not find her. I found ... wraiths."

Brynhild groaned. She was younger than many of the other valkyries. Bold, rash. She'd betray him, one day.

Sigrún already had. Odin had come back from the farthest reaches of Utgard to find she'd married Sigmund's son Helgi without bothering to ask her master's permission. Even younger than Brynhild, Sigrún had followed her heart, much like Olrun before her.

Odin could have allowed her to live out a decade or so with Helgi, but it set a bad precedent. And so he'd arranged for her death and reclaimed her ring.

"First Sigrún and now Hrist," Brynhild complained.

The other way around, actually, but it hardly mattered. Nor had he told her of Svanhit's death. Odin was down three valkyries. He could find more, of course. All it really took was a strong woman, a shieldmaiden, who wanted to extend her life beyond mortal bounds. Anyone willing to wear the ring and pay the price could have wings and a glorious future.

For a little while.

All futures were transitory, like all hopes.

Odin's now rarified visions had forced him to acknowledge that unpleasant truth. A great many unpleasant truths, in fact. About himself. About his role.

Someone, in some distant era, had dubbed him Destroyer. It ought not to have surprised Odin that, time and again, he would live up to the name.

"You have Sigmund's ear," Odin said.

"I whisper to him as he sleeps."

"Get him to treat with King Eylimi of Styria. Convince him he must marry Eylimi's young daughter."

Brynhild frowned. "Didn't Eylimi's daughter die long ago?"

"He has another, only sixteen winters old."

Now the valkyrie turned on him directly. "And you'd have this girl—a princess—marry a man old enough to be her grandfather? Perhaps it ought not to surprise me a man such as you holds no care for a girl's free will."

The more Odin's visions revealed, the more he began to question whether anyone truly possessed free will. Or were they all puppets of urd, trapped in roles demanded by what had gone before in an endless procession, enslaved by the past and future alike? "You forget yourself, valkyrie. Do not repeat Sigrún's mistake."

Brynhild glared at him, hands clenched in fists, one edging closer and closer to the hilt of her sword. But she wouldn't draw it. Her betrayal would come, but not yet. She had more left to do first.

"You had no need to visit vengeance upon her, either. And now you've let Fitela die, as well. Your wild passions drive you to make senseless choices."

Odin sighed and turned back to the landscape spreading out before him. Midgard, frozen and poisoned and dying though it was, had its own beauty. It was the world mankind had, and all Odin's steps had to ensure they kept it. "Fitela no longer mattered." Not that he'd been the one to order Sigrún off his watch. "And your sister made the dire error of thinking herself free to turn from her oath as the mood took her. The rings bind you in my service, and mine alone."

Even without looking, he could feel Brynhild's glare boring in the back of his head. "I had dared to hope that you —a human—might prove a better lord than the one we had before this. I had not yet begun to fear your cruelty might exceed even his."

"My desperation exceeds all others. See that Sigmund marries Eylimi's daughter Hjordis."

The long trek back to Midgard had given Odin uncounted hours to delve into visions of bitter futures. So many revelations. So many half-understood truths now clarified.

He'd thought Sigmund would be the one to return Andvari's Gift to him. Odin had placed all his hopes into the man.

But it had never been Sigmund who would gain the ring and destroy the Niflungar.

It would be his yet unborn son.

51

A platform surrounded the inside of the palisade around Peregot, with archers rimming it. Grimacing, Sif stared out at the gathered Serklander army. Just out of bow range. They stood in blocky formations, dozens of blocks. Hundreds upon hundreds of men, with their big round shields, spears. Some mounted cavalry.

They had swept through Aquiene like a wildfire, crushing what forces the Vall King had left to guard it. By the time he'd returned, half his land was lost. Part of the Serkland army would break off from time to time. Probably conquering or raiding other villages. Maybe engaging whatever Vall forces remained free.

And Sif had come here, fleeing Asgard, to find this cause as hopeless as the one she'd left behind.

A jotunn bitch whelping Thor's son. A betrayal that left a rock in Sif's stomach. A stone that would not pass. Instead it bounced around her gut, turning her insides to a bloody pulp. Crushing her heart with every move she made.

He'd pled with her to stay. And yet he'd claimed the bastard child as his own.

And Sif had fled, to find her daughter. To find her half dead. Broken by abuses no woman ought to suffer. Maybe Sif should have taken her and fled. But it was too late now. Maybe it had always been too late.

The Serklanders might have razed Peregot if they so desired. Instead, they cut off all access to food. To water. Supplies dwindled. People got sick.

Men lay in alleys, groaning in agony as pustules wept foul fluid all over their bodies. Others shit themselves to death. And the Serks just waited, letting them suffer.

With a last disgusted look, Sif trod down the stairs off the platform.

They'd come sooner or later. They'd come and they'd slaughter everyone who refused to bow down to their Fire God. Such they'd done in Andalus, and already in towns and villages throughout Aquiene. Sif didn't plan to convert. Thrúd was all she had left to live for, and the girl wanted to fight.

Despite it all, despite the awful scars. Despite the horrors she'd endured.

The bitter rage of it all choked Sif.

She trudged through the town, wrinkling her nose at the stench. Even before the siege, enclosed places like this suffocated in their own foulness. But now ... now it was like drowning in a sea of filth. Flies buzzed everywhere.

The people didn't bother with separate pyres anymore. Instead, every night there'd be a pile of corpses to burn. Sometimes two.

She found Starkad Eightarms in the small house he'd claimed. The man refused to sleep in the barracks where his father stayed. Just as well. Tyr had let Thrúd get hurt when she was supposed to be under his care. Sif had no desire to see that troll's arse. There was only so many times you could slap a man before it lost its satisfaction.

Starkad stared hard at her when she entered. At night, he leapt over the wall. Snuck out among the Serks and killed a few. Probably didn't do much good, but he never got caught. The how and why of it, he never said.

Sif shut the door behind herself. Starkad always kept the windows shuttered too. She turned around and pressed up against the wall, setting her hips for him. They never talked about it.

She felt it, as he strode silently over. He unlaced her trousers with practiced ease and was inside her in a moment. And then she was grunting in time with his thrusts.

Hard. He used her hard. That was the agreement.

A moment of relief.

And then she'd lace up her trousers and leave. Not a word between them.

Because none of it meant shit.

HER DAUGHTER LOOKED up when Sif entered the room. She'd been staring at a metal hand mirror, but hid it behind her back as Sif came in. How in the gates of Hel had the girl gotten hold of that? No one ought to have provided it …

Tyr had given Thrúd a private chamber in the fort—small consolation—and she spent most of her time here. Sometimes she still went out and practiced with weapons. Sif tried to encourage her whenever she could.

But Thrúd had good reason to want to hide away.

Vicious scars marred her face where Hödr had branded

her. A handprint, permanently burned around her mouth. The skin had melted and warped, becoming a wrinkled mess. Thrúd had told Sif that her Great Aunt Sigyn had saved her life. Given that Sigyn's obscene child had done this, that admission was all that kept Sif from throttling her aunt.

The woman—wisely—seemed to avoid Sif whenever possible.

Had Thor been here or learned of Thrúd's fate, he'd like have killed Sigyn and Hödr both. Maybe he still would, should they live through the siege. Unlikely as that now seemed.

Sif sat down beside the girl and patted her on the knee. "It doesn't matter so much as you think."

Thrúd rolled her eyes. "I heard a story that Father almost killed Great Uncle Loki for cutting your hair." Actually, Sigyn had done that. And Sif had probably deserved it. "Hair grows back. I can't even close my godsdamned lips."

It was true. They had burnt away, leaving a permanent gap exposing her teeth. A twisted one, that made it seem like she forever sneered.

Sif rubbed Thrúd's knee. "There is more to life than your looks, Thrúd."

"Like what?"

"Like ... family."

Now she snorted. "Father betrayed you with another woman. And now you've got some secret lover, too." Sif opened her mouth to object and Thrúd leveled a gaze filled with such scorn she gave over the idea. "And Hödr was basically my cousin."

Hearing that from her daughter, fourteen winters old ... it was a lance of ice through Sif's chest. It stole her breath. Blasted the thoughts from mind, save for a wordless, soundless anguish. Desperately, she worked her mouth trying to find something, *aught* at all, that she could say. "So live for ... vengeance."

"What?"

"Ram a spear right up that bastard's arse and don't stop until the point scrapes his teeth."

Thrúd stared at her a moment. Then she chuckled. Shook her head. "Show me how."

Sif met her daughter's gaze. And she nodded.

SIF PASSED among the soldiers in the lower level of the fortress. Evening had settled in and all had given over training for boasting and gossiping. So much less boisterous than they'd been a few moons back. Back then, they'd still had some wine left. Now, even the water was running low. Now, they'd seen so many of their own drop dead from illness or dehydration.

Slow, horrible deaths. And those who lived knew the same urd lay before them.

Or they could open the gates and make a hopeless final charge against their foes. At least then, maybe some of them might make it to Valhalla.

It was madness, the waiting. King Lotar seemed to hope his brother's army would ride in to break the siege. But Prince Bernard's army was either not coming, or mired in their own battles against the rest of the Serklander forces.

Sif stared at the downtrodden soldiers. In truth, it was less gossip than griping. Bickering. These men were nigh to broken.

How long would it last before riots broke out? Another fortnight? A moon if they were lucky?

No. No, she wasn't going to sit here and wait to die.

Shaking her head, Sif started up the stairs for Lotar's chambers, her words a jumble in her mind. They had her and Tyr, plus Hermod, and they'd all had apples of Yggdrasil. Three Ás immortal warriors. Hel, even Sigyn was rumored to be a masterful archer. Starkad Eightarms was ... well, not quite an Ás immortal so far as Sif knew. But clearly something more than a normal man, still.

They faced superior numbers of the enemy, true. The greater concern seemed to be these Sons of Muspel which she'd heard were a match for an Ás immortal, hard as that was to credit. So they just needed to make certain where and how many ...

Lotar's door guard was asleep at his post. That sort of thing could get a man whipped. Of course, he probably hadn't had a proper meal in a moon. No, she didn't need to report him. Everyone was wrung out like linens. Worn thin. Seeing one of their own beaten for it wouldn't do the soldiers' morale any favors.

Instead, she slipped past the guard and into the king's study.

Lotar himself was also asleep, slumped over his desk, papers splayed this way and that. Not even the king was getting proper nutrition. His was like to be a short reign.

She should go. Just turn around and let him sleep and take this up in the morning.

Hand on the door, she paused. Was she just putting off the difficulty of this conversation? Would she lose her nerve come daybreak?

With a sigh, Sif drifted over to Lotar's desk. Then faltered. Blood had seeped into his papers.

"What the ...?" She lifted his head.

His eyes were open, glazed over. Blood dribbling from his mouth.

"Oh. Oh, fuck." An assassin? How had he gotten into the fortress? The guards. She had to get the—

A hand slapped over her mouth.

A blow struck her in the side. Heavy. Stealing her breath. Burning pain lanced through her an instant later. Sif yanked against the arm, but even with the apple's power, her assailant was as strong as her.

She clapped a hand to her side. Hot blood seeped through her fingers. Gushing out.

She'd been stabbed.

The room swayed. An iron grip held her in place.

Sif jerked her elbow back into her assailant. Her foe let out an *oomph* and stumbled backward.

Sif turned and tried to cry out. Blood gurgled up from her mouth, choking her scream. A cloaked figure dashed into her, bearing her to the ground. Her head slammed the floor.

A haze of white filled her vision.

Another punch in the ribs. Followed by more pain. A hand slapped over her mouth again.

Her vision came half into focus. Her enormously strong foe lay atop her.

Beyond the hood of her cloak, blonde hair fell in loose strands. A glimpse of her eyes.

Sigyn?

Sif had lost her grip on the apple's power. Losing too much blood.

She felt it, as the blade opened her throat. Couldn't get air in through Sigyn's hand. Couldn't breathe.

Her own blood welled inside her throat. Choking on it. Convulsing.

Everything fading. Even the pain.

52

*J*n the back of an alley, surrounded by putrid filth and chittering rats, Sigyn wept, arms wrapped around herself. She wept even as the rats crawled over her skin. Even as they sniffed her with their itchy whiskers.

Sobbed, until all her tears had run dry. Then she convulsed in silent anguish, unable to arrest her tremors.

She ought to have killed herself. It would've spared everyone a great deal of grief. She ought to plunge the same dagger that had slain Sif into her own heart.

But then, Hödr would be lost.

And was his life worth Sif and Lotar's?

It had to be. She was his mother.

And because Sif had walked in on her, Sigyn had murdered her own niece.

For that, she would writhe in eternal torment in the pit of Nidhogg. A kinslayer. Murderer.

IN THE WAKE of Lotar's murder, Tyr had taken command.

He'd begun a search for the assassin, his men combing the city seeking a Serklander. Of course, they'd not find one. Sigyn watched them, going house-to-house now.

Did they see her looking at them? Could they hear the pounding of her heart? Surely guilt was writ plainly upon her face. Yet they passed her by with barely a glance.

Maybe it was worse. Getting away with it.

And in the end, they gave over the search, claiming the assassin must have slipped over the wall.

Which was true, in a way.

The swan cloak made sneaking out of the fort possible, if never easy. Twice, archers had shot at Sigyn, no doubt seeking to stave off starvation for even a day. Already, they'd begun slaughtering their horses. Any not fit to ride into battle, they'd roasted.

Sigyn almost wished the archers had succeeded. A fitting end to her treachery. Instead, she snuck out of the fort every so often, transferred her reports to one of Scyld's men. And he promised her Hödr would remain safe.

And then he'd ordered her to murder Lotar.

Maybe he expected it to break the Valls' spirit. Maybe he expected it to make them open the gates and lead a suicidal charge. Either way, he'd told her to choose between her son's life and that of a foreign king. Hardly a choice at all, much as she despaired over it.

Sigyn sat blessedly alone in the tiny house she'd claimed. Sadly, Peregot had a great number of empty houses these days, even with the refugees. Whole families died of pox, and no one wanted to take up where they had stayed.

Mundilfari had claimed one such home, prompting Sigyn to take one too.

As much to stay clear of the Mad Vanr, who now followed her far too oft for her liking. Sometimes, out of nowhere, he'd ask if she'd mind him sticking his cock in her. In public, he'd ask, as if it were something one did in the market. Not that she'd consent to *ever* lay with the delusional Vanr.

No, she'd claimed a place he didn't know of and whiled her days away in there. Slowly choking on her own wretchedness. Suffocating from toxins born within her breast.

Yes, her house lay across from the gates of Hel. The Queen of Mist—her husband's daughter—stared at her. Waited to claim her stepmother.

And when Sigyn could stand it no longer, she'd go to the fort, to Tyr. And gather more intelligence to share with Scyld's spy. Because it all had to mean something. If Sigyn were to stop now, to refuse ... then Sif would have died for naught.

The door to her new home opened, slowly, as if in nervousness.

And Loki slipped inside, shutting the door behind himself.

Sigyn blinked. She was hallucinating now. Her guilt or despair had driven her mind to collapse and conjure up shades of her own desires.

"Sigyn."

"Are you real?" Her breath caught as he nodded. He couldn't be here. He was gone ... for so long. He and Odin had disappeared in their quest for Mimir's well. She'd begun to fear she'd lost him too. "I ..." She couldn't speak. Couldn't get enough air.

She sucked in great lungfuls but it wasn't enough. She was suffocating.

Lying on the floor.

Loki's warm hand fell on her shoulder, rubbing. "I'm here now. I'm here."

The tide broke in her, and she wept, curled in a ball. Sobbed on and on as he held her in his arms. An eternity, it seemed.

"I ... I ..." She couldn't think. The haze of despondency had left her in a fugue from which she'd never expected to pull free. "I ..."

"Yes, Sigyn."

"I ... murdered ..."

Silence. A pause. Then he squeezed her shoulder again. "I saw. I just don't know why."

He knew. Of course he knew. The flames told him things. So many things.

Panting, Sigyn pulled away to look into his crystal blue eyes. "They have Hödr."

"Who does?"

"The Sons of Muspel. They told me to do as they bid if I wished to see him again. The spy, he ... he said I must kill Lotar. And uh ... Sif came in before I could escape. I didn't know what to do! I j-just acted. I had to protect my son and I ..."

Loki leaned forward and grabbed her shoulders. Hard. Squeezed, until she met his gaze once more. "Whatever you did is done. You must live with it. Bury the guilt as best you can."

"I should confess ..."

"No!" Loki shook her. "Sigyn ... I can't lose you. Not again."

Again ... Such a muddle. Her mind wasn't working right.

"Listen to me," Loki said. "Maybe you did as you had to, maybe not. Either way, it's done. You can't change it. Sometimes we make impossible choices. Sometimes ... a bad choice forestalls an even worse possibility. Urd is cruel." He shook his head.

"Aquiene is lost. They'll take Peregot soon, I think."

Loki stared hard at her a moment. "Arrange another meeting with this spy."

"To what end?"

He fell silent a moment, even shut his eyes. They twitched as if he was in pain. "With everything you sacrificed to save Hödr ... we must get him back. Let's find our son."

53

*H*jordis, daughter of Eylimi, alone could be a match for Sigmund. This thought echoed in his mind over and over, as it had for a moon. It resounded in his dreams. It filled his waking hours. As it had every day on the road to Styria.

Long enough had passed since Borghild had died, and Sigmund would not spend the rest of his long life alone. It was not fit for a king to live thus. No, he needed a queen.

He could not say exactly how or when the idea had settled upon him, but once it had, he could not shake it. It consumed him.

Tale had reached him of Hjordis's beauty, said to rival even great Freyja, the fallen Vanr goddess. Surely the great king of Hunaland must have such a beauty for himself. Surely.

And so he came to Eylimi's hall, along with his retinue of men and shieldmaidens, leaving Hamund to rule over Rijnland in his absence.

Eylimi, having gotten word of their coming, received

them in grand fashion. After all, he remained one of the last true supporters of Sigmund's crumbling kingdom.

Menzlin had withdrawn from the empire, even risking war. Garth had died in grief at his daughter's bloody slaughter in the Myrkvidr, and Hildebrand had declared Rijnland their foes. Sigmund had fought several bloody skirmishes with Menzlin before Baia too withdrew and entered into an alliance with Menzlin, under their newly declared king, Lyngi, son of Hunding. A son who had managed to escape Helgi's slaughter of his line.

Two men with much reason to hate the Volsungs.

War would not rage in the winter, but by next summer, Sigmund expected more than mere battles to divide the kingdoms of Hunaland. Everything was falling apart.

King Eylimi fed him plate after plate of steaming bear flesh and leeks, keeping it all washed down with a steady flow of drink.

"Do you know why I've come?" Sigmund asked when he had eaten all he could stand and more.

"I can think of a few possible reasons," Eylimi replied.

His daughter milled about behind him, ordering around the slaves who catered to the guests. Her flower had truly blossomed, with luscious golden hair and a healthy curve to her form. Even looking at her had Sigmund's cock straining against his trousers.

"Your daughter is of marrying age," Sigmund said.

The girl flushed and turned away, obviously pretending not to hear.

Eylimi nodded. "Yes, and I've received a number of offers for her hand. Jarls loyal to me and their sons. Even a Vall noble if you can believe that. And of course, kings …"

As if introduced, another man across the table rose. A young man, but a scar across his chin spoke of battles.

"This is King Lyngi of Baia," Eylimi said.

Here? Now? Sigmund's first instinct was to leap the table and slay the traitor king with his bare hands. Doing so would violate all rules of hospitality, though, and Sigmund could never act so dishonorably, even if it would *not* have cost him his very kingdom. And it would have.

Instead, Sigmund offered Lyngi a nod of moderate respect—the most he could manage. "King."

"King Sigmund," Lyngi said, voice tight. If only Helgi had managed to slaughter the last of Hunding's brood ...

Ironic. Siggeir Wolfsblood had made the same mistake in allowing Sigmund to escape, and it had brought down his line. Would such a dark urd now befall the Volsungs? No. Sigmund would not allow Lyngi to become the undoing of his kin.

Eylimi cleared his throat. "You see my difficulty, here. With so many great offers come to me, I must disappoint someone. Disappointing a foreign noble means little, of course." A few chuckles. "And my jarls are used to disappointment, I'd think." A couple of groans accompanied by some nods. "Kings, though, have been known to take disappointment badly."

So they had.

"I bring to your daughter far more lands and greater wealth," Sigmund said.

Lyngi snorted. "I bring a husband who's not ancient and who—may I add—did not spawn a murderous bastard accused of being a varulf."

Sigmund leaned heavily on the table, staring hard at Lyngi. One day soon, he warned with his gaze. One day soon, the king would fall on Gramr. Sigmund would drive the runeblade through his chest. She would feast upon his blood.

Eylimi cleared his throat. "Be all that as it may, I see only one impartial way to decide this. Let Hjordis herself claim the man she wishes to marry. She is wise beyond her years, and I will abide by whatever decision she makes."

Sigmund barely stopped himself from glowering. Ask a young girl, barely a woman, to choose between a handsome young man nigh to her age and one three times it? It hardly seemed impartial to *him*.

Hjordis drifted to her father's side, silent as a ghost, and looked from Sigmund to Lyngi and back. To her credit, she didn't look down or turn away. He could almost see the thoughts racing behind her eyes, as if she truly gave consideration to both parties. Did she?

Sigmund cocked his head slightly at her. What did this woman think, truly?

"A difficult choice, Father," Hjordis said after a long pause. "I think I must choose King Sigmund. Though he is old, he is also famed throughout the North Realms. Who does not know the glory of the Volsungs?"

Lyngi groaned, and Sigmund cast a triumphant smirk his way. The other king rose, wiped his mouth with the back of his hand, and strode out, a great retinue accompanying him.

It made Sigmund smile all the wider.

Perhaps urd was not so cruel to him after all. Perhaps he might enjoy one last chance at love in his life.

54

The child in Skadi's belly kicked, drawing a grunt from her as she trudged up the stairs inside the Thunderhome. The ice palace would soon be hers again. Loki's seed had finally taken hold. Things moved well now, and she need but convince Thrym of it.

However, once she entered the throne room, the king stared at her oddly. "They told me Skadi had returned."

"I have. You asked for a larger body. One able to accommodate your lusts."

Thrym snorted. "Still seem tiny from where I sit. And much like someone else has already plowed you deep enough."

Skadi smiled. "Indeed. A spawn of chaos if ever there was one. A child of the line of Hel herself."

The jotunn king leaned forward, grasping his armrests. "You tread dangerously nigh to blasphemy, ghost."

"But I tell you the utter truth." Skadi continued forward until she stood mere feet in front of the massive king. "The child is but one of many tools at my disposal. I now also bring you the throne of Vimurland."

"King Geirrod rules Vimurland. I find it hard to believe he bends the knee to you."

"He's dead." And even so, he served her, or had, until that Hel-damned Thor had destroyed his body. That particular thorn would need to be addressed, and soon. Thor and his hammer might well prove the largest obstacle in their path save Odin himself.

Thrym grinned at that, exposing fangs. So wolfish, this one. Bold and calculating at once. A terrible foe or a glorious ally. "You intrigue me, ghost. What is it you seek? To see Brimir restored to its former glory?"

Skadi continued toward him until she could lean on the armrests herself, staring up at the king. "Brimir is gone. I would build a kingdom of eternal winter. The other jotunn tribes must follow us or be crushed as though men."

The jotunn cupped her chin between his thumb and forefinger, leering down at her. "Do you know our cousins in the south move now, bestirred to make war on the empires of man?"

Skadi smiled, hiding her surprise. The eldjotunnar, the fire ones, had been troublesome even in the days of Brimir. They'd barely held the peace then. She could not expect to establish one now. Now, she'd need to crush them too, eventually. "Perfect."

"How so?"

"We let them and the humans exhaust theirselves while we marshal our forces here. We call all the kingdoms of frost jotunnar. We call the mountain jotunnar and the wood jotunnar. We call the sea jotunnar. And we tell them the war has begun again. The Vanir are *gone*."

"Gone?"

"These petty Aesir you may have heard of? They did not

merely join the Vanir. They banished them from the Mortal Realm."

Thrym lurched from his seat, sending Skadi stumbling backward, clutching her belly and barely stopping herself from pitching onto her arse. "The Accursed One?"

"Mundilfari has been missing for a thousand years."

"Frey and the flaming sword?"

Skadi didn't know the whereabouts of Lavaeteinn, but that hardly mattered. "The children of Njord ..." She growled the foul name, almost choking on it. The bastard king of the Vanir was dead. "They are gone. The king himself cast into the dark."

Thrym rocked back on his heels. Then he chuckled. A low rumble, like an angry mountain, growing in vibration until the entire chamber seemed to tremble with his dark mirth. "Gone ... the betrayers who cast us out. Truly gone?"

"Our concerns now are their successors. The would-be god-king allows his son to feast upon jotunn souls, feeding his accursed hammer."

Thrym nodded, flakes of rime showering down from him as he did so. "This I have heard of. If we are to strike, it seems, we need to lay into motion plans to remove the weapon from his hand."

"Indeed."

Thrym chuckled again, shaking his head in apparent disbelief. "After so long ... Well. It seems I have found my queen after all. And together ... we shall be what Aurgelmir once was. Like a force of nature we shall wash away the corrupt lands of man."

Skadi allowed herself a tight smile.

The reign of winter had now begun.

55

*I*n swan form, Sigyn alighted upon a hill beyond the sight of the Serklander army. She always met the man here. Beneath a beech tree, she settled down to wait.

Most like, someone would have seen her flying over-head. Word would get back to Scyld's man.

And indeed, after an hour, the spy came trudging up the hill. He was an Andalusian, not a Serk, his skin fairer than the Utgard soldiers—though still darker than Sigyn's. An unassuming figure who could pass among the Valls without much suspicion.

His route took him up the steeper side of the hill, and he was huffing lightly by the time he reached Sigyn. "Well? You have more information? Will the new commander surrender?"

Sigyn almost laughed. Tyr was even less apt to surrender than Lotar had been. In fact, he was probably among the most stubborn foes Scyld could have possible arranged. "No. But I do have information."

"And?"

"I found my husband."

Loki dropped down from the tree like a shadow.

The spy had time to utter an aborted shout before Loki's fist connected with his jaw. Sigyn's husband drove a knee into the man's back, then punched him once between the shoulder blades.

Sigyn flinched. That was painful to even watch.

Still, Sigyn had to admit a grim satisfaction. Every so often, urd delivered justice.

SNEAKING the spy back into Peregot was like to have proved impossible. Sigyn wasn't even sure how Loki had gotten in and out and—as usual—he remained somewhat cryptic on the topic.

Without another good alternative, they'd taken him deep into the woods and bound him to a tree.

Loki sat kindling a small fire while Sigyn stared at the prisoner.

Twice she opened her mouth before finally managing to get it out. "Will Hel have my soul?"

Loki groaned softly, but didn't answer until she turned around to face him.

"Was that a yes?"

He shook his head. "Life and death are more complicated than anyone understands, Sigyn. We are all forced to balance—or gamble—our souls against the needs of a tumultuous present and even more perilous future."

"A profound way of entirely circumventing the question."

Loki rose from the cook fire and drifted over to the prisoner, then knelt, and pushed the man's chin up.

He must have just woken, for his eyes were open, staring hateful daggers at the both of them.

"Do you know who I am?" Loki asked.

The man scoffed. "Apparently her husband. And more like than not, a dead man once Scyld learns of this."

"Scyld." Loki drew in a breath and sighed. "We are always haunted by our mistakes."

"You have no idea."

Loki shook his head. "I'm afraid you're the one with no idea. Your greatest mistake was in thinking Scyld is the most terrifying manifestation of flame. Where is our son?"

"Why don't you march down to the army and ask for him?"

Loki frowned, exchanging a look with Sigyn. Then he moved to the fire and stuck his hand in. It came out with flames dancing around it, swirling about his fingers, rising up from the back of his hand like a torch.

The prisoner sputtered. "Y-you're a caliph?"

"No." Loki returned to the Andalusian and knelt in front of him once more, holding his hand up before the man's face. "In the most distant sense, though, I might claim responsibility for their existence. I stole the Art of Fire for man in days long lost. I can no longer say with certainty whether actions that then seemed expedient actually shall prove so. Regardless, the true child of Muspel lies within me. Fire is *life*. But it is also painful, purifying death. Speak now, or touch the tongue of flame."

The man drew in short, ragged breaths, whimpering. Sigyn could hardly blame him. The hair on her arms stood on end at Loki's words. He spoke of something she couldn't quite understand, something beyond her.

When the Andalusian gave no answer, Loki pressed his thumb into the man's forehead.

That drew forth bloodcurdling screams that had Sigyn cringing, looking away, even if she could not block out the terrible sound. The screams melding with the sizzle of flesh. The acrid stench of it overpowering her superhuman senses and leaving her ready to retch and implore Loki to release the man.

But who was she to ask such a thing? She, who had murdered her own niece for this. She, who had crossed all bounds, could not now shy away from inflicting torment on those who had brought her to this precipice.

Loki withdrew his hand, exposing a charred black mark around where his thumb had been. The Andalusian's skin had bubbled and popped, frying under the awful torment. Sigyn clenched her teeth to keep from crying out.

The prisoner whimpered between choking, ragged gasps.

"Where is Hödr?" Loki repeated.

"With the army ..." The Andalusian's voice had become a raspy thing, seeming nigh to breaking.

"Scyld holds him in his very camp?" Sigyn asked. How many times had she flown overhead and never realized.

Tears dribbled from the man's eyes. "Scyld serves him."

"What?" Sigyn gaped at him. "How would ... what?"

Loki groaned. "Eldr is the spawn of Surtr, blessed with a portion of his progenitor's power. A fragment of Muspel himself."

None of that made any sense nor served to clarify the deluge of questions assaulting Sigyn.

"He is the caliph in charge of ... the conquest of Valland." The man gasped in obvious pain. "It will be his to rule ... when Bernard falls like his brother."

Loki glowered a moment. Then he lunged toward the campfire and thrust both hands inside. Before Sigyn could even react, he flung his hands toward their prisoner. An orb of fire shot out of his opened palms and slammed into the Andalusian.

A wave of heat struck Sigyn and hurled her backward even as a deafening explosion wracked her senses.

Everything grew dim for a moment.

Then Loki helped her up. Her ears were ringing. She couldn't hear whatever he said.

She looked to the prisoner. Now a charred mess of bones.

Sigyn truly wanted to retch. But this wasn't done. Not in a long way.

56

*A*fter long days of feasting and celebration with his new father-in-law, Sigmund had returned to Rijnland to find the unrest had only grown. The summer was nigh to ended, and he'd need to use the winter to consolidate his power.

And thus had he spent the past moon in consideration of all options.

He sat, staring at Barnstokkr, Hjordis beside him, while Hamund spoke.

"Obviously Styria has become our most staunch ally." Hamund nodded at his new stepmother. "And Swabia remains loyal. Unfortunately, Styria lost a great number of men due to raids by trolls last winter and, already they expect a recurrence in the coming moons. This leaves us to call levies only from Rijnland and Swabia."

Sigmund waved his hand. "Yes, call them."

"My king," Keld interrupted. "Swabia has just committed a number of men as mercenaries in Valland. The South Realmer emperor offered a fair mountain of silver for Hunalander warriors to hold back the advance from Serkland."

Sigmund groaned. Hel damn it all. "Inform those who remain we'll call the levies before the end of winter."

A messenger raced up to Keld and whispered something in his ear. The thegn's face fell, and he exchanged a few words with the new man, who nodded grimly.

"What is it?" Sigmund leaned forward on his throne. He could afford no more dire news at present. All he'd built was crumbling ...

"The men we sent to Njarar returned, my king," Keld said slowly.

"And?" Hjordis asked. "Will Helgi not come to his father's aid?"

"No, my queen."

"Ingrate," she mumbled under her breath, no doubt unaware Sigmund could catch it.

"He cannot come," Keld said. "My king, Högne's son Dag has murdered Helgi in an attempt to reclaim his father's throne. They say Sigrún cursed him with seidr and he fled into the woods, mist-mad."

Sigmund's mouth had fallen open, but he couldn't shut it. The news sounded impossible. Like some fell dream spawned by spoilt fish or far too much mead.

"Helgi?" Hamund said, stumbling backward until he bumped into Barnstokkr. "Helgi?"

"We have no choice ..." Sigmund said. His chest felt at once numb and filled with acid eating away at his insides. "Send men to help Sigrún."

"We have no men to spare," Hjordis pointed out. "If you send away any part of the army, you risk losing Rijnland. And *Styria*."

Keld cleared his throat and stared at his feet. No. How could it get worse? "Sigrún is dead as well, my king. She took her own life, so talk says."

This wasn't happening.

His whole world was crashing down around him. Had some vile curse befallen the Volsungs?

First Fitela, now Helgi. And Sigrún too, whom Sigmund might have at least dared hope carried Helgi's blood within her. "They had a son already ..."

"We don't know his fate as yet. Civil war ravages Njarar. I'm led to believe the babe might live in hiding with those loyal to Helgi still."

He had to go. Had to find his grandson ... had to ...

Sigmund slumped back on his throne.

The wolf's howl had become a beating drum inside his head. Demanding he release it. Let it come to the surface and run, despite the crowd. Despite even the daylight outside. "I ... I ..."

Of course, he could not release the wolf if he wanted to. Not in sunlight, but still ...

Sigmund rose, brushed past Keld and Hamund, hardly even seeing them.

He strode from his hall. He strode from the town, breaking into a run before he'd even cleared the gate. He ran and he ran.

⚶

MYRKVIDR'S thick canopy made it seem almost night even in daylight. Almost free enough from sunlight to let the wolf run. Sigmund pushed ever deeper into the wood, until at last the sun did set. He tore off his clothes and shifted, then dashed in a wild sprint, howling at the night.

Other howls answered him, varulfur, perhaps, or just normal wolves.

Either way, Sigmund sought no companionship this night.

His wolf eyes made sense of shadows no human sight could pierce. The deeper he ran, the more twisted the forest became, as if the trees themselves expressed the torment ravaging Sigmund's mind.

His dark urd.

Maybe this was his place all along. Varulfur out in the wilds went savage, lost touch with their human roots.

An escape he longed for.

AFTER TWO DAYS, Sigmund returned. Despite the depths of melancholy, he could hardly ignore the duty to the kingdom he had built, the son he had left, or the wife he had newly married.

It took time to find his discarded clothes.

Weary, and despairing, he plodded back through the fields and toward his hall. As he drew nigh, however, he found the whole town abustle.

War bands gathered outside, men forming up with their thegns. Sigmund passed among them until he found Keld, the man already clad in mail and mounted on a horse.

"What's happened?" Sigmund demanded.

"My king!" Keld leapt off the horse and caught Sigmund by the forearm to drag him away. "It's good you've returned. We did not know where to look."

"Despair seized me." Not that it had ever released him.

Keld nodded grimly. "Would that we could allow you the time to grieve. But Lyngi has brought an army against us. Even now they march into Rijnland. They've already pillaged the outlaying villages and wrought uncounted slaughter among the common folk. Jarl Arvid is dead."

Sigmund glowered. They had attacked *now*, on the cusp of winter? A move bold to rashness. It meant if they did not find swift victory, they risked being caught out by winter storms, unable to feed or shelter their warriors.

And his hand shook with the all-consuming need to offer Gramr their blood. If Sigmund could not be allowed to despair, at least he could be allowed to rage.

57

*a*rrows rained down over Peregot. Most fell short. A few unlucky warriors caught one. Hit in the face or torso, most of them, half concealed by the palisade wall. Tyr stood up there anyway. Beside his archers.

Bertulf had command of them. But Tyr had to see.

Couldn't say why the Serks had decided to close in now. Had to come from Lotar and Sif getting murdered. But the connection—Tyr couldn't figure it. He grimaced as another volley showered down on them.

Serks were losing twice as many men. Maybe three times as many. Soldiers in the fort had elevation, cover. But the Serks could afford the losses. Still, made no sense them attacking now. Another fortnight and his people would've broken, most like.

Tyr had sent Hermod to call on aid from Queen Frigg. Whatever she sent was like to be too late though. Had the Serks known Hermod got past their lines? Even Tyr didn't know how he did that. So how could they? Unless they'd caught him.

Dire thought.

Aquiene was doomed. Valland soon after, no doubt.

Maybe Sigmund of Hunaland could stop them at the Rijn. Elsewise, the Serks would just keep coming until they took all Midgard. No one really had the strength to stop them once they broke through here.

Bastards could've taken the town if they wanted. They were just draining away his archers to save their infantry. Wouldn't be long though. A few days more, at most. Then they'd charge.

A bloody fight, and any who didn't swear to their Fire God would die.

Tyr spit in disgust, then trod down the wooden stairs off the wall. He needed to see Starkad. They were all like to die soon, and things needed saying.

Didn't get far though. Sigyn of all people was tromping over his way, beckoning him.

With a frown, Tyr directed her inside an abandoned tannery. Place stank of stale piss despite being disused. Owner must've abandoned it when the arrows started flying.

Sigyn crinkled her nose. "How does it look out there?"

Tyr grunted. "Like someone threw wide the gates of Hel. Open and welcoming. Seen at least five eldjotunnar out in their ranks."

Sigyn frowned, shaking her head. "They'll have a caliph among them."

"Fucking sorcerers." He shook his head. Then paused. How would she know that? Woman was twice over too clever, true enough. But still. How?

She didn't give him much chance to ask, though. "We can't hold out until reinforcements get here, can we?"

"No." He cracked his neck. Always hurt the worst right before the violence started. So stiff. "Truth is, I'm not sure the Queen could send enough to stop this. Lot of our warriors were already in Valland. Or off across Midgard, trying to prove themselves. Not like we have a standing army just waiting."

"If we take the caliph, we might be able to end this."

A caliph commanded the Serks, no doubt. Still didn't answer how she knew for certain one was outside Peregot. "Can't see much way to arrange that. Wouldn't know him if I saw him and couldn't get to him, regardless."

Sigyn winced, looking like he'd spit on her boots. "It's Hödr."

"How's that?"

"I told you … he's possessed by a Fire vaettr."

Tyr groaned. "Never said how that happened."

"I-it … that … doesn't matter." She shook her head. "The important thing is, I've got Mundilfari here with me." Tyr had heard rumor some Vanr First One was in the town. Seemed like nonsense. "He can exorcise the vaettr. We save Hödr and deprive them of their leader."

Tyr snorted. "Got an army between you and him. Unless he can fly."

Sigyn grimaced. "I need you … I need you to draw them into open conflict."

"Didn't notice the arrows flying everywhere? We're in open conflict. Not like to last too much longer."

"Open the gates and charge them."

Woman didn't seem to have a clue how war worked. "Walls are the only advantage we have. As long as our archers hold them, Serks risk awful losses to charge. It's why they waited this long."

"We'll lose anyway. Your archers are dropping a few at a time. If you charge, they'll be in chaos. It'll give us the chance to slip behind their ranks."

"Fucking mist-madness. Lose Peregot in a matter of hours."

She cringed. "I know."

"But you want your son. More than all these lives, right?" He shook his head in disgust.

"If you take away their caliph, they lose their ability to advance, at least for a time. Long enough for you to coordinate a defense and choose a more advantageous battleground. You said yourself—you'll lose the city anyway in a few days more."

Tyr groaned. Woman talked too much like her husband. All cold reasons for every action. But he nodded.

TYR DIDN'T SEE much of Starkad. Boy sometimes came on the walls at night. Stared at the Serks like he thought of charging them all by himself.

Once before, Tyr had tried coming to the man's house. Learned quick enough he wasn't wanted.

Still, found himself banging on the door that afternoon.

When it opened, his son squinted against the sunlight. Hardly even bright through the mist, and Starkad was blinking like they were on Asgard.

"Wouldn't bother you as much if you didn't spend all day in the dark."

Starkad sneered at him, but stepped aside. Let him in. And shut the door the moment he passed. "What do you want?"

"Sigyn told me her son leads the invasion. A caliph, now."

Starkad just kept glaring, eyes narrowed.

"We're going to have to charge them."

"Now?"

"City is lost either way." Sigyn had that much right. "Woman thinks she can get Hödr. Take their leader. Like to get herself killed though. Needs someone good with a blade to watch over her."

Boy snorted. "Fine. I'll do it."

Tyr nodded. Always so damn hard. "Son ..." He reached for Starkad's shoulder.

The man slapped his hand away. "Being on the same side does not make us family."

Maybe naught ever would again. And Tyr was no good with words. Never had been. All he could offer his son was a nod. "Don't die."

Tyr turned. Paused at the door. The boy could say something. Aught at all ...

But he didn't. And Tyr left.

58

To lose oneself in the currents, to look forward or backward until the now vanished entirely, therein lay the peril of the Sight. The more powerful one's Sight became, the greater that peril. Odin, with his abilities augmented by the Well of Mimir, oft found himself lost in a trance, barely aware of the happenings around himself.

He needed to return to the High Seat, to look across the world and take in events happening at this moment. And still his visions drew him ever into far flung times.

Upon Sleipnir's back, he let his mind drift, trusting the horse to guide the way back to Hunaland, as they sped along.

A YOUNG MAN sat in the shelter of a ruined keep, huddled close with his arm around Brynhild, the both of them unclad. He traced a lazy finger along her collarbone, watching where she pointed rather the results of his attentions. The woman taught him runes and secret words mortal man was little meant to know, even as Odin watched her betrayal.

Even as he knew where it must inevitably lead.

That boy, Sigurd, he had such potential. Such a grand and terrible urd before him. The delirious raptures of love and victory that preceded a yet more woeful end.

From the shadows of the Penumbra, Odin saw their ill-fated tryst, watched the lessons and the lovemaking. In the intermingling of their flesh, how could he not see himself and his days with Freyja?

But found himself forced to extinguish the last of his pity. For neither urd nor history afforded the least mercy to their victims. And Odin was as bound to those forces as any other.

Perhaps more so.

And thus, though Sigurd bore that which Odin so needed—and truly tempted him to strike the both of them down—Odin forestalled his hand.

Let them have their moment. For a moment was all anyone could ever have.

FROM ACROSS THE FIRE, Odin stared hard at the young man. Lost in his own thoughts, much as in the boy's questions.

"You know my fate, Uncle," Sigurd said. "Yet you won't tell me."

"Because it will not become easier for the knowing."

"Still, I would have it told to me."

Odin grimaced. He'd known the words would come. He'd seen it in visions long ago. The conversation playing out over and over in his mind. Was it happening now? Was he watching it or living it? Or perhaps for an oracle, no such distinction yet remained.

Finally, Odin nodded. The boy wouldn't be dissuaded. He never had been in all the times they'd played out these events. "It begins as these tales so oft do ... with avenging your father ..."

SIGURD CAME to him as he sat on the edge of a forest, staring at the currents of a river. He could so easily lose himself in their flow. How pleasant to imagine the procession of time would carry ever onward like the river's currents, rather than face the reality that urd warped everything and time became not a river, but a tide, washing back on itself.

"Who are you old man?" the boy asked.

Almost, he could forget the answer to that question as well. He was everyone. He was no one. A thousand lives blended in the tide until he could no longer be sure where one ended and the next began. Was he the men he'd be? Was he the ones who had gone?

And had this happened yet? How was he to order his visions, if order even mattered?

"Are you well, old man?"

Odin. He had been or would be—Odin. At least for a while longer. "You go to choose a horse for yourself, yes?"

The young man raised a brow. "How can you know that? Did Regin send you?"

In a strange way, perhaps. In that way in which all urd moved through the tangled web.

"You want to know the best horse?" Odin smiled, not quite aware of the source of his own amusement. "Let me tell you of Sleipnir ..."

"YOU SUMMONED ME," Brynhild said. The valkyrie had stepped out of the Penumbra beside Odin, as he'd known she would. Nevertheless, her appearance jerked him from his prescient memories, lurching him through time and leaving him momentarily dazed.

They stood upon a hill overlooking Sigmund's camp. The Volsung king's cluster of tents dotted the edge of the forest, visible mostly from the bonfires between every two or three tents. The mist was thick this night, especially for summer, but the fires held it at bay.

The old Volsung king was badly outnumbered by his foes. Odin sympathized. How often men conspired with one another to bring down those in positions of great power, as if the conspirators themselves had the wit or the will to do what the glorious had done.

Such plots had nigh brought down Odin's reign on Asgard and had left him with fewer allies than he'd once believed he could rely on. And now, similar, weaker men banded together to bring down a champion.

Odin turned to Brynhild, leaning heavily on his walking stick. The past few winters had weighed more heavily on him, even though he no longer aged.

Your soul ages ... falling into decrepitude and decay ... until you can justify aught you wish ... I would know ...

"You've done well," he said to Brynhild. The poor woman who could not begin to imagine her own dark urd. "Hjordis is with child. And you've protected Sigmund just enough these past years. Ensured he did not meet an untimely end."

Brynhild nodded, clearly not expecting a compliment and uncertain how to respond.

"You have done well," Odin repeated. The words seemed to speak themselves. Fortunate, as he'd feared he'd have otherwise choked on them. "But now this task is at an end."

The valkyrie pulled off her helm—spilling her braids down her back—and tucked it under one arm. "What does that mean?"

"It means you are not to further interfere with Sigmund. His urd is his own to decide."

Was it, though? Given that Odin had already foreseen that fate, that he knew what would happen even if some details remained hazy, did that fate already exist? And if it existed, was it still Sigmund's decision at all?

"What the fuck are you on about, old man?" Brynhild demanded. "I've not just spent the better part of two years watching over the man to see him die pointlessly now. His enemies have an overpowering force out there."

"Sigmund is an overpowering opponent."

"He's a varulf, yes, but that doesn't make him invincible. Fitela's death proves—"

Odin waved his hand. "You are to leave now. Do naught save claim the most valiant slain on both sides and bring them to Valhalla. Make no effort to spare the lives of *anyone* on this battlefield."

The valkyrie glared. Then she jammed her helm back on her head. Then she vanished into the shadows of the Penumbra.

Sigmund had played an invaluable role. But that role had run its course.

Sometimes, even the words came to him in the visions. The things others would say. The answers Odin must give them.

All of it, shadow play.

59

*S*creaming echoed outside. Clanging of metal. Cries of pain. All of it assaulted Sigyn's enhanced senses as a maelstrom of anguish and suffering. At a woman's wail, Sigyn winced.

With Mundilfari, Loki, and Starkad, she sat alone in the fortress dining hall. Others—everyone who hadn't gone out for the fighting—had locked themselves in the chambers or in barracks or larders, as if anywhere might prove safe.

The truth was, sending Tyr out there had been a ruse. The chances of them sneaking past the tumult of the battle, finding Hödr, and getting hold of him long enough to exorcise a vaettr approached naught.

Their soldiers would lose. And Hödr would come here to claim the fort himself. Just when he thought they'd won, she'd save him.

There was no redemption there. But she'd have her son back.

Starkad had claimed it was better to wait for nightfall. Which was when it had hit her. He always preferred to move or fight after dark. Watching him close, she wasn't certain how she'd missed it before.

The lack of regular breathing. The lack of sweat. And when she focused her senses, she still heard no heartbeat.

Because Starkad was dead.

He didn't seem to rot as draugar so oft did, but he must share their aversion to sunlight. It stole the powers of the dead. And so he'd prefer to fight at night or inside, where no light from the sun could reach him.

As here, in the dining hall.

A meaningful glance with Loki had confirmed he'd realized the same conclusion. But he hadn't spoken of it, either. It made no difference, maybe, so long as the man was on their side. Tyr didn't know—Sigyn was fair certain of that.

Mundilfari milled about the dining hall, mumbling to himself, and occasionally painting runes on the walls or the floor. He'd bemoaned not being able to reach the ceiling.

Starkad kept to himself, sitting in a corner, eerily still. One more sign she couldn't believe she'd missed when she first met him.

Loki's hand fell upon hers and curled around her fingers in a gentle squeeze. A small comfort before a terrible end. Only at his touch did she realize—she'd been trembling.

A TREMENDOUS CRACK resounded through the fort—the sound of the barricade breaking. The cries of battle had begun to dim outside, replaced by the screams of slaughter and rape throughout the town. Sigyn forced herself not to listen, instead, rising to her feet and unshouldering her bow.

It was time. He was coming.

Loki and Starkad had flipped one of the great tables on its side already. Sigyn took up position behind this, for cover. Mundilfari sat down beside her, still talking to shadows, while the other two men drew blades and flanked the entryway. Starkad bore a runeblade, Sigyn suddenly realized. A faint, almost imperceptible light seeped from the grooves carved along its length.

She prayed it would be enough.

Moments later, Serklander soldiers came bursting through the door.

Starkad tore into them with unrivaled speed and fury, his blades reflecting the light from the brazier in the instant before blood coated them.

Loki grabbed a soldier and bodily hurled him aside even while he hacked at the legs of another.

Despite the two men's ferocity, the Serklanders surged into the hall faster than either could cut them down. In the space of a few heartbeats, Sigyn lost sight of her allies in the melee. She loosed an arrow at the first Serklander to break away.

The shaft took him in the mouth.

Already she was nocking another. Draw. Loose.

She had to trust her instincts and her enhanced senses to guide her shots true. She had no time to take aim with care. Another shot, and another.

And then they were too close. Surging over the table.

Sigyn dropped her bow and jerked a knife from her belt the instant before a swordsman closed in on her. Drawing her pneuma made her fast and strong. It didn't make her an expert in combat. She dodged away as he swiped.

How was she to close in against his superior reach? All she could do was keep leaping backward. Relying on pneuma-enhanced reflexes to dodge his swipes. After the fifth one, his swings seemed to slow ever so slightly. Fatigue in his arm. If she could keep this up, she could—

His next swipe came too fast, tearing into her thigh and sending her tumbling to the ground. She lay prone before the pain even hit. And it hit *hard*. As if his blade had been aflame. The agony of it screamed in her head drowning out all other thought.

The Serklander raised his blade high, intent to cleave her head in twain.

A blood-drenched, empty-handed Loki flew over the table and collided with the man, his weight bearing the Serk down. They slammed into the floor. Rolled past Sigyn.

Mail scraped on stone. Loki had hold of the man's coif and slammed his head upon the floor twice. The second time, blood splattered.

Sigyn scrambled to her feet. Her leg gave out at once, and she toppled back down.

"Block the pain!" Loki shouted at her.

Easier said than done. Sigyn flooded the pneuma into her limbs, relying on its power to keep her up. Hands slick with blood, she crawled to her bow. Forced herself to stand and nock another arrow. To rise.

"Scyld," Starkad said. He faced off against the burn-faced Son of Muspel. Waiting for no answer, he launched himself at the man. The Son moved nigh as fast, and the two of them fell into a dance of blades Sigyn could hardly track.

"Keep the rest off him!" Loki shouted, snatching up a curving sword as he charged back in.

Right. Starkad had his hands full with the Son.

Sigyn took a bead on another Serklander and fired. Her arrow punched through his right eye and dropped him in front of his fellows. One of them stumbled. Sigyn put an arrow through his throat.

Her fingers brushed her quiver without looking, felt only a handful of fletched shafts left. Far less than the wave of men rushing in here.

Beside her, Mundilfari was mumbling to himself, seeming to argue with someone she couldn't even see. Hel-damned mist-mad sorcerer! More fighting raged outside—she could hear it, but couldn't tell who yet fought the Serklanders.

She loosed again and again. Two more Serklanders piled up on the floor.

Another man broke around the side of the table.

Sigyn scrambled to nock an arrow.

From nowhere, Mundilfari charged forward and pressed his index finger into the man's forehead. The Serklander stopped dead, quivering in place. Spasms wracked him. His eyes clouded over and blood began to seep from them, and from his nose and his ears as well.

The horrible sense of wrongness crept up on Sigyn, churning her stomach and threatening to draw tears of profound terror to her eyes. It choked her with foulness.

The soldier dropped into a heap on the floor, continuing to twitch there.

Mundilfari shook himself, blinking as if dazed.

Fucking sorcerers. Forcing herself to look away, Sigyn loosed her last arrow, dropping another man who tried to charge Starkad.

Tyr's son was still tightly engaged with Scyld, both seeming evenly matched.

And then, through the doorway, stepped Hödr, treading among the piles of corpses as though they meant naught to him. Flames swirled around one of his hands, a white-hot inferno that drove even his own men away.

Hödr jerked his arm back and a whip of flame arced out like a lash, surging for Starkad's neck.

Loki intercepted it, catching it with his bare hand. Almost blindingly white fire flared between them. Then it erupted around Loki in a wave that forced Sigyn to shield her face.

When she looked up, Loki had been blown clear into the far wall, his clothes a scorching and smoldering mess. The Serklanders who'd stood around him had been reduced to ashes flitting about the room.

Hödr was on his knees, panting.

Her ears were ringing. Over that whine, she caught wind of Mundilfari chanting in Supernal. The exorcism.

Shit. She had to keep Hödr busy long enough.

And she had no more arrows with which to achieve that. Lacking another option, she vaulted the table. Landing after even that short hop sent fresh agonies surging up her leg. She toppled down to one knee, grunting with pain.

Hödr froze mid stride then jerked violently, his face a mask of rage and perhaps even pain. He looked to her then past her, to where Mundilfari chanted so fervently.

"Hödr!" Sigyn screamed. Just keep him busy. Keep him occupied a moment longer.

Her son glared at her, baring his gritted teeth. He took a step forward. And then another. Each slow, as if he pushed against the tide. Flames from the brazier began to swirl. They streamed toward Hödr's hands in arcing bands, like a loose woven braid, spiraling toward each of his splayed fingers.

Oh fuck.

"Hödr!" He wasn't listening to her. Barely even seemed to see her.

Sigyn flooded as much strength into her legs as she could. Then she launched herself at her son. He whipped a flaming hand at her and those streams of fire washed over her head. In an instant her hair, even her eyebrows ignited. Searing pain engulfed her face and she fell, gasping, rolling on the ground as agony beyond aught she knew bombarded her. It drove the pneuma from her grasp and left her reeling, consciousness threatening to slip away beneath the conflagration of pain.

Her vision dimmed.

Flailing, she caught hold of her pneuma again, using it once more to reinforce her body. To block the pain for even a moment.

She managed to roll over.

Mundilfari's voice had become a thunderous roar, reverberating off the walls and seeming to ring inside her head.

But Hödr was still advancing on him. He'd moved past Sigyn and was making slow progress, hands now fully engulfed in spiraling firestorms.

He'd had an apple. He could survive most aught that didn't kill him.

Wanting to weep with the agony, Sigyn snatched up a fallen knife. And lunged at Hödr, planting it in the back of his calf. Hot blood jetted over her arm.

Roaring, he spun, flaming first raised above her. Sigyn dropped onto her back and tried to crawl away. The heat from those flames seared her face as it drew nigh, blistering and scorching her. But Hödr hesitated, a hairsbreadth from immolating her head. With a growl, he turned away, again advancing on the chanting sorcerer.

Letting loose an inhuman howl, Hödr lunged, swinging his arm as if it held a sword. The flames surrounding his hand launched at Mundilfari in a spinning disc. They crashed into the sorcerer and the table and exploded in a boom that stole even the ringing in Sigyn's ears. It burnt away the air and left her gasping.

The sorcerer detonated, flesh and blood burned away to cinders in an instant. For a heartbeat that burned into Sigyn's eyes, he stood there, charred bones. And then those too turned to dust and blew away in the currents of the explosion.

Sigyn's mind rejected the sight, unable to reconcile it. It was impossible. Naught burned so hot.

And ... and ... they needed Mundilfari. He was the only one who could save Hödr. But his chanting had stopped. The echo of it gone all at once.

The exorcism had failed.

The explosion had sent everyone, Hödr included, crashing onto the floor.

Sigyn lay there gasping. This wasn't happening. It wasn't ...

And then the chant took up again, the same timbre, the same discordant rhythm that set her every nerve roiling and praying for it to end once more.

Loki was chanting, stumbling over. Sigyn tried to rise. Could he finish it ...? Just pick up where Mundilfari had faltered?

Her husband dropped knees first atop Hödr as their son tried to rise, pinning the boy's shoulders. He slammed one hand atop the boy's forehead and pinned it to the floor. The other was wrapped around Hödr's throat.

Fuck, he was choking him. No! No, Loki, please ...

All the pain faded to a distant spot in her mind as Sigyn dragged herself across the floor, leaving trails of her blood in the process.

No. Hödr. Please ...

Her little warrior ...

Not this. And not by Loki ... Urd could not be so cruel.

Please.

The whine began to return to her ears, still drowned out by the alien chanting that suffused her senses with the utter foulness of the Art.

Hödr bucked beneath his father's grasp. His head tried to thrash from side to side, but Loki held it still. Smoke was rising in tendrils between Loki's fingers, as if he were burning her son's skull clean through.

Hödr's screams of agony cut through even the obscenity of Loki's invocations.

Flames erupted from Hödr's eyes like tiny volcanoes, burning upward as her son wailed and spasmed.

Loki toppled off him, screaming himself, jerking as if caught in a maelstrom. He rolled along the floor. Streams of blood seeped from his ears and smoke billowed from his mouth. A ring of flame shot out from his body as he thrashed.

Beyond him, Scyld too had dropped to his knees, clutching his head. Screaming.

At least for the instant before Starkad's runeblade sheared clean through his skull.

The remaining Serklander soldiers surrounded them, but none seemed intent to close in and face whatever madness unfurled here.

Unable to form words or even give voice to her screams, Sigyn crawled to her son's side. His eyes had burned away, leaving gaping blackened holes where once they'd been. The flesh was charred around them, blistered and oozing blood.

Sigyn threw her head on his chest, rocking back and forth. Unable to weep.

Unable to aught do save moan.

THEY TOLD HER, later, that the spectacle of such horrors had broken the morale of those Serklanders in the fortress. They had fled, spreading their fear to others. And Tyr had broken through their lines, coming into the fortress to see what had transpired.

The Serklanders named Peregot accursed and set to burning the whole town. But none pursued Tyr as he led the refugees away. Indeed, they fell back into the Andalus Marches, perhaps seeking orders from another caliph.

Loki and Hödr lay in the back of a cart, Sigyn sitting between them. The two people she loved best in the world, both caught in feverish fits while she remained uncertain whether they'd live or die.

THE FOLLOWING NIGHT, Loki woke with a groan, eyes red. Sigyn rushed to his side and eased him back down. Still burning with fever, but surely he'd recover now.

But a terrible look had come into his eyes. A horror she could not unsee.

"What happened?"

"It's ... gone." Loki stared at her, his crystal blue eyes too wide. "Surtr. He's escaped me."

60

*S*igmund knelt over Keld's broken body. His thegn lay in the mud amidst the still raging battlefield, already stinking of his own shit.

No time to see to the man now, but Sigmund swore to himself he'd give Keld a proper funeral. Along with all the others. A field of carrion composed of men and shield-maidens Sigmund had known and loved for long years.

Blood dribbled from Gramr's point as Sigmund charged back into the fray. A Menzlin warrior came at him with a great, two-handed axe. Wild swings, any of which could have cleaved a man in twain. But each blow narrowly missed Sigmund as he weaved from side to side.

He kicked the warrior in the chest, sending him hurtling several feet through the air before landing in the mud with a squelch and a sputter. Sigmund lunged forward and drove Gramr through the warrior's heart.

He bellowed a war cry. How many had he slain this day? Two dozen?

Obvious reluctance marred the faces of two foes around

him, and neither gave charge. One, a spearman, looked to his fellow who bore a battleaxe.

Sigmund raised Gramr high, shrieked, and raced for the axeman.

The man faltered, falling back several steps like a fucking craven. He raised a shield too slowly. Gramr sliced clean through his forearm and cut his face in half.

Sigmund spun even as the spearman charged. He knocked the blow aside with his shield, and stepped inside the man's reach all as one movement. A fell, fey instinct had seized him this day. Every move his foes made seemed whispered in his ears. Every blow they would have struck fell short or scraped off Sigmund's mail.

He rammed Gramr through the spearman's sternum. The runeblade punched through mail, flesh, and spine as easily as linen. His fury had become a sun, burning inside his chest. Consuming him in an inferno that could only be extinguished with blood, and then, only for a few heartbeats.

The wolf sang in his mind, lending him speed and strength no mortal man could hope to match.

A terrible vengeance for two murdered sons and a shattered empire. For dreams heaped onto a pyre. A lifetime of losing all those he'd cared for.

The voice in his head warned him as another foe raced up behind him. Sigmund spun, whipping Gramr around in a low arc. Her blade sheared through a shieldmaiden's waist from one side and out the other. Utter disbelief colored her face for a brief instant. Before her torso toppled free from her legs and blood bubbled up as if from a mountain spring.

"I'll kill you all!" Sigmund bellowed into the mist.

The carnage confused even his keen wolf senses, but still he knew where foes lay. He raced up, over a hill, to find the corpses of more of his men. Beyond them stood a trio of axemen, all with giant shields. Those who had slain so many, now defending the hill.

That voice suddenly told him to move, and move he did, lunging to one side. *Thwack.* An arrow stuck in the mud where he'd just stood. The bowman stood beyond the axemen, already nocking another arrow.

With the best howl he could manage in human form, Sigmund charged up that hill, right into their midst. His shield jerked up of its own accord. *Thwack.* The impact of an arrow against it sent vibrations shooting up Sigmund's arm.

The arrow's weight unbalanced his shield arm, but Sigmund's strength meant he could still move it faster than his foes would expect.

He whipped the shield around first, thrusting it at the first axeman's face. The man hefted his own shield to block the wild blow, which served to at least break off the arrow shaft and send his foe stumbling a few steps back.

Twisting, knowing the other axemen circled him, Sigmund whipped Gramr around in a wide arc. The pair of them fell back though, and his blade met only air. Which was fine. Sigmund continued his arc, twisting it into a thrust at the remaining man who had now charged, axe high.

The runeblade rammed through his face and sent blood and brains splattering over Sigmund as he tore it free.

A heavy blow cracked down between Sigmund's shoulder blades and sent him crashing into the mud. Everything went hazy, dim. He rolled, tumbling, unable to arrest his fall down the hill. He hit a corpse, bounced over it, then landed on level ground.

Streams of pain coursed through his back, his neck, his shoulders. Even his arms for some inexplicable reason. The voice hadn't warned him of that. He barely had time to form the thought before the war cries of another man forced him back to the moment at hand.

Growling, drawing on the wolf's strength, Sigmund shoved himself off the ground and into a lunge in one swift motion. Gramr sliced out one of the charging axemen's guts and sent him stumbling down to the spot Sigmund had just risen from. Shrieking, he turned and faced down the last of the warriors.

The man hesitated a bare moment, then raced in, his guttural scream filling the air.

Sigmund blocked the axe on his shield, the impact numbing his arm and suddenly stinging more than a dozen others had this battle. Fatigue must be taking him, stealing his rage. And he needed that rage. He needed that voice turning him into the invincible Sigmund. None dared stand before him!

He knocked aside another attack with his shield, then launched into rapid swings of Gramr. The runeblade tore a chunk out of his foe's shield. That left the man gaping for a heartbeat. Long enough for Gramr to cleave through his skull.

Panting, Sigmund spun, seeking more foes. "By Odin, I'll kill every last one of you myself! I will tear your halls down, Lyngi! Do you hear me!" He paused, catching his breath. He'd finish what Helgi had started and thus honor his son.

Another man drew nigh, stepping out of the mist, clad not in armor but a cloak and wide-brimmed hat concealing his face. Sigmund could catch naught but a glimpse of a vicious scar where one eye should have been. The man held a spear and seemed to be singing to himself.

Mist-mad fool of Lyngi's?

The spearman advanced on Sigmund.

Come to die, fool? Roaring, Sigmund charged forward.

He raised Gramr high over his head for a chop that would cleave the old vagabond in half. The man raised his spear in both hands to block, little good though it would do him.

The runeblade bit into the spear.

And Gramr snapped in half.

The force of it was like a wail in Sigmund's mind, a cry of the damned in agony, beyond the gates of Hel. It drove him to his knees, gaping at the shattered runeblade. The indestructible sword of the Old Kingdoms. Broken upon an old man's spear ...

Sigmund looked up, expecting that spear to run him through. But the old man had vanished back into the mists.

Gramr ... The gift of Odin ...

Sigmund let the sword fall from his trembling fingers. This couldn't happen. It could not.

Metal clashed on metal. Men screamed. Dying all around. The battle still raged.

Desperately, Sigmund cast about himself, seeking another weapon. A fallen sword lay nearby. He grabbed this, rose, and rushed onward into the mist.

Before the next hill, he came to a contingent of Styrian warriors, desperately holding back a Baian onslaught. Surrounding their king ... Eylimi knelt in the mud, hand holding his gut. Hjordis's father would not last long.

Sigmund threw himself amidst the Baian warriors. His blade hamstrung one. His shield shoved another out of position. He fell into the dance with them. Cleave, strike, dodge, parry.

A spearpoint scraped along his mail, bruising the flesh beneath before punching through a link and wedging into the gambeson under the chain. Sigmund grabbed the spear with one hand and shoved, his varulf strength sending the owner stumbling away. A blade crashed into Sigmund's shoulder at the same time. The fingers of his shield arm went numb even as crushing agony lanced through his shoulder and upper arm.

His shield fell limp at his side.

The pain of it sent him down to one knee.

A war cry behind him. A man moving in for the kill. Premature.

Sigmund twisted around and thrust his sword through the groin of his would-be murderer. It did not punch through easily as Gramr would have. It carried the task though, sending his attacker toppling over sideways, hands clutching his mauled stones.

Gasping in pain, Sigmund crawled to Eylimi. The king stank of shit seeping out from his bowels, mingled with the blood and intestines. His father-in-law was not dead yet, but a fool could see no hope remained to him.

"I'm sorry ..." Sigmund's tongue was heavy in his mouth. Words slurred.

So many dead.

He struggled to his feet. The least he could do was make Lyngi pay for this. Pay in blood.

Vision blurred and uncertain which way he trod, Sigmund stumbled through the mist, dimly aware some of Eylimi's warriors had followed him. Eager to avenge their king, no doubt. Well, Sigmund would grant them that much.

He had to. He owed Eylimi. But without Gramr ... how had the runeblade shattered? She was a gift from Odin. And if he had lost her ... had he not then lost Odin's favor as well? Had the god forsaken Sigmund?

How was a man to live on, knowing he'd once been loved and favored by an Ás and had lost that grace?

Sigmund stumbled into another melee, unable to even tell one side from the other. At least until some few men broke off and charged him. The first he cut down. The second, he drove back. Unable to use his shield arm, he dodged a blow from a third.

A fourth man rushed in, shield-first, and collided with Sigmund's chest. The impact sent him flying backward, crashing into the muck. Someone leaped on him, swinging a battleaxe meant to cleave his skull.

Sigmund caught the man in the gut with both legs and kicked, sending the attacker sprawling away. He rolled to the side, cleaving his sword into another man's shin. A third crashed down atop him, hacking away with an axe.

Blow after blow landing on Sigmund's mail, cracking ribs beneath, crushing his guts. Unable to get his sword around, Sigmund dropped it, then lunged forward, catching the man with a hand around his throat. If only night would fall.

If only he could unleash the wolf.

Sigmund squeezed until his attacker fell still.

Then he collapsed back into the mud.

He needed to get up. He had to keep fighting. He could do this ... Just find Lyngi and cleave his head from his shoulders.

Just keep going ...

But the world had gone dim.

61

*N*ight fell upon the Myrkvidr. In the darkness, the forest grew so very black Odin could scarce make out the two women crouched at the edge of the hollow. A small cave hid them, in case any should come looking for them, though neither did.

Hjordis and her slave Vada both looked to Odin, probably unable to see more than shadows around him.

"Why did you help us, Gripir?" Hjordis asked.

On Odin's advice, the Queen of Rijnland had fled along with Vada, carrying the greater portion of all the gold and jewels Sigmund had owned. Odin had warned them the battle had turned against her husband and the castle would no longer offer safety.

Of course, Lyngi had seized that castle and ransacked it searching for Hjordis and even more so, the golden treasures. The Baian king's men had slaughtered Hjordis's remaining guards, claimed her slaves, raped her women and taken the livestock. All the things one expected from a conqueror, really. Odin could have predicted that without prescient visions.

Rather than answer, Odin pulled a torch from his satchel, then struck flint to steel until the oil caught flame. Through the flicker of torchlight, he could clearly see the fear etched on the women's faces. They probably were not sure even why they had trusted him.

Groaning with the effort of rising, Odin made his way to Vada. "Take this." She grabbed the torch with some obvious reluctance. "Queen Hjordis, your husband yet lives, but he has suffered a terrible wound. If you go to the battlefield now, you can meet with him."

Hjordis blanched, then swallowed hard, shaking her head. "Sigmund is ... no. You cannot know such things. This is a trick."

"Go to the battlefield."

Glowering only a moment, Hjordis took off at an unsteady gait, forcing Vada to chase after her.

Odin too followed, albeit at a great distance, and glamoured to further conceal himself.

He followed the women out onto the site of the massacre. The field had turned into muddy slush, dirt mingling with blood and piss and voided bowels to create an overpowering stench. Buzzing insects zipped among a sea of corpses, broken spears, and discarded weapons.

A handful of looters pried mail from rigid corpses or searched bodies for aught else of value. A great many more of these people would return here, come morning. For now, most of the army remained occupied with their plunder of Sigmund's home.

It had taken a great deal of speed to reach Hjordis in time. Once Odin had broken Gramr and detained Brynhild, he'd known it would be only a matter of time before Sigmund fell under the onslaught.

With the Volsung king lost, Lyngi's forces would have

quickly overcome the remains of the Volsung army. So many pieces had to align for this. Indeed, Odin had to trust that Altvir had done her duty with Prince Alf in Reidgotaland.

Hjordis picked her own way among the fallen, shouting for her husband.

Eventually, a pained, raspy voice answered.

The queen rushed to her fallen husband's side, wailing, heedless of the filth that caked her dress as she knelt beside him. "We have to get you to a völva."

Leaning on his walking stick, Odin frowned, shaking his head. He felt Altvir's presence when she drew nigh, and embraced the Sight to reveal the valkyrie.

She stared at Odin, disapproval plain on her face. Unlike the younger Brynhild, though, Altvir seemed wise enough not to castigate her master, whatever her thoughts on the matter.

"It's too late ..." Sigmund said. "Gramr is broken, in any event. A gift from Odin ... and the god no longer wishes me to wield her. Such can only mean my time has come. I fought ... so many battles while it pleased him."

Hjordis pressed her face against Sigmund's chest, weeping muffling her voice. "I'd lack for naught were you to rise and avenge my father." She sniffled. "Avenge this loss."

"I ... can't. Our son must do ... as I did ... and avenge his father. Up on the hill ... the shards of Gramr fell. Take them and guard them well. One day, a boy may become a man and come to ... claim them. With that, I'm content. I ... want to see my father and brothers once more."

Odin flinched. Sigmund would not rejoin his fallen kin. Volsung and the others had died decades ago and passed unto whatever urd had claimed their souls. Naught Odin could have done would change that.

Hjordis wrapped her hands around Sigmund's and lay

on his chest. Vada knelt beside her mistress then, head on her back. The three of them stayed like that long, until Sigmund's breath had fled. Until the hour grew late.

Odin nodded at Altvir, then trod himself up the hill, to claim the shards of Gramr. The broken runeblade had been one of the greatest works the dvergar had ever wrought. Strange paths the future took, rushing ever toward its inevitable end. Before, Odin had never imagined the sword would break, much less that he would be the one to do it.

He wrapped the shards in a cloak, folded over, then hurried back down the hill. "My queen. I bring you the pieces of Gramr, as Sigmund wished."

Hjordis looked up, red-eyed in the already dimming torchlight.

"You must hurry, now." He handed the bundle to Vada. "Go to the north shore, where men from Reidgotaland will be sailing past. Go with them and find safety from Lyngi. Win the favor of Prince Alf and he shall be kind to you and your unborn son."

To the woman's credit, she rose and rubbed the tears from her eyes. Then nodded. "Thank you. I don't know how or why you've helped us, but ... thank you. On behalf of myself and my fallen husband."

Odin barely suppressed another flinch. Would Sigmund thank Odin for all he had wrought? Well, it did not matter. Odin did not do what he did in order to receive thanks. He did it because no other choices lay before him.

Hjordis turned to Vada. "Exchange clothes with me and wear my jewelry. I'd rather not be discovered for who I am by the prince."

Odin concealed his smirk. Hjordis's precautions were wisdom, after a fashion. Even so, they'd prove both unnecessary and pointless.

The queen looked to him. "I'll always consider you a brother for what you've done."

Odin nodded, then turned his back so the women could change.

When they had, he followed them to the shore, where already Prince Alf's men had disembarked to examine the aftermath of this battle. Altvir had done her part well. Another valkyrie would have a little more prodding to carry out, of course. Odin had already recalled Skögul from Andalus. She'd need to make sure Alf would learn the truth about Hjordis, marry her, and raise her son as his own.

He was a good man—at least as good as men could be in such times. He'd ask for the treasures of Volsung, and Hjordis would lead him to the hollow. Then they'd sail away to safety and Sigmund's son could be born free from Lyngi's grasp. Indeed, Lyngi would think all the Volsungs dead, the same mistake once made by Siggeir Wolfsblood.

Time always seemed to move in these circles.

Odin watched as the Reidgotalander king and his men met the two women, too far out of earshot to catch their words, though it didn't matter. Odin already knew these events. He'd seen them play out many times in his mind.

Satisfied, Odin returned to the battlefield and embraced the Sight.

Dawn was not far off, and looters would be out in force. That hardly mattered, as Odin would be gone soon.

He walked to where Altvir stood, a dozen ghosts standing around her, split into two groups. The greatest of the fallen in this battle, divided on both sides of the conflict. Were Odin not spread so thin, he'd have arranged additional valkyries to claim more of the mighty.

On one side, Sigmund stood, his form misty and slightly etheric, but hail, showing no sign of his bitter wounds.

433

Altvir had spared him that. The man watched Odin now, able to see him clearly once Odin had embraced the Sight. Sigmund stood there, shaking his head, seeming at a loss whether to believe Odin had truly betrayed him.

"You were Vofuth ... way back then. You helped us overthrow Wolfsblood." He straightened and bowed his head. "My lord, Odin. And I never knew."

Odin favored him with a sad smile. "Yes, old friend. You did well, all the bitter years of your life. Now your burdens are lifted. For a time ... Tell me, Sigmund, would you like to see your son Fitela again? He's waiting for you in Valhalla. The valkyrie will take you there. She'll take you all."

"You'll not come?"

"I will, soon enough. First, I have one more thing to attend to."

BRYNHILD MARCHED BEFORE ODIN, casting hateful glances over her shoulder at him. Of course, he'd known she'd betray him. And he'd known he would cast her down, strip her of her powers and her ring. Leave her a mortal woman. He could have bound her hands as well, but she knew better than to try to attack him or try to run.

So, huffing slightly with the exertion, she climbed up the slopes of Mount Hindarfjall. "Why not just kill me?" she snapped at him.

Odin plodded along, feeling the ache in his knees and lower back, and relying more heavily on his walking stick because of it. How was he to answer such a question? Some fragment of the truth, perhaps, little though it would avail Brynhild?

When she dawdled, he prodded her back with his stick.

"Even when disobedience is expected, still it demands an appropriate response. Aught less would be to treat you as but a child."

Brynhild sneered over her shoulder. "You mean you want to keep the other valkyries in line. Whatever you do to me will serve as a reminder of the price of trying to master our own lives."

There was that, as well, and if such an answer satisfied Brynhild, such she could keep. It would not serve Odin's ends to try to explain the future to the woman, nor to expound upon the needs of urd or the way it must unfold, even would she have believed him. More like, she would have thought him mist-mad. Perhaps he was, laying plans that would take nigh two decades to come to fruition. Nevertheless, what he'd seen would unfold if he could get all the pieces in the right places.

Atop the mountain they reached a ruined keep, with shields lining its ramparts. A Sikling fortress, later claimed by Volsung's ancestors. A place of great import, now long forgotten. Men forgot almost all things, in time.

The former valkyrie paused, and Odin shoved her forward, toward the keep's entrance.

The woman's shoulders tensed, but she did stride inward, coming to rest in a great hall.

The Siklings had carved a mighty table from stone here. Once, heroes and warriors had dined with kings in this place. Goblets raised in boastful salutes to those who had passed and those who yet lived. Their shadows played across Odin's vision, almost like ghosts. Memories of men and women gone a thousand years and now but echoes for those few like Odin, who saw what others could not.

Oh, if only Odin could have claimed their souls for his

einherjar and added their ranks to Valhalla. What an army that would have made.

The woman turned now, arms spread as if to demand what the point of coming to this empty place had been.

"You will marry a man who will come to you."

Brynhild spat on the floor a mere foot in front of Odin. "I swear, I shall marry no man! None, save a man with no fear. Even you have fears, old Ás. I've seen it."

Oh, Odin had so very many fears. The jaws of a wolf, closing upon his throat. Tearing it out. His own death, horrifying. His son dying alone ... calling out to his father. A world aflame.

Yes, Odin knew fear.

Some men thought fear came from the uncertainty of the future. Odin rather found the opposite.

"You have forsaken your oath of service," Odin said. "And oathbreakers are damned to feed the dark dragon with their corpses. As you tried to interfere in my choice of victors, so shall you never again enjoy the sweet mead of victory, woman."

Odin withdrew a small thorn from his pouch, keeping it tucked in the palm of his hand where Brynhild could not see it.

"Why bring me *here*?" Brynhild demanded once more.

Odin shook his head. Then he lunged at the woman, caught her arm and pricked her neck with the thorn. "Because here you will lie in deathless slumber for eternity. Choked by your own mail and drowning in nightmares of your dark deeds and the darker urd lying before you."

Brynhild fell back a few steps, hand to her neck, eyes wide. She pulled away her hand, gaping at the blood welling there. Surely, she knew he'd told her the truth. Part of it.

The woman stumbled and Odin surged forward to catch

her. He swept her up in his arms, then carried her to the stone table. There he laid her out prone. Brynhild blinked over and over, moaning, obviously trying to fight the sleeping spell.

Odin preferred to avoid the use of sorcery when possible. But some situations demanded it.

Such was urd.

Brynhild's eyes shut.

Odin straightened her arms and legs by her sides, then left, and turned back to take in the keep on the mountain slope.

In the time of the Old Kingdoms, sorcerer-kings had carved runes into these walls. Cleverly concealed, unless you knew where to look for them. Brynhild would have, had she been in her right mind.

The runes called to vaettir which had now long laid dormant. Waiting for someone to waken them once more.

Odin chanted, invoking those vaettir, drawing them close to the Veil. Long he chanted in that ancient language, until, at last, a ring of white fire sprang up around the entire castle. A barrier to ensure Brynhild's sleep went undisturbed. A moat no man would dare cross.

None, save the one to come.

EPILOGUE

*A*ll the long walk from the shore to their hall, Sigyn held his hand, and Hödr's too. It was well, of course, since Loki might have blundered over the side of the cliff otherwise. No matter how oft he caught himself in this daze, staring at his hands, he couldn't seem to shake it.

For era after era he'd borne the weight of flame inside his breast. A bulwark against the darkness and the mists, even as it burned him. Even as it seared him to his soul he'd held on so very tightly.

Most of his life, really. Ages other men could not have dreamed of, stretching back almost to the beginning of it all. And now Surtr was gone. Worse than gone—free, and no doubt wrathful at his millennia of imprisonment.

At their house, Sigyn eased Hödr into a bed shelf the boy hadn't occupied in years. Loki watched them, his precious family, caught in their own pain. And yet the both of them somehow relieved. Grateful it was over? But it was only beginning. They'd freed Hödr from this torment, but his life would surely find yet more anguish.

No one would forget the things he'd done.

Only when Hödr rested comfortably did Sigyn again take Loki's arm and lead him out back. He let her guide him to the cliff's edge and sit there, watching the ocean. As if looking on water would offer him respite from flame.

A worry had niggled at him since then, a fear that, in looking into fire, he might find even fewer answers than before. Would that offer some relief? Would it lessen his burdens? No. The darkness remained in either event. The merciless procession of the future toward a doom the others had not yet imagined.

Loki had the Sight even before he'd stolen the flame. He'd have it still, even if it did prove weakened. It would only make things harder.

"You're frightened," Sigyn said finally.

Lost in his musings, he'd almost forgotten her burdens. She'd feel responsible for both Hödr's suffering and Loki's own doubts. The lines of her face confirmed as much. Had she heeded his warning back then, had she chosen not to pursue the Art, things might have played out differently. But recriminations served little purpose to either the accuser or the accused.

Besides, the future was what it was. The web of urd had little room for divergence from the path of its strands. Knowing the darkness lurked ahead didn't mean he could stop it. Nor could Sigyn have.

Loki swallowed, uncertain what to say to her. That it would be all right? A lie, of course, and he didn't believe in lying, least of all to her. Even if he could never tell her everything, he'd not lie. "I bore that responsibility a very long time ... for eons. So long I cannot much remember what life was like without it."

She drew him close, arm around his waist. "We'll figure it out. At least we're still here, the three of us. Together."

Yes. For now. Naught lasts forever.

And she could not yet imagine the suffering her actions would lead to. The weight Loki himself would one day bear because of her mistakes.

Such pain stung all the more—when others paid for one's own errors.

"I relied on flame to hold back the darkness and the mist. And now, for the first time, I have no power to fall back upon. How am I to protect you?"

Sigyn squeezed him tighter. "Same as the rest of us, I guess."

Loki shut his eyes and shuddered.

Should he tell her?

No.

Knowing the future and remaining powerless to avert it, that was the worst of torments.

The Saga continues with *The Radiance of Alfheim*:
books2read.com/radianceofalfheim

SKALDS' TRIBE

Join the Skalds' Tribe and get access to exclusive reader rewards like *The Ragnarok Era Codex*, as well getting free books like *Darkness Forged* and notifications on release dates and sales.

https://www.mattlarkinbooks.com/go-ragnarok/

Want maps, character bios, and background information on the Ragnarok Era? Look no further.

AUTHOR'S RAMBLINGS

I mentioned that *The High Seat of Asgard* was one of the most challenging books I've ever written. This one is a close second, as indeed, I suspect this entire second trilogy to prove. One of the main difficulties here becomes how to structure interlaced events taking place over a span of time greater than those of typical novels and at the same time carry forth the scope of so many characters involved in these myths.

As before, my original outline went through a lot of revisions, with the essence of the story remaining unchanged, but the telling of it reorganized. Among these changes, up until I had actually begun writing, I'd intended to tell Fitela and Helgi's stories through Fitela's point of view. Once I was deep in the guts of the book, however, I realized that while those stories connected to the others, they way they did so was so tertiary as to risk seeming disconnected from the main narrative.

The difficult choice to remove those chapters did, however, allow me a bit more space to further flesh out some things that otherwise felt pushed to the side. Even so, there remains so much more I *could* develop, which I comfort myself in supposing I might someday write as another series. For *Gods of the Ragnarok Era*, I felt I needed to keep the tale as focused on Odin and the Aesir's struggles as possible.

Which said, fans of the *Runeblade Saga* no doubt see numerous callbacks to it.

Additionally, of course, this second trilogy sees significant focus placed upon Sigmund and his son Sigurd (as arguably the greatest heroes of Norse myth). Sigmund's tragic death was always a part of the inspiring myth and thus had to become an inevitable destination for this arc, even if Odin only realized it later on. What we see of Sigmund's (and forthcoming Sigurd's) saga will naturally be the parts that best relate to his interactions with the Aesir and his uses to Odin.

Relating to the Aesir, one thing that I—and others attempting to retell myth—have sometimes find necessary is amalgamating originally distinct characters for the sake of a cohesive narrative. For example, Gridr is the female jotunn who warns Thor of Geirrod's treachery. She is not, however, originally a daughter of Geirrod (those were Greip and Gjalp). And while there is reason to believe Thor may have had an affair with Gridr as well (as did Odin), the mother of his son was actually Jarnsaxa. This convoluted mess of giantesses served to create a narrative jumble without any cohesion. Consequently, I merged them into a single jotunn female.

Other aspects of the tale also required adjustment based on the tenuous and sometimes contradictory chronology of Norse mythology. For example, a great many poems make reference to the death of Balder (Baldr), including the one involving Vafthrudnir. Balder's death is usually the first spark of Ragnarok and thus Odin *might* have gone seeking all this wisdom after it. Logistically, though, it becomes questionable that the father would go off on all these adventures after his son's death but before his funeral or the consequences of the murder.

On a thematic level, *The Well of Mimir* dives deeper into one of the underlying conceits of Norse mythology (also found in many Indo-European myths): that of fate. Knowing the future does not allow mythic heroes to avoid it. Indeed the very knowledge may often create a self-fulfilling prophecy. It has been argued that the moral decay and compromises the Aesir make as their desperation grows ultimately lead to the beginnings of their own destruction. Along with an idea in the Prose Edda regarding the "gods" being human, this idea became one of the fundamental conceits I relied upon in retelling and re-conceiving the story of the Aesir. The characters in this series are most often responsible for their own tragedies and—in Odin and Loki's case—perhaps all the more so because of their foreknowledge of the future.

And no character comes out unscathed. Every mistake or misdeed necessitates another, leaving no one's hands clean. There are no saints. We see this in the desperate and often despicable actions Odin, Sigyn, and Tyr take.

With the fifth of nine planned books complete, we are now more than halfway through that tragic end. I have sometimes thought that a good book (or movie) is one where you're still thinking about it the next day (or for several days longer). In that vein, I hope you'll be thinking about this tale for a while more.

For unwavering support, I want to thank my wife. I couldn't have gotten here without you, Juhi. Thanks to Clark for helping me work out some of these tricky plot points.

Also, special thanks to my cover designer (because holy shit!) and to my Arch Skalds (in no particular order): Al, Tanya, Kimberly, Jackie, Dale, Missy, Grant, Lisa Marie, Bill, Rachel, Barbara, Bob, Kaye, Mike, and Regina.

Thank you for reading,
Matt

P.S. Now that you've read *The Well of Mimir* I would really appreciate it if you'd leave a review! Reviews help new readers find my work, so they're very helpful. Thank you in advance for helping me build and grow my author career!

Follow me on BookBub:
https://www.bookbub.com/authors/matt-larkin

BOOKS BY MATT LARKIN

Gods of the Ragnarok Era

The Ragnarok Era is a dark fantasy retelling of Norse mythology, chronicling Odin's rise to godhood. If you love old legends, tragic mythology, and action-packed reads, check out The Ragnarok Era now!

https://www.mattlarkinbooks.com/series/ragnarok/

Legends of the Ragnarok Era

Legends of the Ragnarok Era expands on the world developed in The Ragnarok Era series by delivering dark tales outside the main series narrative. Fans of mythology should not miss this epic series.

https://www.mattlarkinbooks.com/series/ragnaroklegend/

Runeblade Saga

The Runeblade Saga is a series of dark fantasy sword and sorcery adventures set in the world of The Ragnarok Era. Filled with plenty of grim action, tragic heroes, and more than a bit of horror, these books are for fans of mythology and sword & sorcery alike.

https://www.mattlarkinbooks.com/series/runeblade/

For Juhi. For not giving up.

Made in the USA
Lexington, KY
21 September 2018